FORBIDDEN

FORBIDDEN

Roberta Latow

HEADLINE

First published in 1995
by HEADLINE BOOK PUBLISHING

10 9 8 7 6 5 4 3 2 1

British Library Cataloguing in Publication Data

Latow, Roberta
Forbidden
I.Title
813.54 [F]

ISBN 0-7472-1346-1

Typeset by Avon Dataset Ltd, Bidford-on-Avon, B50 4JH

Printed and bound in Great Britain by
Mackays of Chatham PLC, Chatham, Kent

HEADLINE BOOK PUBLISHING
A division of Hodder Headline PLC
338 Euston Road
London NW1 3BH

For Felicity and Peter

'Desire me, encounter us
in your secret night.
I kiss you'

– *The Epic of Artimadon*

SONNING ON THAMES, BERKSHIRE

1994

Chapter 1

'I am really looking forward to seeing you eat humble pie.'

'You should know better than that, I never eat humble pie.'

'After nearly three decades you really think all you have to do is appear like a genie from some magic lamp and gaze into her eyes? One brief glance, one of your more seductive ones, and Amy Ross will believe you never stopped loving her? That it will be enough for her to fall in love with you all over again?'

'You doubt that's possible? You shouldn't. How many times during our marriage have you done it?'

'Me, and how many other women? What a cad you are to remind me! How arrogant.'

'You want to see her walk away from me, as if our love never existed.'

'You couldn't be more wrong. I want to give you back to her. For her to know we're through with each other, and for her to meet Tennant, the son *she* never gave you. Once you two are reunited, I want *all* of us to become a part of her life. You can claim her for love. I want her, maybe not as a friend but certainly sympathetic towards me. I don't want her to see me as a rival for your affection. Not good for my career or Tennant's.

'But of course you wouldn't be thinking that way for yourself, would you, Jarret? The great lost love of your life, you claim. The woman you can no longer live without. She was your one true love at the happiest time of your life, you claim. Recapture her? Relive that exciting, happy time you had together? And without having to eat a fat slice of humble pie? I think not. Unless she's a bigger fool than I've heard she is.'

'You really can't bear that I love her, have always loved her.'

'That's just vanity speaking. This is an amicable divorce, remember? We're friends who know each other too well. Your love for her means

3

nothing to me now that we have agreed to go our own separate ways. Once I might not have been able to bear your loving her, but certainly not now. After twenty years of living with you, I can bear anything. If I couldn't, what would I be doing here now?'

He raised a hand and fingered some strands of hair that had escaped the sleek French twist at the nape of her neck, tucking them neatly into place. The gaze that passed between them was curiously dispassionate. Genevieve looked at him assessingly. It had been a very long time since she had loved him. A short time since she had left him. But still she could see it all there in his face, those very things that had seduced her, enslaved her to him.

He still had those same alluring good looks. The dark blond hair had hardly a thread of silver in it, and the eyes, once a deep violet under those long, thick, dark brown lashes, though somewhat faded with age were nonetheless enchantingly seductive for the reticent expression they held. The large square face, fleshily soft, still had the sensitive look of a poet or painter, and was made dramatically handsome by a patrician nose as seen on white marble busts of Ancient Roman nobles. Lips were sensuously shaped, seductive for the enigmatic smile that promised hidden passions. He was tall and broad-shouldered, but more fleshy than muscular, a soft rather than strong-looking character. Yet, like those noble senators or officers representing the Roman Empire, dressed in their leather and silver armour, who drew attention centuries later in courtyards and museums, he carried himself like a god.

She had yet to find a woman who did not succumb to the quiet, self-absorbed Jarret Sparrow. He could still create an aura round him that drew towards him men and women alike. And could still swallow them up whole as he had in his younger days. In that one respect, time had stood still for Jarret. He was as adept at that as ever, maybe even more so.

Oh, Amy Ross, let's see what you're made of. Not sugar and spice and everything nice, I hope. And with that thought in the forefront of her mind, Genevieve Sparrow rang the doorbell.

She rang it again, and yet again, and still no one came to the door. By this time Tennant, who had been following his parents on the footpath that led from the road through a small wood under a cathedral of leaves – orange and ruby red, a multitude of russet shades, golden yellow, bright and jewel-like from a warm October sun beating down through the tall hundred-year-old trees – had caught up with them.

4

Genevieve turned to look at her husband and son. The three stood in silence in front of the handsome wooden boat house, grand for its size and three-storey turret, its peaked stone-tiled roofs. It had not been what they had expected, although none of them really knew what they'd expected, only what they hoped to accomplish.

'Well, she wouldn't be inside on a day like this,' offered Tennant.

They walked down the several wooden steps from the front door. The wood thinned out to a carpet of lawn in front of the boat house with on either side of it a romantic English garden and herbaceous borders and rose bushes right down to the river's edge. Amy was just tying up *Arcadia*, a small steam boat of honey-coloured wood and brass fittings, with a tall and slender smoke stack.

Tennant sprinted away from his parents. 'It's a beauty,' he told her. 'A little jewel of a boat. Here, let me help you.'

'It's done. I have it down to a fine art,' she told him, and having completed her task looked up from her work to see who had made the offer.

Amy was somewhat taken aback to see the handsome young man. His smile, his eyes. Time suddenly ran backward and she very nearly lost herself, reached out to caress a cheek that seemed familiar to her. Tennant had had no idea what Amy Ross would be like; he had felt curious about this woman his father had once loved, but that vanished with their first gaze into each other's eyes. What he saw in them was something sensuous, a quiet mystery, kindness, love. He wanted her.

Time stopped rushing backward for Amy Ross. Instead, the moment she looked past the handsome young man to see the couple walking across the lawn towards her, it stood still. She recognised Jarret at once. First by the figure of the man walking towards her; then by his walk – sure, determined, but a solitary entity, cutting a path for himself wherever he went. It was still the walk of a big, beautiful man even after so many years.

She was taken aback. Struck dumb. She had all but forgotten his existence. In thirty years she had thought of him, what, five or six times? Yes, maybe that. And only in the context of the art world of the sixties in New York, and then only because he was part of the best and the worst times of her life.

After their last encounter she had never once wondered what it would be like if their paths crossed, how she would handle seeing him again. She'd somehow known that that was unlikely to happen, they moved in different circles. Only now, seeing him, did she realise that she had

5

seen to that. There was no doubt about it, Amy was shocked. This was her private world, one she had fought hard to create and live in, and he was violating it. What was he doing here?

When they had been together she'd thought she knew him down to the marrow of his bones, but in fact she hadn't. Not until he left her did she really know the man. Devastated once by his leaving her, she was shattered a second time by what she subsequently learned about him, finding it unbelievable that she should have loved so deeply a man like Jarret Sparrow. However, she knew him well enough now to see that he was very nearly as shocked by this meeting as she was. He seemed dazed, merely stood there looking bruised, at a loss as to what to do with himself, unable to speak. She had seen it all before; it was part of his charm, drew her towards him as it had so many other women in his life. Only this time Amy knew it was happening and how devastating it could be.

It was Genevieve who finally broke the silence. 'Hello, I'm Genevieve Sparrow. I've brought you a gift – my husband. To be more accurate, my former husband. It's an amicable divorce, we're still friends. He has claimed for years that you are the great lost love of his life. I dispute that, but it's neither here nor there at the moment. I wanted to meet a great lost love of Jarret's, and I also wanted to meet you. I read your book *Pop Goes The Easel*, and liked what you had to say about Pop Art. And I wanted you to meet my son, Tennant. Like father, like mother, he too is a painter. For years I thought *I* was the great love of my husband's life. Well, at least our love was fruitful. Too bad you never had his child.'

'Genevieve, that's enough! Do shut up.' At last Jarret had found his voice.

'That was a bit bitchy. I didn't intend to be bitchy, Amy Ross,' Genevieve said, with more of a smirk than a smile.

Amy finally managed to speak. 'How did you find me?'

'You're angry. Please don't be angry with us,' said Tennant.

Amy turned to face him. 'I'm not angry. Just surprised to see your father after so many years of silence on both our parts.' Then, turning to Jarret, she told him, 'I would have appreciated a note asking to see me, a telephone call, some warning if you felt you wanted a meeting. You might have asked if I wanted to see you again.'

'I was afraid that there would be no reply to a note, you would put the receiver down on a telephone call. Would you have agreed to meet me?'

6

'I doubt it.'

'We assumed as much. Hence the shock tactics. They have at least worked. We're here and we're talking. My idea, I'm afraid,' said Genevieve.

'I can almost understand Jarret's intrusive behaviour, but you, Mrs Sparrow, what are you doing here? Why have you done this to yourself and to me?'

'Habit. I've been pimping for Jarret for years. He claims he loves you, wants you. Had to see you after all these years to make it right between you, maybe forge a new life together. He's been obsessed with the idea. I have never been able to deny Jarret anything – you of all people should understand that. You've been there, done it. To the death, I understand.'

'Genevieve!'

'I think you had all better go. This is private property and you are trespassing.'

'How very inhospitable of you, Amy Ross. I expected civility at least, even a cup of tea to go with the humble pie I so wanted to enjoy watching Jarret eat. Actually I expected more from you. At least your understanding that if Jarret and I have resorted to such drastic action to make contact with you, you would appreciate how sincere we are about seeking a reconciliation. We are, after all, entering the last productive years of our lives. Is it so wrong to make one last grab for happiness and leave the past behind us? Jarret and I are through with each other but our lives are entwined. Just as yours has been, if not entwined with mine, a factor in my life, though you may not have known it.

'I've had to live with the ghost of your love affair with my husband all my married life. I'm a little bitter about that. It may be wrong of me but at least I'm admitting it. I wanted the satisfaction of dumping him on your doorstep, and saying: "I've had him, now you can have what's left." Tacky, yes. Pathetic that it should give me so much pleasure, yes. But it does. I'll leave, Tennant and I will, but without Jarret. You can have him. God . . .' with that Genevieve looked up at the sky and then back to Amy and Jarret ' . . . spite and revenge are *so sweet.*'

Genevieve slipped her arm through Tennant's and she and her nonplussed son walked away.

Amy watched them vanish round the side of the boat house. She felt as if her world had been shattered until Jarret said, 'Forgive her.

She knows she never had me as you did, as you still do. I need you, now take me back.'

Amy opened her eyes. She had a headache, a dull pain at the back of her eyes, and her mouth was dry, so very dry. She licked her lips. They were parched. She pulled herself up against the pillows and placed a hand on her forehead. It wasn't that she felt unwell, more terribly unnerved.

For several minutes she lay in the warmth of her bed and contemplated the splendid view through the vast triangular wall of window following the roofline of the boat house from the floorboards to its peaked ceiling. She never tired of that view: the river, and on the far side the occasional large rambling house set in a wood or on a carpet of well-trimmed lawn. Decorative gazebos, sumptuous gardens, a decrepit wooden boat house much smaller than hers, in summer covered almost completely with honeysuckle and climbing roses. The occasional boat heading downriver towards Windsor and London in one direction, others up towards Oxford and as far as Wiltshire and the small spring said to be the river's source. Because her bedroom at the top of the boat house very nearly hung over the water she could see a long way up and down the Thames: a splendid sight, English countryside at its best, and only sparsely populated at the stretch of the river where she lived.

Mist was rising off the water and hovered a foot off the grass or in the trees, the sun not yet high enough to burn it away. She heard the quacking of ducks which brought a smile to her lips. Since childhood she could not resist the sound or sight of them on a river, and most especially not below her own bedroom window. Amy rose from the bed and walked to the window. Yes, there they were, busily gliding and quacking below. When in residence, she and the ducks had a morning ritual. Amy flung her dressing-gown round her shoulders and dashed down the wooden stairs to the floor below. Another gallery hung in the vast open space of the seventeenth-century boat house – the floor that housed her library and served too as a second sitting-room or place for the very occasional guest. That floor had a wall of windows on to the river as well and a door that led to a narrow balcony. Amy opened the door and stepped out. The ducks were directly below her, treading water in circles, calling for their morning feed. She removed the lid of a large crock, the ducks' larder, and tossed down handfuls of stale bread and cake. She watched them for a few minutes but the air was damp and with a decided nip in it. Amy stepped off the balcony and back into the library, watching the ducks through the window. Two white swans and one black glided into view. Only when the water birds had gobbled down every morsel of their morning repast did they move on upriver and Amy left her post.

Walking down the remaining flight of stairs and through the drawing-room, the space where once magnificent long barges had been housed by a wealthy lord so that he might go from his country house by river to visit his sovereign at Windsor, Amy was once more aware of her headache and that feeling of unease.

While making coffee, she kept wondering what had happened to give her such a sense of anguish. A restless night. No more than that. She walked with the coffee jug in her hand to sit down in the wing chair at the end of the long, two-hundred-year-old oak table. Years of bleaching and scrubbing had made the surface resemble cream-coloured satin. She ran her hand over it, a habit of hers. She liked the feel of the smooth wood, the solid earthiness of the country kitchen table. Amy placed the jug on it, and then her hands to her temples. She rubbed them gently, trying to concentrate on what was disturbing her. A breakthrough. It had been a dream that had vanished from her mind.

It came back slowly, in fragments. A young man. People on the lawn. Then her clouded mind cleared and all of her dream came rushing back. Jarret! Jarret had come back to claim her. This was the first time Jarret Sparrow had slipped into her dream life. And as if that wasn't bad enough, he had brought his wife and a son with him. The wife *he* had never made her, the son *she* had never given him. She poured herself a cup of coffee and was shocked to see that her hand trembled as she relived that dream.

Amy felt as if she had been assaulted. It had forced itself upon her, violated her against her will. 'Out, out,' she wanted to shout, and wipe it out of her mind. But the dream had happened and Amy had never been good at blocking things out. She didn't much like the fact that it could upset her as much as it had. Was that indicative of something? She had after all been through with Jarret for more than twenty years.

She spoke aloud. 'You were a dream and nothing more. You died and were gone the moment I opened my eyes. A dream . . . you forget a dream. You don't try and deal with it.' Amy smiled, feeling better. When she raised her cup to her lips, her hand was as steady as a rock.

Amy drove her battered four-seater 1937 Lagonda Rapide up to the entrance of Claridge's. The well-worn and shabby-looking soft top of black duck was down. She drove the car open even in quite cold weather, putting the top up only in the rain.

Cars had never meant much to Amy except a means of getting from A to B until this royal blue tourer with its long bonnet and spare wheel in place on the running board had one day been driven up the drive to her house. It was love at first sight. She saw the Lagonda more as a magnificent piece of mechanical sculpture than an automobile. The owner of the car had wanted a Paul Klee watercolour she owned and loved. She'd swapped it for the car.

Amy, her white silk headscarf rippling in the wind, driving her vintage sculpture on wheels, was always a treat to see.

She and the doormen at Claridge's had an arrangement; or rather Sir Charles Henry Grenfell had one. He was the car's former owner, the man who had been so persistent in trying to obtain the Klee for his collection. Amy and Charles had become passionate lovers after the swap. He wanted marriage, she didn't. Now they were friends though he, still in love, believed one day they would return to each other as sexual rather than the platonic lovers they had become. On instructions from Sir Charles, who had for years kept a suite of rooms in the hotel, whenever Miss Ross drove into Mayfair the doormen were to see to her car. That posed no problem for them. They were besotted with Amy's car. The Lagonda Rapide was a universal object of desire.

Amy went through the usual formalities with the doorman.

'Good morning, Mr Craven.'

'Good morning, Miss Ross. Good drive into town?'

She would always give a brief traffic report. He would always comment on the weather. And all this while she was still in the driver's seat, parked in the space where the taxis were meant to deposit or pick up their passengers, or double parked next to some elegant Rolls-Royce.

'Do you think you can do something with the car for a few hours, Mr Craven?'

'I think I can manage that for you, Miss Ross. Shall I send it round for a wash? If you gave us the day, she could have a good polish too?'

'A wash will do. I must think of sending her away for a few minor repairs.'

They exchanged smiles and he opened the door. Amy slipped from behind the wheel and the doorman reminded her, 'She really deserves a new top, Miss Ross.'

The two stood looking at the car together. 'I know, Mr Craven, she

10

deserves everything: shinier chrome, a new paint job. But really I love my car the way she is. She wears her age with such elegance and without face lifts. We both know I'll hold out until it's a dire necessity to replace the top.'

'So much more stylish this way,' another voice agreed.

Sir Charles Henry Grenfell stepped up to Amy and untied her white silk scarf. He slipped it from her head and bent down to kiss her on the lips. Placing an arm around her shoulders, he walked her away from the doorman, saying, 'Thank you, Craven.'

Amy ran her fingers through her hair: shoulder-length, a rich chocolate brown, shiny, healthy-looking in a tumble of soft waves she wore parted to one side and just off her face. It fluffed up and framed her creamy-coloured skin. It was a face still beautiful and seductive, possibly even more so for its maturity: just a hint of a few laughter lines at the corners of the eyes. She smiled now at Charles.

Amy Ross was a woman who looked fifteen years younger than her actual fifty-eight. She had a great deal going for her: a stunning bone structure, the sort that never ages; a long and slender neck, still taut and smooth like the rest of her body. All six feet of it. There was something Junoesque about Amy Ross: the way she walked on those long shapely legs that seemed to go on forever, the slender yet shapely figure with pronounced hips and a sensuous bottom, an ample bosom. When she entered a room or walked down a street, there were always heads that turned in admiration for a second look. She had about her a look of health and femininity, a quiet but sensuous strong beauty that men wanted to possess, at the very least caress, and women to emulate. But the most seductive thing about Amy Ross was the challenge she presented to men: an independent, intelligent beauty who was not easily available.

Charles adored Amy Ross's looks; the way she dressed; the way she moved. With the grace of a long-legged, elegant animal: a gazelle or giraffe, he often teased her. There was never a time when they met that his heart didn't skip a beat on seeing her. Today she was dressed in one of the little black silk dresses she was so fond of wearing in the city, a Jean Muir, with over it a black cashmere shawl draped casually around her shoulders. She wore a pre-Columbian gold necklace: a thick pure gold ring with a large fertility frog in the centre, an antiquity he had bought her one Christmas. She also wore high-heeled black alligator shoes and carried a minute black alligator bag on a gold chain.

'You look ravishing.'

'You always say that. You must have seen me in this outfit a hundred times.'

He gave her one of those looks that she understood so well. Often when he looked at her that way, she too wondered why they could not make it work. It had been so good for them, their sexual togetherness, the way they loved each other. But platonic love and friendship were all she wanted from him now. He was less happy with it than she and lived in hope that things would change.

It was always the same on meeting, one brief glance into each other's eyes, just a hint of question and pain in Charles's, and then it was over, and they were left to enjoy each other's company.

They walked arm in arm into Claridge's. Heads turned. They made a handsome couple, the young baronet and the tall American art historian. She remained, for the young and very eligible aristocratic English girls, the older woman who had a hold on the very eligible Sir Charles Henry Grenfell, a mystery to them and a threat to their happiness. Several of them smiled and greeted the couple. Amy as usual looked embarrassed. She always looked just a little timid or withdrawn when she was out and about in public with him, especially in his circle of friends. They were not hers.

That had not always been the case. It was Amy's nature to remain in the background of things. She enjoyed being the observer rather than the observed, there but not there. But for a period of time after she and Charles had met and fallen in love they were very social; that had been part of their problem, perhaps. They had led his way of life and not hers. But love had taken over and she'd allowed herself to be drawn into the social whirl she had happily retreated from many years before Charles appeared in her life. It was inevitable Amy would finally tire of the fun; it was too much yet somehow not enough to satisfy her. She returned to what she already knew made her happy: work. It was more fun than fun. Living a very private life and not being gossiped about was very important to her feeling of well-being.

They lunched on paper-thin slices of smoked salmon draped like silk over a white dinner plate, and a bird's nest of twigs from which they plucked quail's eggs to be peeled and dipped in celery salt. Roast pheasant with all the trimmings to follow, accompanied by Louis Roederer Cristal. A discerning drinker, that was Amy Ross's favourite champagne. She felt about a glass of that in the same way she did about a glass of the best of the clarets: a Margaux, Petrus, Pichon-Longueville, or one of the great white wines: a Chassagne-Montrachet or Chablis Grand Cru. A little of the best of everything was the way Amy liked to live. She was not a greedy lady, didn't have to dine in the grand manner often, but that did not prevent her from enjoying treats like this when she got the chance.

Over tiny pots of hot chocolate souffle with hot chocolate sauce dribbled over them from a small jug alternated with a trickle of double cream poured from another, Amy told Charles, 'The most decadent, obscene extravagance – how else to describe this pudding?' She raised her chin and gave him a light and sexy laugh, plunging the tiny spoon into the pot with one hand while still pouring cream with the other. He could never resist her laughter and raised his glass in a toast.

'To all the decadent, obscene extravagances of our past, and in the hope of more in the present and future.'

Charles was clever enough not to force the issue and wait for Amy to raise her glass in affirmation that there was still hope she would return to him in that way. He instantly drank his champagne while gazing into her eyes.

The toast made was a *double entendre*, one half of which hinted at all things sexual, and they both knew it. Amy was saved from an awkward moment by the appearance at their table of a man. He was tall and broad-shouldered, with dark hair gone salt and pepper colour and touched with distinguished white at the temples. His face was pleasant and kindly, with brown eyes behind fashionable round steel-rimmed glasses. One look showed he was American: Brooks Brothers button-down blue shirt and J. Press tweed jacket worn with a very smart tie and grey flannel trousers. Very East Coast, New England.

He began by speaking to Charles who replaced his empty glass on the table and rose from his chair.

'I am sorry about this intrusion but I would have known the lady's laugh anywhere.' With that the newcomer turned his attention to Amy. 'Hello, Amy. Do you remember me? Peter Smith? It's been a very long time.'

Amy was surprised but delighted. The moment he had appeared at their table she had felt there was something familiar about him, but had not had the least idea who he was. Until he spoke her name, and gazed into her eyes.

'Peter Smith! How extraordinary to meet like this after . . . how long?'

He smiled at Amy and then returned his attention to Charles who was still standing, napkin in hand. Peter Smith thrust out his hand.

13

'Pete Smith,' he said, and the two men shook hands.

'Charles Grenfell.'

Then, turning back to Amy, Peter answered her. 'How long? Well you might ask! A wife and six children ago. Thirty years or near on. I hope you'll forgive me but I'm at the next table and your laughter drew my attention. I simply couldn't resist coming over to say hello.'

Charles called a waiter to bring a chair. 'Please join us for coffee?'

'I'll sit down for just a minute but I won't stay, thank you. We've only just ordered our dessert. Oh, my mistake. You say pudding for dessert in England. My daughter Cosima, who studied here, would have corrected me.'

Charles liked the man. There was something wholesome and real about him, and though very American, there was an edge to him that one found only in those who travelled with respect for other cultures, absorbed the best of what they found abroad and used it to enhance their lives. Charles could see he was one of those who always gave the best of themselves in return.

'Do you come often to London, Peter?' asked Amy.

'Yes, I have done. I like London, and England. And you?'

'I live here. I have for more than twenty years.'

There was an awkward few moments while they both searched for something else to say. But as youthful memories resurfaced, Amy realised that she had lost something when, grabbing at life with both hands, she had abandoned Peter Smith in her wake.

'What are you doing here in London, Peter?' asked Charles, cutting into the embarrassed silence that had taken hold round the table. That seemed to revive them.

Peter answered, 'Cosima is making her debut in *Lucia di Lammermoor* at Covent Garden tonight.'

'How wonderfully exciting!' There was enthusiasm and genuine delight in Amy's voice.

'Many congratulations,' offered Charles.

'How thrilling for you to have a daughter with such talent.'

'Yes, thrilling. Not bad for a simple Long Island farmer! But, hang on, she's not singing Lucia yet. I mustn't linger though. This is her celebration luncheon party, and then we must all go upstairs and nap to be fresh for the big night. Cosima's instructions.'

He rose from his chair, as did Charles, and the two men once again shook hands. 'How wonderful to have seen you again, Amy.' He raised her hand and gave it a gallant kiss. They smiled at each other and he walked away.

'Nice man,' commented Charles.

'Yes, he always was a good person.'

Amy and Charles left their table shortly after Peter Smith had returned to his family. They smiled as they passed the Smith clan: four handsome young men and two beautiful young women who beamed back at them. Amy glanced briefly at Peter Smith. Seeing him somehow warmed her heart.

Chapter 2

There were many things that Charles found charming about Amy Ross, not the least of which was that she never took herself as seriously as other people did. That was part of her power, and yes, Amy did have a great deal of power. She wielded it in their personal relationship, just as she did in her professional relationships, more subtly than any woman he had ever met.

She did it by standing back out of the limelight and appearing like magic: a puff of smoke, abracadabra, and *voilà*! There she was, at the right moment, for the right reasons, doing the right thing. Amy Ross, in the spotlight, to shine like the star that she was for a rare appearance, afterwards to recede once more into the shadows. That was her style, the way she liked to live.

She was a woman who knew how to retreat in order to advance, in order to win. She was therefore admired, respected, and very much sought after. She had an inner life that shined through her looks, the way she moved, the way she lived and worked.

In his heart Charles knew that he would never win her back to his bed nor to the altar unless some fundamental change took place in her. Most of the time he tried to ignore that fact and just went on living the best way he could under the circumstances. But today, walking with her from Claridge's up Brook Street to Bond Street and Sotheby's where they were going to view a painting, a Rothko he wanted to bid for, he somehow couldn't go on, very nearly said something to her about it, but stopped when she broke into his thoughts.

'How very strange seeing Peter Smith. I had thought it would have been someone else.'

'I don't quite get that. Have I missed something?'

She slipped her arm through his and drew closer to him, neither of them breaking step. 'Oh, it's nothing. Only just a few days ago I had a dream about someone from my past.'

'A man?'

'Yes.'

'The near past or the very past past?'

'A long, long time ago.'

'A lover?'

Amy stopped. She seemed to cling even closer to Charles and gazed into his eyes. He saw something in them he had never seen before. Was it pain, sorrow? Instinctively, he reached out and caressed her cheek, and whatever he had seen vanished as suddenly as it had appeared.

'It wasn't a very nice dream. Nasty, in fact. It was about a man from what seems like another lifetime who returned to claim me. The dream unnerved me and I put it out of my mind. Now, having seen Peter, it's come back. I hadn't thought of it as a premonition of some sort, hadn't thought it was a warning that I would really meet someone from my past.'

'The man in your dream . . . it wasn't Peter Smith, was it?'

They had resumed walking and Amy was very quick to tell him, 'Oh, no. Peter Smith was a very nice and happy interlude.'

They were just walking through the door into Sotheby's. Charles gripped her arm very tightly and Amy stopped short and looked at him. 'And me, Amy? Am I more than Peter Smith? More than a very nice and happy interlude?' he asked her in a voice lowered to just above a whisper.

'What's wrong, Charles?'

'Let's forget the Rothko. Come back to Claridge's with me, to bed. I don't want to be a mere interlude.'

There were people on both side of the glass doors trying to get in and out of the auction house and being held up. Amy and Charles looked embarrassed when they realised they were causing a traffic jam. He pushed the door open and they walked through it into the reception area. Amy took him by the hand and led him to one side.

'You always have been, always will be much more to me than an interlude, and you know that, Charles.'

The relief he felt was enormous. He sighed and all anxiety left his face. He felt suddenly foolish with not the least idea what had caused him momentarily to feel he had lost Amy to her past. He felt enormously sexy, full of lust, but his mind took over and he controlled himself. He would not lose her by forcing the issue of sex. She had made it abundantly clear to him that if and when it was to happen for them

18

again, it would be she who would approach him. He was about to attempt to cover his *faux pas* but was saved when one of the Sotheby's directors approached them.

By the time they were standing in front of the Rothko painting they had been joined by several people and were being observed by Sotheby's staff and art dealers. That was the sort of attention Amy Ross commanded when she appeared at exhibitions in galleries or sale rooms. Her stamp of approval or disapproval, any comment, was closely attended to. Like many an art historian she was used not only as the voice of authority but as a barometer. Her mere appearance, as now, gave weight to a sale.

Her presence at a viewing was always exciting, creating tension, expectation; the mere fact that she had come out to look at the paintings piqued people's interest. Even more so because she rarely said much, and almost never stated an opinion publicly. People tried to get an inkling from her manner or the change of expression on her face, from who she was with or by listening to any interchange between her and the entourage that usually formed to follow her round the gallery.

Amy knew the Rothko. Seeing it once again, she was reminded of the first time Mark Rothko had shown it to her. Her heart took a leap for the sheer majesty and beauty of the work. 'What audacity,' she had told him. He had asked her, 'Why audacious, Amy?' And she had answered, 'Because it's more godly than God, anybody's god.' And then they had both fallen silent and lingered for some length of time contemplating the ethereal peace and tranquillity of the work. It was one of his paintings that peeled away the surface of things and shot straight to the centre of being. It was a painting of pure heart and exquisite soul, a painting that was more alive than life itself. It was life eternal.

How glorious it was to see it again. Of all the works of art she had ever seen, this painting was one of her favourites. It had vanished into a private collection for many years and though the collector who owned it would happily have allowed her a viewing any time she liked, she had never taken advantage of her position and asked to see it. Amy had written an essay on the painting and the painter which had appeared in one of her books on Abstract Expressionism. It was often quoted from and used in other writers' publications. That too had been a long time ago. Now, standing once more in front of the painting, she remembered those words she had written. They too had stood the test of time. If she had any intention of writing about the painting or the painter again, which she did not, there was not a single word she would change.

She and Charles were still engrossed in the painting. Several Sotheby's staff were still very much in attendance, hovering expectantly. They were well trained to know a serious buyer when they saw one. Amy quite suddenly felt stifled, not by the painting but the whole process of art for sale. That often happened to her and was one of the reasons she only rarely emerged from her reclusive life to step into the art world.

A profound sadness for Mark Rothko, that he was dead and gone, came over her. Had he known what a magnificent legacy he was leaving behind? She believed he did and, in some strange way, that it was what had killed him. Those years in the late fifties and early sixties had been so exciting, the best and the worst of her life. She didn't often think about them but the Rothko and the reappearance of Peter Smith, together with that horrid dream of Jarret's return, seemed to be drawing the past back into the present. So what? We all live with the ghosts of our past, she told herself, and the sadness vanished as quickly as it had appeared. She smiled, and felt quite happy to be seeing the Rothko again – happy and privileged. She placed her hands together, their fingertips touching, and brought them up to her lips. One more glance and with a beatific smile on her face she turned away to slip her arm through Charles's.

'Shall we go?' she asked.

They were ushered through the reception area, to the door. Finally outside on the pavement she turned to Charles. 'Well?' she asked.

'It's everything you said it was, and more. What a privilege to own that painting.'

'I knew you would see it for what it is, one of his finest. What will you do?'

'Bid for it. But I don't know that I can afford it. We'll have to see. Who do you think I will be bidding against?'

'Difficult to say, surely a museum or two, but they aren't the ones to worry about. It's the private collectors who will spend more money on it.'

'The sale will be in New York. Will you come with me?'

'I don't think so. Not my scene any more, you know that.'

'Nor mine.'

'You could always handle it from this end, bid by telephone.'

'More than a million dollars?'

'I think you must be prepared for very nearly two million.'

Walking down Brook Street from Bond Street, Charles saw Amy's car being driven up to the entrance of Claridge's. The timing was too perfect for his liking. She would want to get away at once. Had they had to wait for her car, he would have suggested tea, preferably in his suite. Amy and Charles had little routines they lived by and rarely deviated from these days. Both were careful, each for their own reasons, trying to keep their relationship on an even keel: Amy because she didn't want it to change, and Charles because he did and was fearful of losing her altogether.

The doorman tipped his hat to them, and Charles was surprised and delighted when Amy said, 'Mr Craven, can I ask you to keep the car for another half hour? I would like to have tea with Sir Charles.'

He was even further surprised when she agreed to have tea in his rooms. Not the grandest of Claridge's suites, it was nevertheless one of their most charming with a small entrance hall, large sitting-room, pantry, two bedrooms and baths. The sitting-room was elegant in shades of cream and white silk damask with eighteenth-century furniture, books piled on every surface and fresh flowers in every vase. Oriental carpets on the floors and contemporary paintings on the walls: Picassos and Renoirs shared the space with Soutines and Monets, Schwitters collages, a Motherwell, a Pollock, and in the bedroom, hanging over his bed, an Ingres of sumptuous naked odalisques. Charles had come from a long line of collectors of beautiful works of art. Silver-framed family photographs stood everywhere, the white concert grand lid a veritable gallery of them.

Charles had taken the suite over from his father who had had it decorated in the 1930s by Syrie Maugham, first and only wife of Somerset, who had made the white drawing-room fashionable. The suite had been passed on like that, father to son, since the hotel opened in 1898, always a much-loved base for Charles's family when they were in London. In Paris they kept a similar suite at the Ritz, their place in France. The family house had for centuries been and still remained a stately hundred-room palace on twenty thousand acres in Derbyshire. That was home life; otherwise it was travel and hotel residences everywhere else. The Grenfells had always known how to live well.

From the first time Charles had taken Amy to the suite she had liked it, found it utterly charming. Nothing had changed. Charles went directly to the fireplace and put a match to the already laid fire. It caught at once, flared up, and he turned from the leaping flames to face Amy. This was what he wanted: Amy, here in his life. He smiled at her, went to her and removed the shawl from round her shoulders and dropped it on a chair. He took her in his arms and kissed her, stroked her hair. She was responsive. She slid her arms under his open jacket and round him, caressed his back. His hands felt so good on her breasts. She kissed him back and leaned into his body. She sighed with contentment, then stepped ever so gently away from him. She placed a hand on his cheek. He took it in his own and kissed it. Amy moved away to warm herself in front of the fire. A kiss, a caress . . . that they still allowed themselves in this now platonic love she insisted upon.

Charles rarely made an issue of their sexual estrangement; he had in the past and they had almost lost each other over it. He had learned to deal with his sexual ardour for Amy. He excused himself for a moment and went to the bedroom. Closing the door, he went directly to the telephone.

When he returned Amy was sitting at the piano, tinkling the keys. He sat down next to her. They were both high on the Rothko. They had had a grand day.

'Thank you,' she told him.

'No. Thank you.'

And they kissed once more, this time the kiss of two friends who loved each other. Two people who knew they were thanking each other for more than a good lunch and viewing a great painting. She was thanking him for not forcing the sexual issue, he her for loving him the best way she could. They spoke about the Rothko until tea arrived and the Lapsang Souchong was poured and cakes served.

Over tea they talked of other paintings and painters. The excitement kept mounting for them both. Great art can do that: awaken you, transport you into realms other than your own.

Even the telephone's intrusion could not bring them down from their high. Life seemed suddenly more rich and valid. Charles answered the telephone, still with his mouth full of cake.

He chewed and swallowed and tried to talk all at the same time. Amy rushed to his side with his cup of tea. He took a swallow and they both smiled for his greediness.

'Yes, Mother, I am eating,' he said at last. 'You've caught me out.'

Lady Mary spoke for some time. Charles sipped tea and smiled, sometimes interrupting her with a burst of laughter.

He held his hand over the receiver and whispered across the room to Amy, 'She's being very amusing about her dotty sister.'

'You will take a co-pilot?' he asked his mother.

Lady Mary asked about the Rothko painting. Amy enjoyed his enthusiasm in telling her about it. When he asked if he might call her back because he had Amy there for tea, he was obliged to pass the telephone over.

Lady Mary and Amy were very fond of each other, more so since they were in agreement that Amy should never marry Charles. They spoke for a short time and then Amy put the phone down.

'She says to tell you she will call you from the flat in the Ritz late tonight, and to make sure you can afford the Rothko. If need be she will go partners in it with you, but only under duress, and you are to remember that the family Dürer cost only fifty pounds.' They both laughed. The Dürer portrait had been in the family since 1512. Lady Mary never failed to remind Charles of what a good buy it had been, always ignoring the year in which an ancestor had purchased it. The story was told every time he was about to buy anything.

The lift door opened and Amy, Charles's farewell kiss still lingering on her lips, stepped out on to the ground floor of the hotel. Her attention was caught by a very pretty girl who was just finishing a call on one of the house phones. Amy watched her hurriedly put down the receiver and rush towards the lift. She was young and mischievous-looking, a sparkle of expectation in her eyes. She was bound for an assignation, no doubt sexual.

Something instinctively told Amy she was the girl Charles had discreetly called from the bedroom. Amy was well aware of his sexual appetites and that he sated them with sensual ladies who understood love had nothing to do with their liaisons. It didn't bother her; she knew she could change his having other women if she wanted to. She didn't. Normally she was indifferent to his personal life when it didn't include her, but this time she was somehow curious, as if she wanted to confirm what she already knew: that he was sexually active and satisfied without her. And there was something else. If truth be told, that last kiss . . . had she not felt sexual stirrings? Slight as they may have been, yes, she conceded, possibly.

She was several yards away from the lift but turned to see, as the doors closed, that the girl was the only person in it. Amy walked back and watched the needle on the indicator above the lift move until it

23

stopped at number three, Charles's floor. In spite of herself, she felt a pang of jealousy. She recognised it and despised such an emotion so put it out of her mind and heart. One day she would have to let Charles go forever. But that she would think about another day. She was still too high on art and having had such a lovely day.

She was just walking down the steps to the front entrance of the hotel. Seeing Peter Smith and his family had been part of her joyful day, she remembered. On impulse she turned and walked back to the concierge's desk. She asked for a piece of notepaper and a pen and wrote down her name, address and telephone number. Amy smiled at the concierge and asked him to have it delivered to Mr Peter Smith, then hurried from the hotel to her car.

She slipped behind the wheel of the Lagonda and tied her white silk scarf round her head. Then she and Mr Craven went through their usual parting dialogue.

'You'll just about miss the afternoon traffic, miss.'

'Just about. The car looks wonderfully clean. I'll bring it in one day early enough for a proper waxing and polishing.'

'And the top, miss? Before winter, might I suggest?'

'Yes, before winter.'

Amy tried to tip the doorman who always told her the same thing. 'It's taken care of, miss.' He was not a man to pass up a tip, that was after all his livelihood, but so was obeying orders and staying on the good side of Sir Charles who had instructed him not to take money from Miss Ross.

Amy smiled at several people about to enter the hotel who stopped to look admiringly at the Lagonda. A Japanese tourist snapped a picture of it. That set her off. She switched on the ignition and put the car in gear. Mr Craven stepped into the road to hold up the traffic while she pulled into the stream heading towards Bond Street. She was on her way home.

Charles and Tiffany Marsdon had an arrangement. They called each other for sex and fun, that was it. Uncomplicated and very satisfying. They liked each other enormously but loved other people. Sex was the way their relationship started and that was the way they meant it to continue. They were discreet but not secretive.

Charles was unimaginably sexy and decadent, the most experienced man she had had since her first lover. She had become a lady of sexual delights for him as well. The Right Honourable Tiffany Marsdon had

24

been a thirteen-year-old upper-class beauty, an innocent flirt who teased men with her looks and happy-go-lucky charm. Inevitably she had been seduced by a much older man, a friend of her family, who had then taken her under his wing. It was he who had introduced her to the wonders and sublimity of exciting intercourse, unconventional sex and its many manifestations. He had addicted her to sex and when, after several years of their being together in an on and off relationship that afforded her many boyfriends as well, he was through with her, he was clever enough to suggest Charles as his replacement, causing neither Tiffany nor himself any pain or scandal. No hearts had been broken, hers merely corrupted.

The changeover quite suited Tiffany who had understood the difference between carnal love, which she and her first lover had had for each other, and real love, something she had now found with a young doctor. It was mutual. The doctor was sexually besotted with Tiffany but had not nearly such a strong libido as she did, nor was he aware of just how strong hers actually was.

Charles was the solution to Tiffany's sexual drive; she was an admirable solution to his. For the moment they suited each other and probably would long after the doctor returned from a visit to India. Only then they would be even more discreet than they were being now. There was less need for the doctor was working in a hospital in Bombay for a year. He and Tiffany had decided they would seek a future together on his return if they still felt about each other as they had when they parted.

Charles opened the door and Tiffany walked into his arms. He swept her off her feet and carried her to the sofa next to the fireplace. He closed his eyes and held his breath for a moment, so thrilled was he by the feel of her fingers wrapped round him. She hadn't bothered even to open his belt, merely slipped her hand under it. She felt a shiver of excitement just to have that not quite flaccid flesh in her hand. Tiffany adored a man's body, the scent, taste and feel of his sex, and all things erotic – Charles's body and sexuality most especially.

With her free hand she opened his belt and unzipped his trousers. The sound of the zip shattered the silence of the room, focusing their sexual desire. He sprang to life in her hands. Rock hard he throbbed for her. He slid his hand under her skirt and tore away the patch of white silk between her legs. She gasped, and once again, when he thrust eager and searching fingers deep inside her.

'You're bad. God, are you bad!'

He laughed. 'You're delicious, warm and moist, slippery as satin.'

They were gazing into each other's eyes. Lust had taken them over. Nothing in the world mattered for them but the erotic: coming, the taste of each other. They wanted the beat of their sexual embrace. Their hearts and minds were racing towards the pleasure they would give each other; that it seemed no one else in this world could or would give them.

He sat down on the settee with her still in his arms and swung his feet on to the sofa. She placed pillows behind his head and shoulders, and slipped round until she was on top of him. She went to her knees, straddled him, then raised herself while taking him in her hands and directing him until his handsome large knob was where she wanted it. He could wait no longer. He took over and, hands on her waist, with one hard push impaled her on his pulsating member. They were breathless with excitement as she rose up and down on him while tearing off his clothes. She wanted him naked, every inch of his flesh exposed for her to do with as she wanted.

It was no different for him. He disposed of her dress as quickly as possible, had her naked except for bone-coloured stockings with black lacy tops that clung high up on her thighs. Her nipples were hard and erect; her long blonde hair silky and sensuous. Her body, the way she moved on him, seemed to taunt him, as did her blue eyes. He knew that challenge; she wanted him to take her, dissolve her into pools of come. She wanted the entire gamut of sex: ruthless, hard, tender, loving, depraved. Tiffany would endure all things for the sexual oblivion they were seeking together. He quite loved her for that. They had been there many times together, just as he and Amy had once.

Naked and luscious, Tiffany arched her back and rode him. He placed his mouth on her nipples, first one, then the other, and sucked hard. She writhed with the pleasure of exquisite sensations.

He whispered, 'Tiffany, Tiffany,' and his heart beat, Amy, Amy.

He was voracious for her and every penetration was exquisitely deep and tight. He kept the pace of his penetrations even as she came in long and powerful orgasms. Breathlessly she told him in a voice filled with lust and barely above a whisper, 'You're wonderful – we're wonderful. The sex is the best, always better when you have seen her, want her, and use me. You're having sex with me but beating her out of your system. That's why you're so bad. *We're* so bad, and so good together. We know what we are and are not to each other. Bad doesn't matter to us, only adds to the lust we share and the joy of sex together.

26

I want your come, Charles, all you want to give me. You will find no rejection here.'

This time they came together in a long and exquisite orgasm where he pulled on her blonde hair and bit hard into her nipple until he drew a droplet of blood. Simultaneously they let go and called out shamelessly in their lust for life.

Amy drove into the garage, a tumbledown building whose uneven stone-tiled roof was hardly visible for the shiny green ivy that had taken it over as it had the rest of the building. A rambling bush and a small tree were growing where one section of the ridge had collapsed. The garage, more a work of art and flora, had been braced from the inside so many times it had about it more the look of an architectural installation than a covered space. This collapsing shack was home to the Lagonda, and was kept immaculately clean. In some ways Amy did pamper her car. Its shelter was heated in winter, had lights, and unbelievably an old carpet on the floor which Doreen, the woman who did, vacuumed once a month. Amy's friends and neighbours took this extravagance as acceptable eccentricity – the norm for the English though unusual for an American.

After taking the torch from the glove compartment and snapping it on, Amy cut the lights and made her way down the path towards the boat house. The timer switch on the lamps in the library had taken over and the soft warm glow seen through the windows was welcoming. The evenings were drawing in early and she had arrived home at the time of day when dusk was reluctant to give way to night. It lingered, and was unusually beautiful: the blue haze tinged with pink from a setting sun, a pearly translucent mist that hovered, the silhouette of shrubs, and the house dark and brooding in that light but warm and glowing inside. It seemed a perfect ending to the pleasurable day she had spent with Charles.

On entering the house she went directly to the fireplace and put a match to the well-laid fire. Then to the kitchen to put the kettle on, and next to the drinks table in the drawing-room to pour herself a small measure of malt. She drank it down in one swallow. The bite of it in her mouth felt good, warmed her at once, and she shrugged off the chill she had felt in the last few miles of her drive from the city in the open car. Yes, these autumn days demanded warmer clothes riding in an open car. Winter was not far off.

Amy was still feeling exhilarated by her afternoon in London. It seemed a little fanciful but she simply could not shake off the presentiment that something had changed for her during their afternoon together. She could almost have said for them. How? When? Why? All unanswerable questions but she had some good guesses. Was it seeing the Rothko again? Being dazzled by the power of its greatness? Peter Smith? Had seeing him triggered something in her? Or had it been a reminder of being young and discovering sex and the endless pleasure it can be with someone who loves and adores you? Someone who is guileless and good, simple and sweet, yet wild and passionate as Peter had once been.

Yes, maybe it had to do with seeing him again because after that unexpected encounter, and visiting the Rothko, for a moment there with Charles, in his suite, when he had caressed her breasts, she was aroused as she had not been for a very long time. And it was still with her, that desire for all things sexual with a man, something she'd thought over for her forever.

Could it be that it had never been over for her? That this celibate life she had been living these last few years was nothing more than a hiatus because there had not been the right man to give herself to? That she had wanted more than great sex with Charles, or any of the other would-be lovers she had hovering round her, and was stubbornly waiting for it to come along? She wanted sex with a man she could love with great passion, a full heart, as she had very nearly done once with Peter Smith – until she dumped him, coldly, ruthlessly, when she fell in love with Jarret.

What tricks the subconscious can play on one! To dream of Jarret and have Peter appear. Peter, Rothko, Jarret . . . they represented the past, a time in her life that was high, bright and beautiful, and yet a time that ended for her in the depths of darkness and despair. Aloneness such as she had never known. She could hardly bear to remember those times nor how she had lived through them. She had been healed by time and success, real love from several good men. Now it was as if that time had happened to someone else.

She felt enormously pleased that she had left the note for Peter. Whether he called or not, she knew it had been the right thing to do. Amy thought of him and his family, the thrill of having a daughter making her debut at Covent Garden, no matter how small the role. She was happy for him. And Charles? Inescapably he came to mind too – having sex with the beautiful young girl she had seen in the lift. How inevitable that he should have women like her, how lucky the girl was to have such a lover. And how right Amy was to have arranged things so that she might never suffer the humiliation of being set aside for a younger woman.

It was difficult for even Amy to understand why it was so important to her to find a great and romantic passion. To be able to live to the fullest in it one more time – or else to give up sex altogether because she would settle for nothing less. Obviously it was rather more than important, something deep-seated, since celibacy had been so easy to sustain. In some ways it had been a relief to have taken a sabbatical from the erotic, living for pure pleasure and nothing else. At her age she needed more than that. Or, as the case had been, less. Was that age or just maturity?

She didn't have the answer but she did have the good grace to laugh at herself. Age or maturity indeed! No amount of soul searching, the past edging in on her or an unwanted dream, could dull the good feelings she had about herself and life in general. She simply wished she had not grown up in a country whose dictum was: 'Life is a candy box full of delicious sweets, a bowl of ripe red cherries, the rainbow *and* the pot of gold. It's all there for the taking . . .' It had not prepared her for reality. The world as it really is: hard and cruel, where things do not always go your way because you expect them to, and people are evil to other people, and countries rape and despoil other countries. Amy Ross was a happy and lucky lady, who, having learned the hard way the reality of life on earth, was grateful for every good day that came along, seeing it as a bonus for surviving to live another day.

A lingering hot bath, bed, and television – not a bad way to end a good day.

Chapter 3

'Hello.'

Pete hesitated. He had received her note when on the way to the Opera House. He looked at it, felt surprised Amy had left it, then slipped it into the pocket of his evening jacket, and put her firmly out of his mind. He hadn't allowed anything to distract him from that momentous evening. It was Cosima's night. And Annie's. If only she had lived to see it, to be there with them. Well, she hadn't. His wife had died two years before and had missed seeing her dreams for Cosima come to fruition.

The night had been a great success, and the next day and the day after he and the children had more celebrating to distract him from thoughts of Amy. But then, as two of his children left for Paris and Rome, and others made ready to return with him to New York, he found space to think about whether he should or should not do anything about Amy Ross. Clearly leaving the note was an invitation for him to do so.

From the moment Amy re-entered his thoughts and the question was raised he could not erase the sound of her laughter from his mind. How beautiful and sensuous she was still, after several decades. Time seemed to have stood still longer for her than anyone he still knew from that period of his life. What had happened to her? What sort of life had she lived? Was she married? Did she have children? The young man with her, was he part of her life? Curiosity, and no more than that, made him dial the telephone number she had left . . . or so he told himself, and believed it to be true, until he heard her voice. One word, 'Hello', triggered desires in him he had thought dead long since. Did he want that? He was about to put down the receiver but had hesitated too long. She repeated, 'Hello.'

There seemed nothing to do but speak. 'It was nice of you to leave a way for us to make contact again.'

31

Amy was surprised to hear his voice. She had given up on him. It had been nearly a week since she had seen him and impulsively left her address and phone number. He had looked so good, so big and comfortable, still with a sexy macho quality to him. And so American. That amused her – that after all these years abroad she should still find that all-American male look so attractive.

'How nice to hear from you again. I'd given you up, thought you'd returned to Long Island.'

'I'd like to see you, for lunch or dinner, maybe. How about today?'

'I'd like that but it's too short notice, I'm having friends in for lunch. I could make tomorrow.'

'We're leaving tomorrow morning.'

A pause, so long it rang like thunder. It was becoming embarrassing, and embarrassment was the last thing either of them wanted. They broke the silence, both speaking at the same time, which seemed to bridge the distance between them. They laughed and then Amy said, 'Come to me, and bring your beautiful children. Is there a beautiful wife too?'

'I'm a widower. Is there a husband?'

'I've never married.'

'May I come alone and arrange for them to join us later if they want to? I promise that will make life much easier. They're all young adults with ideas of their own as to how they want to spend their last day in London.'

'Fine. Come as early as you like and spend as long as you care to.'

Amy gave instructions and timetables for the best trains and directions for the taxi from there to her house. Having hung up, she was surprised by how excited and pleased she was that Peter had called, that he wanted to see her again, and was coming for the day. She looked at her watch. Nine-fifteen. An early riser, she had already fed the ducks, had been out for a morning walk along the river, and had placed the canvas cushions on *Arcadia*'s wooden benches.

To make lunch for one more person was no problem for Tillie Tyler who was quite used to changes of plan in Amy's household. Tillie had her favourites among the people who came and went through Amy's life, and those were the ones Amy's housekeeper pulled out all the culinary stops for.

Amanda Whately was one of them. She was Amy Ross's best friend. Amanda and her record producer husband were glamorous members of the pop world. They and their three young children lived across the river and upstream about a quarter of a mile, in a rambling Edwardian pile.

Tillie was looking forward to cooking lunch today. She liked Amanda but was dazzled by Dick who always brought her the latest CDs for her children. She could remember him in the sixties when he'd started out with a guitar and had written songs for famous pop groups. The Whatelys were nice, simple, plain-talking people, he with a Geordie accent and Amanda with a very upper-class one. This was his third wife, his third set of children. They came for lunch often but this time had been invited especially to meet Edward Silberzog who wanted to look at their collection of Francis Bacon paintings.

Now Mr Silberzog was a handsome young man, and always charming to Tillie, often bringing her some little gift. He would always tell her, 'For being such a grand cook, and for taking such good care of Amy.' People did worry about Amy and the reclusive life she lived. Her friends all thought her solitude odd for someone so attractive and sought after, someone who enjoyed people and had such a happy grasp on life.

Five mornings a week, Tillie rode in to work on her moped. This morning her mind was on the menu. For the first course, spinach souffle, perhaps. But Amanda was always late, not a good thing for the perfect souffle . . . Tillie had the habit of warning Amy of her arrival by ringing the old ship's bell outside the door. She rang it now as she placed the key in the lock. Then, with a basket of fresh vegetables over her arm, pushed open the door and called out, 'I'm here, Miss Ross.'

'So am I.'

Tillie, taken by surprise, jumped and nearly dropped her basket. 'You frightened me! Lord, did you frighten me.'

It was Amy's habit not to come down from her bedroom or the library before Tillie's arrival. The drill was: arrival, greetings, breakfast brought upstairs, a discussion of the work to be done that day, then each of the women would get on with her workload. Only rarely did Amy go down to the kitchen before Tillie's arrival. It was different on week-ends.

'Sorry, Tillie.'

'Have you had your breakfast?'

'Yes. You have so much to do I thought I'd get it and me out of the way as soon as possible. We're going to have another guest for lunch.'

'Sir Charles?'

'No, someone new. An old friend I bumped into last week in London.'

They sat down and discussed the menu, and Tillie, who had been working for Amy for fourteen years, was very much aware of how happy she was. She seemed to be more exhilarated than usual, and that was always more fun for Tillie. More fun for the luncheon party too. It meant that Amy would not be locked away in the library dealing with the endless stream of correspondence or research that seemed to be such a large part of her work, but popping in and out of the kitchen all morning. The housekeeper and the mistress of the house had an easygoing relationship. One thing they always did together was to dress the table. Amy Ross liked the table to be as beautiful as the food when she entertained.

Two hours later Tillie opened the door to Peter Smith. He handed her a large box of Belgian chocolates. 'Oh, Miss Ross will like these. She's partial to Loeonidas white chocolates,' Tillie exclaimed.

'Well, that was a successful guess.'

The moment he smiled, Peter Smith went on Tillie's A list. 'Come in.'

On the way from the railway station – Edwardian, with tubs of shrubs and wooden benches on the platform, the building itself reflecting the hey-day of rail travel – Pete had been enchanted. He had felt he was stepping back in time to the England most Americans want to see. All that had been missing was a grey day, fog and a chill in the air.

Instead he had found the sun high in the sky and drenching what was left of the autumn leaves on the trees and the carpet of them on the roads with a luminescent light that made them glow dramatically against the evergreens and shrubs. The air had been unusually warm for the time of year. Altogether he had been surprised and charmed but somehow could not equate the setting with Amy. He was even less able to do so when the taxi took a turn off the country lane on to the dirt track that led to her house with its barnlike proportions and unprepossessing entrance. She was still full of surprises evidently. Stepping through the front door, he was jolted into Amy Ross's world and yet again caught off guard by the splendid environment she had created for herself.

He stood with Tillie in the entrance hall among lifesize eighteenth-century terracotta statues, three of them: beautifully draped Roman ladies standing majestically among Kentia palms and flowering azaleas in front of a clear glass folding screen. His eyes could hardly take in everything. Besides the ladies and the pair of armoires, one either side of the front door he had just walked through, there were fishing rods neatly stacked in a rack, huge old baskets filled with gum boots, a pair of eighteenth-century curve-backed chairs with lion's heads for arms carved out of blocks of red marble. Tables – one of wood, dark and rich, round and on a chunky pedestal base; another of grey marble, octagonal, on an elegant urn-like pedestal – were covered with books piled high among fishing reels, a basket of apples, another of pears, several hats, a pair of gloves, and a canvas fisherman's bag.

The one long solid wall was used to display a Hans Hoffman painting, two large Motherwells, three richly framed Matisse drawings, and many more works of art Pete did not recognise, rising one above the other up the three-storey-high wall. The view from the hall encompassed the entire boat house from floor to rafters and exhibited the two galleries, one above the other, as well. It was impressive yet comfortable, exciting and inviting, from the fire in the huge hearth to the many paintings and sculptures, the rare, worn and faded oriental carpets on the floor, and the furniture in original coverings or else upholstered in antique pieces of tapestry and fabric.

Tillie pushed open the glass screen and they stepped into the drawing-room where she called out, 'Miss Ross, it's Mr . . .' She looked to Peter for help.

'Mr Smith,' he told her.

'Mr Smith is here.'

From the top gallery at the far end of the boat house, high above them, Amy called down, 'Peter.'

His name seemed to echo through the house. He felt disorientated, out of his depth, and wondered what had possessed him to make that call and accept this invitation – until Amy appeared at the gallery's balustrade. She waved a shoe at him and called down, 'Just finishing dressing. Your timing is perfect. We'll have some time to ourselves before the other guests arrive.'

He watched her drop the shoe and slip into it. He followed her with his eyes as she walked from what he guessed was her bedroom, down the stairs, across the library and down another flight of stairs, into the drawing-room towards him.

'How are you?' she asked.

There was something in the way she spoke, an intimacy in her voice, that drew him towards her. Finally he managed, 'Somehow I don't know how to answer that. I think I'm suffering from culture shock. England *and* Amy Ross!'

He had always had an honest wit about him that had been endearing. She smiled at him. 'Surely not?'

'Surely yes! This place – it's marvellous. What a setting to live in: English countryside an hour from London, a garden, and on the river. And the house . . . well, I didn't think about where or how you lived, but if I had, I wouldn't have imagined anything like this. Would it be awful to ask for a tour before the others get here? There's so much to see.'

Amy had no idea what made her do it. His genuine enthusiasm for her and her house? There being no awkward moments where there could have been? Or was it mere instinct, happiness at meeting him again, at having him in her home? Whatever the reason, she raised her hand and very gently ran her fingers through the locks of hair that had fallen to one side on his forehead. She smiled at him. That was too intimate for Peter. Very gently he removed her hand and, clasping it in his, smiled at her.

'Come on, I'll show you round. Shall we start at the top and work down?' Amy asked him.

They had two hours before the other guests arrived. And when they did Peter and Amy were not in the house but sitting in the sun on faded, flower-patterned linen cushions on a wooden bench aboard *Arcadia*.

It was a joyous two hours for them both, greatly resembling a first date. They were cautious with each other, flirtatious, accepting of the sexual chemistry between them but cleverly dancing round it. They were two people discovering each other and liking what they were finding. It was not so much that they were avoiding talking about the past as that they were more interested in discovering each other all over again. They talked about many things, none of them intimate. Intimacy did not seem to be on their agenda. Friendship did. And yet . . . there was something there for Amy, something she hadn't felt for a man in a long time.

Edward Silberzog and Amy had never been lovers. Edward had only male lovers. The clever thirty-two-year-old art historian and Amy were close friends, sharing a love of art and the art world. They confided in and helped each other. Therefore Edward was surprised that he had not been told about the mystery guest sitting in the steam boat with Amy. As he crossed the lawn to join them Edward could see quite

36

plainly this was no one from their world but an outsider, a stray. Not like Amy at all.

The Whatelys arrived in a rowing boat and tied it to Amy's dock then the party all went into the house for drinks. Throughout the lunch of souffle, followed by a whole poached turbot served with hollandaise sauce and an assortment of baby vegetables, then bread and butter pudding with lashings of double cream, followed by a ripe Camembert, the conversation was entertaining. There was much laughter, helped no doubt by several bottles of perfectly chilled Montrachet.

Pete found Amy, in every way, to be much more than he'd expected. Maybe too much so. She barely resembled the woman he had once known, though that was to be anticipated. He was certain he no longer resembled the man he had been. They had lived whole lives apart, full and rich lives, but very different – he could see that in the way Amy lived now. She had left him for a great love, for adventure, to grab the world with both hands and shake it. Had it been worth the price she paid? He didn't ask her that, nor if she had found all she had been looking for. Had she been happy? Was she happy now? He had the answer to that last question, could see with his own eyes. Here was a woman content with herself, and her life. What more could one ask for?

He had chosen to take over the family farm, to live in Easthampton where he was born. He had not married for passion or for love. Those were the things he had had with Amy, the things she had run away from. No, he had married on the rebound from those things and had settled for a beautiful quiet woman who wanted the same things he did. He married the girl next door and they had a wonderful life together, raising their children and being a family of substance in a small chic Long Island town. They were the plain-folk friends of their more famed neighbours from New York City. Among those far more sophisticated and creative writers and artists, they functioned as sometime patrons and full-time examples of stability. Peter saw himself during Amy's luncheon as not quite but almost a boring fellow in Amy Ross's world.

But Peter Smith was truly a man content with the life he had made and with himself. And so he felt not insecure in the company he was keeping, just different from them. He didn't mind being ordinary, it had always suited him. But being honourable and ordinary had also lost him Amy.

It was over coffee when he was standing next to the fire with her and they were talking about the tragedy of the former Yugoslavia: the heartbreak that would never be mended, man's inhumanity to man. There was something in her voice, a light in her eyes . . . He was amazed as it came to him like a bolt of lightning: he still loved her, still wanted an erotic life with her. Their differences were the same as they had always been, yet even after all these years they didn't affect how he felt about her, not one bit.

Once that flash of awareness had struck him, Pete's attention lapsed. The realisation truly stunned him. He was a man no longer looking for love. As for the erotic, an uncomplicated sex life was easy to achieve in Easthampton or New York City. He was, after all, a most eligible man.

His wife's illness had been long and incredibly painful; years of nursing her, watching this woman who had never in her life harmed a living soul waste away, had taken a toll on him. He intended never to marry again. Until now, the moment when he gazed into Amy's eyes and faced the truth: she had always been the woman he'd wanted to marry and build a life with. He had always wanted to love and care for her so that she could have everything she wanted in life. And, God help him, he still did. He only heard her words when she touched his arm and asked, 'Peter, are you all right?'

It seemed to snap him back to reality. 'Just a little too much wine, I think. I'll step outside for a breath of fresh air. That will revive me.'

Amy watched him walk away from her. She didn't much like that. She could not remember the last time she'd felt so good about a man. All through lunch she'd stolen glances across the table at him. She wanted him, thought how nice it would feel to be wrapped in his arms, all the warmth and strength of character he possessed enfolding her. How safe she would be with him. He had been a formidable lover in their youth, would he be less than that in his middle age? A strange question for a woman content with celibacy, and who no longer had much interest in sex. She very nearly laughed but instead distracted herself from thoughts of him by paying attention to her other guests.

It didn't work. He remained on her mind. Amy knew he was lying, it had not been the drink. She waited for several minutes before she followed him. He was standing by the river, pensively smoking a Havana cigar. She walked up behind him and slipped her arms round his waist. She would not embarrass him and force the issue. Instead she asked, 'Feeling better?'

He sighed. The warmth of her body against his felt so right, so good. He clasped her hands in one of his and held them there. Without turning to face her, he told her, 'It has really been wonderful, sheer magic, to see you again. A visit I will always remember.'

He was relegating her to the past, she could understand that. A chance meeting of two old lovers, she really didn't expect more, and yet she was somehow sorry. Was he? Amy released herself and moved round to face him. She was smiling, and her smile brought one to his lips. 'That's good since the day isn't even over. I'm going to take us all on a trip upriver to a place for tea. Would you like that?'

'Very much. Does *Arcadia* sail as well as she looks?'

'Better. Peter?'

'Everyone else calls me Pete. I'd forgotten you never did like abbreviated names.'

She ignored that, and though she hadn't intended to say anything, asked, 'It wasn't the wine, was it?'

He hesitated but then answered, 'No.'

'It was me.'

'No, it was us. Will you settle for that?'

'If you'll answer one more thing. Us past or us now in the present?'

'Does it matter?'

'It could, and I think we both know that.'

He answered by placing an arm around her. They smiled at each other and Amy had her answer.

There was something there for them both. Was it gratitude? The excitement of discovering each other again, and nothing more? Time. Each of them needed time to adjust to the possibility of love entering their lives, with each other or anyone else. For they might after all be nothing more than catalysts in each other's lives.

For Amy the day seemed more special, more glorious. They boarded *Arcadia* and she busied herself making ready for their trip up the Thames. Pete watched with admiration as *Arcadia* began building up a head of steam.

Those were the last moments that Pete and Amy would have together that wonderful day because when Amy gave the three blasts of *Arcadia*'s horn that would summon her other guests they came down the lawn with four of Pete's children who had arrived several minutes before. It would be chillier on the river, though the sun was still high in the sky. Thanks to Tillie, the party arrived from the house with a variety of shawls, jackets, woolly jumpers, and hats together with the box of chocolates that Pete had brought, a bottle of Kirsch, and a basket of small-stemmed crystal glasses.

Pete's children were enchanted by Amy's house and lifestyle. Half an hour later, chugging along on the river, they were equally enchanted by Amy herself. The luncheon party seemed to shift immediately into a higher gear with the arrival of the Smith children. Handsome and beautiful young people, intelligent and with a zest for life, they donned some of the warm clothes as did Amy's other guests. Everyone looked at everyone else, and under Amanda's direction exchanged hats and shawls or jackets as if they were dressing for a play or a costume party. There was a great deal of laughter. The chocolates and the bottle of Kirsch were constantly passed round.

'So, this is high jinks on the Thames,' said Edward, enjoying himself enormously.

Several people walking their dogs along the river bank smiled and waved at *Arcadia*. 'What a grand sight it must be, seeing this sixty-foot vintage boat and a jolly party like us in full steam going up the river,' said Cosima.

Tom, Pete's twenty-five-year-old son, said, 'Why do I keep thinking of *Ship of Fools?* That assortment of strangers on a boat sailing to their destinies. Or *Fitzcarraldo*. That wonderful boat plying the river or being pulled through the jungle to bring opera to the natives. Wonderful films.'

'Tom's a documentary film maker, but he'll end up another Jean-Luc Godard. He has a flair for the dramatic and the fantastical,' offered Pete.

'We can't all be farmers, Dad.' And Tom punched him playfully on the arm, then placed his arm round his father's shoulders. 'Besides, look at us. Could we not be some comic opera of our time? *And* we have a genuine opera star with us.'

'And a record producer,' interjected Dick Whately.

At that moment Cosima stood up in the boat and began to sing a few lines of an aria from *The Flying Dutchman*. Her voice rose above the sound of the engine that somehow added drama to the aria and conjured up visions of the ghostly clipper ship: broken masts and sails shredded from the winds, sailing through a swirl of dense fog on a sea smooth and calm as a lake. For a moment as she sang, something mysterious from the netherworld settled over *Arcadia* and her passengers. Everyone on board was transfixed by Cosima's glorious voice, the drama she evoked. She stopped singing as suddenly as she'd begun, and smiled at them. She tore the black, wide-brimmed felt hat with its clutch of white ostrich feathers attached to a crimson satin band from her head, and with a grand flourish made her bow and jumped down from the bench where she had been standing. There was applause, shrill whistles, and calls for more, more!

And there was more, but no more Wagner, and not from just Cosima. Dick told them briefly about the river and Jerome K. Jerome's story of *Three Men in a Boat*. Edward hummed a duet with Amanda, the Beatles' 'Yellow Submarine'. Josh, Pete's youngest child, gave his rendition of 'Old Man River', but was heckled after only several lines into silence and a sulk which vanished after he had been fed several chocolates by Cosima and Amanda. Fred, another son, who was the image of his father, and clearly as besotted by Amy as his brothers and sister, asked what the river had been like in Henry VIII's time. She entertained them with a history of what life on this stretch of the Thames was like in the sixteenth and seventeenth centuries until they pulled up to a dock to have a sumptuous hotel tea: bite-sized cucumber sandwiches that melted on the tongue, rich tea cakes, scones and clotted cream topped by dollops of strawberry preserve, and slices of chocolate mousse seven-layer cake were served at the small inn that had stood on the river for two hundred years.

On the way downriver towards home they stopped off at the Whatelys' because everyone was having too good a time to stop partying. Edward vanished with Dick and Amy for a tour of the Bacon paintings and was quite overwhelmed by the collection and that Dick had bought his first five direct from the artist for a thousand pounds and a case of champagne each, his last painting from a dealer for nine hundred and fifty thousand pounds and no champagne, merely a night on the tiles with Francis in celebration. The Whatelys had a collection of enormous importance and value, Bacons of extraordinary quality that Dick intended to keep as private as possible and at home. A frustrated Edward, who had hoped to get him to lend some of the paintings to a travelling exhibition of Bacon's work which he was organising, was silenced once and for all when Dick told him, 'I don't give a flying fuck about their value! I bought them because I like them, enjoy every minute of them. I feel about them the same way my mother feels about the antimacassars on her chairs. It wouldn't be home without them.' Amy could barely hide the smile on her lips. Edward had been told. Dick had been warned of Edward's intentions and was playing with him adroitly.

Dick walked away from Edward, himself barely able to keep the smile off his face. He did so like playing the Geordie boy made good! 'Have a look at this, Cosima, and then we'll have a sing-song. I have a couple of friends with voices who are neighbours. I'll give them a call, and how about you all staying on for dinner?'

Dick tossed her a score, Leonard Bernstein's *West Side Story*, and added, 'There should be one or two things in there that would suit your voice.'

It was gone two o'clock in the morning when the lanterns were lit on *Arcadia*, and Edward, the Smith clan and Amy pushed off and down the river towards home. The lantern on her dock was twinkling in the night, cold now but with a sky bright with stars and a harvest moon, only a hint of a mist on the water. They steamed towards it, a happy band of revellers.

Once in the house and warmed by the fire, the party was quite suddenly over. It was time for sleep and the new day that was fast coming upon them. Amy offered to put them all up for the night in one fashion or another, Edward offered a ride to London if they could all squash into his BMW. Finally they decided they would all go to London, Amy driving and taking with her Pete and two of the boys, Edward the others.

Once Amy reversed the Lagonda Rapide out of the garage and tied the white scarf over her hair, she had to laugh. The Smith clan were all standing there, silent and agape. It was the final straw. She had won them over hands down. Only her laughter broke the spell the sight of the car cast upon them. What seemed like a hundred questions about the Lagonda later, they were all settled and on their way. It was a short and easy run to London at that hour.

Standing under the canopy of Claridge's, surrounded by the Smiths, being hugged and kissed and begged by each of them in turn to come to Easthampton for a visit, only then did Amy think, They might have been *our* children. I might have lived a whole lifetime in the bosom of this family instead of one night. It was a quick glimpse of what might have been, no more. It hurt for only a second then the pain was gone. Amy Ross did not believe in what might have been.

It was Cosima Smith, Pete's lovely daughter, who, when she kissed Amy on the cheek, whispered, 'You've made Pa really happy. We've never seen him like he was today. Thanks.'

They were all there when it was time for Amy to say goodbye to Peter. She took him by the hands and told him, 'You have a wonderful family, it's been a privilege to meet them.'

42

'I'm a lucky man.'

'Yes, you are.'

'It's been a memorable day, one I'm sure we'll all be talking about for a long time.'

'And for me. I'm so pleased you remembered my laugh and came to say hello.'

'Then let's not say goodbye.' He could say no more. His children were watching, the timing was wrong.

With that he walked Amy to her car and helped her in. She started the engine. One last look at Pete. She half expected him to say something, she wanted him to, something intimate, something with hope in it. He said nothing. Instead, he placed his large strong hand over hers now clasping the steering wheel and squeezed it, and she knew why he was saying nothing.

'It's up to me, isn't it?'

She smiled at him and he smiled back and removed his hand. He stood away from the car.

'There's a lot to think about,' she said, more to herself than to him.

'Take your time,' were his last words to her.

She turned away from him to look over her shoulder and give one last wave to his children before she drove off. She caught a glimpse in the Lagonda's rearview mirror of Pete Smith standing among his children under the lights of Claridge's. She saw a canopy of brightness, shining warmth, an island of comfort and love in the blackness of the night, the loneliness of the deserted, silent street. How many lives can one live in a lifetime? wondered Amy.

Chapter 4

In addition to Amanda, Amy had two other close friends. But these women were career women like herself, in their mature years, having gone through various lovers and husbands. Busy women but far more social and more interested in men than she was. They therefore considered it unfair that it was Amy who attracted the men when it was they who were on the hunt.

They were ladies who lunched together on occasion, saw each other rarely because their work and their lifestyles were so different, and spoke to each other at length at least several times a week. They earned three-figure salaries, spent money lavishly and worried about Amy, who, in their eyes, lived from hand to mouth. In fact she lived from assignment to assignment, book to book or, when desperate, from the sale of a work of art. Her income was tenuous, her life lived in the slow lane. They thought she needed excitement, a man, preferably one to give her financial security because for all the comforts and aesthetic beauty she lived with, she was still a working girl – and no longer a girl at that.

They saw her insistence on staying as much in the background as possible and living full-time in the country as negative factors in her life. Her lifestyle concerned them. They were most certainly not country girls, more Mayfair ladies, and rarely spent more than the odd week-end in the country – and that usually meant the South of France or Tuscany. But they were caring girlfriends. That was why they were all four of them meeting for a quick lunch at Fortnum & Mason. They had heard from Amanda about the fabulous Smiths and the day on the river.

All through lunch they skirted any mention of Pete Smith. Instead they gossiped about the London scene. Amy lived vicariously through her girlfriends' social lives, enjoying every minute of it all as long as she didn't have to be a part of it. They knew it, and so did Amy who only on the rarest occasions allowed them to drag her into their social whirl. The waitress had just finished topping up their cups with coffee. No sooner had she left the table than Frances said, 'Amanda says Pete Smith and his family are great. So who is Pete Smith?'

'I never thought you'd last through to the coffee, Frances. You could have met him, you *had* been invited.'

'That doesn't tell us anything, Amy. Amanda says they were an attractive bunch.'

'And?' teased Amy.

'Very American, apple pie and vanilla ice cream, a farmer,' said Karen, who from the twinkle in her eyes and the intonation in her voice considered those things to be serious drawbacks to eligibility.

'Actually, I did say all those things, *and* that he didn't have a Chinaman's chance with you if you were turning down suitors like Charles.'

'I've known Amy longer than you have, Amanda, and I can tell you, it's all a matter of magic with her. If the magic had been there, he would have had a chance. Was the magic there? Did your heart skip a beat? And who was he really? 'Fess up,' demanded Karen in the nicest way.

Amy laughed, bringing a smile to all of them. 'It didn't take you girls long, did it? What romantics.'

'And I suppose you're not a romantic? That's a laugh! Since I've known you, until you called it off with Charles anyway, it was one romantic interlude after another for you. Of us all, it's you who's the greatest romantic. The men in your life, the work that you do, the lifestyle you've created for yourself in the country . . . You make us three look like tough, realistic mercenaries when it comes to men,' objected Frances.

'Well!' said Karen, and all the women had the good grace to laugh at themselves.

'Did your heart go zing when you saw him again after so many years?' asked Amanda.

'Oh, he was a man from your past. Too bad.' That was Frances again who had claimed many times she wouldn't touch a lover from the past with a barge pole.

'Well?' prompted Amanda, who had been curious and had not in the five days since the luncheon party had time to talk to Amy except to say thank you on the telephone.

'I confess.'

They waited anxiously to hear her confession.

'My heart did *not* go zing. That's not to say that I would not have liked it to, but who knows? Maybe hearts don't go zing for middle-aged ladies. It felt warm, comfortable, I found him sexually attractive – but then I always had. And, yes, I am a romantic.'

'You mean, that's it?'

'What more do you want?'

'How did he feel? Did he make a pass?'

Amy ignored the questions from her girlfriends and asked, 'Amanda, you were there. How did you find him with me?'

This was an opportunity for Amy to refresh her memory of that day. Certain things were becoming clouded. Though Pete had remained vivid in her mind the following day and for several days after, that sense of the sexual chemistry between them was beginning to fade, helped perhaps by Amy's not having heard from Pete since she had driven away from him.

'Attractive, intelligent, sexy. A big, quiet man, sort of like Gary Cooper or James Stewart. The quiet Americans they used to portray in the movies. A good man, interesting in his own very straight way. A little out of his depth or maybe just surprised by the different lifestyle we live. Incredibly happy to be with Amy and his children. The kind of man who's always pleasant to be around. Did he fancy our Amy? Rotten, I would say, but he was holding back. But that might be me wanting her to have such a good man in her life. He was very cautious. Showed nothing. So what's the story, Amy?'

'I don't honestly know if there is a story, Amanda. He walked up to the table in Claridge's where I was dining with Charles, and until he spoke I didn't even recognise him. I had forgotten him nearly thirty years ago – until I heard his voice. We were lovers and in love when we were young. I left him for someone else, someone quite the opposite to him, dumped him without a second thought. I was out of control, had fallen madly, deeply, passionately in love as I had never been before. I didn't let him down easily or very nicely. One day we were everything to each other and the next I walked out on him with barely a word. I shattered his life and his dreams. Truth be told, when he approached Charles and me and I realised who he was, so much time had passed that what had happened between us in the past didn't seem at all important. Not for me, nor for him. It was instant relating instead, as if we never had a past.'

'And?' asked Amanda.

47

'And I liked him as I always had. I had forgotten how nice a human being he is, and was enchanted by his children. I've not heard from him but somehow I think I will. For the moment there's no more to it than that.'

The three women had been listening intently, hopefully, hanging on to Amy's every word. These were not the sort who liked to see a man get away. They were riveted by this peek into Amy's past. Her friends around the table were women who had known her for many years and therefore had some knowledge of her immediate past. But Amy had always been extremely secretive about her life and loves before she had moved from the States to Europe. Oh, the odd reference, but only fleeting. Nothing more.

Amy didn't have that all-American trait of laying out her life for anyone to see. She was always tight-lipped about herself, past and present. Frances had once summed her up as, 'Lots of self-esteem, big libido, little ego, and just the right amount of vanity.' She had been right. Even Amy herself, when she heard it, had to agree.

Riveted by news of a new man in Amy's life, and hearing of the Amy of decades ago, made ruthless by passion, the great, grand love that can destroy, they realised for the first time why she played so loose and so free with the men who fell in love with her. Why she rejected marriage to Charles, and before him Anthony Kramer, a long-time suitor the girls had begged her to marry. Charles was too young while Anthony Kramer was of their generation, an American like Amy, not very handsome but attractive, sexy, erudite. As Frances used to put it, 'Mega wealthy, a man who enjoys spending his money in the sort of ways Amy approves of.' Both men were still around and in her life years later; they still had hope. But she never relented, kept her unmarried state, her short-term sexual love affairs, until she had given up even these. Now the puzzle as to why was suddenly solved. The three women sat silent for several minutes, each looking at the others. None of them had to say anything, each of them understood what they had never guessed: that there had been a one and only man in Amy Ross's life. And whatever had happened to that love affair had left her too damaged for love, the commitment of a long-time relationship. That life she lived long before they met her, that life she rarely spoke about, had caught up with her.

'The other man, Amy. That's the real story, isn't it? Do tell.'

The women were surprised and somewhat embarrassed to see the colour drain from Amy's face. Embarrassed for her, that she had been

48

caught out; embarrassed for themselves for having been so prying and the cause of some anxiety about the other man in that long ago love story: Pete Smith.

'What a clod you are, Frances,' snapped Amanda.

Amy felt cold, her mouth suddenly dry. Frances had given her a fright. The real story? The other man? Those two things had been long forgotten, dealt with emotionally a long time ago. But what they conjured up now was that dream she had had less than a fortnight ago. It flashed through her mind and unnerved her in the same way as she had been unnerved upon awakening from it. A dream of Jarret Sparrow? The arrival of Pete Smith? None of it made sense. What had those two things to do with her life? She took a sip of the hot coffee and a deep breath. She closed her eyes for a second and took another deep breath, sighing slowly, becoming more calm. Or was it a sigh of resignation? When she opened her eyes the anxiety her friends had seen in them only moments before was gone.

Everyone at the table looked relieved. For a short time something unpleasant had settled over the women and they were all glad it was gone. Frances, Karen and Amanda were further relieved when they saw a smile on Amy's still pale face.

'No, she's not a clod, Amanda. What she said didn't upset me in the least. What it did was to remind me of a most unpleasant dream I had some days ago, and that *did* upset me. Now it's passed and I'm all right. It was a dream about that other man – of whom, by the way, I have no intention of telling you the least little thing! He's a man I haven't thought about any more than I have of Peter these last twenty odd years, and no one I care to talk about. The only thing I will say is that to dream of one and have the other arrive is odd indeed. Now can we leave it at that?'

The women didn't mind dropping the subject. Each of them had had in their time some man they didn't want to bring back into their life, even in conversation. They understood, but that understanding was not enough for them to continue their lunch in the same easy way in which it had begun.

Amy was driving. All the way home she and Amanda spoke about any number of things, anything and everything except the hiccup at lunch which had so upset her. When Amy drove through the gates of the Whatelys' house and up the drive she was holding her breath, just praying that Amanda would not at the last minute bring up the incident.

They had, since it was a bright sunny day and still unusually warm weather, driven to London in the open Lagonda. Amanda wore a sable and knit jacket, and a hat with a scarf over it tied under her chin. Amy had her usual white silk scarf covering her hair and one of Charles's gifts wrapped round her: a 1920s full-length jaguar coat in fabulously good condition. There was besides the Lagonda's super hot heater to keep them warm. Now, with Amy still in the driver's seat and the motor running, Amanda was out of the car and reaching into the back seat for her shopping: Harvey Nichols, Harrods, The White House, The General Trading Company. Bags of it. Amy felt relieved, now that they had made it home, that the subject of Peter and Jarret was closed.

It would have been had not Dick Whately come out to greet his wife and help with the shopping. He greeted Amy with a kiss and then, walking towards Amanda, said, 'Had a nice day, ladies? Well, I can see you did, Amanda.' Then, gathering all of her shopping from the boot and the back seat of the car, Dick laughed and teased the women, 'Just a normal girls' day out! Amanda buys out the store, while Amy doesn't even have a new handkerchief. I wish you would use Amy as your example when you're out shopping, my love.'

'It's the same old speech every time he sees a shopping bag,' said Amanda, standing next to the still seated Amy, not the least annoyed by her husband's suggestion. Both women knew he didn't give a fig what his wife spent.

Dick leaned down to give his wife a peck on the cheek and asked the two women: 'Good lunch? Lots of delicious girly gossip, a little true confession, the usual?'

Amanda deliberately stepped on her husband's toes. Rather than interpret this as a signal to be quiet, he exclaimed, 'Christ, Amanda! What was that for?'

Amy realised that she had not fooled Amanda into thinking she was no longer disturbed by the dream or Pete Smith. The two women looked at each other, and in the gaze that passed between them Amy saw Amanda's concern for her and appreciated that she had tried to hide it ever since the luncheon party had broken up.

'Because it was a signal to shut up, Dick. And that was because you were right on the mark. Maybe not true confessions so much as murky revelations.'

'Yours?'

'Dick!' Amanda was distinctly annoyed now.

'Sorry about that, Amy. I'm a clod.'

'Don't be silly, Dick, there's nothing to be sorry about. The girls only got a little to chew over. You can be sure I didn't give much away and have declared the subject closed. Which it is.' Then Amy gave a light flirtatious laugh to ease the awkward moment for Amanda and Dick.'

'Stay for dinner,' urged Amanda.

'No. Thanks, but I really do want to get home. I have calls to Switzerland to make.'

'Buying, selling or consulting?' asked Dick who was always fascinated by Amy's work in the art world.

'Consultation on a Soutine someone in Switzerland wants to sell privately. Bags of discretion. If it does come available you would do well to have a look at it. I think it's very much one you'd be thrilled to have in your collection. I can't say more right now.'

With that Amy blew them a kiss and roared off down the drive. It would take her another twenty minutes to get home, and she did so want to get home.

Once she closed her front door behind her, she leaned against it and gave an enormous sigh of relief. That dream simply would not go away! Why did it still haunt her? The past didn't. Yet she was frightened by that dream. 'Shit,' she called out in the dark, silent house and switched on the lights.

Her whole world sprang into light. A stranger who had not known her had once been brought to her house. The stranger went away and sent a note: 'Your house is an uplifting experience. Thank you.' She looked through the glass screen and saw it in its entirety in one glance, and it was true. It was an uplifting experience and her mood was raised above the darkness of a dream.

Suddenly the energy that had drained out of her at the close of lunch with her girlfriends rushed back. She would no longer sustain unhappiness or anxiety. She had learned how to let it go. Once she had been a woman who never expected upheavals of any kind in her life and could be devastated by them. Now she was a woman who could expect them, could take them in her stride and deal with them, and then immediately let them go. There was a great deal to be said for the mature years of one's life.

Amy looked at her watch, she was running late, and went directly to the library. All the research work on the Soutine: its provenance, her analysis of the painting, letters corroborating her own analysis from a French art historian, and from Edward Silberzog as one of the curators at the Museum of Modern Art in New York, was laid out on her library table.

Amy examined the documents one more time. She looked yet again at the excellent coloured photograph of the painting, a prime example of Chaim Soutine's work. She placed the photograph on the library table again and sat back and closed her eyes, remembering the real painting and the collection in Geneva. She had gone twice to see it. The first time at her client's request, the second at her own. She had had to confirm several things about it. Both she and her client were thrilled by what she had so far discovered. The painting was an extremely rare Soutine, probably the only one of its kind that he had ever painted.

Chaim Soutine had been a Lithuanian Jew who had emigrated to Paris in 1913. Amy's client's father met him a year after he arrived at the time Soutine was being influenced by Expressionism. Amy's client's father, a doctor, was at the time collecting the then new Expressionist painters. He attended several of the poor Montparnasse artists who respected him as a physician but even more as a friend who never sent a bill. When he was called in to attend Chaim Soutine, the doctor had been appalled at the poverty and filth the man lived and painted in, and had befriended him. Not an easy task. Soutine was a difficult and suspicious man who had been twisted by gruelling poverty, near starvation, a darkness of the heart and soul. The painter finally achieved recognition in the 1920s despite his reluctance to exhibit his work. Amy's client's father was rewarded by him when, one day arriving at Soutine's studio, he found the painter in acute distress with an American dealer and his client pressing him for a large canvas Soutine did not want to sell.

The arrival of the doctor settled the problem. Soutine sold it to his friend for the equivalent of fifty dollars in French francs, a pittance compared to the dealer's offer but a fortune in the 1920s to the artist and the doctor. There were accounts in diaries and letters to verify the story.

Amy had studied the life of Chaim Soutine and could almost visualise it: the tortured, unhappy soul, the squalor of his life, the Paris art world of the 1920s. The painting itself? A masterpiece. Amy was thinking about that scene. How humiliating for him to have to bargain for his life's blood, for that indeed was what he painted with. What price could one put on such an elemental struggle, and the great painting which was its result? She conjured up a vision of the artist working on this glorious canvas. Chaim Soutine painted with his guts and his soul, and with thickly applied paint, intense colour, distorted, writhing forms. He was, with Chagall, the leading representative of French Expressionism. Amy remained lost in that painting and thoughts of the artist, the agony and ecstasy of art. She was snapped back to reality by the ringing of the telephone. The interference annoyed her. She was quite happy lost in the Paris art world of the 1920s. The telephone was incessant, ringing several more times before she finally answered.

'Hello.'

'You sound grumpy. I hope I didn't wake you?'

She hesitated for a few seconds before she answered him. Her voice softened. 'No, you didn't wake me. Did I really sound grumpy?'

'Yes.'

'I suppose I was. I was lost in my work and the ringing of the telephone yanked me back to the here and now.'

'I'm disturbing you. I'll call back another time.'

'No, don't hang up. I'm really pleased you're calling.'

'You are?'

'Why are you so surprised?'

He changed the subject rather than answer her question. 'The children want a steam boat like yours.'

That amused Amy. She felt a surge of tenderness towards him. '*Arcadia* was built in 1901.' They were skirting around the real reason for his call and they both knew it.

'How are you? I think about you often,' he told her.

'I'm glad about that.'

'That's encouraging.'

'It was meant to be.'

'That last sight of you driving away into the night all alone – I hated that.'

'Pete, I left with a great deal to think about.'

'You called me Pete, and you hate nicknames!'

'They don't bother me as much as they used to, and you always preferred it. I can live with that.'

'It isn't much but it's a beginning.'

'I guess it is.'

'I'll call you tomorrow night.'

'I may be in Geneva.'

'Oh.' He sounded hurt, disappointed.

She quickly added, 'For my work.'

'I'll try you, and if you're not there I'll try another time. Is that all right?'

'Of course it is, you silly old thing. Seeing you again has made me really happy.'

'Long may it last.'

'Goodbye, Pete.'

'Goodbye, Amy.'

He'd called and that felt good. But why didn't it feel better? She wanted it to. Amy had hoped that when she did hear from him she would feel that surge of excitement for a man that she wanted to feel again in her life. Not obsessive love; she had had that, been there, and it had been terrific but destructive. High on the life of another as well as oneself, there's a great deal to be said for that, but not when it blinds you to all else in life.

It didn't have to be instant love and passion, overwhelming sexual desire. She had had that too, many times. She could wait for it to evolve. Maybe this time round that was what Pete was doing as well. Possibly, had she not been distracted with the Soutine and the call to Geneva, she might have felt a greater surge of sexual excitement at the sound of his voice. But Pete had had a great deal to compete with at the moment when he'd called: the art world and her work, the singular life she had created for herself.

Bad timing, she told herself. She would come round. And then, for a fleeting moment, wondered what it would take. She thought on that and deduced there must be something to her and Pete because he had stirred sexual feeling in her, the desire to be outrageously sexual with a man again, which had not happened for a very long time. That in itself was exciting, something to ponder on. Especially since she had truly believed she was through with sex and love.

She was still immersed in thought when the telephone rang again. She answered it and pushed thoughts of Pete from her mind. The sale of the Soutine was uppermost now. She had suddenly made her decision as to the three people she would approach on behalf of her client, and that was her preoccupation when she heard Edward Silberzog's assistant at the Museum of Modern Art in New York explaining she was calling on his behalf. He was flying in to London for a day and then on to Paris. Could he possibly meet her at her place on Monday afternoon, briefly? He would be bringing a friend along for her to meet.

Amy was only barely listening to the young woman. Her mind was on the Soutine and the coup of dealing with this great find of a painting. She said absently, 'Yes, thank you, goodbye,' and jotted the date down in her diary.

'Then that is a confirmed appointment, Miss Ross?'

'Yes, I did say that, Penelope.'

'Please, did you write it down, Miss Ross? He asked me to ask you that. It's very important to him, you see. He's only stopping off briefly in London to meet you.'

'Yes, it's down in my book. Look, I don't mean to be rude but I do have to go, Penelope.' And Amy put down the telephone and again, almost immediately, picked up the receiver and punched in the Geneva telephone number.

The following day, when Tillie was putting together thin sandwiches of brown bread, sparingly buttered and thick with smoked salmon topped with several screws of freshly ground black pepper, for the small basket Amy used to picnic with on air travel, and she was checking her briefcase for the fourth time to make certain she had forgotten nothing, the ship's bell outside the front door was loudly rung.

Amy ignored it. She was switched off from everything but the project in hand: getting to her client in Geneva. Her mind was filled with the Soutine painting of two nude reclining women, and the fact that the world believed that he had only painted one nude, prudish and flurried. It had always been assumed the reason had been a discreet and unpublicised romantic life. This new discovery would change history. The sale of the painting, and the book she had decided she would write on the history of it, were all running wildly through the forefront of her mind. She would try and tie its publication in with the exhibiting of the painting if it was sold to the Louvre or the Metropolitan Museum in New York, two of the three buyers she had in mind. This was just the sort of thing that Amy enjoyed: to deliver a coup to the art world, make a client happy, earn enough money from her work to live well for the next two years, *and* be able to stay in the background of it all. She was thrilled to be going to Geneva, and that said a great deal. She didn't much like Geneva.

Tillie answered the door. The clear cellophane box of flowers was enormous and tied with a white satin bow. The end of the box had been removed and from it protruded the stems of three dozen white roses. They had come by courier from Constance Spry's shop in London. She took them to the library at once.

Amy was just closing her briefcase. Delight at the sight of the flowers shone in her eyes; she could always find time for flowers. She assumed that they had been sent by Charles but then remembered that his florist was Moyses Stevens. Anthony Kramer never sent flowers. A bauble from Tiffany's from New York, something from Hermès in London or Loewe in Madrid was more his style.

A new admirer? How flattering. What fun. 'The Lalique vase, Tillie, they should look magnificent in it.'

'These are the longest stemmed roses I have ever seen. Someone is smitten, Miss Ross,' teased Tillie, and hurried off to fetch the antique piece that seemed to have been made for white roses – or so Miss Ross thought because she never put any other flowers in it.

Amy pulled on the ribbon and the bow disintegrated in her hands. She removed the box's lid and the small white envelope lying across the stems. The signature made her sit down and look once more at the roses lying in the box. She leaned over them and gathered them into her hands, pushing her face down among them. The scent was sweet. Amy was surprised and delighted at the extravagant gesture. She plucked a single rose from the box and sat back in her chair to contemplate its beauty. Then she read the card:

> *All the flowers in the world are for you, Amy.*
>   *Pete*

Geneva was a great success. This was the second sale that Amy would be handling for Annette and Pierre de Boulet. It had not been an easy decision for them to sell the Soutine but needs must. The proceeds would ensure that the rest of their art collection would remain intact and could be housed in the small private museum they intended to create on the ground floor of their Geneva house. It would still boast eleven Chaim Soutines. The doctor's love of art and his access to the painters in Paris at a time just before the Great War had laid the foundations for a now large private collection. After the decision to sell the Soutine came another. The de Boulets asked Amy to compile the catalogue and to write a book on their collection in the distant future.

These were the things occupying Amy's mind now as she sat in a first-class seat on the plane from Geneva to London. Her meeting with the de Boulets could not have gone better. The de Boulets appreciated her discretion in handling the sale. They were not ostentatious art collectors; even their museum would be by appointment only, and requests for admittance judiciously considered. Amy would not let them down.

Her mind was racing. She tried to think of other things to slow it down. The staggering beauty of those three dozen white roses in the Lalique vase on her library table came to mind. And slowly she calmed down. This was the first time in days that she'd allowed herself the luxury of setting aside the Soutine business and the art world; she could afford to now, having accomplished all that she had set out to in Geneva.

Pete had indeed surprised her. The call the night before they arrived had been nice, but the flowers, and the card with them, had nothing to do with *nice*, they were most decidedly romantic. And she liked him even more for that gesture. It was what she needed, and he had instinctively known that and had done something about it. To be fair she had been touched very deeply by his words, '*all the flowers in the world are for you, Amy.*' But at the same time a shiver of apprehension had gone through her, and the hand holding the card had trembled. It had been as if someone had walked over her grave and she had known it was not Pete Smith, it had been Jarret Sparrow, because immediately on reading those words she remembered something quite contrary that Jarret had once said to her. She heard his words as clearly as if he had been standing before her uttering them. 'All the flowers in the world are for *me*.' And amazingly she had loved him so much, she had agreed with him, and would have laid every living flower on earth at his feet if it had been in her power to do so.

Amy had placed the card in the pocket of her suede skirt, and put Jarret and Pete firmly out of her mind. There had been no time to deal with emotions, those dead and gone, or those new and tender that with the right nurturing might one day flower. The tremor had left her hand, and a Chaim Soutine painting, Geneva, and the international art world she loved so much had taken over her life.

Now, the art world set aside, Amy reached into her pocket and drew out the small white card to re-read Pete's words. She had a window seat and stared through the glass into November sunlight and billowing white clouds. Her mind kept drifting back through the years. She didn't much mind the memories flooding back, it had been a long time since she had allowed them to. Maybe now was the right time to review those years, see them as a mature woman, when as a young one she had lived and almost died only by a *grand amour*. She closed her eyes and drifted back to Jarret Sparrow and Amy Ross's beginnings.

VENICE, ISTANBUL, PARIS, NEW YORK

1958–1962

Chapter 5

The tourists were gone, the travellers had arrived, and it was the best time to be in Venice: early October when the children were back in school, and a cross-section of the world's most interesting people were visiting. They were there to spend time in this splendid city of mystery, intrigue, and irrepressible beauty. Romantics and poets, painters and writers, this was the time of year they passed through the city for a fix of inspiration, to sit in the sun in St Mark's Square and drink in the Venetian way of life over a Negroni or an espresso.

It was Amy Ross's third day in Venice. She was journeying towards she knew not where exactly but she did have a final destination: Egypt. She was in Venice for the same reason that she had been to Paris or that she was going to Athens – because she had woken up one morning and there was a deadly sameness about it as there seemed to be about every morning of her life.

It was a good life, a safe life, a fun life. She had an exciting and rewarding job, a good man, great sex. She had worked hard to get those things and even harder to keep them going, but suddenly Amy realised that though she was content, the world had to be bigger than the one she was living in, and she wanted a peek. It was that. Nothing more, nothing less.

'It's not that I want to change my life, it's more that . . . no, don't look at me that way. I don't want to change *you*. I love you, Peter.'

And Amy had meant that when she had said it and still meant it now as she listened to the sounds of Venice, felt the warmth of the sun eating into her flesh, burning away ambition, purpose, seeking. From the moment she had walked away from Peter at the TWA terminal in New York he had vanished from her mind. He and everything else in her previous life: work, friends, hopes and desires, all gone. It was odd and somehow wonderful, like leaving your baggage behind and travelling light, in total freedom.

In Paris, she had stayed in one of the city's hundreds of small, unprepossessing, just a little on the seedy side hotels. This one, in a seventeenth-century building, was just round the corner from and behind the Place Vendôme. Her room had been small and depressing, but that hadn't bothered Amy in the least. It still had the floral wallpaper on the walls that had been hung in the 1920s, an old brass bed whose mattress was lumpy and caved in in the middle. Its floral cotton bed cover and matching curtains were worn thin from years of wear and tear, but it smelled of potpourri, and had a very French old world charm. The staff, what there was of it, had been accommodating. At breakfast the croissants had been fresh and the coffee strong, the milk for her *café au lait* hot and the peach preserve thick with fruit.

Amy loved Paris from the very first moment she saw it, and liked it all the more for being there alone. She had walked the streets from early morning until dark, and had been to see again the Monets at the Jeu de Paume, to the Louvre for several hours, and then had done the galleries on the Rue de Seine. She sat and read the *International Herald Tribune* over an aperitif at the Deux Margots, lunched at the Brasserie Lipp, and then, after several days, reluctantly, but because an art dealer friend of hers in New York had arranged it, she had called on an American painter, Richard Olney, living and working there.

Her birthday had fallen on the last Sunday in September and she had spent a magical day with Richard and his friend Jimmy Baldwin in Chartres. What a thrilling birthday: spent with a good painter and a famous and inspired writer, enjoying a cathedral of incredible power and beauty, and a rose window whose colour and design had burned themselves into her mind forever. A great deal of drink at a small table set outside in the sun and then they had dined on a sumptuous lunch with a fabulous view of the cathedral looming up in front of them. What a birthday those two intelligent, erudite and amusing companions had given her! They had given her Chartres as few others would ever see it, given her Chartres and themselves for a day. Later she had given her newfound friends supper in a small cafe in a rough and poor section of Paris where Jimmy was living.

The two men had opened their lives and their world to her and taken her in as one of their own. Quite used to being round artists, Amy knew about the sacrifices, the poverty, the obsession to create, but somehow on her birthday with those two men in Chartres she understood it, felt it deeply, and knew that she had never had the passion or the lust to live on her own terms, or fought as these men did and

62

would do to the death for what they were and wanted to be. She had been somehow reborn in Chartres that day.

Sometime during the night in Paris, just before she had fallen asleep, she had wished that she had allowed herself to be picked up by one of the handsome young Frenchmen who were constantly paying her attention. Sexual desire kept her awake. To be taken over by a penis, to come in glorious orgasms . . . she would caress her breasts and close her eyes and imagine it and fall asleep. Amy was not promiscuous, had never been, was afraid to be. She believed in love and marriage, one-to-one relationships. That's what most women like her believed in in the late fifties. Sex without love? A great idea but a far-off dream for a New England girl who had little taste for jumping into the unknown.

Jimmy Baldwin had given her the name of a small and cheap *pensione* where writers and painters who went to Venice took up residence. It was in one of the back streets of the city, a place that rarely saw the four-day tourist, though it was only a twenty-minute walk through winding narrow cobblestoned streets from St Mark's Square, even less by gondola. From the canal side the old and beautiful but crumbling *palazzo* was impressive and not far from a handkerchief-sized piazza with a thirteenth-century fountain in it, a good, cheap, small restaurant where one might meet just about any of the expatriates living in Venice and most of the Venetian artistic world or the more interesting travellers spending time in the city.

She had called from Paris but the *pensione* was fully booked until today and so Amy kept her reservation at the Gritti Palace and for several days had enjoyed being in the lap of luxury, though it was an extravagance that only a holiday of a lifetime would allow. They had not seemed at all surprised when she had checked out of the Gritti and asked to have her luggage sent over to the *pensione*. The concierge merely gave her a knowing look. A love affair that demanded discretion was assumed. Ah, the romantic Italian mind. She had been amused.

Only four or five more days in Venice and then on to Athens. Amy was thinking about that when she removed from her purse a charming note that had been waiting for her at the Hotel Gritti Palace on her arrival. It was from a friend of an architect friend of hers in New York who awaited her arrival in Athens and would be delighted to meet her. She was to call upon her arrival at her hotel. Her friend was a sophisticated lighting designer who worked with the great architects

63

of the time: Frank Lloyd Wright, Walter Gropius, Mies van de Rohe, Le Corbusier. He needed no other clients, indeed had no other apart from one of the New York City museums when it ran into problems over how to light an exhibition. A handsome, fascinating man whom she saw quite frequently for lunch or a drink, who travelled six months of the year and several months ago had returned with his friends from a camel trek across the Sahara. To be shown round Athens by a friend of his was not a thing to be missed, especially after receiving such a charming note. Amy sensed that she had yet to discover Venice and fleetingly had thought to put Athens from her mind and remain longer in the city. Re-reading the note, she changed her mind. Five more days would have to do for this trip. There was far to go and much to see.

It was a strange sensation for Amy, travelling alone. People perceived her differently from when she had travelled with her lover Peter, a group of friends, or with her mother. As she sat in the square she began to understand that she too was perceiving things differently – not only people and places but herself as well. Her solitude was somehow affecting her. There had been moments in Venice when a strange melancholy would grab hold of her and then let her go. She found that disconcerting. Amy was not a melancholy person. She put these feelings down to loneliness, to having no one to share these great experiences with. Strangely Peter, whom she loved, did not even enter her mind as a solution to this loneliness, nor did anyone else.

Amy had always been an acute observer, able to discriminate about what she saw and absorb only what was relevant to her. On this trip she found herself more deeply involved with everything and everyone who crossed her path. She understood what it was to be a woman alone in the world because she was being treated like a woman alone. All her life she had been loved and protected by people. Even now she had a mother who selfishly would not let her go, a lover who unselfishly would. Amy, this woman out roaming the world alone, knew better who and what she was because she *was* alone and in a strange land and allowing herself to be open and vulnerable and free. She felt a new strength in herself; that strength that others saw in her that she had never quite believed was there. She believed it now. It felt great.

How can it happen, she wondered, that you can suddenly get smart sitting in the sun watching hundreds of pigeons swoop down in a cloud of feathers to forage for food or swirl up and away to ride the breeze like circus performers entertaining their keepers? Everyone was a sucker for the pigeons in St Mark's Square.

She called for the bill, paid it, and rose. Two attractive men at the next table who had been flirting with her stood up and asked her to have a drink with them. She declined but thanked them and gave them a ravishing smile. Amy was suddenly happier with herself than she could ever remember being. Life seemed more wonderful. She felt she had freed herself from the fetters that had been holding her back. She struck out across the square towards the *pensione*. A pigeon landed on her head, one on her shoulder. She made the fatal mistake of stopping and several more swooped down on to her arm, another clung to her back, one stood on her hand. She shooed them away. 'Don't you forage on me! Go be aggressive with someone else. Tomorrow, maybe tomorrow – or maybe never,' she told them, and then dropped her handbag. With a swoop of her arms and tossing back her head she gave a peal of happy laughter that echoed round her. The pigeons released her and flew up into the air, the sound of their fluttering wings like muffled thunder.

En route to the *pensione* Amy discovered places she had not yet been: a *palazzo* exhibiting antique glass which she enjoyed immensely, a small cluster of antique shops near one of the hundreds of arched stone bridges that crossed the canals. She was aware of how much quieter it had suddenly become. Away from the Grand Canal there were fewer gondolas and power boats; more Italian and less English was spoken here. It seemed suddenly a different Venice, one for the Italians, one where people lived and died like people in any other city in the world, only they were buried on a separate island and their roadways were water and they travelled on foot or in a boat. The beauty and wonders of their city were taken for granted and here were people just getting on with their lives.

Amy felt herself being swallowed up by this other Venice. It seemed even more mysterious, all this living going on behind the tourist scene. She suddenly understood that Venetians were a very different breed of Italian: born equally of a modern and historic city.

Amy wandered the streets from one shop to the next, one church to another that had to be seen. To several exhibitions in small galleries: Greek icons, Etruscan sculpture, Venetian sixteenth-century miniatures held her attention particularly. She was amazed to see several one-man exhibitions of New York contemporary painters. Why she should be surprised had more to do with her preconceptions (she had left the contemporary art world, her world, behind) than their being there. Venice was after all the home of the Biennale, the great exhibition that drew people from all over the world, the venue that every painter she knew wanted to be chosen for.

It was dusk and she had tarried too long. Night was descending and she was lost in the maze of narrow paved streets. The shops were no more. Aged buildings and huge *palazzos* silently looming in the half light were their replacement. It was silent except for her footsteps echoing on the cobblestones. She was wearing a beige linen skirt and blouse and with the sun gone was feeling cold and disorientated, just a little frightened.

Quite suddenly she stopped. She could go on no further. Several minutes and a few deep breaths later she no longer knew why she had panicked. After all, how lost can one get in Venice? More composed now, she continued on her way until she came to a three-storey house wedged in between what appeared to be the street entrances of two large *palazzos*. A glimmer of lamplight showed in an upper-storey window. A sign of life. It made her feel foolish for the anxiety she had put herself through. She saw an ancient wooden door, and in its centre a massive black iron lion's head knocker. Amy used the ring that protruded from the lion's mouth. The sound was loud and echoed through the quiet street. She rapped several times before she heard a window open at the top of the house. She was relieved to hear a voice call down to her.

'*Buona sera, chi è?*'

Amy walked backwards across the narrow street and pressed herself against a building, the better to look up and tell the man of her plight.

'*Buona sera.* Do you speak English?'

'Yes. What do you want?'

He spoke perfect English and with a charming accent that Amy did not recognise as Italian. 'I'm sorry to disturb you. I'm looking for the Palazzo Davanzati.'

'You're lost?'

'Yes, I'm lost. Can you help me?'

'Wait there, I'll be right down.'

Several minutes passed with not a sign of life from the house, or any other on the street. In fact the upper window went dark. What seemed like an age but was more like five minutes passed and just when Amy thought the man had not understood her, or had simply decided against helping her, there was the sound of an iron bolt being shot and the front door creaking open on its rusted hinges. It swung back to reveal a young man whose features she could just about make out in the dim light spilling on to the street.

'Hello,' he said.

Amy crossed from where she was still standing to greet her saviour. 'I thought you'd changed your mind.'

'I don't understand.' And there was puzzlement in his voice.

'Never mind. Hello, I'm Amy Ross, and I'm sorry to disturb you.'

'It's not a problem. I'm sorry it's taken so long but I'm renovating my house and the workmen have left it half torn away. Oh, the delay? You thought I wasn't going to come down, now I understand. Come in.'

Once Amy was in the entrance hall she was able to get a better look at the young man. He was incredibly beautiful, there was no other word for it. Somewhere in his mid-twenties, he had straight thick black hair that just covered the rim of a collarless white shirt, an old-fashioned shirt, one that Lord Byron might have worn: the finest of cotton with voluminous puffed sleeves that buttoned tight on his wrists and tails tucked into tight, well-worn jeans. He was not exactly delicate, not exactly feminine – in fact, not feminine at all – just a sensitive-looking male beauty, the sort that ancient Greek sculptors might have used for models when they carved Greek youths for posterity. He was sensuous the way a woman can be when she moves, but with a masculinity to him that was undeniable. He was, too, enormously erotic-looking, as if sex was his life's blood. He was very slim but with broad shoulders and a tight, rounded and muscular bottom. She wanted to see him nude, she wanted him. Amy guessed males and females alike fell in love with him on sight. He was irresistibly alluring, deliciously decadent – or at least one imagined he might be. Either that or asexual, as pure and fresh as driven white snow.

It did not take her long to understand that he was too a beautiful person, someone very unusual. He smiled at her and there was something genuine and sweet in his expression. Here was a man with not a malicious bone in his body.

'I think you're cold. Follow me. The drawing-room at least is liveable. I'll light a fire, and you'll have a drink to warm you, and then I'll take you to the Palazzo Davanzati. Oh, let me introduce myself. My name is George Constantakis, a Greek from Egypt. We are the best of the Greeks, you know, the Egyptian Greeks,' he told her teasingly.

He was gazing into Amy's eyes. His were pools of black, sparkling

67

and sensuous, and he had the longest, most sexy eyelashes she had ever seen on a man. He appeared to speak with them. His skin was the colour of tea and his nose perfect and noble; his lips such as any woman would have wanted for her own.

The hall was crammed with packing cases and paintings leaning against the wall, candelabra with candles in them stood on top of steamer trunks. She and George squeezed their way in and round things until he opened the drawing-room door. They stepped into a beautiful sixteenth-century room with a wall of windows, some of which still had their original glass. It ran the width of the house and faced on to a canal. Lamps were lit. It was furnished with bits and bobs of Venetian things, most of which appeared to be past restoration. But it was the room itself that was amazing, by *palazzo* standards perfection in miniature. Through the windows she saw a pair of lions on either side of marble steps leading down into the water. Across the narrow canal a private gondola was tied to a pole striped with colour. For several minutes she stood entranced by what she was seeing and the silence all around save for the rhythmic lapping of the water against the marble steps.

George lit the fire and soon it flared up. He took a deep, rich scarlet velvet jacket from a chair and placed it round Amy's shoulders. That pulled her from her trance. George smiled at her, a knowing smile. Here was a stranger who understood the magic of Venice. George liked her; she had a soul to match her beauty and ripe sexuality. He went to a table covered with a silk velvet cloth and from a decanter poured them both glasses of brandy. 'Drink this down, it will warm you. You must be careful in Venice this time of year when the days are still hot and the nights are cold.'

Amy drank her brandy in one gulp and found George was right. It instantly warmed her. 'This is an amazing room,' she told him, looking up at the twenty-foot-high ceiling with its intricate carving, faded colour and gilding.

'Yes, it is. It's the perfect Venetian *palazzo* for one. It has wonderful views of Venice. In the daytime through this window you can see a larger canal. After some distance it turns rather sharply and you can catch a glimpse of the Grand Canal. From the rooms above the best domes and spires, roof tops and canals of the city that are never photographed can be seen.

'This house is wedged between two marvellous *palazzos* that are still lived in by the same families that built them. They commissioned this house to be built at the same time as their palaces to keep a quite violently mad brother close to them rather than incarcerate him. He lived here in splendour with his keepers and servants. They say that soon after he was moved into this house, quite suddenly the demons that had haunted him from birth vanished. All the violence and most of his madness was dissipated. He lived to be seventy-two years old, a very old age four hundred years ago, never leaving this house except for rides in his gondola which were taken late at night or at dawn when few people were about, or else when he walked in the small garden. Diaries I have seen claim that for the last thirty of those years he was quite sane. They believe here in Venice that this is a house with a healing spirit.'

'Have you lived here long?'

'No, not long.'

Amy had so many questions she wanted to ask George about the house and how he came by it. But she knew it was rude and had the feeling that he would be offended by her prying, so she asked nothing.

Shortly after her arrival he offered to take her to the *pensione*. She realised after five minutes that she had done well to ask for help. The way to the *pensione* was through seemingly endless twisting and turning streets and several small piazzas. After twenty minutes they were at her *pensione*, the Palazzo Davanzati.

On entering the courtyard through wooden doors set in a wall that faced the street she was immediately enchanted. It was filled with potted tropical and Mediterranean flowering trees and shrubs, a palm tree and creeping vines, all overgrown. A curved flight of rose-coloured marble stairs rose magnificently to the first floor and the second of the two main entrances to the building. The first and equally as grand entrance was on the canal. The *palazzo*, though crumbling, was impressive by any standards.

George and Amy entered through the front door. This was nothing at all like any *pensione* she had stayed in or heard about before. She had imagined something quite modest, having heard about the place from Jimmy and Richard and others of the sort of clientele that frequented the *pensione*. In fact the Palazzo Davanzati was at least as large and as grand as the Hotel Gritti Palace, the only difference being that this *palazzo* was still a private house that took in recommended-only paying guests, and then only ones who were interesting and amusing to the owner.

George found a servant dressed in a rather smart white jacket with a family crest emblazoned in gold thread on the cuffs. He wore white cotton gloves also, and was in his seventies at least. The two men spoke in Italian for several minutes and then Amy and George followed him through several magnificently furnished reception rooms to an inner circular hall with a vast marble staircase that wound its way up several floors under a dome that Amy would later find had been painted by Tiepolo.

She all but pinched herself to make certain she was not in a dream. She felt more like Alice having walked through the looking glass than Amy Ross in Venice. George looked amused.

'You might have warned me,' she whispered.

'Yes, I might have, but then you wouldn't have been surprised.'

'It's not exactly what I would call a *pensione*, George.'

'That's what's so amusing – it is. Marina, the princess who owns the place, adores meeting interesting people. She collects them the way some people collect fine china. Her charm and generosity, and the high regard in which she is held by the Venetians, are just some of her saving graces. She's not a snob, more a noble lady. You'll like her. Marina is an unusual Venetian. She likes foreigners, takes them into her home as paying guests, and the money she earns goes towards the upkeep of the *palazzo*, which as you can imagine is an endless project and very expensive. I doubt she makes anything, she takes care of her guests too well for that, and will rarely take anything from a writer or painter or any struggling artist. I actually think she opens the house to people because she likes to see it full and alive and can't afford to keep it that way without them.'

They were on the second floor now and walking down a corridor hung with family portraits. The butler stopped in front of a pair of doors and pushed them open. The three entered a sitting-room, large and elegant, with windows on to a small balcony overlooking the canal. There the butler had a conversation with George after which he beckoned to Amy and took her through to the bedroom, equally as large and with an impressive four-poster canopied bed hung with sixteenth-century silk velvet damask in a colour that could best be described as silvery moonbeams.

Amy's luggage had been unpacked and her clothes hung in an armoire in the dressing-room. Her nightdress had been laid out on the bed, her dressing gown draped elegantly across a chaise longue. The bathroom was all marble and mirrors, and her toiletries and cosmetics had been placed neatly on the dressing table. The butler then escorted

Amy back into the sitting-room. After talking for a minute more with George he left the room.

'Pleased?' asked George.

'Need you really ask?'

'No. Just teasing. Silvio says I am to tell you that drinks are served in the library on the first floor at eight. Dinner is served at nine and apologies have been sent by the Princess Marina. She is not in this evening, but there will be five other people at the table. He has also asked me to tell you how things work here. You come and go as and when you like. There are no rules about dress. Breakfast is served in your room as and when you want it but you must tell the waiter or the chef what you want the night before. Lunch is served at two o'clock and you are expected to say if you are not in for it or if you have invited guests to join you. You must say at breakfast if you plan to have an evening meal in. That's it. Oh, and though Silvio has not said so, I happen to know that guests who have the occasional overnight visitor are not frowned upon – that's taken as the norm here, part of the Palazzo Davanzati's charm. Well, now you are no longer lost, I'll be on my way.'

George took Amy's hand in his and lowered his head to place a kiss upon it. They gazed into each other's eyes and smiled. He knew very well that this young woman was stepping into a new, more decadent world, and had no doubt, even after being with her for so short a time, that she would make the most of it. She had about her a hunger and passion, repressed but struggling to break free. Otherwise what was she doing there?

'George, thank you very much for coming to my aid, but it doesn't seem enough merely to say thank you. Please let me invite you to stay for a drink?'

'I would really like that but I can't. I'm invited out this evening.' He slipped his velvet jacket from her shoulders and draped it over his arm. 'Oh, and just a word of advice – most everyone who stays here is in for lunch. It's usually amusing, and the food is always excellent. But for dinner, when you want to go out somewhere close by, in the piazza only a few steps away from here is the restaurant we all go to. It's cheap and good, you can't miss it. It's called Rimboccare. You'll find struggling poets, writers like myself and painters turning up there when they have a few pennies to spare. It's our lifeline for meeting, eating and drinking. Now I really must go.'

Amy sat on the end of the bed and thought about the beautiful

George; she could hardly get him out of her mind, nor his strange but wonderful house. Finally she decided on a long and luxurious bath. In the hot steamy water she dozed on and off and tried to make some sense of the excitement that seemed to have taken her over, swept her up and away from everything she felt safe with and sure of. She found this alien world, the real Venice, fascinating. It was like being drugged and taken a million miles from being a tourist in the Piazza San Marco. She felt as if she had stepped back in time to a world where everyone was just a little eccentric, just a little too self-involved, living for the fun of living and creating. Enthralled with Venice, they were drugged by its beauty and mystery, intrigue and history, and seduced by the city. She felt utterly bourgeois, as if she had many skins to shed. A brief peek into this world seemed not nearly enough.

In the library where drinks were served (American martinis, French champagne), she was not surprised to meet one of America's most famous playwrights and his entourage, in Venice for five days of fun. He was very drunk or drugged and not very pleasant. A manic depressive – you could see it in his eyes, hear it in the sharpness of his wit. Several other names that she had heard of but never met were present, altogether less tortured. Two couples from Paris, another from London. Half of them went elsewhere to dine. Those who remained and Amy sat at the long dining-room table, splendid with family silver and flowers, set at one end for them.

George had been right: the food was sublime, the best she had had since her arrival in Italy. But the company was only mildly amusing and after dinner Amy went directly to her room. On her pillow she found a note from George. He would come to the Palazzo Davanzati after siesta tomorrow to take her to see one of the hidden wonders of Venice.

They met the next day and George took her to see a small but splendid church. It was closed to the public, but he had made arrangements to borrow a key. Inside they saw fourteenth-century frescoes that were the finest she had ever seen. That night Amy invited him as her guest to the restaurant he had suggested to her. There several people who knew George greeted him with delight, and surprise that he had been wrenched from his house. One man's eyes filled with love on greeting George; an older woman, still ravishingly beautiful, embraced him and whispered something in his ear. Everyone she was introduced to seemed to be just a little bit in love with George, to want him, and Amy could understand that. She wanted him herself.

Another day they went to the small islands of Murano and Torcello, and that evening George took her home to his house and they ate bread and cheese and drank wine in front of the fire. He read poetry, she told him about American Abstract Expressionist painting, and they spoke to each other about passion, faith, and love. They kissed and fondled each other. He was a sexy man to be with and one who obviously knew his way round women. Amy wanted more: to shed her clothes, for them to be naked in each other's arms. She wanted a taste of the naughty sex he promised. He was a seducer very much in control of what he wanted, and when, and from whom. Amy could have let herself go, become besotted with George, but she never went where she wasn't wanted. They talked all through the night and got to know and like each other, then they watched the dawn come up over Venice.

Early in the morning several days later she went to George's house again. It had undergone an impressive transformation. The rooms had been stripped bare of furnishings except for essentials. In the drawing-room were a pair of chairs, a table, cushions scattered on the floor, lamps on low tables. Nothing more.

'What's happened?' she asked.

'I inherited the house from an admirer, someone who loved me very much and wanted me to have a place to live and work in. I had always visualised it as pure space, clean, beautiful space, for my soul to wander in. I had too many things so I gave them away. Isn't it wonderful now?'

And it was true, the house was a thousand times more beautiful, and this minimalist living suited George. Brought out another dimension in him, one that was more spiritual.

'Yes, George, the house has a more powerful presence now. Something ethereal that goes straight to the heart, touches the soul,' Amy told him.

'You understand, I knew you would. Everyone has to clean their house out one day. We all do it in different ways.'

That was the thing about George that until that moment she had not figured out. He was more, much more than merely physically beautiful. He was a good person, incredibly wise but silent about it. He was on a path of greater awareness in the Buddhist sense, and that above all else was what set him apart from most people. That was his charisma, what drew would-be lovers to him, what made people want to be part of his life. The realisation quite took Amy's breath away.

It was several minutes before she was able to say, 'It's my last evening in Venice, George. I'd like it very much if you would dine with me at Rimboccare. Please don't say no?'

That afternoon the weather quite suddenly turned cold and it began to rain. The downpour continued all afternoon and evening, and there was a wicked wind. The streets were running with water and people vanished into their houses. Tourists never left their hotels. As good as his word, George arrived at the Palazzo Davanzati and together Amy and he braved the weather and made a dash across the tiny piazza to the Rimboccare.

The place was deserted except for one couple at a table in the window and another in the back of the small restaurant. The proprietor fussed over Amy. He had taken to her and was, like everyone else, extremely fond of George. They were shown to their table, against the wall, midway down the narrow room. A waiter greeted George and lit the candle in the centre of the table. A bottle of wine was placed on it, glasses upturned.

They had ordered their meal and were just settling down when Amy was suddenly aware of the couple sitting in the shadows at the back of the restaurant. It was the man who drew her attention. Amy and he were facing each other, and she found it difficult not to keep stealing glances at him. He was a big man with fair hair. Quite the most handsome she had seen for a while. His looks were cool and charming. She felt an enormous attraction to him. It was inexplicable but she wanted to be near him, a part of his life. More than once she caught him gazing at her and sensed that he found something in her that he wanted. Amy thought herself fanciful and tried to forget him, but his mere presence in the room would not allow that. She turned her attention to George and the food.

They were on their main course: *osso bucco* and polenta, served with a mountain of slim strips of courgettes pan fried in olive oil. George was pouring from their second bottle of wine.

He told Amy, 'I think there's someone here you might like to meet. He's a fellow American living in Venice, a painter. I know he would like to meet you. I'm surprised to see him here, Jarret almost never comes to this restaurant. His is a more grand circle of people than the artistic element that frequents this place. I really think he comes here on occasion to get away from them. He is after all an artist, and all artists need their peers for feedback. I'll ask him and the lady he's with to stop by for a coffee on their way out.'

Amy wanted to ask, 'Am I being obvious? How do you know he

wants to meet me? Is *he* being obvious?' She wanted to say, 'No, don't bother', or 'I'd rather you didn't'. But she said nothing, merely looked blankly at George who took her hand in his and patted it. He told her, 'Just don't fall in love with him, that's forbidden.' Even then she could find no words to reassure him that she wouldn't.

When George approached the table at the rear of the restaurant, the man he had called Jarret rose from his chair. His smile was devastating, filled with charm and terribly seductive. He was tall and big and very elegant in a slightly shabby way, like a prince in pauper's clothes. Amy tried to shake herself free but the manner in which he lowered his eyes and then stole glances at her made that impossible.

After several minutes George returned to the table and his meal. He took several forkfuls of food before he said, 'They would be delighted to join us for coffee.'

He changed the subject and for several minutes Amy did manage to forget Jarret, though the sensation of being drawn across the room to him was still very much there. It spiked her natural vivacious charm with a sensual seductiveness that she usually kept well hidden. Few men had ever discovered the erotic Amy Ross and none but Peter Smith had ever been able to set her free sexually enough to enjoy that aspect of herself to the fullest. She was feeling a new sureness of self and enjoying it.

Amy and George were not quite finished with their meal when Jarret appeared at the table. He spoke directly to Amy. 'Hello, this is Sophia Minetti. I'm Jarret Sparrow, and you're Amy Ross.'

'And we all know and love, or have loved, or want to be made love to by George,' said Sophia Minetti with a smile much too knowing for Amy's liking. Here was a woman who was not just peeping into this mysterious, sensuous and exciting world but seemingly part of it. What had she meant? What was she insinuating? Had the three been lovers of each other at one time or another? Sophia Minetti made Amy feel very straight, very dull, and certainly not exciting enough sexually for either George Constantakis or Jarret Sparrow.

George rose from his chair to kiss Sophia, and the two went into a dialogue in Italian for some minutes. As for Amy and Jarret, it was a *coup de foudre*, as if they had received a blow that had momentarily stunned them. Once they came back to their senses there was no escaping the chemistry at work between them, that same something she had been sensing all evening from across the room. Amy tried, even while it was happening, to tell herself that she was imagining it, being fanciful. They tried to break the spell.

'I'm sorry, you've not finished your meal.'

'It doesn't matter.'

'Are you long in Venice?'

'No.'

'Is this your first visit?'

Banal, it was all so banal, and they both knew it. They were not fooling themselves or Sophia or George. Even they were aware of the invisible magnet that was drawing Amy and Jarret together.

He moved his chair closer to Amy's, snapped his fingers for the waiter and ordered two coffees, and then turning back to Sophia told her, 'We mustn't stay long.' And that was all the notice he paid to anyone at the table other than Amy. The banal was dropped. He went right to the point.

'You're a magician – you've returned George to us. He's been very reclusive of late. You must be very important in his life.'

'Oh, I hardly think that. We've only just met.'

'Tonight?'

'No, a few days ago.'

'That can be enough.'

'Would it be enough for you?' Amy could hardly believe she'd said that.

The look that passed between them gave her the answer she wanted. She was flummoxed yet ecstatic with happiness. Nervously she looked to see if the others at the table were aware of what was happening between her and Jarret. George and Sophia seemed deep in conversation.

Jarret chose not to answer Amy. Instead he asked, 'Who are you, Amy Ross? What's brought you to me?'

'I'm an art historian, working in New York. And I have always questioned fate.'

'I'm a painter, I live and work here in Venice and Istanbul where I share my houses with another painter. And I do believe in fate. It's fate that I should have come out on this foul night. Fate that I should have come here when we had planned to go elsewhere. And it's fate that you should be here. I saw you come in and shed your wet things and we've been together from that moment on. That, I believe, is fate at work.'

The sound of his voice, and his words, were mesmerising. She hung on every one of them. He was expressing her own feelings about him.

76

There was a tremor of emotion in his cultivated mid-western voice, mellowed by years at Harvard, of living in Europe and speaking foreign languages. It cast a spell over her, made it difficult for her to keep her feet on the ground or to face the reality of the situation. A holiday flirtation and nothing more.

'Tell me about your work? Where can I see it?' Amy wanted to know him, wanted him to fill the void in her life. Oh, yes, from the moment Jarret Sparrow spoke to her, she knew what she had never even suspected before: there *was* a void in her life.

'I'm having a one-man show in New York sometime this year. I'm in a group show in Paris but that's for others to view not you. Come to my house. I want you to see my house and my work. What day will you come?'

'I'm leaving tomorrow.'

'You can't.'

'Oh, I can and I must. I'm meeting someone in Athens tomorrow evening.'

'Tell him you've had a change of plan.'

'No, that's not possible.'

'Then you won't get to see my work, my house, be a part of my life. You don't believe in fate.'

Amy was not ready to give him up. The very idea of losing him was already frightening. She felt quite mad, not in control of herself.

'I don't leave until after lunch tomorrow, I'll come in the morning.'

Joy in his face, a sigh of relief. Signals as to how he was feeling about her that went straight to her heart. He smiled and it was as if the sun came out and burned away any resistance she might have to him. He raised her hand from where it was resting on the table and lowered his lips to kiss it. When he lifted his eyes and gazed into hers there were tears in them. He was choked with emotion. Neither of them could speak. He knew she was his. Finally he managed to bring himself under a semblance of control.

'Where are you staying?'

'The Palazzo Davanzati.'

'I'll come for you, or you'll never find your way. Early, very early, so we can spend your last hours in Venice together. I'll see you off tomorrow. Until then you're mine. Go home now. Pack. Get Silvio to send your luggage on. He knows very well how to do those things. Settle up there, your bill and all that, you won't be back or ever stay there again. Seven o'clock. No, not seven. I'll be at the Princess

77

Marina's door, the street side, at six o'clock, just when Venice is waking up.'

He did not wait for an answer but turned to Sophia and spoke to her in Italian. George rose from his chair. Jarret gave him a farewell hug, and said, 'Thank you, George.' Then smiled at Amy and told her, 'I'll see you in the morning.'

Sophia kissed George and turned to Amy. She smiled at her. By that time Jarret had already left the table and was waiting impatiently to be gone from the restaurant. Sophia looked at him and then back at Amy. 'It's a long time since I've seen Jarret as happy as he is right now. He's smitten. It shows on his face, the way he moves. New life flows there. And what about you? I don't believe in fate, Jarret does. What I believe is that Jarret Sparrow has made a conquest, and you, Amy Ross, have fallen in love.

'Venice . . . Remember, it plays tricks on people, it's famous for its masquerades.' That was her goodbye to Amy, that and a kiss on her own fingers which she blew across the table.

Chapter 6

He was there in the hall waiting for her when she came down the stairs. After a night of tossing and turning and having very little sleep – full of the excitement of leaving Venice, a moment of infatuation with a stranger, and the new adventure that lay before her – Amy was more calm about Jarret. That was not to say that she felt no reaction to seeing him; quite the opposite. Her heart skipped a beat. She found him, if anything, even more attractive than the night before.

Amy still felt drawn to the excitement of being with him on her last day in Venice, of entering his world, seeing his work. This feeling she had for him was different from any she had ever known and quite inexplicable. She would have liked him to have taken her home the night before and made love to her then. It was obviously sexual, this something between them.

'Venice is at its most glorious this morning. The light is miraculous after that dark and hideous rainstorm yesterday. The sun has come out for us, Amy Ross.' Those were his first words to her: polite words, charming words, but where was the passion he'd had for her, that he could hardly hold back the night before?

Jarret seemed calmer but he hadn't fooled her. She sensed it at once: that the sexual attraction was still there but that he was repressing it. All during her restless night she kept rationalising him away because soon continents would be separating them, and they lived such different lifestyles. She sensed that he had done the same. They had to save themselves from each other, she told herself. One look across a room does not make a lifetime of love, sex, security, and marriage. Or does it? And what had George said: 'forbidden'? And what had Sophia Minetti been trying to tell her? Had that been a warning? Those were the things that were crossing her mind when she put out her hand to greet Jarret. But what the mind dictates the heart does not necessarily follow. The moment his lips touched her skin Amy knew that she had

79

a fight on her hands to keep her relationship with Jarret Sparrow a holiday flirtation and not a romance.

'I hardly slept last night, I was so looking forward to seeing your work.'

'*I* spent most of the night arranging the house to give you an exhibition.'

'Is it far, your house?'

'It's faster by water, but I don't spend my money on gondolas and only in emergency on powerboats. All my money goes on paint and canvas.'

They hurried away from the Palazzo Davanzati. Jarret closed the wooden street door behind them and looking at the high walls that fronted the *palazzo*, told Amy, 'Now that world's behind you, I'm going to take you into a new and better world, more wonderful than you've ever known. That's what you want, isn't it? That's what you've been looking for?' Jarret was full of enthusiasm, his eyes filled with excitement. It was there again, that special togetherness, two people wrapped up in each other, wanting each other. She very nearly gave a sigh of relief.

He slipped his arm through hers and they hurried along the narrow streets, crossing stone bridges, and seemingly going deeper and deeper into the heart of Venice. He fired questions at her, about her work. Every time she told him something interesting about the New York art world they found yet another point of communication. Their footsteps echoed through many twisting and turning narrow cobbled footpaths and small, quiet piazzas; little squares with architectural treasures from the fourteen and fifteenth centuries – fountains or a sculpture worn away by time, a bench of stone, a chair of marble, a single column, a carved capital lying on a plinth. By the time they arrived at Jarret's house, which was not a house but a *palazzo* of twenty-five rooms with water frontage, she was lost again with absolutely no idea where in Venice she was.

They stopped in front of his door. 'I feel like fate did send you to me, you know, that you've come at just the right time in my life. I'm not a novice, I exhibit my work all the time, but the excitement I feel about showing you it . . . well, I haven't felt like this for such a long time, if ever. I don't know what you expect, and I don't know that you'll like it, but I do know that you'll understand it, that you're with me.'

Jarret's words touched a nerve in Amy, a tenderness, an unbelievable gratitude to him for feeling that way about her. She was about to say something but he stopped her. 'I think every canvas I've ever painted has been for you; every drawing, every collage, they've all been created for you. No, please don't say anything now, just look.'

He hadn't needed to silence her, she couldn't have said anything anyway, she was too emotionally unbound, falling very nearly helplessly in love.

Amy had wondered whether he was a good painter, whether he might even be a great painter, instinct had told her that he would not be a bad painter. She had met enough artists to follow her instincts about them and their work. She had occasionally been surprised but rarely, if ever, had she been wrong. She forced herself to set her emotional feelings for Jarret Sparrow firmly aside for the time being.

Amy stepped into the hall of his *palazzo* stunned by the emotion in his voice, the passion for her in his eyes. The moment he closed the door behind them he locked out the world as she knew it, and Amy entered Jarret Sparrow's world.

All the while they had been making their way to the *palazzo* she had been aware of him as a man and her sexual attraction to him. His cool, sensual handsomeness and charm had seduced her, and she had to keep fighting that seduction, had to keep trying hard not to lose herself in an infatuation that was doomed to end in just a few hours. With the click of the lock Jarret the man vanished into the recesses of her mind and Jarret Sparrow the artist took over their lives. Amy Ross, art historian, adviser, sometime dealer, scuttled the Amy Ross who was falling in love.

Amy was immediately aware of a massive body of work, that of a prolific artist who worked in many media: collage, construction, watercolour, sculpture, oil on canvas, paper, wood. The *palazzo* was not so many rooms as *palazzos* in Venice go, but they were enormous rooms with high ceilings and beautiful proportions. The walls were painted white and hung with his work and his work alone. Huge, small or average size, framed and unframed Jarret Sparrows. Abstract paintings, some better than good; strange surrealistic collages – exciting works of art that sometimes worked and sometimes did not quite. They were powerful paintings, full of colour and action and yet static at the same time; that was their uniqueness and possibly what made them not quite work. Jarret Sparrow had a yearning to be a great painter, that was the message Amy received from room after room of his work, cleverly hung, excitingly displayed. Yearning is one thing, a great

81

painter another – thus spoke the professional Amy Ross to the woman already in thrall.

The *palazzo* had a large inner courtyard one could look at through the open loggia on the first floor of the building. Even that was hung with his work; painting on heavy silk was another of his media and these flag-like paintings were slung over the balustrades into the garden.

In contrast with the abstract works of art, the courtyard garden was formal and grand in design and planting, the equal of the finest in Venice or anywhere else in Italy. Even this late in the season it was blooming, a miracle for a garden in Venice. And the house that was not a house but a *palazzo* was still beautiful. One could imagine it in its glory during the fourteenth or fifteenth century when everyone who was anyone owned a *palazzo* in Venice. When Jarret's palace had been constructed, Venetian power was at its height. The sumptuous and splendid in all things was encouraged by the Venetian Senate, the better to impress visiting merchants and ambassadors. Both façades and interiors were matched for magnificence. Amy had seen many examples of that during her stay in Venice, had actually lived for a few days enjoying the luxury, the history of another age. There it had seemed natural: here at Jarret's it was extraordinary.

The paintings were one thing; the furnishings, the manner in which he lived, another. To Amy it seemed as if he had spent his years in Venice raiding not the antique shops but the junk stores of the city. Anything that had some age, from Art Deco back in time and style: a clock with one arm and no glass; a bowl chipped enough to be called a design of its own; silver plate that had, in places, long ago lost its coat of silver; teapots without spouts, and some without handles; chairs that had lost an arm or at the very least whose caning had been worn or punched out. Sofas lumpy and smelling of damp – shabby furnishings rather than works of art, room after room of pitiful junk arranged in decorative salons. A palatial residence created from trash and hung with canvases that turned the *palazzo* and Amy's visit into a happening. The house of a rich talent but a poor man keeping up with the Joneses? Only in this case the Joneses were the princes and princesses, the marquises and marchionesses, the dukes and duchesses of Venice and Europe. Or was this the house of an artist who had a passion to be a prince, and lived as the only prince he could afford to be?

'I'm dazzled,' Amy told him.

'That's what you're supposed to be.'

He took her by the hand and they moved slowly from room to room.

Amy was genuinely overwhelmed by the work. She began asking questions about the paintings, relating far more easily to them than to his collages. She found the large collages disturbing, so different from his work with the brush, as if two different minds, two separate people, had worked on them. Hours later Jarret's work had taken them over. It was nearly one o'clock when he had pulled the last painting from a stack leaning against the walls of his studio.

Those hours had not passed in silence. Painting and all works of art were a part of these two people's lives; they had been schooled in art and what each of them had to say about Jarret's work had substance and intellect behind it. Inevitably the conversation went from his work to the new and exciting painters in the New York contemporary art world; to those great painters alive and dead who had influenced their lives; to the shift from Paris as the centre of the modern art world to New York. The talk was heady stuff, they were high on it and each other.

All the while they were drawing closer together but time was driving them apart. It was a strange sensation, this constantly having to put the brakes on, but that was what Amy was doing. 'Don't fall in love.' Were George's words advice or a warning? 'Venice . . . Remember it plays tricks on people, it's famous for its masquerades.' Sophia's words. Seeds of doubt planted in her mind. They were making Amy cautious, and now that she had seen the way Jarret lived and his work, she felt more unsettled than anything else.

Had he made one overtly sexual move towards her she would happily have thrown all caution away and taken the hours they had left to consummate the life force throbbing between them. She wanted orgasms with this man. She had a burning desire to be sexually one with him, to experience the little death with him, the dying in that moment of coming. And she wanted to make love to him, for him to come, give himself up to that exquisite moment of bliss. She sensed a mysterious significance to her being with him that was beyond anything she had ever felt with another human being. His looks? His charisma? His devastating cool and yet sensual charm? He had them all and was practising on her. She had seen this in other men but never one like Jarret.

And there was something more. Something she saw in his eyes, the looks he gave her: desire. With every breath he took, every word he uttered, in every way he moved, he was telling her he wanted her. The elaborate display of his work, the wanting her to be there with him; he

83

could not lay enough of himself out for her to take up. He had sexual lust for her. One minute it was there in the manner in which he gazed at her, and then it was gone, in the way he kissed her hand, took her by the arm and led her away from one painting to another. The sexual tension was electric, yet nothing happened, neither in word nor action, not even a hint of promise or innuendo.

When at last they were in his bedroom he pulled her into his arms and they gazed into each other's eyes. All worlds, art or otherwise, vanished in those few seconds when he placed his lips upon hers and kissed her. The warmth of his body, the scent of his skin, the lips that trembled with passion. Enfolded in his arms, the Amy Ross she had always been died and she was born again in that kiss. He released her, never taking her to his bed, never saying a word of love or desire or expressing any erotic passion for her. Instead, he took her by the hand and led her from the room. Several rooms away he stopped. For the first time he spoke about the man who shared his house.

'This is Fee's room. He never shows it to anyone, but I know he wouldn't mind your seeing it. I'm so sorry Fee – his real name is Firuz Yolu but everyone calls him Fee – isn't here to meet you. He would adore you, and I know you would like him. His room is the only one in the house with his paintings in it. He doesn't paint any more. He should, he's a terrific painter.'

'No!' Amy was emphatic.

Jarret looked amazed. 'What's wrong.'

'Selfishness. I don't want to share this experience of you and your work with the sight of anyone else's paintings. We have so little time before this is over. Do you mind?'

She could see in his eyes that he didn't mind in the least, that he was flattered. Jarret told her he loved her more for her sentiments by taking her in his arms again and giving her another longer and more lingering kiss. She could hardly miss the emotional effect her words had had on him. They bound the two of them even closer together. Arm in arm, in silence, they walked through the *palazzo* to the kitchen, the poorest room in the house. There Jarret finally spoke.

'There's hardly a crust of bread but I can offer you a coffee.'

'What time is it?'

'We have two hours left.'

'You make it sound so final.'

'I don't mean it to be. It won't be. I'm going to be in New York in a few months.'

84

'You will call?'

'Yes.'

Suddenly there seemed hope for them. The realisation reached both of them at the same time. Smiles crossed their faces, happiness, joyfulness came forth in a burst of laughter. 'This is a celebration, I was so afraid we would never see each other again,' she told him.

'I wish I could offer you a sumptuous lunch in the best restaurant in Venice with a view that will never allow you to forget me or the city and will make you always want to return, but I haven't the means.'

'Then let me offer you lunch, I have holiday money.'

Before they left the *palazzo* he rushed Amy back to his studio. There he selected a watercolour, one she had admired. 'I never give my work away. I mean that, *never*. But this, I *lend* to you, to have something of me with you. I don't want to be forgotten.'

They had their lunch and over it told each other about their day-to-day lives, their hopes and dreams. They exchanged telephone numbers and addresses and gave each other their travelling schedules. Soon Jarret too would be gone from Venice to Istanbul where Fee was opening the house. Istanbul! That came as a jolt to Amy. It would make Jarret even more remote from her than his being in Venice. Before they had even parted, this magical day she was living was receding, becoming a dream or something of the imagination.

They had no friends in common so he spoke of his: Madame Grès and Schiaparelli, Salvador Dali, the Countess this and the Count that, and half a dozen millionaires. High society names. Even their artist friends were different. The outside world was pulling them apart. All that was left was how they felt about each other. They returned to that and clung to each other until lunch was over then walked across St Mark's Square, a cloud of fluttering wings hovering round and above them, following their every footstep to a water-taxi stand on the Grand Canal.

'Thank you for a wonderful day. You have the watercolour to remind you,' he told her.

'I'm sorry I can't break my date in Athens this evening.'

'Should I be jealous?' he teased.

'Of James Crier, a man I've yet even to meet? No, I don't think so.'

Jarret began to laugh, and told her, 'Neither do I. What a relief! I know James and his sister. You'll like him, but you'll not love him as you love me.'

'Are you so sure of that?'

'Yes, and so would you be if you believed in fate as I do.'

Amy thought he was about to take her in his arms when a middle-aged woman, still a great beauty, approached them. She shimmered with elegance and held out her hand imperiously to Jarret. He immediately took it and lowered his head in a kiss. Immediately he seemed to change, become the courtly society man. They spoke in Italian and finally she turned to acknowledge Amy. Introductions were made and the woman switched to perfect English. The boatman kept pointing to his watch and telling Jarret they must leave if they were to make Amy's train to Rome. But there was no *they* taking the water-taxi, just Amy. Jarret had yet to tell her that he hated emotional exits and entrances.

It seemed to her their farewell was over before it began. He was helping her on to the boat, wishing her a *bon voyage*. All warmth and intimacy had gone from his voice, except for a squeeze of her hand, a look of sadness in his eyes, a few whispered words: 'I'll come and claim my watercolour.' Then he was gone on the arm of a Venetian lady. She heard their laughter as the powerboat gave a mournful blast of its horn and eased smoothly into the traffic plying the Grand Canal.

Amy had no sinking feeling, she was not shattered by the way she and Jarret had parted, it was more that she was so very sorry it had happened at all, that her magical day with him was over. If anything she was grateful for the experience of Venice and Jarret, of love on the run, passion dampened down by bad timing; appreciative of a separation that might have been far more painful had they given in to how they really felt about each other. Even with her eyes still on him and unable to see his handsome face, watching the charismatic Jarret with another woman as she sped away from him, Amy began to ask those irritating questions. Had she read too much into his feelings for her? Did she imagine he wanted her because she wanted him so much? Had she misunderstood his words of admiration, taken them to mean more than they did? Had they indeed been words of adoration and love or merely a fantasy on her part?

He had after all not bedded her. Seduced her but had not taken her. Why? would have been a good question but Amy didn't ask herself that. Indeed her heart took over her head and all she could do was stare after him, keep him in sight for as long as she possibly could, holding on to love's lost dream.

She ran to the stern of the boat the better to keep him in sight and there she remained until she could no longer distinguish him from anyone else in the square. Amy remained alone there when even the square itself, with its famous bell tower, was out of sight. She had watched him with keen eyes, but eyes that had not been sharp enough. She had missed seeing him turn to look over his shoulder for the boat that was carrying her away from him. Nor could she imagine the profound sense of loss he felt at her departure.

The Principessa on Jarret's arm did. She smiled at Jarret and spoke to him in Italian. 'Americans like that pretty girl are so innocent. Children really when it comes to real life. Had I interrupted something? We know it couldn't have been love.'

'Someone to do with the New York art world.'

'Ah, that would explain it. Shall we go home to bed?'

'And Carlo?'

'In Rome.'

'Then your place?'

'And you must stay to dine. I'm having people in.'

'Much as I would like to, I don't think I can.'

'Go to bed and have sex, or dine with us this evening?'

'Both.'

'I saw love in that girl's eyes, Jarret.'

'So did I.'

'Oh, Jarret, my dear Jarret, you're treading on dangerous territory here. Girls like that do not bring *palazzos* with them, and titles, nor do they further men's careers. Not at least the men they love. I am surprised at you and so will Fee be. I never beg, Jarret, you should know that by now, but I do think you would do well to come home with me.'

It was true the Principessa never begged. She commanded, and most of her young lovers obeyed. So did Jarret, and had been doing so discreetly for many years. They shared a sexual depravity that had no need for love or emotional involvement, and she had been good to Fee and Jarret. But it was none of these things and all of them that made him change his mind and go with her. It was too an incredible need to have sex with a woman, lose himself in a warm, moist and willing female. That was what he had wanted from the very moment he set eyes on Amy Ross in Rimboccare. The Principessa Carina Dondolo offered what was needed at that moment: a distraction from the loss of Amy Ross. And it was a loss. The day had had its magic for him as it had for Amy. From the moment he set eyes on her he was struck with desire for this woman, who seemed immediately to fill a void in his life. He had been honest when he told her that he thought she had come into his life at just the right moment.

Sex with the Principessa had been a delightful distraction. By the early hours of the morning, when he left her, Jarret had Amy Ross in a proper perspective vis-à-vis his life and was more himself. He crawled into his bed and slept a dreamless sleep, the sleep of a child, without a care in the world. But the morning sun and the sound of the bells ringing across the city and his stroll through the rooms of his house to the kitchen were to remind him of the day before and Amy Ross. Her enthusiasm for his work, her attraction to him, her passionate beauty, her rich and loving soul; those things lingered in the very air he breathed like a strong perfume. Like some sweet ghost they floated through the *palazzo*, embraced him and would not let him go.

He sat down in a chair and gazed through the window into his beloved garden. He had been planning his trip to New York for months. Jarret knew he must get that one-man show he had been working towards for so long, that the excitement in the contemporary art world was now in New York and he had yet to conquer that world.

He had chosen Europe years ago and Europe had been good to him. It was his home, the place he lived and worked best in. It had embraced him as the poor struggling American painter and brought him Fee. Together the two men, the odd couple, the American and the Turk, had come a long way as painters and friends, partners in the search for fame and fortune.

Later, when Fee had played matchmaker and Jarret had married Savannah Lee, the three had charmed their way into the lives of the wealthy and aristocratic titled Europeans living in Paris, Rome, Venice. Jarret Sparrow became the link between that world and New York high society when abroad. He and Fee made of these people patrons of Jarret's work that had brought him dealers and exhibitions, and retired Fee from painting so he could manage their lives. Stepping stones, all stepping stones to the New York art world, fame and fortune – obsessive desires that were gnawing now at Jarret's bones.

Now that he had met Amy Ross he had even more reason to make the dreaded trip to New York. It was dreaded because New York was not easy for Jarret. It embraced him socially for his handsomeness, for being a painter, for the lifestyle he lived. It martyred him for his connection to a burdensome wife, and grieved for his having to divorce her to save them from each other. Americans saw him and his sad story of love and marriage as shades of F. Scott Fitzgerald and Zelda.

Amy Ross was new and fresh and had the vitality and passion for the art world he loved, for life itself. For a few hours it had rubbed off on him and he wanted more of it and much more of her. It had been, still was, sexual. He had wanted to throw her down before he had even spoken to her, and had nearly done so several times during the time they were together, but he was a greedy man, and a taste of her sexually would not have been enough. He wanted to possess her sexually but not only sexually, totally. When he saw her off, he saw it in her eyes. He had won, he had taken possession of her. The next time he saw her they would reap their reward, he for having seduced her, she for her submission to a fatal attraction. They would have sex and she would be his forever. The very idea was enough to arouse him. To feel himself erect, pulsating for her, surprised Jarret. He was usually a master of sexual control, a habit formed to get him what he wanted.

Amy brought him new life and hope and he thought of her now and wanted her and wondered where she was, what wonders of Greece she was seeing. She was thinking about him no matter where she was, who she was with or what she was doing, of that he was certain. He had seduced her as no other man ever had or could. It had all been there in her eyes. And much to his surprise, in his hand was proof that Jarret Sparrow had been seduced by Amy Ross.

Amy was in Athens, walking on the stones of the Acropolis with James Crier at her side at the time Jarret was in his kitchen coming to terms with the possibility of having fallen in love.

It seemed to her that every step she took on this magical journey of hers was like stepping off a cliff. She felt as if she were in free fall all the time. Paris was Paris and Chartres had been France. Venice had been Italy, there had been no culture shocks there, but from the moment her feet touched the ground in Greece she was transferred into the unknown, another new and wonderful world. Greek culture took her over and James Crier eased the way, softened the shock. Jarret was very much there too, she couldn't get him and their time together out of her mind. She did make an effort to keep her feelings about him in perspective, and most of the time was able to do that by telling herself, 'This is madness, love for a stranger, a man I might never see again. A man I know nothing about.' Suddenly she wanted to know who this man was. A glimpse of his life had only confused her. Her desire to be with him, add something to his life, disconcerted her.

Amy and James had the Agora to themselves and were very much aware of each other as well as their surroundings. Here was a man more suited to her. Tall and slender and very handsome, erudite, well-dressed, a Greek scholar, a wealthy, sophisticated man with great charm, a romantic who was interested enough in her to send flowers and take time to be with her, a man interested in *her* work. He was all the things she could ever want in a man, but the chemistry she had instantly felt with Jarret was not there. They were memorable, these days and nights with James, but she was a woman in love with another man.

James wanted her to see at least one Greek island before she left for Cairo and took her to Patmos where he had a house. On the boat going there Amy found it impossible to keep Jarret locked up in herself any longer. Reluctantly she let him surface and asked James, 'Do you know a painter called Jarret Sparrow?'

'Yes, I do.' James was too much of a gentleman to allow surprise to come into his voice, though he was surprised.

'I met him in Venice.'

'My sister introduced us in Paris. She lives there, and was friendly with him. More so than with his wife.'

How can one word wield such a blow? Amy felt winded by it. Jarret had not mentioned a wife, there had been no sign of one. She managed to conceal the shock she had received from this news.

'His wife wasn't in Venice.' That was not what Amy had meant to say.

'Well, she wouldn't be. It is, I understand, a bitter separation. In fact, I think by now it might be that they have divorced.'

'And his painting, do you know his work?' asked Amy, trying to keep the relief from her voice.

'Yes, I do. My sister has a gallery in Paris and has shown him in group exhibitions. She likes his work better than I do. I only quite like it. He's not consistent. Sometimes I like him better than other times. Did you get a chance to see his work?'

Amy was aware that James knew what he was talking about. He was the head of a department at the Whitney Museum and with an eye that was as refined as one could get. He was a man respected for his critiques and knowledge of contemporary works of art. A shy man, who kept out of the limelight and politics of the art world, he was very much a behind the scenes person. An aesthete, remote from the outside world but never from his friends, was how he had been described to Amy. And it was true, you could see that in him, in everything he said and did. It was so much of his character it was even in his walk.

'Yes, I did.'

Thankfully James did not ask her opinion of what she had seen. In fact he asked no questions at all about her meeting with Jarret, but went back to the book he was reading. He had had his housekeeper pack them a picnic and a few hours later, when they unpacked it and he had opened a bottle of champagne and they were nibbling on fried chicken drumsticks, he asked Amy, 'Did you meet Jarret's friend Fee?'

'No. He was in Istanbul.'

'He is the better painter of the two but he no longer paints.'

'But still not a great painter.'

'True.'

'It would have been nice to have met him too. I had such a magical day with Jarret.' There, she had said it. It was out in the open. James did not seem at all surprised.

'Yes, you would have. He's a charming man. Possibly too charming to be a great painter.'

Chapter 7

Amy had several days in Athens and mainland Greece in the company of James, and then on the island of Patmos. It was an island of ethereal beauty that emanated an aura of a greater power than man's or life's itself, a halo of light shining down on it. The simplicity of this place rising wondrously from the depths of the Aegean Sea, a purity, embraced Amy with its otherworldliness, and her feelings for Venice and Jarret, in spite of what she might have wanted, waned like the moon.

On her arrival in Greece Amy had for a very short time suffered a degree of culture shock. Her first country with an alphabet that was hardly recognisable, a country that lives its life in the streets yet is not Mediterranean. It was to her mind the last outpost of western civilisation, only a hop across the sea to the East.

If it had been difficult to leave Venice, it had been even more sad for Amy to leave Greece. The country and its islands cast a spell on her. She was aware of there being something of life there that suited her, that she wanted to see more of, be a part of. She promised James one day she would return and they would make more trips together to the archaeological wonders the country had to offer. She would return when she had real time to travel, months, possibly years, to live in Greece. Here she imagined she would find her dream island as James had found his.

He saw Amy off at the airport and it was his enthusiasm for Egypt that spurred her on. That, and because in Cairo were waiting yet again friends of her friend in New York and James's who were ready to receive her. She marvelled at the kindness of strangers who took her in with extravagant hospitality and respect for her need to experience a broader world than the one she was successful and content in. Through them she was discovering an Amy Ross she had never had a true picture of before. She had never thought of herself as particularly interesting

93

or vivacious though she did know she was neither dull nor boring. She was the type of person who got on with her life but never evaluated herself or it.

Riding through the streets of Cairo from the airport to the hotel was an education in itself. This was her first African country, her first Arab experience. The noise, the heat, the dust, the people: dark and sultry-looking. Women hung from tip to toe in black muslin, their dark laughing eyes and nothing more revealed. A few wealthy, upper-class society beauties were very chic, dressed in the fashions of Paris, Rome and London. Men wore caftans, turbans and sandals. The jam of traffic and populace on foot, and flat carts, donkeys and camels, rattling lorries and rusting cars, bicycles, tricycles and motorcycles, the occasional sleek chauffeur-driven Mercedes, Jaguar or Rolls, ferrying coffee-coloured, handsome men dressed by Savile Row tailors or French designers.

Only a few hours after her arrival, Amy met her new Cairene friends and was swept away to a dazzling first evening in Egypt. A Rolls-Royce sped past the three great pyramids of Giza looming mysteriously under a sky studded with stars to a party in a Bedouin tent in the desert with an array of beautiful and interesting guests.

A ride on a camel round the pyramids at that moment of dawn where the full white moon is still visible and the sun is just breaking over the horizon. Amy sat mounted on her camel surrounded by a dozen other beasts and riders from the party, watching the Sphinx hiding in the darkness of night slowly come to life in the light of a new day. All chatter and laughter stopped among the mounted revellers as this great mysterious being of stone enveloped them in the power of its presence. No one could possibly fail to be moved, changed in some way by the experience of the Sphinx and Egypt entering their life. Amy certainly was. She fell in love with Egypt and it did not take very long for her to understand that she would return there many times during her lifetime.

Open and vulnerable to the country and the people, whom she found to have a sweet and easy nature, she travelled as widely as she could. Her new friends took her to Memphis, which was not very far from Cairo, and she saw the natural scenery of the place: the mighty Nile with its band of green on either side, forests of palm trees, the fauna of the river and desert, above all the colour of Memphis. Amy would never forget it – something between putty and sepia, as in an engraving – and the stillness and heat. Those things would stay in her soul forever.

She would be able to reach down, pull up the vision of Memphis and the monumentally large stone reclining Rameses whenever she needed to be reminded of perfection, timeless beauty, eternity.

She travelled alone, south to Luxor, the Valley of the Kings and the Valley of the Queens. And it was there when she was watching dawn rise over the Nile that she had what she could only later deduce was a mystical experience of some sort. The light, the Nile, her own emptiness, who was to say what it was, but those things merged and she had a vision of the Nile rising until it vanished into the sky.

Over breakfast in the dining-room of the Winter Palace Hotel she decided she had seen enough and wanted time and space away from Egypt to absorb, etch into her mind, what she had already seen. She returned to Cairo and said goodbye to her friends.

The plan had always been that she would return to Athens for a farewell dinner with James and tell him about the wonders she had seen. She was packed and ready to leave the hotel when a cable arrived telling her that he had to leave Athens for Paris. Her travel plans had been one night in Athens with James and a last look at the Acropolis the next morning, lunch at Zonar's, and then the plane to Paris for three days' shopping, a few galleries then home. It was a disappointment to miss James, she had looked forward to seeing him and telling him all she had seen and experienced, but there was still the Acropolis to be experienced again.

Cairo airport was chaos and there were long delays on some of the flights. Athens was one of them. Until the cable from James this had been a magical journey with nothing but surprises and wonders. It had gone smoothly, had all been more, much more, than she had ever expected, and with no hiccups to her plans until now. She had been spoiled and knew it but still felt sad that it couldn't end without this frustrating delay. The chain of events from one long-delayed flight meant her tight schedule was falling apart. Never mind, she kept telling herself. As she sat in the uncomfortable metal folding chair in the airport, for the first time since she had left New York she thought about the city and Peter. Somehow they seemed strange to her now. Not her holiday or Paris, Venice, Athens, Egypt, nor the people she had met who would stay her friends all her life. She thought about James in Paris, and Jarret in Istanbul because that's where he would be by now. Would he call her in New York? She smiled to herself. Oh, yes, he would call her, the chemistry was there. She had him in a proper perspective now, this artist who still remained for her the same

95

handsome, sexy and interesting man she'd seen across a dim and nearly deserted room in a restaurant in Venice.

Venice. How nice it would be to spend her last few days roaming the back streets and canals, discovering more of the undiscovered city that George had shown her. One last look to etch into her mind the place that had brought her that unforgettable day with Jarret Sparrow. How could a shopping spree in Paris compare with that? Well, the travel plans were set and that was that.

In that hot and massively overcrowded terminal hours ticked by with no answers to Amy's queries about when her flight would leave. Over the crackling tannoy system came an announcement at last. But that was a flight to Rome. It would do, anything would do to get out of that terminal. She could certainly get a flight from there to Paris even if she had to suffer the loss of another look at the Acropolis. That leg of her journey had already been affected anyway by James's absence.

Amy rushed to the Alitalia desk and with what seemed like an inordinate amount of fuss changed her ticket. The plane was held for her, she made a dash for it, and only realised what she had done when she was buckled into her seat and they were soaring at a near forty-five-degree angle into the sky.

Nine hours later, and thinking she was slightly mad, she was in a gondola watching the sun set over the Grand Canal as she glided up to the entrance of the Gritti Palace Hotel where she was met by the manager and several staff, the usual welcoming ritual initiated by the call of the gondolier.

The very first thing she did on entering the hotel was to hand her air tickets over to the concierge and ask him to change them for a flight from Italy that would get her to New York four days hence. Then she wiped the thought of travel from her mind.

It was difficult to analyse the way she was feeling: excitement, incredible joy at being in Venice again, a kind of out of control madness of love and passion for Jarret, who wasn't even here. She was re-experiencing feelings for him that had been forgotten, at least on such a scale. Amy was feeling giddy with happiness that she could let go, give in to such irrational feelings and behaviour. It also made her feel incredibly sensuous, sexually ravenous.

A room had been found for her, which was incredible in itself since she had no reservation. It was large and sumptuous with its windows facing on to the Grand Canal. A Canaletto come to life.

The maid unpacked Amy's clothes while she stood by the window wondering at the view and the fact that she was even here. She revelled in that feeling of being in love. She wanted to rush to St Mark's Square and watch the night with its myriad of stars take that wondrous place of beauty into its grasp. But it was too late, and she was too tired, too over-excited to gather her energies or even hold her passions in check. Instead she chose to bathe and wallow in them. After a long and luxurious bath in scented water where she got in touch with her body with caressing hands that she pretended were Jarret's, and came to terms with just how much she yearned for a man, she changed into her most elegant dress and went down to the bar for a celebration.

That was somehow what this messed-up journey now seemed to her: a celebration of her freedom, her capacity to love and be loved on a grand scale. She ordered a champagne cocktail, and then another, and after the third, alone at the bar, was able to acknowledge after a look in the mirror that it was all there showing in her face, the liveliness in her eyes. She was a luscious-looking woman in love. Never had she so enjoyed admiring glances as she did that night in the bar.

When she was called to the dining-room Amy suddenly felt extraordinarily tired. She asked for her meal to be sent up to her room and there dined alone in front of the window with the lights of Venice like diamonds strewn across the water.

It was late morning when she woke from a deep and untroubled sleep. She ordered breakfast and had it in bed. White peach juice, scrambled eggs and Parma ham, hot buttered toast and strawberry preserve. She had the window open a crack and a light breeze ruffled the sheer white curtains. The sounds of Venice filled the room. At one point during her breakfast she put back her head and laughed aloud. This was the last place in the world she had expected to be having breakfast this morning.

Having finished her repast, Amy rose from her bed and dressed. She caught herself being very particular about what to put on and finally settled for a very full skirt of mocha-coloured suede. She pulled on a cream silk knit jumper that clung to her naked torso like a second skin, too provocative for the shadow of her nipples and the swell of her ample breasts showing through it to be worn without the short cognac-coloured polished leather jacket with its turned-back cuffs of suede and bronze buttons. It was perfect for the weather which had turned much cooler than it had been three weeks before when she had last been there. Though the sun was out, a great deal of its heat had gone.

Amy took a long time checking herself in the mirror. She had changed, seemed to herself to be sparkling with a new kind of sensuous beauty, and liked herself that way. She clasped a leather belt round her waist with an antique Navajo silver and turquoise buckle. Only her shoes looked wrong, worn out from her travels and ready for the dustbin. She made up her mind to buy shoes in Venice, having remembered from the last time an exclusive shop that had tantalised her the very first day she had arrived from Paris.

She climbed into a powerboat, wanting to see St Mark's Square from the water rather than bursting in on it from a narrow street. It was a strange sensation being there alone, so different from when she had last walked through it on Jarret's arm. She had not expected it, but was suddenly sad to be here without him. She was without a man, without a lover. She could not understand why that was so important. It hadn't been all through her travels until this return to Venice. Now she felt, to the very core of her being, a kind of emptiness, of only being half alive, half a person in search of the other half of her soul. She felt for the first time in her life incomplete. It was a feeling so profound that she was quite shaken by it and had to fight off spiralling downward into a void, at the bottom of which was despair. Never before had she felt such a need for a man, for Jarret. She fought herself like a demon to get back her equilibrium, refusing to accept that she could be so foolish on nothing more than the chemistry that passed for a few hours between two people.

She tried to reason with herself that it was Venice, one of the most romantic cities in the world, mistress of the Adriatic, not her or Jarret or what they were or were not to each other, that was eating away at her. She began to see the city as both romantic and yet mysteriously death-like, the canals and its magnificent *palazzi* more embalmed than preserved as the tides tried to reclaim them.

Over a Cinzano, at a table in a sea of others set out in the square, she realised that she was taking a melancholy pleasure in the subtle decay that infested the city. But Venice basking in the extraordinary light reflected off its lagoon and canals, and moving in its very own and special time-scale, was conspiring to make her appreciate the city in spite of her sense of decadence, decay and death.

Amy felt better having come to terms with the place. Looking round her in the square, filled even now way out of season with visitors, she saw more clearly those same tourists she had avoided before in order to experience the city in a different way. She could accept now, was even relieved that, though she did not behave as they did, she was the same as they were, a tourist in Venice and nothing more. She would feed the pigeons, commission a bad charcoal drawing of herself from a bad artist, have an even worse photograph taken from a worn-out box camera on a tripod. She would no longer ignore the plastic flowers stuck in the prow of a gondola or the over-pricing as she had before. She would gripe as the tourist hordes did and forget the real back-street Venice that had swept her into love.

She had imagined living there the way George and Jarret did, the way the Princess Marina did, and it had seemed rich and glamorous and exciting and filled with mystery. No longer. Now it just seemed curious that they were not affected by Venice as she had been.

Venice was a city of visitors even to those who were born or who chose to live there. Venice was a dream, an escape from reality that should happen to everyone at regular intervals. But it was a place with an unreal quality and short stays there were long enough. How could Jarret have chosen to live here? Why? She pondered these questions and her own motives for returning. One last look into dreamland before her return to New York and Peter and reality? To put an infatuation to bed – well, at least to place it in its rightful context? Whatever the reason, centred once again, looking round, she knew that as much as she would like to be, she never could be one of Venice's average tourists, or even play a Miss Average Tourist role. She bloody well would not feed those pigeons!

Amy threw back her head and laughed aloud until tears actually came to her eyes. Being able to laugh at herself released the enormous tension and unhappiness that had been building in her. She no longer questioned, was merely relieved that her uncertainty had vanished with her laughter. Instantly, she felt wonderful, absolutely on top of the world, and put it down to having opened her eyes to Venice and herself. She was thrilled that she was a traveller and not a tourist, and that she could still make a fool of herself over a place and a grand passion for a man.

Amy called for her bill, paid it and started weaving her way through the mass of tables, thinking that she would go to the Lido for lunch. That was just what she felt like doing. She had yet to see the Lido or Burano, the small satellite islands circling Venice. Distracted, she didn't see the man until he stepped in front of her and spoke.

'You're Amy Ross, aren't you?'

He was not very tall, slender and balding, and his skin was tanned and smooth with an incredibly polished look to it. His eyes were dark brown and bright, clever, smiling eyes, and he was dressed in black flannel trousers and wore a black blazer with bright silver buttons over a black silk shirt with a collar that was too wide and too pointed and worn open at the neck for several buttons. A small black silk scarf was tied in a knot round his neck and on his chest could be seen a silver coptic cross on a gold and silver chain. The clothes – well-worn but impeccably clean and well-pressed – had seen better days. He looked smart if a little sinister. All that black in the sunshine. He carried his clothes with too much flair and wore much too much scent. Amy was astonished.

'Yes, I am. I don't think I know you?'

'You don't. We don't know each other but I feel as if you have already become a part of my life. I would have known you anywhere. Jarret has not stopped talking about you since you left Venice.'

Amy's heart raced at the very mention of Jarret's name and to know that he had spoken about her, and continually, to this man was more than she could have hoped for, more than the vain hope she had been carrying in her heart that he had not forgotten her and would call when he was in New York.

All she could manage to say was, 'Good things, I hope?'

He raised her hand and lowered his head to give it the perfect continental kiss. 'Frankly I've never heard him rave about anyone as he has about you. Or about having such a thrilling day. He thinks you have somehow changed his life and has been feeling very sorry for himself for letting you go.'

They were standing among a sea of small tables covered with white cloths and metal and wooden cafe chairs but not many people. This seemed to be *the* hour for all of Venice to take their break because people were coming and going past them. A man jostled Amy and quickly took her by the elbow and excused himself. He recognised the stranger she was talking to and excused himself to him, then greeted him and kissed him first on one cheek then the other before leaving. Amy was grateful for the intrusion, in which she was able to calm herself.

Then Jarret's friend took her by her arm and suggested, 'I think we should walk on.'

'This is incredible – that you should know me, pick me out from the hundreds of people around.'

'Well, frankly I was first attracted to you by your laugh, when you were laughing at yourself, and then I knew it was you almost at once.'

Amy found that a little eerie, that he should know she had not been laughing at something other than herself. Few people after all sit alone laughing at themselves. Rasputin came to mind. She was amused and wondered if she was such an open book or if this friend of Jarret's was incredibly perceptive. She realised who he was.

'So you're Fee?'

'Yes, I'm Fee, and thrilled to meet you, though I had not expected it would be in Venice. Jarret will be so pleased to see you.'

'He's here? In Venice?'

'Yes.'

'I had no idea, I though he was in Istanbul with you.'

'Change of plans.'

'How extraordinary. A last-minute change of plan is what brought me back to Venice.'

'That's what you may think . . .'

'Now you're going to tell me that it's fate at work?'

'Now I don't have to.'

'But that's what you believe?'

'Fate and Jarret is what I believe brought you back to Venice. Fate and Amy Ross is what changed our plans and is, I believe, why we're still here. But does it matter what I believe? You're here and I'm thrilled to meet you and bring you home to Jarret. He will be incredibly surprised and happy.'

It suddenly became very real to her. That she would be seeing Jarret, that they were somehow a part of each other's lives. She felt weak-kneed, incredibly emotional. The weeks of setting aside her feelings for him, of trying to rationalise him, keep him and her emotions in proper perspective . . . she could drop all that now.

She could hardly wait to hear his voice, to see his face. 'Shall we call him?' she asked Fee.

'Oh, no. We'll surprise him.'

'Do you think that's wise?'

'Very. Now where were you going? What were you going to do today?'

'I was going to buy a pair of boots or shoes in a shop near here and then I was going to go to the Lido for lunch.'

'I'll come with you to the shoe shop. I know it and the owner very well. The Lido for lunch – how lovely. You mustn't change your plans.

After lunch I'll take you to Jarret. You would like that, wouldn't you?'

'Oh yes. But what of your plans?'

'I had no plans for today.'

'Then you must be my guest at the Lido for lunch.'

'I don't want to impose. Are you sure?' asked Fee.

'Quite sure. We could call Jarret and he could join us, celebrate the workings of fate?'

'He's out or I would have taken you directly to him. I will join you for lunch. I don't eat very much.'

'It doesn't matter.'

'What fun,' he said, and arm in arm they headed for the shoe shop.

Fee seemed to know everyone, and everyone who greeted him seemed to be an intimate of his, as if he were somehow a part of their lives, a part of the Venetian scene. He was amusing and solicitous and flattering. He took Amy over in the nicest way, made the day she had planned much easier by arranging everything effortlessly.

From a basket hung on the arm of an elderly flower vendor, he chose a minute bunch of violets tied with narrow streamers of satin ribbon and pinned them to her jacket. Amy could not help but notice that the woman refused his money. It seemed enough for her to chat with him and to serve him. Her fondness for him was obvious.

Amy and Fee had great fun in the shoe store and Amy bought shoes and a pair of boots. He had taste and was interested in her shopping, and it was he who arranged for the shoes she purchased to be sent round to the Gritti.

He got a good price for a boat to take them to the Lido and they had the luxury of not having to share it with anyone but each other. En route he had the boat slip briefly down several canals to show Amy views of exquisite buildings that she might never have seen without him. He had called through to the right hotel for the right table and they were received enthusiastically. Fee seemed to be well known and respected here as well.

And he was amusing. There was something quite fey about him, as if he were not quite ordered in his mind and possessed a strange kind of over-confidence, but all in the nicest way. A touch of madness, artistic madness, was what Amy finally summed it up as.

Over a stunningly good lunch she could not help but notice that he was indeed frugal with his food and drank no alcohol.

Ever since he had made himself known to Amy, every other sentence he spoke was about Jarret. Of course that was wonderful for her. All she really wanted was to talk about him or have someone else tell her about him, his life and his work. She was gaining a picture of Jarret Sparrow that only drew her closer to him.

Fee raised his glass to her. The toast he made was, 'To you and Jarret, Amy.'

'How generous of you, but might you not be a bit premature, Fee? I do hope not, but you might be.'

'No, I don't think so. You have to remember, I know him better than anyone else in this world. We have lived and worked together for years. I've listened to him talk about you for weeks. Jarret is a man in love, and I'm thrilled to be the one to bring you back together. Now that I have met you and like you, I find it exciting that you're going to be a part of our lives.'

It was true then. Jarret loved and wanted her, and she certainly wanted him. All this was heady stuff, almost too much for Amy to cope with. Fee made her believe it was true and what she wanted most was going to happen: she was going to be part of Jarret's life, not just a holiday romance. She could feel it in the marrow of her bones. Amy was overwhelmed by his generosity. There could be but one toast. She corrected him. 'To us, the three of us, may all our dreams come true.'

'How nice to be included. I had hoped we would get on, and we do. Did he tell you about his wife?'

'No. He never mentioned he had a wife,' she answered nervously.

'Well, legally he doesn't any more. But I will always think of Savannah as his wife. We got on so well, Savannah and I, it's still difficult for me to accept that it should all have gone so wrong. We tried so hard to make her happy. I never thought he would love like that again, but here you are. New beginnings, new happiness. You have no idea how thrilled I am for you both, for all of us. To see Jarret happy is to be happy myself.'

Of course there were innumerable questions about Savannah that she wanted to ask but somehow Amy sensed that these should be set aside for the time being. Fee had brought Jarret from the realm of possibility to reality. Jarret was so alive for her that she felt to pose any questions about him or his ex-wife would be a betrayal of some sort of the man she loved and who loved her. If there were any questions she would address them directly to him.

Instead, she changed the subject and said, 'Fee, all afternoon we've done nothing but talk about Jarret and me. What about you? I'd like to know more about you. I only know that you're a painter who no longer paints, and that Jarret is your best friend.'

'Friend and partner in work. In all things, in fact,' he corrected.

Amy did not quite understand what he meant. Rather than question it, she told him, 'I stand corrected.'

'Firuz Yolu. I am Turkish.'

'Is that the name you paint under?'

'*Painted* under. Yes, when I did paint.'

'Will you paint again?'

'Who knows?'

There was something in the way he answered her, a look in his eyes, the way he moved uncomfortably in his chair. Painters and painting Amy understood and was intuitive about, and she didn't like what her intuition was telling her now. Fee was lying. She sensed that he knew very well that he would pick up his brushes again, and that he was biding his time. He was a painter being cagey about his work, and she guessed he was working to some plan. It was at that moment that she made up her mind that whatever Fee or Jarret were to do with their careers, she would never become involved professionally. Talk about art and their work with them, yes; art was after all the stuff of their lives in one way or another.

Fee shocked Amy when he added, 'At the right time, for the right dealer. If not the big one-man show for a top international dealer, then never. It's Jarret's career we're working on at the moment. Partners in everything, I did tell you that.' It was as if he knew that she had caught him out.

Amy realised that he played fey because he wanted people to think that was all he was. She didn't mind that particularly, so long as she hadn't been taken in by his act. And she hadn't been. Amy did believe that Fee was genuinely a fey character but also sensed that beneath that lay an oriental mind, clever and quick, possibly devious. It prompted her to ask, 'Where did you meet Jarret, Fee?'

'In Florence on a hot summer's day in the Uffizi, in front of a Donatello. He was a very new arrival. The handsomest, most sensitive and interesting American I had ever met, and so full of enthusiasm for art and Florence. His Italian was atrocious, mine very good. I came to his rescue. I was with a French friend. We three were very poor, living off the hospitality of wealthy friends in high places, and our small allowances: mine from a brother, Jarret's from an old aunt, and Jean-Paul's from his mother. We decided to pool our resources and travel together. Jarret and I have been together ever since, much more than

104

friends, more like brothers. We have had a marvellous life full of adventure, good times and bad. And Jarret has become a fine painter with a considerable following who will make it big one day.'

'I would like to have known him then.'

'He was exactly the same as he is now. He's still an innocent – we both are when we shouldn't be. He's still very much the naive American in spite of all his years away. We are in many ways simple souls, artists, who see too late when people are taking advantage of us. We still suffer for the love of art, and take care of each other. Our relationship is designed to further our careers. Sometimes it's Jarret's we work on. Sometimes mine.'

'You sound like partners in art and crime against anyone who threatens your alliance.'

Amy hardly realised what she was saying until it was out and then she had no time to consider her words because Fee jumped in with a laugh and told her: 'Jarret kept raving on about how quick and clever you are. Well, it's certainly true you don't mince your words! Be assured you are absolutely correct. That is exactly what we are.'

'Should I be worried about that, Fee?' asked Amy, who was feeling that she had stumbled into something she was not prepared to deal with.

He rose quickly from his chair to take the few steps to her side. He kissed the top of her head and raised both her hands, kissing one and then the other. Then gazing into her eyes, he told her, 'I don't think you have a thing to worry about. I could have not spoken to you in St Mark's Square. I didn't have to tell you Jarret is in Venice, nor deliver you to him as I intend to. And if that's not proof in itself then try this: I like you and hope we will be the best of friends. I already feel that we are.'

His words made sense and the look in his eyes gave her the feeling that he meant them. It prompted her to confide in Fee, 'I'm nervous about you springing me on Jarret as a surprise. It might be embarrassing for him.'

'You just leave that to me. I promise I'm going to make you the happiest woman in this world.'

'An artist, a prophet . . . what more can I ask for in a man who picks me up in the most romantic city in the world?'

'It's the oriental mind, my dear. I am after all a Turk. It would be great fun to show you Istanbul. We could travel together. I could show you my country and its wonders. You may not think so now but I can assure you that there are vestiges of the Ottoman Empire that exist even now, and we have a marvellous house on the Bosphorus.'

'I somehow don't think of you as being Turkish, more an exotic European: the languages, the houses, Paris, Venice, Istanbul . . . You have come a long way from the poor starving artists who met in Florence all those years ago. Your life is more glamorous than other painters' I've met.'

'I think of myself as an oriental by birth and a European by taste. I could never give up one to be the other. I am actually one-quarter English. My mother's mother. I was educated in Istanbul and Paris. Until I met Jarret I had no interest in America, but he changed all that. I find New York amazing, and like Americans. They are so hospitable.'

At that point Fee dropped names from the social register that she had only read about. He was amusing and gossipy about these people and she sensed that he did not take them particularly seriously. By the time the pudding was served Amy began to realise that Fee took very little seriously, that he played with life. Somehow she had to admire his audacity.

Amy found his ruthless honesty about himself impressive, especially when he told her, 'I've always liked women and the female mind but loved men. I have many women friends and used to have lots of male lovers, but I no longer do. I've been celibate for years. Sex holds no interest for me though it still does for Jarret. I suppose the reason we'll always be friends and partners in life is because he's heterosexual and I'm homosexual. We have a life together and ones apart from each other. We own houses and things together, pool our money, share our debts, what's mine is his and his is mine, but the sex thing never looms its irrepressible head to cause any problems between us. That does not, however, mean that I'm not dazzled by beautiful young men – I am. I just never bring them home.'

It seemed that once Fee started talking about himself there was no stopping him and Amy was riveted by all he revealed. Here was a character the like of which she had never met before. His was a world of which she had scarcely any knowledge. It was not at all hers or the way she wanted to live, and yet she could appreciate it, was fascinated by it.

At last he got round to Savannah. 'It was I who introduced her to Jarret. It is usually I who am the one to find people to amuse us. Jarret is quite shy as I'm sure you have already noticed. I feel very sorry that I no longer see Savannah. We were great friends and had many good

106

times. She is a delicate thing, and oh, such a beauty! A real southern belle from one of the South's most aristocratic families. Savannah Lee was her name before she became Savannah Sparrow. I still see her occasionally.

'When we first met her she was rather a pathetic little thing with a very handsome mother who dominated her. Well, she had to really, Savannah had been born with a heart murmur and always lived a rather restricted life. Her mother, Aurora Lee, a doyenne of Southern high society, really never quite knew what to do with Savannah. Then Mummy Lee found Europe, and I found them. The rest is history, but I'll let Jarret tell you about that. All I will tell you is that after a lavish wedding she left her mother and the South behind her and practically overnight in Jarret's arms became a new woman. We set her free and they had a wonderful life, buying houses and fixing them up. We all had a marvellous time and then it was over. Well, hey ho.'

Amy couldn't resist asking, 'And the heart murmur?'

'We healed her. After the divorce it vanished.'

'And where is she now?'

'London. She works in a shop on Bond Street, as manageress. Christian Dior got her the job.'

'She lives in London?'

'In a small rented flat off Berkeley Square. You see, her mother disowned her after she went through all her inheritance and divorced Jarret. The Lees never divorce or botch up their lives, which was what the dragon lady expected of Savannah – I always call Aurora Lee the dragon lady. She should have told us how dependent a wife Savannah was going to be. Oh, well, she seems happy enough living in her modest circumstances and travelling in the most illustrious of European society, playing the penniless, desperately injured Southern aristocrat done wrong by her husband. That does on occasion cause us problems . . . Silly woman. None of it is true. A woman scorned and all that, I suppose. Still, I've always hoped that Jarret and she will make it up, find love again. That is, I did until a few weeks ago when I returned to Venice to find out about you.'

Chapter 8

Amy felt herself being carried along by Fee's enthusiasm at being the instrument of her and Jarret's coming together again. And why not? It was true. If not for Fee, would she be walking through the narrow street to their house? But much as she wanted to see Jarret and hear in his own words how much he'd missed her and wanted her, she was incredibly nervous about this reunion. More than anything else because she might be let down, the chemistry might no longer be there. She wanted it to be the same as it had been when she was struck by love for him the moment she laid eyes on him in Rimboccare.

Fee and Amy had taken the motor launch from the Lido to a canal only a short distance from the *palazzo*. 'Jarret would be certain to hear us if we arrived home by way of the canal and used that entrance. The element of surprise would be spoiled,' had been Fee's explanation.

The sun was out and the light a miracle, like no other Amy had seen. It had a magical, unreal quality to it; made her want to raise her arms and grab it, hug it to her. She wanted never to forget it. Its warmth seemed more intense than it had been because the day had barely a whisper of a breeze left in it. She walked arm in arm with Fee through the streets and felt like one of the children who had followed the Pied Piper. Unable not to. Charmed by Fee, grateful to him for leading her to her heart's desire, she felt giddy with happiness as those same children might have.

Several times she had suggested to Fee that they might accomplish this reunion in some other way than surprise, but to no avail. Now, as they approached the *palazzo*'s door, she stopped short, stricken with nerves.

Fee fussed with her hair, adjusted the violets on her jacket, then graciously kissed her hand and said, 'Be very quiet, on tip toe so to speak, and not a word. I'm going to take you into the garden. He'll meet you there.'

Fee opened the ancient wooden door and they stepped into the hall. Amy was surprised by how little she had remembered of the beautiful hall and briefly took notice that there were fewer of Jarret's paintings there now. Stealthily they crept through the hall and from there, after pushing Amy out of sight into the library, Fee called out, 'Jarret! Jarret, are you in?'

No answer. Fee walked Amy through the library and into the garden, to its very centre. 'Here. You stand here – he'll come to you.' He smiled at Amy and patted her shoulder then mounted the stone staircase that led to the open arched loggia on the first floor. Once more he called out, this time asking, 'Jarret, where are you?'

Amy heard his voice and had to close her eyes to calm herself.

'In the studio.'

'Come down to the garden. I've brought you something, something you've been wanting.'

There was no reply. Several minutes went by before Amy heard a door open, and another close. In those several minutes she was alone in the garden, she experienced the strangest sensations: disorientation, emptiness, child-like dependency.

Jarret opened the door to his studio and stepped out into the loggia. Walking straight to one of the half walls set under each arch, he sat down on it and looked into his garden. There was nothing child-like about the Amy Ross he saw. The sun shone on her hair which gleamed like silk. Once more that tall, slender but voluptuous figure he had longed for these last few weeks took possession of him. She had removed her jacket, rested it on her shoulders, and her full breasts, the shape of their nipples through the fine silk knit of her jumper . . . she might as well not have worn anything at all. Amy had been looking in a different direction. She turned and gazed directly up at Jarret and smiled. Her eyes were filled with a wild passion, matching his own sexual desire for her. Neither of them seemed capable of saying a word. It took several seconds for Jarret to collect himself. When he did, he rose from the wall and dashed down the stairs, taking them three at a time.

He was half running through the garden to her. Amy wanted to dash into his arms but felt too unsteady on her legs to move. He wasn't less but more, much more, attractive even than she had thought when she had been with him before. The chemistry between them was if anything more potent. There was an intensity between them that was undeniable. All that Fee had told her about Jarret's feelings for her was true. It was right there in his eyes, on his face, in the way in which he was moving in on her. She wanted to call out his name, to say something, anything, but words wouldn't come. And not for him either. He rushed into her arms.

That first kiss, lips trembling with passion, was a foretaste of sexual delight. His lips against hers set them aflame. Wrapped in each other's arms, it was as if their entire beings were focused in that meeting of lips and mouths and tongues. Amy felt like molten gold, all fluid and out of her normal form. Everything she did in that kiss was more natural, more real and genuine, than she had ever experienced before. Involuntary almost, without thought, prompted by pure instinct. She was sensitive to the tiniest thing, as if the skin had been flayed from her body.

He placed his hands on either side of her face. He held her and studied her face as if to make sure she was real. Then slowly he pulled her towards him and placed his lips upon hers once more. She felt his tongue licking the inside of her lips, searching. He sucked her tongue slowly, pulling strongly on it, into his mouth and out, into his mouth and out. Oral sex by way of a kiss. Amy felt such exquisite sensations, she wanted to call out as she came in a short sweet orgasm.

He slipped his arm round her waist and walked her through the garden and up the flight of stairs. 'Speak to me. Say something, anything, just so I know this is real,' he said, choked with emotion. There were tears in his eyes.

'It's real enough,' she told him, neither one of them taking their eyes off the other.

He placed his free hand to his forehead and shook his head. 'I was here waiting, every day waiting for something to happen, and I didn't know what. Now I know it was you. Fee found you and brought you to me. He said he would. I claimed it was impossible, that you were not returning to Venice. But you're here, Amy, and I'm the happiest man in the world.'

He swept her off her feet and into his arms and carried her over the threshold and into his bedroom. Putting her down on her feet, he closed the doors to the loggia and stood looking at her. He watched her put her jacket on a chair and unbuckle her belt. Jarret went to her and removed the belt from her trembling hands, tossing it on to a settee. He pulled the silk knit jumper up over her head and dropped it on the floor. She waited for his hands to caress her breasts. They ached for him. Her nipples were long and slender, the nimbus round them a halo of a creamy peach colour, provocative for their nearly blending in colour with the heavy, firm, and magnificently shaped breasts that looked ripe with milk or honey – something delectable. But he didn't touch her breasts. Instead he tore off his own clothes.

He was erect. Amy did not play coy, the thought never entered her mind. Her eyes remained riveted on his phallus. It was as noble as the rest of Jarret's looks. His penis was long and thick, its head a very large knob. She could think of nothing else but being possessed by Jarret and his more than ample penis. She had not known what she expected but his sex was so perfectly formed and beautiful, so forceful, the succulent-looking scrotum that hung voluptuously beneath so handsome and dignified, so incredibly sexy, that she could not think of anything else. She undressed with only Jarret's sex in mind, Jarret's sperm taking possession of her until they both dissolved into puddles of their own come mingled together.

She was down to her white lace garter belt holding up sheer cream-coloured stockings. She walked backwards to the bed, actually retreating from him in the hope that he would follow her quickly before she came again. That was her signal to Jarret that she was ready for him, that she wanted him.

He did follow her. She lay down on the bed and he followed her again, to lie quietly next to her for a very few seconds before he picked up her hand in his and kissed it as he slipped on top of her. Skin to skin, their scents mingled. The weight of him on top of her, even that was unimaginably erotic for Amy. It honed her lust for him to the point where she had to hold her breath not to call out in the pain of her desire.

She opened her legs wide and he raised them and placed them high on his shoulders. She lay there, open and vulnerable to him, and trembled with anticipation. With one hand he gripped her shoulder and with the other he slid his penis teasingly up and down her soft pink cleft. He was there, ready to plunge. He gave her no comfort of words or declarations of love to ease her lust but moved his hand to her other shoulder. He caressed it and then held both her shoulders in a tight grip as if to reassure her that she was safe, he was in control. He lowered his head and laid his cheek against hers, caressing her face with his.

Jarret watched the tears form in her eyes and knew he had possession of Amy. That excited him further. It fired his love for her even more. Now his lust was as much out of control as hers. He pressed his lips

112

upon hers. They parted. Their tongues and mouths moved together and he thrust the knob of his penis very deliberately into Amy's soft and warm vagina. Jarret eased himself slowly into her. He filled her tightly but continued plunging deeper and deeper. A more exquisite sensation he had never felt. She was so very much alive for him, using herself to grip him, creating a rhythm of her own to please him.

Jarret pulsated with life, throbbed with lust, and for Amy it was as if she had never had a man before, so marvellous was the sensation of having sex with him.

Jarret rested for a few minutes inside Amy before he began, slowly, with finesse and controlled lust. Deep and languid penetrations for a very long time, getting the feel of every morsel of warm, moist, satiny flesh, marking her for himself forever. That was what he was most deliberately doing and that was what he was whispering to her.

Amy could not hold back. One orgasm followed another and another. He had her relaxed into sexual submission to a man, a phallus, and sex, as she had never known it. With every orgasm she had he seemed to be renewed and continued, changing his pace when it suited him. It was as if it were impossible to get enough of her, as if they had found it impossible to get enough of being locked together in sexual oblivion. Half a dozen times she asked him to come with her but he didn't.

He would answer her with, 'Not yet. This is what you want, isn't it? This is what you came back for. This is what I've been thinking about since you left me. This is what we should have done that night we met and the next day.'

Time and place vanished. Lost in lust for each other, they entered another realm of being, a place Amy had never been before. They had achieved a kind of sexual nirvana. And there they lived on a higher plane than either of them had ever known. Far after they reached that place of no return and had dwelt in their lust for as long as they could maintain it, it happened. They came together in a powerful, long and blissful orgasm. It was like the moment of creation for them and they spilled forth in love.

Jarret slipped from Amy's body and lay quietly on his side next to her. She turned to face him and searched for his hand. He brought their hands to his mouth and kissed her finger tips. They gazed into each other's eyes. In his moment of orgasm, Jarret had called out again and again, 'I love you! God help me, how I love you,' and that's what she saw now in his eyes – that he did indeed love her. Amy wanted to hear him tell her again that he loved her, but he remained silent.

113

She was spilling over with love for Jarret. She had not held back during intercourse. Repeatedly she'd told him of her love for him, how wonderful he was. She needed to know that what they felt, what they had said to each other, was not said in the heat of passion, although she knew in her heart that they were more than in lust, they were in love with each other. Yet he said nothing.

Instead he kissed her lightly, sweetly, on the lips, then moved his mouth from hers to her nipples. This was the first time he had touched her breasts. He sucked deeply on one then the other. The sensation set her tingling, made her lustful enough to forget her need for words of love and commitment.

Amy had nipples that were extremely sensitive and reacted to a man's mouth, to deep and sexy sucking. They became rigid and seemingly longer and she squirmed with pleasure. It was as if Jarret wanted to suck her breast whole into his mouth. He too was lusting again. Now, for the first time, she felt his large rough hands cupping her breast while he fed himself on it. He caressed and squeezed it and Amy could see that he derived tremendous sexual pleasure from it. He was driving them both into a sexual frenzy. Amy was writhing in lust. He tried to hold her still with his hands on her waist while relentlessly clinging to her nipple with his mouth. Amy's body stiffened and she came in a long and intense orgasm. He could hardly not have noticed it. Only then did he remove his lips from her breast and speak.

'I wish that your tits were filled with a rich creamy milk for me, milk sweetened with honey. That I could suck nectar from your nipples, that you could nurture me from your breast in the same way you gave your orgasms up to me.'

'Would that I could,' she told him. And her heart melted that little bit more for Jarret Sparrow.

Amy saw him rampant and ready for her and caressed his penis with her hands. Only moments before he took possession of her nipple again, he raised her leg to drape it over his hip. He covered her hand that held him with his and together they directed it. They teased her soft moist flesh and found the entrance they were looking for. Together they pushed and both gasped with pleasure as he sank to the hilt inside that place he wanted to be. Only then did he tell her, 'Amy, I love you. You're like some exotic forbidden fruit that I can never have enough of.'

Then his lips wrapped themselves round her nipple and he sucked and licked ravenously for the milk that could only come as orgasms. Much later, when the moon and the stars had come out, to satisfy his

114

thirst for her, she taught him how to drink her come, the milk of her lust, using her as a cup.

An elixir he had never sampled before, the mere taste, the act, he had never considered before he met Amy Ross, drew him ever closer to her and into an unrivalled passion for this woman who surprised him at every turn.

In the morning with the sun streaming in on their faces, it was Amy who awakened first. She turned on her side, leaned on her elbow and watched him sleeping. She wanted to cry for the sheer handsomeness of this big man lying fast asleep next to her. Amy wanted to move away a lock of the hair that had fallen on his forehead, to touch his cheek, kiss the lashes on his eyelids, lick his lips with the point of her tongue. Of course she did none of these things, didn't want to wake him, just lay there believing that she was the luckiest woman in the world.

This handsome, talented, extraordinarily sexy man was hers. There were to be many other mornings like this. It was hard for her to believe. She had no doubts now about Jarret loving her, he had told her so continually while they were in the throes of their lustful coupling.

He opened his eyes. The moment he did Amy realised that she and Jarret were back in the real world. Their reunion had been so intense and thrilling, a miracle really, that they had somehow forgotten the real world.

Jarret turned on his side and leaned on his elbow, taking the same position that Amy had been in for hours. They gazed into each other's eyes. 'Good morning,' he said, and a smile crossed his lips.

'Good morning,' she replied.

'I'm famished, and so must you be.'

'Yes, I am actually. What shall we do about it?'

'We'll have breakfast in bed. Would you like that? Or else in the garden?'

'The garden.'

'I'm so happy you're here,' he told her, and kissed her on the lips. 'It's frightening to think that we might have missed last night if fate had not been in our favour.'

There was a tap at the bedroom door. Jarret wrapped himself in a blanket and went to see who it was.

Fee and he exchanged some words in French. When Jarret finally closed the door he told her, 'Fee seems to have anticipated our wishes. Breakfast awaits us in the garden.'

Jarret was no longer there when she returned from bathing. The room had been put in order, her clothes gathered up from the floor and laid neatly on the bed. She dressed and went out on to the loggia. The view was remarkable. The magnificent large garden in the inner courtyard below, and beyond it a canal that merged into another much wider, with beyond that the crumbling buildings, domes and spires, towers and roofscapes of Venice – so different from the topography of New York City or Easthampton, the places where she worked and lived.

She recognised the music of Vivaldi coming from somewhere in the house. Several minutes later, while she was admiring the magic world that Jarret and Fee had created for themselves, she came to understand in a flash of enlightenment that she was a stranger in a strange land when it came to their life. How much would they all have to change to make it otherwise? That became the burning question, the imponderable. The other and even more burning question was, could they? And yet more questions – did they want to? Would they?

Jarret entered the garden, a piece of bread in one hand and an apple in the other. Just the sight of him and all questions were automatically relegated to the back of her mind. Amy hurried along the loggia and down the flight of stone steps. He heard her coming and turned. The light was playing on his blond hair: a Greek or Roman god, that must have been his role in another life. A statue of one at least. Yes, there was something very still and statue-like about Jarret, maybe an indifference to the world, certainly a coolness, even a timidity, that was incredibly seductive. She gave him a hug and kissed him. It wasn't returned. Instead, he broke off a piece of his bread and handed it to her.

'I thought you'd never come out of your bath. I missed you. I hope it's not always going to be that way, my missing you to the point of distraction.' And he smiled at her.

'Words that would make any woman's heart race,' was her answer to him.

Jarret popped the remainder of the bread that had been spread thick with butter and dribbled with honey into his mouth, and taking her hand in his they walked together through the garden to a table that had been set for breakfast.

It was vaguely reminiscent of the Mad Hatter's tea party, that breakfast: the small table had a gold cloth on it with an edge that was frayed, and another cloth that was half eaten away and worn through

116

in several places to show the wooden surface of the table beneath. No two pieces of china on the table matched, the tea pot had a broken spout, the creamer had lost its handle. There was a loaf of rough bread on the table, a bread knife that had lost its rippled edge and was dull, the bowl of honey had a crack in it and oozed on to the plate beneath it. The apple basket's handle was broken.

Just as Jarret gallantly held out a chair with a broken back for Amy, they heard Fee call out, 'Hey ho.' He was walking across the garden towards them dressed in a black caftan, a black silk turban round his head, and carrying a platter covered with paper-thin slices of smoked ham and luscious-looking purple figs. Behind him followed George, dressed in jeans and a white shirt open at the neck, carrying a platter of fried eggs.

'A breakfast for lovers,' said Fee, a smile on his lips and his arms open to embrace Amy once he had placed the platter on the table.

'Oh, Fee, it looks marvellous. How kind, thanks so much.'

George was placing his platter on the table and embracing Jarret with a manly hug when Fee answered Amy with, 'Not me to thank or Jarret. We hate food and cooking in the house. It was George. I told him you had returned to us and he offered to cook breakfast for you.'

Beautiful, calm and sweet George with whom everyone fell in love. He seemed like an island of sanity and reality in this amazing world of Jarret and Fee's. And yet she knew that he lived in just such unreality as they did. It shocked her to think of even using George as a scale to measure Jarret's life by; there was something way over the top about it. In her overwhelming erotic passion for him, and for the sake of their love for each other, Amy was trying to accept Jarret and Fee's lifestyle as just another world. A lifestyle as valid as hers or anyone else's, one she could be happy living.

George placed an arm round her and gave her a kiss. 'Welcome back to Venice.'

He and Fee fussed over her, and Jarret looked pleased if not just a little aloof from it all. Ravenous, the two lovers sat down immediately to eggs that were cooked to perfection.

'Fried eggs – the one thing George has learned to master in the kitchen. We should be more than honoured that he's cooked for us, Amy. You see, he no longer cooks breakfast for anyone,' said Jarret, a teasing note in his voice.

Amy had the feeling that Jarret was trying to tell her something more about George. People seemed always to be dropping innuendoes about him. She could not understand what they were trying to say or why they were so displeased with him on the one hand and so admiring of him on the other.

The two men refused to join Amy and Jarret for breakfast. George wandered round the garden after telling her, 'This is Jarret's pride and joy. This garden is one of the treasures of Venice.'

'Savannah loved this garden, she was its inspiration. It was somewhere for her to sit. She never could quite get over a city without grand gardens as in the South. It's filled with cuttings she and Jarret took from their travels round the world – that's part of its exotic charm. Jarret's as devoted to this garden as he is to painting. He says it's his sanity *and* his love. It's too bad Savannah's so bitter about it. Well, what are you two going to do today?' asked Fee.

Amy found it oddly disturbing the way he spoke of Savannah, as if she were still part of Jarret's life, and Jarret, who had not even mentioned an ex-wife's existence to Amy, merely listened expressionless and without comment. Indeed, as if he were endorsing the fact that she was still a factor in his life. Amy waited for Jarret to say something about Savannah directly to her: 'She's my ex-wife' would have been enough to ease her anxiety about the power she sensed Savannah still wielded over him. Nothing, not a word. It had been his opportunity to mention and dispense with her in their lives. His not doing so made it clear to Amy that if Savannah wasn't there in the flesh, she was certainly there as a ghost to haunt them.

Instead he answered Fee with, 'We haven't thought about that. What are you going to do?'

'I'm going to stay with Alfreda and leave you two alone.'

Jarret said nothing, merely handed a fig to Amy, having first turned the skin inside out so she could suck the luscious ripe flesh from it.

George left soon after his walk through the garden. Fee hovered over their breakfast but refused to sit down and join them. Instead he ingratiated himself even further with Amy and eased her anxiety considerably when he told her, 'I can hardly believe this is the same man who was stomping round here unhappily, unable to paint, besotted by a lady art historian he might never see again. Now here you are, and what a joy to see you and have Jarret out of the doldrums. I don't think we should ever let you go. You're his happiness.'

Fleetingly what went through Amy's mind was embarrassingly trite: love could conquer anything, certainly ghosts from the past. Trite and wrong, very bad thinking. But she was hopelessly in love so she ignored

118

all the warning signs and asked Jarret, 'Is that true?'

He laughed. 'It would seem so, according to Fee.'

'Never mind according to Fee. What about according to you?'

'Fee and I most always think the same. Be satisfied with that.'

It never entered Amy's mind not to be, and when he said, 'Let's go to the studio. I want to show you what I've been working on since you left. It seems you're my muse as well as my sensual delight,' she could have wept for joy.

Fee had been flitting about the garden like a rare species of black butterfly. He hovered over Jarret now. 'Amy's leaving in three days' time, Jarret, so you sort yourselves out before she does. I want no sad faces or sulks from you, and no more changes of plan. Paris and Istanbul, the sooner the better, remember?'

Before Jarret could answer, two people entered the garden and he rose from his chair to go and meet them. It gave Amy an opportunity to realise that to love Jarret was to take on Fee. There was a bond between these two men which she could not quite understand. She had never had a friendship or known one between two people as strong or as complicated as Fee and Jarret's. The realisation that Fee was an enormous influence over Jarret became an immediate concern for her, and though she liked Fee and was grateful to him for finding her and delivering her to Jarret, she recognised in him, for all his fun and wit, an ambitious and Byzantine mind. Amy saw herself as a problem in Fee's life, and Jarret's love for her as an even greater problem for him. Unless Amy fitted Fee's requirements – and she hadn't the vaguest idea what those might be – she sensed her love affair could be short-lived. She knew in her heart that for them both this was going to be the love that was meant to be and forever, but that it was a fragile thing.

Amy felt suddenly quite frightened for them both. It was a gut feeling for she really had nothing to base her fears on except the way Jarret and Fee were conducting their lives together. Fee was quick to see the colour drain from her face. He was standing close to her and asked, 'Is something wrong?'

Never one for artifice or for looking to add troubles to her life, Amy asked, 'Fee, do you mind Jarret and I loving each other?'

'If I minded, would I have brought you to him, Amy?'

'I don't know.'

'I'm your friend, and a good enough one to tell you that Jarret's falling in love with you is a great surprise, as much to him as it is to me. It would be best for you to remember that Jarret has only one great love and that's painting. All other loves are sexual, temporary or forbidden, so you see you're no long-term threat to our lives. That's why it was easy to pick you up and bring you home for Jarret's amusement.'

'You make yourself sound like a pimp, Fee.'

He laughed. 'Calling me a pimp, though I am and have always been that for Jarret, is clearly not the way for you to ingratiate yourself with me, Amy. You're a clever and beautiful woman and Jarret's in love with you, and rightly so. You're terrific. He's sexually besotted by you, will give you all he can of himself, and you can have a great time, especially in bed. I suggest you make the most of it and let me be your friend as I was Savannah's. We can have a good time together, and we will. Just play by the rules of the game.'

Amy could hardly believe that she was too much in love with Jarret not to just walk away from Fee. He was not exactly sinister but instinct told her he was dangerous for her to have as an enemy. She would have to stand up to him, be civil, and cope with him because he was and would always be a part of her life as long as she stayed with Jarret.

'What rules?' she asked.

'Give Jarret what he wants, no more, no less, and we'll all be well and happy.' Fee took her hand in his and kissed it.

Was it as simple as that? Was Fee telling her it was not him nor her but Jarret who was in control of his love affair with Amy? She had no time to ponder these questions because Jarret returned to introduce her to the two people who had arrived – a Greek painter and her friend, a sculptor, who lived in Paris.

Their arrival sparked off another glorious day with Jarret. His friends were amusing, charming, and very talented and clever artists. Looking at Jarret's work with them, talking art, going to the painter's studio and looking at her canvases, then on to a small inexpensive restaurant where they were the guests of the new arrivals, was exciting and fun. They drew Amy out and found her to be as Fee had told them she was: a clever New York art world player who knew all about the contemporary scene there.

The communication between herself and Jarret, rich and interesting although not overtly emotional, was passionate enough for the Greek painter to whisper in Amy's ear, 'How did you do it, capture that elusive heart of his?'

It was close to midnight when they arrived not back at Jarret's *palazzo* but the Gritti Palace Hotel. There the concierge fussed not over Amy but Jarret. She could not help but wonder how and why he had become such a well-known figure in Venice. The night manager offered them a bottle of champagne in the bar and there Amy and Jarret sat alone except for a man at the far side of the room.

'When Ernest Hemingway was here in Venice, chasing after a beautiful young Italian girl and writing *Across the River and Into the Trees*, between his rooms here at the Gritti and above Harry's restaurant on Torcello, we often met. He would have liked you, found you beautiful, and been enchanted by this romantic love idyll of ours.'

'Is it just an idyll, do you think?'

'Maybe we shouldn't question that, and maybe I was wrong to try and define what we have together.'

Jarret was such a different man with her when the sexual chemistry was working between them as it was now that they were alone and in the peace and quiet of the bar. She could see the lust and love for her in his eyes. Something in his entire being seemed to change. Both were equally aware of their erotic passion, so much so that words were not necessary. Theirs was an overwhelming desire to be intimate with each other, to seek a world of sexual oblivion together that was once more taking them over. And that was when Amy liked Jarret best.

'What's your room number?'

Amy told him, and there was a tremor in her voice. He squeezed her hand. His was trembling. It was then that she realised Jarret was just as emotional about their love affair as she was. That was an odd confirmation to her, but a confirmation none the less, that neither Fee nor Savannah could change their feelings for each other. It somehow reassured her that their love was theirs, and that together, no matter who or what, they would make it work.

'You get the key. I'll follow in a few minutes. I'll wait until there's no one round to see me,' he told Amy.

'And what if they did? You don't actually think they would make a fuss about me having a man in my room, do you? I'm sure Ernest Hemingway felt no need to sneak his amours up the back stairs. Really, Jarret, this is 1958. How very old-fashioned of you.'

He looked surprised. 'In Venice it's always better to be discreet. Venetians love a scandal, and we can't have that.'

'Is this love affair always going to be top secret?' asked Amy, who was not much liking the idea of his sneaking up to her room.

'Not top secret, but we should keep it to ourselves and not let the outside world come in and spoil it. Discreet will do, and that will be

121

difficult enough. Amy, I'm a selfish bastard, I want you for myself, for us when we're together to enjoy a haven away from people and places and things. You're an oasis where I can quench my thirst, an island unto yourself where I can bathe in your sunlight.' He bent forward and whispered in her ear, 'And when I come inside you, it's like finding the home I never dreamed I would have, and all the passion and excitement of my life at its peak, having those two things at the same time. I think about fucking you all the time but it doesn't mean I want the world to know about it.'

That was how Jarret felt, but what about her, Amy? Strangely not very different from him. Her love for Jarret, their sex life, was intensely personal to her. Only his expressing their intimate life so well made her realise that while she wanted the world to know she and Jarret were lovers, she didn't want to shout it from the roof-tops. She found that somehow perverse, odd, not a very solid foundation to build a life together on.

He smiled and kissed her hand and rose from his chair. She left him in the bar and went to get her key. It was early days in the love stakes. She adored him and wanted him. He could say anything, do anything, as long as they were together.

Amy showered very quickly, and brushed her hair, and had time to make up her face. She looked incredibly pretty and sexy, just the way she wanted to look for Jarret. She slipped into her black crêpe-de-chine nightdress: an expensive extravagance she had treated herself to in Paris, a birthday present to herself which she had not as yet worn. It had thin shoestring satin straps and was low in the back, very nearly to her waist. The bodice had inserts of black lace and her breasts could clearly be seen through the lace. She looked in the mirror before she slipped the dressing gown, a kimono of the same black crêpe-de-chine, over her shoulders and slid her arms through the wide glamorous sleeves. She was quite overwhelmed by what she saw: an Amy she had never known before. She liked this sexy, beautiful woman waiting for the man she was giving herself up to so completely.

She was no stranger to great sex, long and luscious orgasms, completely satisfying, but she was unused to sex such as she and Jarret were having, where a man controlled her with his thrustings, demanding that she dissolve in orgasm after orgasm. A man who loved her with a powerful passion that was more than sex, more than love even. Her heart raced in anticipation as the door opened and Jarret walked into the room.

122

He walked directly to her, dropping his jacket on to the floor, pulling at his tie, unbuckling his belt. 'You're always surprising me, seducing me with being more than I want you to be.'

He slipped the kimono from her shoulders and it fell to the floor. Jarret turned her round once to look at her and then, taking her by the hand, led her to the bed. It seemed impossible to Amy that this was only the second time that they would have been to bed together. It was for her as if they had been having sex all their lives. She wanted him desperately and saw that same desperation in his eyes. There was no kiss, no caress. He was erect, rock hard. She had only to see that and she lay down on the bed, her knees bent, legs wide apart, the luscious black silk draped sensually round the paleness of her thighs.

Jarret pulled her up against the many pillows on the bed and then lay on top of her, placing his enormously engorged sex against the softness of her cleft. 'I like to watch your face while I'm fucking you. It's your hunger, your greed for sex, your love for me, that excites me. Your writhing in pleasure, how you hold your breath before you come, and then your release. I like to watch all that while I feel the warm gush of your come flow over me.'

A little vulgar, a lot sexy, this talk during sex from the usually silent Jarret. There was no doubt that his words excited them both, made them feel even more raunchy than they already were. Without any foreplay or hesitation he thrust violently into Amy. Unable to hold back she opened her mouth to call out, not in pain but pleasure, but he anticipated her and placed a hand gently over her mouth to keep the sound at a minimum. He kept it there for some minutes while he took her slowly, exquisitely. She picked up his rhythm and went with it, contracting and easing, and using her pelvis in dances of pleasure for him, wanting always to give as much pleasure as she was receiving.

All the while he was generous with his praise of her sexual abilities, telling her, 'You feel so warm and wet and luscious. It's so thrilling the way you embrace me with your sex.'

He was no less generous about himself, telling her, 'For all the rest of your life, no man will ever fuck you better.' His confidence was well founded, she never doubted it was true.

Once again, after he came and only then, he caressed her breasts, taking a nipple in his mouth and sucking until he dozed off. Amy was asleep when he awakened her with a kiss. No words of love or passion for her, he merely rolled her over on to her tummy. Still half asleep, she instinctively raised her bottom by going on her knees, her arms

123

and head resting on the pillows, her eyes still closed.

She felt Jarret raise the silk of her nightdress up over her bottom. As if by instinct she imperceptibly rocked slowly back and forth on her knees. To see that luscious rounded bottom simulate the act of being fucked was for Jarret a tantalising tease.

Amy was still dwelling in that land between sleep and awakening when Jarret placed his large rough hands on her firm, fleshy, rounded orbs. A brief caress before his hands slipped under her bottom. Slowly he sank his erect and pulsating phallus into her tight, warm and satiny place. With hands holding her firmly by the waist, he was able to keep her very still while he screwed her down with sex, brilliant fucking, where he left not an inch untouched by his probing penis, changing the tempo when he chose to. He rode her to a song of sex where he was both composer and conductor. She his muse, his blissful delight. He was marking Amy with sex, for himself, for life. It was obvious to them both that that was the way he spoke to her of love. It was during that early-morning intercourse that Amy realised how intensely private his love for her was.

He was gone when she awakened. She reached out. He wasn't in the bed next to her. Amy felt a sense of loss so painful she had to cover her face with her hands and take several deep breaths to calm herself. Tears stained her cheeks; her sobs broke the fragile control she had over herself.

That he was gone was one thing, but the premonition that he would never be anything but temporarily there for her was another. Knowing that was pain for a woman in love, was an attack on the heart that was very nearly unbearable. When two people love each other as she and Jarret did, there was a need for continuity, a sharing of all things, the good and the bad to the end of their days. That was how Amy imagined life dealt with true love. Was that so wrong? Too romantic? With Jarret it was, came the answer.

After some time, she was able to calm herself. It was then that she realised she was helpless to do anything other than follow her heart, but that she would also have to remember: no matter the intensity of the love she and Jarret had for each other, theirs was the long-term love that would change his life. Of the three kinds of love that Fee said Jarret dealt with: sexual, temporary and forbidden, she sensed theirs fell into the latter category: *forbidden*.

How could one be so happy and so sad at the same time? Was she over-reacting? Of course she was over-reacting. She would wait for

Jarret to tell her their love was forbidden. Until then, love each other they would.

Amy made up her mind to be strong-willed so as never to suffer the pain of loving Jarret. She would expect nothing, ask nothing of him, wanted only what he wanted to give her. They would live each day, each hour and minute, as it came. She had arrived somewhere with that thinking, a place that made her feel immediately relaxed about loving Jarret as she did. She reached out to place her hand on the pillow where his head had rested and found a piece of notepaper.

I'll be in my studio working, and waiting for you.
Jarret.

Chapter 9

Amy took a water-taxi from the Gritti to the *palazzo*. This was the first time she would have entered Jarret's house from the canal. It was a grander façade and in better condition than the rest of the *palazzo*. Somehow, it didn't go with the interior and its decadent and faded, broken and shabby furnishings, trying to be antiques of quality. It was impressive. The building also made Amy wonder how artists such as Fee and Jarret could afford to live in such a place. By their own admission they were struggling painters, and poor as church mice.

The taxi gave several short blasts of the horn as the driver helped Amy out on to the first dry marble stair rising out of the water. She took two more stairs and was standing at the entrance to the *palazzo*, flanked by a pair of age-old and weatherworn marble unicorns that appeared to be guarding the door. Amy used the heavy bronze knocker several times. The echoing sound broke an eerie silence except for the lapping of water against the stone stairs.

There was something unreal about her being here, in the same way that there was something illusory about her being so very much in love with Jarret. Standing in front of that door, waiting for him to come and answer it, she realised that in love as she may be with him, and willing to turn a blind eye to many things as she might be, only his behaviour towards her could provide the ultimate reassurance.

She heard footsteps, Jarret's footsteps. A smile crossed her lips. Elation swept through her body. Jarret was there on the other side of the door. She was empty-handed. How silly, she should have brought flowers, sweets, something. She heard the bolt being shot and a key turn, and her heart raced. The door creaked open. She thought, Never mind, I've brought myself. The iron-studded door was pulled back and Amy readied herself to rush into Jarret's arms. Only just caught herself in time.

'Oh, dear, am I such a bad replacement? That's what it says on your face, Amy.'

'Replacement?'

'Temporary replacement is what I should have said. Come in, come in.' And Fee bent forward and kissed Amy on each cheek.

The sight of him dressed all in black – turtleneck jumper, trousers, well-polished boots and a Moroccan caftan heavily embroidered in silk braid – brought her up sharp. A necklace of chunky amber and silver beads hung nearly to his black leather belt. Fee looked bright-eyed and happy. She had never seen him look otherwise.

'I thought you were going to stay with your friend Alfreda?'

'Change of plan, and a good thing too. If I had gone to stay with her then you would have had to spend the day alone. There would have been no one to take you round Venice today, *and* I got us an invitation to lunch at our friend Principe Marino Colonna Bouccati's *palazzo*. He longs to meet you and show you his collection of contemporary paintings along with some of the best Italian Renaissance works you will see anywhere. Most of Venice is talking about Jarret and Fee's new friend, the art historian from New York.'

They were by now walking through the ground-floor rooms. Amy stopped Fee. 'Where's Jarret? And why am I not spending the day with him?'

'He's up in his studio waiting for you. He's leaving for Paris with Peggy Guggenheim in two hours' time. He couldn't say no to accompanying her there, and had to go anyway.'

'He never said anything to me about it last night.'

'He didn't know last night.'

Amy knew the house well enough to break away from Fee and head for the studio. She burst in on Jarret who was calmly rolling up some canvases. Just seeing him, the warmth of his smile for her, centred her. All anxiety vanished.

'I missed you this morning.'

'And now you know you're going to miss me today. Fee really does talk too much. I wanted to tell you myself.'

'Do you have to go?'

'Yes. But all's not lost. Fly to New York via Paris. We can have tomorrow together.'

'You mean, fly with you and Peggy Guggenheim?'

'No, there's no time for you to get yourself together before we leave.'

'Do you have to go?'

'Yes.'

'And what about me?'

Jarret stopped what he was doing and went to Amy, took her by the hand to sit with her on the settee. 'Peggy is not a woman easily gainsaid. We're neighbours here in Venice and she's an influential woman in the art world. She wants me to travel with her, so travel with her I will.'

As much as she wanted to disagree, Amy knew Jarret was right. Peggy Guggenheim was a legend in the art world. A woman with an eye for modern painting who did something about it, with a New York gallery in the late 1940s that showed Jackson Pollock when no one else did; who sponsored him and so many now famous painters and sculptors so they might keep painting while she stockpiled works of art.

She was many times over a millionaire who recognised true art and bought from and supported what would turn out to be some of the greatest of the modern painters of the twentieth century. She had steeped herself in modern art and the men that painted it, had managed to have them as friends and lovers and even to catch Max Ernst as a husband.

The New York art world knew all about her genius as well as her legendary tight-fistedness when it came to money, her eccentricity, vanity, power and charm. She in her own right was one of the big names of the art world of the twentieth century, constantly looking at paintings, collecting, and still with an eye for art and an intelligent word about it that everyone listened to. She kept the bulk and best of her paintings in her *palazzo* in Venice, along with a collection of yapping little Chinese dogs, that was a museum all its own and sometimes opened to the public. Peggy Guggenheim was a formidable woman.

She had chosen Jarret to accompany her, and even a man in love could not turn down such an offer. Was he her lover? Amy hated herself for even thinking about that, but she had seen Jarret and his charm, his sexiness at work, with the Greek painter and her friend from Paris. Jarret had the seductive charm of a virile man who was also part child, a victim of his talent, a fragile being in a hostile world, and would not a much older woman with a penchant for painters find him attractive?

It was knowing in her heart that Jarret and Fee were ambitious for themselves and their work, and her unease about how far they would

129

go to get what they wanted, that compelled Amy to ask herself: Prey on an older woman, make love to a famous name, was Jarret capable of that? No, she answered herself, not the man who had made love to her the way he did. In spite of what she believed, she asked him, 'And?'

Amy detested the way the question came out. It made her seem jealous, and she was for a moment, insanely so. Once she recognised that she snapped out of it. Jealousy was an emotion she had no time for. She had seen it in others and found it despicable. Having never experienced it before, she found it a destructive and horrid feeling and one she would never allow herself again.

Jarret's eyes were cold as steel and fixed on Amy's when he answered her, 'And I hope one day she'll buy a painting of mine for her collection.'

Art was one thing, his and Fee's hustling was another. She had no doubt that Fee had had his hand in this, but the passion between Amy and Jarret was set apart in its own way. Amy was determined to stand up to Jarret's treatment of it. 'If you had called me, I could have been ready to travel with you,' she responded.

'You weren't asked. I was. Don't make more of this than there is. Subject closed, I think, don't you?'

Amy thought, Closed but not forgotten. A lesson well learned? It was obvious there were to be Jarret and Amy in a secret world all their own, Jarret and Amy together and apart in public. His life, her life, their life. And who was to know, maybe she could be happy in that sort of love affair? And maybe they could make it work? And when she wasn't happy? And if it didn't work? Well, she could always leave.

Jarret was no fool, he saw everything she was thinking in her face. He had not expected to be so disturbed by her anxiety over the situation, nor fear that she was not as much in love with him as he'd thought she was. He was a hardened seducer of women and had always made it a policy never to explain himself or his actions; that had always worked to keep the women who wanted him quiet and unquestioning for fear they would lose him.

He hardly realised he was breaking his policy when he told her, 'Look, she wants me to escort her to a gala in Paris tonight. All the art world will be there. How could I say no? And I didn't want to say no. That doesn't mean that I'm happy to leave you, I'm not. I know you must be in New York the day after tomorrow. Get to Paris tonight and

130

take a night flight to New York tomorrow. That way we can have all day together in Paris.'

It was nearly midnight when Amy checked into her hotel round the corner from the Place Vendôme. She very nearly sighed with relief when the concierge recognised her, greeted her warmly, said that he could accommodate her with a room for that one evening only, and made no fuss about her having no luggage.

Once she was shown to her room she fell exhausted on to the bed. Emotionally drained, confused from the mixed signals she kept getting from Jarret and Fee, happy to be back in Paris and strangely relieved to have left Venice behind, she wasn't at all sad that this was the last night of her travels abroad. Though she was not ready to leave Jarret, she was quite ready to return to New York and life as she knew it. Or rather as she had known it. She had been on an odyssey that was rich and filled with wondrous experiences, and now needed time and space away from them to evaluate.

Amy was far from being a foolish young woman, she was very much aware that the life she had been so content with could never be the same. A larger world was what she'd been looking for, and a larger world was what she had found. That and a deep and profound love for a man who professed to return that love. She had changed, expanded as a person, and her New York life and work would have to follow.

Amy lay there, eyes closed, relaxing from the frenetic but fun day she had had with Fee in Venice and her harassing journey to Paris. There were so many imponderables when she was away from Jarret. She was always finding new ones. Odd, for example, that he had not asked her to stay with him in the flat he'd told her he owned on the Left Bank, in St Germain.

Was it only this morning that she had said goodbye to him in Venice, only last night that he had made such magnificent love to her, that sex and orgasm that had taken them over and done more than consummate their relationship? It had changed their lives and made them the richer for having found each other.

Amy pulled the scrap of paper with his Paris telephone number written on it from the pocket of her skirt. She rolled on to her side and, taking the telephone, asked the concierge to get the number for her. Her heart raced at the very idea that she was about to hear his voice. His telephone rang and rang. There was no reply. Amy replaced the receiver and made excuses for his not being there. He had said he would get away from Peggy as soon as possible.

She called at one, and at two, and at two-thirty in the morning, and then she began to cry. Disappointed, frustrated, feeling stupid for being in Paris at all, she fell asleep.

Amy had asked for a call at eight o'clock and now the ringing of the telephone was incessant. It pulled her from a deep sleep, but once she was awake she was very much awake. She asked for Jarret's number to be tried again. Almost immediately he was on the line. It was outrageous but she almost burst into tears from sheer relief that he was there. His voice . . . she had almost forgotten what a marvellous voice he had.

'*Bonjour.*'

'Hello, it's Amy.'

'I've been waiting for your call. I've been so worried that you hadn't managed to get here. All sorts of terrible things went through my mind – that we might not have today together, that you couldn't make plane connections, that we were destined to be parted before we could make plans for the future. The very idea was like a light going out of my life. Where are you?'

'At the hotel where I said I would be.'

'Give me the address. I'll be right over. And don't bother to get dressed.'

Amy gave him the address and he was off the phone without even a farewell. She had had her chance before she gave the address to tell him that she had called until three in the morning, that she could have been waiting for him in his bed, in his flat, so why hadn't she been? Why had he put them both through the misery of being apart longer than they had to be? But it all sounded so churlish after his words, the expression of his anxieties, revealing to her how much she meant to him. The light going out of his life.

It wouldn't take long for Jarret to get to the hotel. Amy went into top gear. It was not a matter of not getting dressed but of getting undressed. She had fallen asleep in the clothes she had travelled in, had not unpacked her shoulder bag. From it now she took her Paris-bought nightgown and black silk kimono, a tooth brush, a small make-up bag, and started peeling off her clothes.

She bathed, and was changed and looking incredibly relaxed and beautiful, standing by the window looking out across the rooftops of

132

Paris, when his knock on the door came. The timing was perfect, the maid having just finished laying a small table next to the windows with breakfast for two. She had only to leave the room.

He didn't wait for an answer but opened the door. They stood there, he still in the hall, Amy standing by the window. They gazed at each other for what seemed like an age, and often after that meeting Amy would remember those moments as a turning point in their young but intense love affair.

Something was implicit in their being alone together. If there had been any doubts whatsoever on either of their parts that the feelings they had were other than genuine they vanished once and forever in those few minutes in that hotel room. It proved to be such an emotional moment for them that neither of them could speak.

Not even when Jarret crossed the room to stand before Amy and take her hands in his, and kiss first one and then the other, and then drop to his knees, wrapping his arms round her while he laid his head against her belly, could Amy speak. She merely placed her hands on top of his head and ran her fingers through his hair. Jarret opened the kimono and rubbed his face against the crêpe-de-chine of her nightgown. His lips sought her mound beneath and he pressed a kiss upon it, and another. Amy took him by the arms and pulled him up off his knees.

Standing wrapped in each other's arms, they kissed and then Jarret smiled. He took her by the hand and they walked to the small table by the window.

'I'm famished.' That seemed to break the emotional spell that had all but crippled them.

Amy laughed. 'And so am I. Starving actually.'

He removed his black cashmere overcoat with its smart velvet collar and threadbare cuffs, tossing it on to the bed. It was impossible for Amy not to feel some pride that this big, beautiful artist standing in his worn tweed jacket, shirt with frayed collar and cuffs, trousers that shone with age and wear, had chosen to love her.

A silver pot of coffee in one hand, hot milk in the other, Jarret filled large breakfast cups while Amy whipped away the silver domes covering their plates.

'It seems you're always there for me with everything I need, and just at the moment I need food most. An extravagant breakfast! It seems you're always nurturing me in one way or another.'

'Didn't Peggy feed you?'

'Peggy! She's meaner about buying people a meal than I am.'

Jarret had dramatic gestures. He raised Amy's hand and kissed her fingers, then drew the chair out and stood behind it attentively while she sat down. He took his seat across from her and smiled. Was it her imagination or did he seem happier in himself? Here, in Paris, there was something more alive about him than she had seen in Venice, except for that first morning they had met in his *palazzo* and had talked art while she looked at his work.

On their plates were poached eggs on toasted brioche, tiny sausages and mushrooms, and on the table a mound of hot croissants and a bowl of peach preserve. She had never had a cooked breakfast in this small hotel and was sorry now she hadn't. They both delved into their food. This was the first time that Amy became aware of the strength of Jarret's appetites: food, sex, life as he wanted it. Why hadn't she noticed that in Venice?

'When do you go?' he asked.

'I must leave for Orly no later than four o'clock this afternoon.'

Jarret took a swallow of his coffee and gazed across the table at Amy. She waited for him to say, 'Stay. Don't make that plane, change your plans. We need more time together to decide what to do with our lives.'

It was a foolish, girlish thing to think, and unworthy of her. She knew that but couldn't help herself. The romantic Amy, who had never until she had met Jarret thought of herself as being all that interested in love, had taken over. That shocked her into standing outside herself and looking clearly at the scene being played out. She was not embarrassed; nothing but thrilled at the seediness of seeing herself dressed and ready, anxious even, for sex with her lover in a second-class hotel in Paris. But she was astonished that for all that she and Jarret had together they were still strangers, and whatever romantic notions she had vis-à-vis Jarret, or him for her, in a very few hours they would be parting, and with too much unsaid.

She had so many questions, wanted so many answers. There were things she wanted to express about his work and his lifestyle, and things that she desperately wanted to understand, but Amy could not find the right time or the correct place to approach him on such matters. Was this the place? The time? Hardly. Talk of such nature would kill the moment. Passion and sex had bound them together with invisible threads. All the intimate words she craved from Jarret, she could have, but she knew by now they would only come while they coupled: when

134

her orgasms flowed, and he was thrusting towards a climax. At that moment Amy wanted that more than mere conversation.

As if reading her mind, Jarret placed his fork down on the empty plate, his napkin on the table, scraped back his chair and stood up. He walked to the door, opened it, and placed the 'Do not disturb' sign on the door handle outside. Amy watched him crossing the room towards her, dropping his clothes as he approached her.

She wanted to touch him, hold his erect penis in her hands, but she did nothing. It was Jarret who liked being the aggressor, Jarret who enjoyed sexual power over her, and she, as much as she wanted to enjoy the feel of him in her hands, liked even more his sexual dominance over their sex life. She went to the bed and lay down. He raised her nightgown and turned her on her side, and that was the way he took her.

Unable to hold back, she came the first time, at the very moment he had penetrated her fully and she felt his genitals lying warm against her. From that first orgasm she found herself undone by Jarret, unable to stop coming.

'Jarret, Jarret,' she whimpered.

'I know, I know,' he told her.

Finally they came together and after he slid off Amy and on to his side, he took her in his arms and held her quietly for some minutes before he told her, 'You would have enjoyed last night. Peggy was at her best, and Dali was there, and Dubuffet, Yves Klein. Lots of heated discussion on how and why the art world after the Second World War shifted to North America, how the New York school of art has all the vibrancy and power and talent, but still hasn't produced a Picasso or Matisse. Just the very same things you were telling me in Venice that first morning we were together and you saw my work. All the things we talked about filled my head and I heard myself saying, as you had, that at the moment New York and American art is where art's life blood is, where its heart beats the fastest, where inspiration is running high. They all listened and exclaimed at the change of ideas I'd had, and thought they saw a new enthusiasm. Was it in my work? Dubuffet asked. Yes, I told them, I feel my work changing, my concepts shifting, feel I have opened up. Peggy was frightfully impressed. Yes, you should have been there.'

'Then why wasn't I?'

'You were. In my heart and my very soul. I kept thinking about you. Later I went back to my flat with Dubuffet and showed him some of my new canvases. He was surprised and impressed by the change. Peggy said they were a departure from the collages which she had always liked but would never have give a serious one-man show. The new canvases, the ones I've painted since I met you, work on those she told me, and play your dealers right. She feels I might have a chance of a one-man exhibition with Walter Cordigon in New York. I've been cultivating him for years, entertaining him, introducing him to the aristocracy of Europe. And now with this new direction my work seems to be taking, he should come through for me. I told you, you're my muse.'

Jarret kissed Amy. She was of course thrilled for him. Excited that his peers were enthusiastic about his change of direction, though it was still early days and he had far to go. The art historian and critic, not the lover, was talking here. She was overjoyed to be a muse to her lover. What woman would not be? But this time those positive aspects did not blind Amy. She was still seeing things the way they were.

Feeling emboldened, she spoke up. 'I'm going to ask you again, Jarret. Why wasn't I with you last night? And don't tell me about Peggy. I mean later, when all the formalities were over, after midnight, until three in the morning when I stopped calling. Why are we in this hotel like a pair of illicit lovers and not in your flat in St Germain? You're not taking me into your life, Jarret, and in a few hours we're going our separate ways. What am I to think about that? Surely you must know we're in love, and unless we nurture that love it will fade away? Is that what you want? Am I being some kind of a fool, misreading your feelings for me?'

'You're a surprise. You dropped into my life from nowhere. I have a whole life going for me outside of loving you. You mustn't be greedy about me. Not now, not ever. I had that once and will never allow it to happen to me again.'

'I feel there's someone else. Is there someone else? If there is, and you are committed and want to stay with her, this is just a fling, then say so, put me straight.'

Jarret looked surprised and seemed to take a defensive attitude. 'I don't know what you're talking about.'

'Savannah?'

The very mention of her name changed the expression in Jarret's eyes. They grew cold and hard, and yet he visibly relaxed, seemed almost relieved as he answered, 'She was my wife.'

'Are you still in love with her?'

'She has nothing to do with us. I thought you understood that what is happening between you and me has nothing to do with her or anyone else? We're something very private and very special, outside everything else in this world. Don't tell me you don't sense that?'

'Yes, I do. It's something more powerful than I've experienced with any other man.'

'Then how can Savannah come between us, or anyone else for that matter?'

'Are you telling me they can't. That's all I need to hear, Jarret.'

'Yes, I'm telling you they can't. And if they try, we won't let them.'

What sublime words for a woman in love! Once Jarret had committed himself at least to let nothing come between them, colour came into his face. He seemed somehow embarrassed and quite fidgety. He became his usual taciturn self, as he and Amy dressed.

After she paid her hotel bill she slung her bag over her shoulder and they walked together round the corner to the Place Vendôme. To walk the streets of Paris with a lover is to see the city with different eyes. To love someone as Amy loved Jarret, and be loved as he loved her, was a tremendously uplifting experience. It gave her a new lease on life, as if she could take on the world, love it that little bit more. She was bursting with the power of love and joyful for herself and every living creature that crossed their path: a tiny black twittering bird perched on the back of an empty chair, a squirrel nibbling crumbs from a cafe table, the beautiful and very chic women or the handsome men rushing to their next *rendezvous*, an angelic-looking child scampering across the street with her nanny.

As they walked towards the Tuileries they would occasionally stop just to look at each other. Unable to contain their happiness, they would smile at each other, putting out of their minds the fact that in only a few hours they would be parted.

'What would you like to do? Where would you like to go? What would you like to see?' asked Jarret.

'I'd like to have the best and most fresh oysters for lunch, and a bottle of the best Chablis. You do like oysters?'

'Adore them, and I know a little restaurant famous for oysters round the corner from my flat. It's been a fish restaurant and oyster bar for two hundred years. A man stands outside on the street in front of the place in a straw boater and a black rubber apron, and shucks the oysters from a mound lying in a bin of crushed ice.'

'It sounds marvellous, let's go there. But first, I'd like to see where you live in Paris.'

Amy saw the hesitation in Jarret's face. 'Is it really important to you?'

'Yes, actually, I think it is. I want to be able to visualise you living and working here. Is that a problem for you, my going to the flat?'

'No. Not if that's what you want.'

They had a long and brisk walk from the Right Bank of Paris over to the Left and St Germain, then to the narrow street where Jarret lived. It was a crisp and sunny day and Paris had never looked more beautiful, more exciting: the vibrancy, that individual and unique French chic, one could see it everywhere, it was in the very air they breathed.

In a small eighteenth-century house on a street busy with smart art galleries and chic little shops was Jarret's French home. The street had a village quality about it with its *boulangerie* and *charcûterie*, the *chocolaterie* with a flower stall in its doorway. Several people greeted Jarret as they passed him on the pavement.

He placed a key in the street door and they walked up four flights of stairs to the flat. More thrilled to be there than puffed out by the climb, Amy could hardly contain herself once they were inside. It was utterly charming: small rooms leading one into the other and filled with sunlight from the skylights above. But like the *palazzo* it was chock-a-block with things. Only here in Paris they were anything but shabby. It was a little jewel of a place, but somehow too precious.

After Amy's original impression of the flat, she began to notice that on every surface there were framed photographs of people. Many were of an attractive but not particularly beautiful delicate-looking young woman with tremendous sadness in her eyes. Long after Amy saw the same young woman flanked by Fee and Jarret in other photographs, she guessed it was Savannah Sparrow. Amy's first reaction was one of pity and a profound sadness for this woman. She tried to ignore her but that was difficult. Her presence in that flat was everywhere. By the time Jarret had finished giving Amy a tour of the rooms, her curiosity about Savannah was ungovernable. Savannah's loss of Jarret as husband and lover was Amy's gain, and somehow that seemed to make her uncomfortable. Had Jarret once loved Savannah as he loved Amy now? Do ex-husbands always keep their homes a shrine to an ex-wife? Not if they are through with them.

'It even has a small terrace, come and see,' suggested Jarret, who

138

seemed unaware of what was going through Amy's mind.

She stepped out on to the terrace. 'It's an utterly charming flat, Jarret. I would guess a very sought-after property?'

'And you'd be right.'

'Where's your studio?'

'I rarely work when I'm in Paris, and when I do it's on small things. I use Fee's room if he's not here, or the bedroom. Sometimes a friend's studio for a day.'

'I suppose the only drawback is the kitchen. It's the size of a postage stamp.'

'It is never a drawback. We always eat out or are invited.'

'Didn't Savannah ever want to cook or entertain?'

'She was very spoiled. She has never even boiled water for tea.'

'How long were you married to her, Jarret?'

'Do we have to talk about my ex-wife, Amy?'

'Yes, I think we do when you keep her around, silver-framed on every table, when you have sex with me in a second-class hotel instead of your flat, when you would not have brought me here if I had not insisted. Yes, I think we do have to talk about Savannah, for both our sakes.'

'I don't have sex with any women in this flat, any more than I do at the *palazzo* in Venice or the house on the Bosphorus. You are the first woman I have ever taken to *my* bed in *my* house, except for my wife.'

'Am I supposed to be impressed by that?'

'You certainly are, and flattered.'

They were gazing into each other's eyes while having this conversation and Amy was very much aware that he was being sincere, trying to tell her how important she was to him. He placed his hand under her chin and tilted it upward.

There was nothing for it but to be equally as sincere. 'Well, I am,' she told him. Jarret knew how to extract everything he needed from Amy.

It was then that he rewarded her with a kiss. 'What do you want to know? Let's get rid of the questions.'

Jarret walked Amy to a settee and they sat down together. Then he told her, 'You have five minutes. Ask anything you like and I'll answer, but then no more questions, not ever. Agreed? If not there is no point in our being together. It's called trust.'

It was an ultimatum and it frightened Amy that he should be delivering one, but the very thought of losing him frightened her even more. Amy knew he was right. Trust. Without that, where could their love go?

Reason told her she must agree. Love insisted upon it. 'Agreed,' she told him.

'Good.'

Amy was relieved that he looked quite relaxed and willing to satisfy her curiosity. Pleased even to be talking to her about anything she wanted to know. 'About Savannah and the divorce then. Why did you divorce her?'

'I didn't divorce Savannah, she divorced me. Always the gentleman, I allowed her to. It seemed less unsavoury.'

'What happened?'

'I married a semi-invalid, spent years healing her, dragging her round the world for treatment, a fragile flower of Southern society. We made our home here in Europe, and Paris and Italian society took us to their bosom. We were, as you can see, a beautiful couple, a charmed threesome with Fee. Very sought after by fun people wherever we went. With me she found her health, and a stubborn spirit she had hidden very well, to capture the hearts and minds of everyone who crossed her path – and of course to get everything she wanted. She used it to gain attention with the least little effort on her part. And sex . . . I married a reluctant lover, a sexually ignorant virgin, and turned her into a woman – only to catch her in bed with an old French aristocrat.'

'You must have been shattered?'

'No, not shattered. Angry. Very angry.'

'What did you do?'

'I threw her out, into the street, with nothing but the clothes on her back. Two days later all Paris was talking about how she was driven into the arms of other men because of how I neglected her, abandoned her for months on end, never provided for her. All untruths. Not everyone believed her, and then even fewer when I defended myself by naming the man. I was prepared to do so in court to divorce her. Her mother pleaded with me not to make such a scandal and allow Savannah to divorce me. We came to an amicable arrangement. I took everything we owned between us, this flat, the house in Venice, all our possessions, in exchange for Savannah's divorcing me. It was, still is, messy, both of us playing the injured party. I lost my wife but it cost *her* dearly.'

There was no bitterness in Jarret's voice, no hurt, he was without

140

anxiety or anger in telling Amy this. She wished he had shown some sign of at least one of those sentiments. That would have seemed to Amy to have been somehow normal for a man who kept his ex-wife's photographs on display everywhere. But it was cold indifference that he displayed, and an uncharitable thought crossed Amy's mind. Jarret kept the flat this way so that visitors could see him as the injured party trying to get on with his life. Had Peggy, visiting the flat the night before, not felt some sympathy for him? And Dubuffet? Even Amy herself? He had been the injured party, but there was something not very nice happening here. Amy wasn't sure what it was. What she was sure of was that she didn't want to know any more.

Jarret interrupted her thoughts. 'No more questions?'

'Yes, one. Fee says he hopes that you'll get together again, that you made a good couple. Do you still love her?'

'No. I don't *still* love her, I never loved her. I felt sorry for her. She was like a crippled princess and I saw myself as the handsome prince who could kiss her beautiful and whole and well and then we could live happily ever after. All the ingredients were there and it was all working except that I never realised that she was at the same time eating away at my life, enslaving me to her as her husband, only to betray me. Now can you put her in the past, Amy?'

'I can, if you can?'

'Not quite yet. She's trying to get this flat back from me. She won't, I can assure you. As I told you before she has nothing to do with us. Now that was your last question.'

Amy wanted to shout: 'Christ, give her back the flat and all this stuff in it! It's clogging up your life, it's stifling you, and what has this all to do with your work?' But instead she leaned forward and kissed him lightly on the lips.

They rose from the settee and a look passed between them, one that they knew well. It was there for them again, sexual desire. Savannah, Fee, Venice, the flat, all vanished. To be petted and kissed, caressed, would have been nice but too tame for these lovers. They knew what they wanted. He took her standing against a wall. She clung to him with her legs tightly wrapped round him. He took his time with long and exquisite penetrations until he felt her dissolve again and again.

'Tell me you'll be there for me in New York?'

'I will. I will,' she answered breathlessly. And then she lost control of her orgasms and called out as she came. Jarret had to place a hand over her mouth to muffle her screams of passion. He loved

141

her for them; they excited him and he thrust into her wildly until they came together. Their legs grew wobbly and, Jarret still inside her, they slid down the wall together, and landed in a heap on the floor.

It took them several minutes to regain themselves and when they did, he told Amy, 'Never doubt how I feel about you. Always remember what we are to each other, promise me that?'

Afterwards they were shameless: they ate two dozen oysters each and every one was sublime. They drank the bottle of Chablis and talked about art and his work. Amy looked at her watch. There was so little time left for them. Jarret, who was well known at the restaurant, had the waiter order a taxi for four o'clock. It was deserted by now, but no one asked them to leave. They were too high on each other to think about the minutes ticking by or about being parted. And then suddenly it happened, the taxi arrived.

They saw it draw up in front of the restaurant and both fell silent. Jarret made not a move, said not a word. It was left to Amy. She rose from her chair and that galvanised Jarret who rose from his. Silently he slipped into his overcoat and Amy into the beige cashmere three-quarter-length jacket she had been wearing, but then she suddenly froze. He came to her aid. It was a wrap-round jacket with wide lapels. He adjusted it and tied tight round her waist the soft belt that held it closed, then fussed with the lapels, turned the collar up. He touched her hair, stroked it several times, and then slid her bag on to her shoulder. Now it was Jarret who seemed to have control of the situation. They said goodbye to the proprietor and walked out into the street. The oyster man was gone, his bin covered over with a green canvas. Amy felt as if everything round her was closing. Determined not to show her distress, she smiled.

They stood together for several minutes by the taxi before he opened the door for her and Amy ducked down and slid across the seat to make room for him. He leaned into the taxi.

'I can't do this.'

Amy slid back across the seat. 'It would mean a couple more hours together.'

'I'll write to you.'

'Please?' Amy hated the desperation in her own voice.

'Don't ask me to go with you. I'm bad about farewells and airports. It's been too perfect a day. I want to remember it from here.'

'Will you come to New York?'

'Yes, I've made up my mind. I'll be there as soon as I can, a matter of a few months. You'll call me?'

'Yes.'

'Amy, I have to go and so do you. God bless.'

He closed the door and was gone before the taxi had left the kerb.

Chapter 10

One thing about New York City – you have to get on with your life or die. Even worse, it can swallow you up whole and spit you out in pieces. It's a city filled with romantic lovers, happy, and unhappy relationships, illicit affairs, hopeful love, desperate love. No matter who you are, you have to get out there and live any way you can in spite of your love life if you want to survive.

The most exciting and unique city in the world is a hard task master, makes enormous demands. But there's adrenaline in the very air you breathe, and a buzz that stings you like a bee, makes you jump and run. Through the glass and steel canyons that criss-cross Manhattan run millions of people from all walks of life trying to make it, live life to the fullest and not hit the skids. New York hates failure, loves the big winners. It sucks out the very best or the very worst in people. It was sucking the best out of Amy Ross.

Leaving Paris and Jarret behind had been a wrench she had hardly known how to deal with. On the flight across the Atlantic she had relived this remarkable love affair she had stumbled into. Very carefully she had gone over it just to make certain she was not reading more into it than existed. Chance: her return to Venice, and chance again: Fee discovering her and returning her to Jarret. All that had been taken into account before the wheels of her plane had touched the tarmac in New York.

Amy could thank the city for keeping her on the straight and narrow path and from behaving like a desperate fool in love. Just to get through the airport terminal and into a cab, to see, as she inched her way through the traffic, the skyline of New York come up over the horizon, had been to come back to reality with a thump. Amy had, and the past weeks of love and sex and Jarret Sparrow had all fallen into place like the pieces of a puzzle. Though her love for Jarret had not diminished in the least, she kept it in proportion to the rest of her life.

By the time she had stepped from the taxi to the pavement in front of the brownstone house on East Eighty-ninth Street where she lived in a one-room flat, Amy was more grateful than ever that she had found love, but was very much in control of her life.

There was about her a sexually awakened air, strange and thrilling for a woman who had enjoyed a steady lover for years. Erotic imaginings haunted her; the desire to come in strong and thrilling orgasms where she was out of control of herself and her sexual desires was held in check all day until those moments before sleep when she could conjure up a vision of herself and Jarret having sex. He had marked her, changed her for life, not only with sex and love but in a powerful and constructive way. They communicated through art, their chosen life's work, as well as on the most intimate and personal level.

It did not take long after her arrival home for Amy to understand that it was not enough to tell Jarret what was missing from his work: courage, sacrifice, giving a hundred percent to take that next step up the ladder if you wanted to climb higher, be special, make a difference. Those things that Amy had preached to Jarret she had to put into practice herself because she realised that in her own work it was time to move on, take major steps.

And so she was using the courage that love and passion had given her to expand her life and work. The changes she was making like a small snowball on the move kept gathering impetus and growing bigger and more impressive. It was thrilling, every day an adventure. In some cases it meant her taking chances that were frightening because Amy was not a gambler, though now she realised she had always been a closet adventurer.

It had been her policy to spend three days a week in New York staying in her bed sit. She taught five classes on Contemporary Painting of the Twentieth Century at Parsons School of Design and Cooper Union, and filled in for several of her friends, more established and respected art historians than herself, at more prestigious schools and universities. It had been hard going getting a foothold and she had been in the habit of taking whatever jobs were on offer to get herself established. She did have a considerable reputation as an authority on American Art after 1900, and for being *avant-garde*. Amy had the ear and the eye of several dealers for whom she did consultation work, spent most of her time researching for other art historians and critics, well-established names in the New York art world. A friend of many of the unsung but up-and-coming artists in the city, she on occasion acted as agent for them.

It was hard but exciting and extraordinarily rewarding work, but Amy had a few things against her vis-à-vis the academic art world and getting a contract for herself to teach at one of the better schools of art: Princeton, Yale, or a museum position as curator or assistant curator. There were other contenders for such positions with better academic qualifications than she.

She had attended Smith College but never gained a degree thanks to family pressure for her to leave and earn a living. Family pressure for her to take on the responsibility of helping a hypochondriac mother care for the family during her bouts of illness. A father who did not believe in educating daughters. Early on she realised that she would have to work harder and faster and with more tenacity to make up for that lost degree, and she had. She had become a respected art historian but it hadn't come easy. Until her return from her European holiday and love on a grand scale she had remained quietly in the background of the art world, beavering away while others reaped rewards from her efforts. It was more than time to move forward in every aspect of her life, and move was what she was doing.

Some people applauded this new assertive Amy Ross, others did not. Those she worked for realised what they had lost but respect for her abilities and their fondness for her allowed them now to treat her more as an equal and less as a flunkey. Amy Ross was cleaning house. Shuffling people and projects round to make them work in this new life of hers. There were casualties.

For weeks after her return she had avoided big and handsome, wonderfully sexy, quiet, conservative Peter Smith, the man she'd thought she would marry. They had met when she'd rented a small wooden house on the beach in Easthampton.

Amy had known a few painters who lived in Easthampton on Long Island because it was relatively secluded and the rents were cheap. The lifestyle was small town and very much like New England where she came from. Its attractions were many for an art historian who needed peace and quiet to work in, not least of which was that it was an easy train ride into New York City. It was a small town of affluent old-time money and high society summer people, locals who had been born and bred there for centuries, and a few artists and writers who had homes and studios there. The three groups kept to themselves and rarely met socially.

Peter Smith and his forefathers had always been farmers and landowners and were a well-known and respected family, with Peter the most eligible bachelor in town. Only he wasn't, because he fell in love with Amy Ross. It had been instant attraction, and then admiration for her, and then love. Each found something in the other that satisfied them, his stability, her ambition. She was the excitement of his life, he was the ardent lover of her dreams. They had been happy together and happy with the thought of each other when they were apart.

Though they had been together a long time and had been a couple in every sense of the word save a marriage certificate, they had led separate lives of their own, had remained individuals apart from their togetherness. Each of them had experimented with other partners during their years together, but they had been discreet, and had never discussed their infidelities. These had never been betrayals because Peter and Amy had agreed on an open relationship, freedom to see other people. Their youth and uncertainty about settling down in a one-to-one relationship for life, and Amy's ambition, demanded that. But those other liaisons had been few and far between and had never been important or better relationships than the one they had together. Until Amy met Jarret Sparrow.

Peter and Amy had agreed many years before that if ever someone or something came into their lives that changed how they felt about each other, it would be short, it would be quick, they would cause each other the least amount of pain possible and would part as friends. They were proud people who wanted a hundred per cent love from each other, and if they couldn't have that and all the passion and excitement they had known together, they wanted nothing. No compromise love would be good enough for them. But as in all things theory works only until one has to put it into effect. Peter Smith was one of the first casualties of Amy Ross's new life.

It was unfair and wrong, but he had vanished from her life, her heart, her mind, when she'd experienced that *coup de foudre* with Jarret Sparrow one dark and stormy night in Venice. He never reappeared. She was utterly through with Peter Smith. Jarret was *the* man in her life to the extent that she had not the least thought of Peter until the day after her return when the telephone rang in her New York flat. Her heart leapt in the hope that it was Jarret missing her already, and then felt flat when she heard Peter's voice instead.

She had said nothing but hello but the enthusiasm and happiness in her voice said much more. Peter picked up on them at once. 'You're home! Thank God you're home. You sound marvellous, I've missed you horribly. It's been too long this parting, too long to feel only half alive. Never again. I'll be on the next train and at your door as fast as I can get there, and you can tell me about your travels then. In bed.'

Amy was hearing all the things she wanted to hear from Jarret. The wrong man! The wrong man! That was the message that kept tripping over again and again in her mind. She very nearly screamed with frustration, disappointment, fear, because he was not Jarret. Whatever path she had chosen to go down with Jarret, there was no turning back. Hearing Peter's voice only confirmed what Amy already knew in her heart.

'No,' she told him.

'No?'

'It's over between us, Peter. Let's just leave it at that. We said it should be short and quick.'

'Hang on, Amy. Let's just at least talk about this.'

'There's nothing to talk about.'

'Well, I think there is.'

'Then you would be wrong.'

'I think at least an explanation . . .'

'What happened to "short and quick when love dies"? That's what you said you would find civilised and acceptable if ever it were to happen to us. It's dead, we're dead. Please don't call again.'

'At least tell me why?'

'A man, a greater love than I have ever known, or will ever know again.'

She had put the receiver down on Peter and never again thought about him or what she had done. He was the past, it was as if he'd never existed. Amy could not explain her behaviour to herself or anyone else. This new surge of creative energy and freedom that was sweeping her along new roads had taken her over and was absorbing her completely. She sensed that it had to do with being in love with Jarret, but was more, much more than that. Every day she was shuffling about people and friends, work, the many facets of her life. Like a fan of playing cards held in her hand, she would pick and choose and rearrange for the best working combinations until she knew what to keep and what to discard. She was out for a winning hand. Only one thing remained constant: her passion for Jarret.

New York, that city of get on with it, and the merry-go-round art world, kept the degree of loneliness she allowed herself vis-à-vis Jarret pretty much in check. That did not however preclude her all but tearing the post box open with her bare hands every morning, looking for a letter from him.

The first picture postcard came barely a week after her return but that had been from Fee, telling her they were still in Venice and that Jarret spoke about her constantly and they missed her. She read that card a hundred times, until the corners were worn from picking it up and putting it down, from holding it in her hand for what amounted to hours while she tried to read between the lines, read into it what she wanted to hear, while she pressed it to her bosom and told herself pathetically time and time again, 'He hasn't forgotten me, he loves me.'

Two weeks after her return the first letter arrived. The handwriting was large, bold and flowing.

Istanbul

My Dearest Amy,
I left Paris the day after you did. Returned with Peggy to Venice, then there was the packing up, the closing of the house for the winter. People to see and say goodbye to. Thank God Fee has already opened the house on the Bosphorus and my studio awaits my arrival. I long to get back to work. Write to me there. If money allows, Fee and I will travel to Damascus for Christmas, visiting Aleppo first, but at this time of writing it seems a remote possibility. A cruise up the Nile on a friend's yacht in February might be managed.

I am determined to come to New York before spring, alone, without Fee. He disapproves, thinks New York this year is not necessary, but I will win him over. It's you who have stirred my resolve, you who have inspired me to new things in my work, and you who have revived my lust. Now only you can satisfy it. I have more to go to New York for than ever before. Write to me, about yourself and the New York art scene, and love me and no other. I cannot bear to think that it could be otherwise.
Love,
Jarret

All through the winter there were picture postcards of Istanbul from Fee, always amusing and flattering and reminding her how much Jarret loved her. There were other cards from them both, some written separately, some together, from Cairo and Luxor, raving about the wonders of Egypt, but none ever said 'Wish you were here'. And she began to wonder why that was, and why for two people in love with each other, two people who had so much in common to build on, Jarret made so little effort to include her in his life. But when a woman receives love letters such as Jarret was writing to her, she makes excuses for being momentarily left out of her lover's life.

As the months passed Amy's life and work were taking monumental strides. She became an acting agent for several modern painters and was arranging a world tour of paintings and sculpture, 'The New York School of Art After Abstract Expressionism', sponsored by a Dutch publishing house and a Swiss and a Dutch museum. She had worked hard and pulled out every stop even to get in the running for such a project. It was a coup to have been awarded the job which included writing the hardback book on the subject and the catalogue for the exhibition. It would make her reputation.

Though contracts had not yet been signed, the gossip was out on the streets that a relative unknown had been chosen to head the project, and a woman at that. Amy insisted on anonymity until she was ready to give a press release, and that included merely giving hints to Jarret about an interesting new project. Too many high-powered curators from the Whitney and the Museum of Modern Art would have their noses out of joint. And the art historians round town? They could be bitchy, and especially since they were for the most part divided about whether there was a rising new art movement after Abstract Expressionism or not. The New York contemporary art world of dealers, collectors, and museums was in a crisis of sorts – the 'where does art go from here?' syndrome. They needed a new impetus in American art to keep the market fresh and buoyant. That was part of the excitement of the New York art world as it readied itself for a new decade, the 1960s. Amy had three years before the first showing of the travelling exhibition was to open in Amsterdam.

Such a commission, and the reorganisation and escalation of Amy's other work, were cause for a revaluation of her living and working arrangements. Amy had always been hard pressed to make ends meet. Like hundreds of millions round the world, she worked to live, with no cushion of money to fall back on. The rented Easthampton house, her real home, the place she was happiest in, would have to go because she needed the money allotted to that for larger premises to live and

151

work in in New York City, essential now to accommodate the changes in her life.

That was a tremendous wrench on several levels. Amy was a very private person who enjoyed her anonymity, and the lifestyle of a lazy and quiet community. The pace of Easthampton suited the private side of her nature. The other side, her passion for painting and the art world, the excitement of artists and galleries, dealers and academics and art history, enthralled her on all levels except the endless social and hustling side of that world.

She avoided it whenever possible, which was strange because when it was not possible and she was in the throes of it she handled it very well. It was the bitchiness she was unable to stomach. The clever, ruthless social climbing she was unable to do, finding it too much hard work, and unnatural, dishonest, ugly, soul-destroying. Several times, thanks to peer pressure, she made a feeble effort but Amy wasn't able to sustain social hustling long enough for it to be effective. Too anxiety-making, working against her grain. She happily gave it up, got where she wanted to go with her career the hard way, by being true to herself. It was thanks to a few amusing people – and they could be very amusing – her friends and the artists, dealers and curators who knew her for her work and what and who she was, that she was able to pick and choose the social events she attended. She gained a reputation for sincerity and a certain naïveté in the art world, a courageously good eye, a scholarly understanding of art.

At a large and crowded private party in a loft in Greenwich Village one evening, when everyone was very high on booze and laughter, jazz and art, a big handsome bear of a man, the sculptor David Smith, placed an arm round Amy's shoulder and whispered in her ear, 'A Dutch collector friend of mine has leaked the word. What a coup for you! I'll say nothing of this to anyone but I want you to know: you're too nice, not hard, ruthless or dishonest enough for the art world. Be careful, get tough, hop on the band wagon, deal dirty, or the sharks will get you. The Betty Parsons and Amy Rosses of this art world are few and far between. Take my word for it, I know what I'm talking about.'

Amy didn't. David could see it clearly in her eyes: the passionate belief in art, that it could rise above the machinations of commerce and man. He stroked her hair and then kissed her and walked off to greet Barnet Newman.

Amy thought about that now while looking round her room. The second blow to her home life: her plan to give up this flat that had been a haven for her in the city. There had been many good times here, and still there would be many more, the best ever. Jarret was arriving in a matter of hours.

More than four months! Now that Amy's separation from him was nearly over she allowed herself the luxury of dropping her guard and gave in to thinking of nothing else but lying in his arms, their losing themselves in lust and love, just being together, allowing him to come forward and occupy totally her heart and mind. There was so much to talk about, so much to catch up on, not least of all to see his new work and what he had done in these last months.

She was nervous, filled with anxiety: would he feel again as he had felt about her in Venice and Paris? This was New York, the real world they would be walking into together. Jarret without his *palazzo* and his *yalis* on the Bosphorus, his Paris *pied à terre* and Fee – and hopefully with Savannah well and truly out of his system and not there like a ghost on a haunting.

It had been Fee and his postcards during these last months that had made her understand and sense Savannah's continued presence: watching in the background of Jarret's life. Amy had come to wait very nearly as anxiously for Fee's postcards as she did for Jarret's letters. It had been Fee not Jarret, with his snippets of information on those postcards, most of which she found disturbing in one way or another, who kept Amy informed about the side of his life Jarret never wrote about.

Thinking about them now, Amy went to the drawer where she kept Fee's postcards and Jarret's love letters. She removed them from their ivory box and went to sit facing the fireplace on the large French Empire *lit en bateau* in the middle of the room. The cherrywood bed had the look of an elegant, grand, old-fashioned sleigh with its equally high curved head and foot board, and its claw feet. Enriched with occasional ormolu escutcheons, it held pride of place in the centre of Amy's bed sit. A beautiful and rare object, it was impressive not only for its beauty but for acting as a bed for two at night and a sofa for herself and guests in the daytime.

Placing the letters in her lap, she leaned against some of the many embroidered cushions on the sofa-bed. She held out her hands to warm them before the heat of the fire blazing in the hearth, and listened to the sound of crackling logs break the silence of the room. There was a scent from the Regal lilies in a glass vase on the square walnut

153

eighteenth-century French library table in the bay window overlooking the street, now set for dinner for two.

Amy's mind was drifting back in time to her first meeting with Jarret. Before she had seen the *palazzo*, heard about the two-hundred-year-old thirty-room wooden house on the waters of the Bosphorus, the *yalis*, another sort of much sought-after palace, and all the things, the very many things, Jarret and Fee filled their homes with. Amy had not been daunted by any of it, it had meant little to her because in a matter of minutes Jarret had meant everything.

Only now, as she looked away from the flames and round her one room, did she realise how disappointing her lifestyle might be to Jarret. Sparsely but elegantly furnished, her room was comfortable for basic working and living in for one person, not so easy but possible and comfortable for two with no one working. Only now did it enter her mind that it was not what Jarret was used to.

Amy had lovingly made room for his clothes in the wardrobe, allocated a drawer in the chest, a space for his things in the bathroom. As she looked round the room while fondling his letters lying on her lap, she came to understand that hanging on to love on paper your dreams grow bigger and brighter, while reality diminishes.

In a matter of two hours or less, Jarret could walk through that door, his ardour having cooled. Amy was no masochist in love. If that was to be the case she would know instantly. The very thought made her feel queasy. A knot formed in the pit of her stomach. She clutched the letters in her hand as if hanging on to them for dear life. She took several deep breaths, trying to calm herself and make that dreadful sick feeling go away.

She looked at her watch and felt chained to the ticking of every clock in the world. How could he do this to her, keep her waiting an extra two hours before setting eyes on him? How could she do this to herself, enslave herself to a watch and grow more impatient and unsure of herself with every glance at it? His insistence that she should not meet him at the airport had been a blow. His excuse had been he wanted their reunion in the privacy of her flat.

When his letter had arrived giving her the time and date of his arrival, she had called him. His very words had been: 'No! I insist you don't come to the airport. Too public for us. All this pent-up love and passion . . . can you be so sure you can control it? I can't.'

Those words had disarmed her. Remembering them now calmed Amy considerably. It also caused her concern, Jarret having to bus in from the airport and then bus again to get to her in the cold and sleety night that carried a bitter wind. He would never spend the money for a taxi, of that she was certain. And so once more she looked at her watch and waited. She decided to re-read his letters, those letters that had kept her going all the months they had been apart. Eight or nine letters – not very many for a man in love. But the contents gave her sufficient love and hope, enough for her to make excuses for there being so few of them.

Amy,
A letter in haste. Work fills my days and my nights. All my nights seem empty, a desert, without you in my bed. So everything I am, can be, could be, goes into the painting. With every brush stroke I tell myself: This is for Amy, for us. Love can be such a lonely business, lust addictive, the withdrawal symptoms painful. Let's just hope this separation has been character building because it's been hell. Your letters are marvellous, they keep me close to you.
   Jarret

Dear Amy,
I think of you, and of our nights in Venice. Love me.
   Jarret

Amy dearest,
Your letters about the New York art scene are riveting and amusing. I like so much hearing about it, and your life, what you do, where you go, that there is no other man in it whom you will allow to love you as I do. Work has been interrupted by visitors. We'll be going to Damascus for Christmas and later on to Egypt. What will you do for Christmas?
   Love
      Jarret

Amy, my dear,
It was wonderful to receive your call and to hear your voice. Almost too wonderful, it made me miss you all the more. I too am sorry we can't be together for Christmas and the New Year. I will make it up to you (I'm sure you can guess how) when I am with you in New York. If New York doesn't come off, we'll find

155

another way to be together somewhere. Fee sends his love.
   Jarret

Amy,
Well, it's settled, I will be in New York the first week in March.
Fee's attitude about this determination of mine is: Fine, as long
as I get a show arranged then back to my old self and Europe as
soon as possible. He's known me a long time and sees a change
in me he can't quite comprehend. Neither can I. He sees it as a
passing phase in my life. I on the other hand am not so sure
about that. You've cast a spell on me. More than lust, but very
much that. I think about you and fucking you all the time. I don't
mean to be crude but that's the truth of it.
   There are several people I can stay with but I have made no
plans, merely announced to them approximately when I will be
arriving. I will come to you directly from the airport. Dinner at
home, just the two of us, please. No people, just candlelight and
the god Eros hovering over us. I leave the rest to your imagination.
   Love has always been there for you from the very first time we
came together.
   Jarret

Amy placed the letter back in its envelope and looked at her watch.
They loved each other, a love that neither of them had been looking
for, something different from and more intense than anything either
of them had known before. Something Amy knew neither of them
would ever find again in another partner. And yet she sensed that
her love for Jarret was as forbidden to her as his love for her was
forbidden to him. She could not shake from her mind that they were
star-crossed lovers. The great mystery to her was why? Why should
that be? The questions were there but Amy wasted no time trying to
find an answer. She knew that, like a good mystery, all would be
revealed in time.

Amy had no desire to push herself into his life any further than he
was prepared to take her. Jarret wasn't prepared to give her a 'they
lived together happily ever after' ending, that had been demonstrated
by the lack of invitations for her to join him, not even one in all their
months of separation.

She now believed that she had sensed forbidden love was the name
of the game with Jarret when she had gone off to Greece and Egypt

and tried to kill her feelings for him. To sense something is one thing, to love another.

She rose from the bed and placed the letters back in the ivory box, but before she did she looked through Fee's postcards and read several of them aloud.

My dearest, beautiful Amy,
Miss you. What fun we could have
if you were here. I thought of which
room you could sleep in, it's directly
over the water. Jarret loves you,
I've never seen him like this.
    Love, Fee

The weather is marvellous for
this time of year on the Bosphorus.
Bread and honey and strong black
tea in the sun on a balcony hanging
over the water. We send you love.
    Fee and Jarret

Amy dear,
Jarret in Athens for a few days
with friends. Savannah
is there. I am always in hope of a
reconciliation. Foolish? But it is my
fondest wish for us all. Be well.
    Fee

Amy replaced the picture postcards in the box and the box in the drawer. In Venice, she had not been able to make up her mind whether Fee was a true friend or a villain. Whether he was more honest with her than Jarret was. She received mixed signals from Fee, sometimes disturbing, sometimes flattering, at other times informative but coloured by his involvement in Jarret's life. The one thing that she was sure of was that he saw the love that she and Jarret shared as less important than they did.

Since her return to New York, the few people to whom she had mentioned Jarret and Fee found them an odd couple, and an even odder threesome when Jarret and Savannah were married. A curator of

157

drawings at the Metropolitan Museum of Art, a friend of Amy's, described Jarret as having been an angel of a man to his wife. Before, during, and after marriage, Jarret and Fee had lived and were still living more like impoverished princes than artists. No one knew quite how they managed it, but there were wild guesses, some unsavoury. Another person told Amy they were powerful social climbers with Jarret being the adored one for his looks, talent and charm, which he used unmercifully on the many men and women who fell in love with him. Fee, known to most people by his proper name of Firuz Yolu, was seen as being eccentric and with a Byzantine mind that only Jarret really understood. Such comments had made Amy very cautious about letting people know how involved with them she was. Opinions? Rumours? Truths? She would only believe what she could hear with her own ears, see with her own eyes.

Amy placed a log on the fire, then went to the full-length mirror elaborately framed in ivory and mother-of-pearl Damascus work and checked herself in it. What to wear had been tricky. She'd wanted to wear something sexy and glamorous, an at-home thing that Jarret would want to rip off her in a moment of uncontrolled lust. But that had seemed too obvious, and could be embarrassing if they no longer felt the same erotic passion for each other.

Now, looking in the mirror, she knew that she had chosen well. The long-sleeved wine-coloured silk velvet wrap-round dress that plunged low between her breasts, and with its sarong skirt that invisibly hooked on the hip, was simplicity itself, yet sophisticated, sexy and festive.

Amy ran her fingers through her long, silky chocolate-brown tresses, hair that was rich and luxurious and worn off her face. The excitement of the moment shone in her violet eyes. The mirror showed that she had never looked prettier or sexier. Jarret did that to her, brought out the very beautiful and female side of her nature, that side of her so few men had ever been able to tap into. She smiled. Jarret had never seen her looking so glamorous, and she knew that she would not be a disappointment.

Once again a look at the time. She felt that anxiety that comes from a reunion with a lover. It was now a matter of minutes rather than hours and time to put the dinner in the oven. Rib of beef and roast potatoes, a green salad with a vinaigrette dressing, chocolate mousse for pudding. She had changed the menu so many times, having wanted it to be the perfect meal, their first in her flat, and was still unsure that she had chosen well. She had really splurged on the wine, a fine Petrus.

Twenty minutes later she was standing at the window looking into the street. Taxis came and went, cars, a few people braving the weather. The scent of cooking meat sent her to the kitchen to check the oven. She was just walking from there to the fireplace when the screeching sound of the buzzer split the silence of the room. Amy actually jumped. Her heart began to race, her mouth went dry. The waiting was over.

Chapter 11

How many times had she imagined what this moment would be like? Truly, she had lived it to death. In the last week, try as she might, she could no longer imagine what Jarret's arrival would be like. What she had never imagined was that her legs would feel like lead and screwed down to the floor. She couldn't move. A rush of heat went through her body. She pressed the palm of her hand over her heart and tried to still its racing. She quite suddenly lost all memory of Jarret's face. She had not the vaguest idea what the man down in the street pushing the buzzer looked like. Were they two strangers meeting for the first time? Those letters, what were they? And the few days that they had been together, and the sex, what was all that about? The months of keeping love alive, of sexual hunger for his phallus, his heart and his soul, all gone. Had she been crazed? She walked to the intercom on the wall by the entrance door to her flat. Amy could find no voice to speak into it, merely pushed the small white button that released the front door catch, opened the door to her flat and stepped into the hall.

She heard the front door close and his footsteps on the marble floor. Amy walked to the balustrade and looked over it and down into the stairwell. Someone was coming up the stairs. He wore no hat. The sight of his bare head, a gloveless hand on the stair rail, was enough to send Amy back into her flat. There she stood in the safety of her home, facing the open door, the hall, her future.

Looking through the row of balusters she saw first a flash of his head, his shoulders. He was taking the stairs two at a time, then rounded the last few that curved on to her floor. And suddenly he was there, walking swiftly towards her, wearing his black overcoat with the velvet collar and carrying a small case in his hand, a smile on his lips. He should have had a scarf, he should have had gloves, but instead he wore the cold, and looked half-frozen.

Once more they were struck: the shock of love, the same *coup de*

161

foudre, they had experienced before. The handsome and quiet, elegant and charming Jarret, looking every inch a Fifth Avenue gentleman-artist, was walking towards her, but she didn't rush out into the hall to meet him. Instead she remained where she was, standing still while a new and fresh sense of joyfulness took her over. Never taking his gaze from hers, he entered the flat and closed the door behind him, placed his case on the floor in the small vestibule that led into the sitting-room, not slowing his pace as he walked towards her.

He stopped a few feet from Amy. Jarret was re-acquainting himself with her, she could sense it: the way his eyes lingered on her hair, her eyes, her lips, the happiness she was wearing like a light film of powder on her face. She saw his expression change from pleasure to delight when his gaze lingered on her body: the way the wine-coloured silk velvet wrapped itself softly but seductively round her breasts, the narrow waist, the hips he had found so voluptuous. The long shapely legs shod in high-heeled wine-coloured lizard shoes made her look more glamorous than he had ever seen her before.

Amy stretched out her arms in a greeting, offering him her hands in welcome. Only then did he step forward and take them in his, lower his head and press his cold lips against them.

'You had forgotten me,' she told him.

'Not so much forgotten as my vision of you had dimmed. Seeing you like this is like discovering you all over again,' he told her.

'Your hands are freezing. Welcome home. Give me your coat, and go and stand by the fire.'

He gave her his coat and did go to the fireplace to warm himself. She had noticed that his hair was wet and so after hanging his coat in the wardrobe went to the bathroom and returned with a towel. There was an awkwardness about this reunion that she had not expected. Too much distance or possibly too much time had elapsed to dispense with it easily. Or maybe they were just too overexcited, too nervous. Amy knew she was. She wanted to get on with loving him, with his crushing her in his arms, his being unable to hold back his lust for her. What had that to do with taking coats and being cold and wet?

Amy began to towel dry his hair. After several minutes he removed her hands from his head and the towel with it and ran his fingers through his hair.

He was wearing a dark suit, very well tailored but worn, a white shirt and a dark tie that had seen better days too. Jarret removed his jacket and dropped it on the wing chair. While they were gazing into

162

each other's eyes, he shrugged the wide red braces off his shoulders. They hung limply by his sides.

The distance between them seemed to vanish like the mist when the sun comes out. He loosened his tie and Amy went to him and undid the knot, slipping it from round his neck.

'Hello, Amy Ross.'

'Hello, Jarret Sparrow.'

Amy placed her arms round his neck. Jarret slowly drew her to him, then tightly up against him, his hand on her bottom, pressing until she could feel the swell of his penis straining against his trousers. She sighed and whispered in a husky voice, 'How lovely to feel you so alive for me. I've waited so long, been so lonely for you and for this.'

What they felt for each other was still there and confirmed by their tears of relief. Here was a love that was deep and profound. They understood that, possibly for the first time. A moment so filled with emotion was inhibiting, words failed them. All energies were silently directed to dealing with the realisation of their feelings and the repercussions of them.

Jarret placed his lips on hers and gave her the most passionate kiss of their affair. He licked her lips, touched the tip of his tongue to hers, and then licked her lips again, sucking them into his mouth and nibbling on them. Amy searched out his tongue and sucked it into her mouth, moving her tightly puckered lips on it. Sensual kissing gone wild: she sucked as if she were giving head. This was the most aggressive she had ever been with Jarret and her aggression seemed to gather momentum: she wanted to bite into his lips, his flesh, to give him head – take his penis erect and throbbing into her mouth, lick and caress, suck him deep into her throat. But Jarret cut short all of that when his eager kisses were directed from her lips to her eyes, the tip of her nose, the side of her neck. He caressed the silk velvet covering her breasts and slipped a hand beneath it. Together they walked from the fireplace to the bed. Sitting there with Amy in his arms, Jarret moved aside fabric and exposed Amy's breast. Cupping it in his hands, he sucked the erect nipple, the puckered nimbus into his mouth.

Amy felt herself slipping into submission, all aggression gone. Her only instinct was to nurture this man, to let go whatever she was clinging to and come. He had both breasts exposed now and was moving between them with his mouth. Limp in his arms, she whimpered as she came in light, sweet orgasms. Never leaving her breasts, he placed her against the pillows. The sarong skirt of her dress parted, she was naked save for the lacy garter belt holding up her stockings. Her legs open wide now, he went between them and pinned her arms back above her head. Jarret held them there with one hand while he unzipped and directed his engorged phallus with the other. The penetration was languorous and exquisite, his thrusts slow and forceful, until she picked up the rhythm and went with it, doubling his pleasure as well as her own.

Jarret was where he wanted to be, doing what he wanted to do. All barriers down, he could now tell Amy in whispers husky with lust what he felt, what she wanted to hear. 'I love you. God help us, how I love you. You've been there every minute of every hour of every day, even when I was denying you. This is what you want – my fucking, to be fucked to oblivion by me. If it was only enslavement by lust . . . but it isn't, it's love. It's you, Amy Ross.'

When they came together they went limp in each other's arms, Jarret lying on top of her, still erect inside her. Amy could feel him shrinking back. It was instinctive; she clasped him tight to hold him there for as long as possible. Finally he slipped from and off her and on to his side facing her.

It was inexplicable, natural, primeval, her overwhelming desire to hold within her every drop of his semen and her come. She would have liked to keep it in her womb, to hold him forever within her body. She wanted never to part with a drop of his life's force. It was lustful and more than that – it was utterly private, and extraordinarily thrilling to love a man enough to want to hold him inside you for all eternity. Even too intimate to express to Jarret.

Amy watched him adjust himself and zip up his trousers. He gazed into her eyes and told her as he adjusted her dress to cover her breasts and her nakedness from the waist down, 'Violet eyes. God has indeed blessed you, I'm a lucky man. Now tell me, my violet eyes, how did you like that for an ice breaker?'

Amy laughed and so did Jarret. 'Fine, just fine. For a moment I was worried we were going to be reduced to no talk, or even worse small talk, or even worse than that indifference – "let's just be friends".'

He took her by the hands and pulled her up from the cushions she was lying against. They sat there for several minutes, hand in hand, then he told her, 'That wasn't how you looked.'

'How did I look?'

'Very chic, very New York, glamorous for an art historian, not at all anxious for a woman waiting for her lover, cool, composed, yet hungry for sex with me.'

'You were very sure about that?'

'Yes.'

'And that I had remained faithful to you?' she teased.

'Yes.'

Amy threw back her head and laughed. 'How were you so sure?'

'Because you love me, and couldn't give yourself to any man the way you give yourself to me. I did tell you that you would never replace me.'

'I might have found a stand-in.'

'It was never even a vague possibility. Admit to me that's true?'

Amy found herself caught out. For some reason she could not understand, she would rather not admit to Jarret that it was true. A blush appeared on her cheeks. She rose from the bed and straightened her dress over her hips with the palms of her hands and busied herself plumping up cushions on the bed. He stood up immediately and took her hands in his, lowered his head and kissed one then the other. Gazing into her eyes, he said nothing.

She leaned against him. The warmth of his body, his scent. She was awash with his sperm and their comings together . . . she was helpless to do otherwise than tell him, 'It's true. Of course it's true.'

He ran his fingers through his hair and sighed. Was it with triumph or relief? He detached himself from her and went to the fireplace where he placed several logs on the ashes. The fire, very nearly out, began to smoke. He knelt down and blew on it for several minutes then it caught and flared up. He turned from the fire and looked round the room.

'Do you like it?' she asked.

'Very much. I don't know what I expected, but it's more.'

He walked to the table set for two in the bay window and put his face among the flowers, the better to draw in their scent. Amy joined him. The bottle of wine was unopened. He picked it up and asked, 'May I?'

'Of course. I meant to offer you a glass but somehow got distracted.'

'A fine wine, perfect flowers. And dinner?'

'Oh, God, dinner. I forgot about the beef.'

She ran to the kitchen and opened the oven. A blast of heat and the powerful scent of roasting meat filled the kitchen. The potatoes were crisp and the colour of caramel, the layer of fat on the top of the rib of beef crisp and browned to perfection. It sizzled and spat as she removed the roasting pan from the oven shelf.

He was right behind her. He slipped his arms round her waist and pressed up against her, looking at the food over her shoulder. 'You've thought of everything, the best of everything, and all for me. I think I'm going to enjoy being spoiled by you, Amy Ross.'

It was a tight squeeze for them both in the kitchen but she managed to turn round to face him. 'For us, Jarret, for us.'

He laughed and told her, 'It's all right for you to spoil me, Amy, and even to admit to it.'

'And what about me?'

'I've already spoiled you for sex with any other man, I dare say I can manage to keep that up. Every painting I paint is for you. A more than fair exchange for all the flowers in the world, and roast beef and fine wine,' he teased.

But was it a tease? There was something, a look in his eyes, that was just a little too intense for a real tease. She had a brief mental impression of the *palazzo* in Venice chock-a-block with things, the Paris flat, and the *yalis* on the Bosphorus, and realised that her lover was a very greedy man. So greedy, she almost laughed aloud. To Amy, who did not understand real greed, something she herself had no feeling for, it was more funny than pathetic. She simply could not take it seriously and so was not disturbed by it.

'I'm famished,' declared Jarret.

Over food and drink conversation came easily to them. Each was curious about what had happened in the other's life since last they had been together. There was chatter and laughter. What little serious talk there was was constructive and interesting. He was charm itself and flattering, open and more informative than he had ever been with her. The evening went from great to sublime not just for Amy: here was a Jarret she had seen only flashes of in Venice and Paris, one completely at ease and happy, full of vitality and without artifice. He was whole, hers and hers alone, and they both seemed to revel in that. Yet when it came near to any talk of love, any declaration of his passion and commitment to her – 'I love you, Amy. No matter what happens in our lives, you have to believe that I love you, God help us' – that only came much later during his long and exquisite erotic thrustings, and when Amy was lost in lust for him, exhausted from the many orgasms he was able to bring her to.

Even the sex was different, more raunchy and adventurous, but always with Jarret in control, Amy submissive. But no matter how submissive, she held him enthralled sexually. It seemed that he could not get enough of her, they could not get enough of each other.

Amy awakened long before Jarret. She lay on her side leaning on her elbow and watched him sleep, overwhelmed by how much she loved him, wondering that one human being could love another so completely. She didn't wake him, would simply lie there very still, gazing at him until he wakened naturally. That would become one of the patterns of their life together. Some mornings it could be a matter of minutes, occasionally it was hours. It never mattered to Amy. The warmth of his naked body next to hers, his scent and steady breathing, his extraordinarily handsome good looks in repose, she could never get enough of. These were some of the most intimate minutes they would ever have together and Amy was sometimes moved to tears of joy and gratitude to have him for a lover.

Many was the time while he slept that she wanted to lay her head upon his chest or place her head in his lap, her lips upon his flaccid penis. She never did, didn't want to break his sleep, for him to wake and ruin this special secret time she had alone with him. In all the time they lived together he never once awakened before she did.

That first morning after his arrival when he did awaken it was nearly noon. They never left the flat. By dinnertime Jarret had already marked it with his presence: a jumper lying over a chair, a jacket hanging on a door knob, his white shirt draped over a lampshade. Looking away from the library wall where he was checking the titles, he caught her observing the scene and most charmingly told her, 'My way of making it my own? Because I feel so at home and think it is mine? Take your choice.' Then he went to her and sat on the arm of her chair and stroked her hair, running his fingers through it.

The intimacy they shared that day made Amy wonder how she had ever lived so happily without it. Never had she experienced such a sweet sensation. Not even as a child, as an adolescent growing up in the bosom of her family, not even with Peter, only hints that such intimacy might possibly happen. All ambition and striving gone, here were two people totally centred, in utter bliss, living in the moment. It was as exciting and vital as anything Amy or Jarret had ever known. Yet they were not children. They understood that they could not stay locked up in an elegant bed sit a few doors off Fifth Avenue on the upper East Side. Their greatest challenge was to keep what they had alive. Each of them knew that but daren't speak of it.

At one point during the afternoon, while lying on the floor in front of the fire and taking tea and cakes, he asked, 'Is it everything you dreamed about, our being together?'

'More. It's perfect except for one thing.'

Jarret looked more puzzled than surprised. 'You're disappointed about something?'

'Yes. Your paintings. I was so sure this place was going to be filled with them, I long to see them and you didn't bring any.'

He looked relieved. A smile crossed his face. 'Didn't I?'

Amy sat up on her knees. 'You beast, you have! Where are they?'

'I brought enough canvases for a one-man show. I can't wait for you to see them. I want you to help me choose the ones to be stretched.'

'But where are they?'

'I dropped them off at the gallery yesterday afternoon.'

'Yesterday afternoon?' Amy felt sick in the pit of her stomach, puzzled, confused. 'But you were in the air over the Atlantic yesterday afternoon.'

'No. I took an earlier flight.'

'I don't understand this. When exactly did you arrive in New York, Jarret?'

'Around three o'clock.'

'Then you didn't come directly from the airport?'

'No. Is that a problem for you, Amy?'

She wanted to say, 'Yes, it is. If you had a change of plans then why didn't you call and tell me? Why keep me dangling like a foolish schoolgirl in love, counting the minutes, waiting for a phone call, the doorbell to ring?' But how could she? It was she who'd assumed that he was rushing from the airport directly to her. She who had dangled herself. She was too ashamed of her obsessive love for Jarret to answer in any other way than she did.

'Why would that be a problem for me?'

The cold look that came into his eyes, the not very nice tone that had flared up in his voice, had come from nowhere. Now they vanished as suddenly as they'd appeared. 'You will be the first to see them, even before Walter.'

'Then you are going to have a show at the Walter Cordigon Gallery?' said Amy with genuine enthusiasm and delight for Jarret since she knew very well how difficult it was to get a one-man show in New York.

'He hasn't said yes yet, but he will. He wants to see the paintings first and he had no time or space to do that what with people coming in and out of the gallery yesterday. I told him I would be there in the morning and make a selection of the paintings I want stretched. The

168

gallery will pay for the stretchers, an advance against future sales. Fortunately Walter won't be in tomorrow before one o'clock so you and I can have the back room of the gallery all to ourselves. I can hardly wait to hear what you think of the work.'

'And I can hardly wait to see it,' she told him.

Shortly after tea when Jarret dozed off in front of the fire Amy gazed round the place that was no longer her room but theirs. He had invaded her space the way he had invaded her heart and it was paradise. But she was acutely aware that something was wrong in paradise, part of which was that she loved Jarret too much. It was probably at that moment that she realised, living with him, she would have to work twice as hard to keep him in proportion to the rest of her life. He had already taken possession of her and, shockingly, she believed that having done so, he was capable of taking over her life; that he would make her, if he wished to, vanish into a dark corner of his. Fanciful? She wondered. In her erotic life with him she could cope with that, but their erotic life was apart from the love he professed to have for her, and it was this love for her that concerned Amy.

She too dozed off and when she awakened felt strangely secure in herself and her love for Jarret. Incredibly, she had come to understand that they might never be together for all the days of their life, whereas before she had dozed off that had been her fantasy. It was at that moment that she made the decision that for as long as they were to be together, she would have the best time of her life.

The following morning they were waiting at the gallery door before it had even opened. When Walter Cordigon's assistant arrived Amy was amused to see how awestruck he was before Jarret. No sooner had Rory unlocked the gallery door and switched the lights on, than he was offering himself as helper. Rory was pleasant enough to Amy but she could see he considered Jarret a star.

The back room was too small for them to spread the work out and the young man suggested, 'Use the main gallery. We don't get many people in this early in the morning. Just don't tell Walter!' Which was what they did.

The roll of paintings was large and heavy but Jarret managed it by himself. A chair was brought out for Amy. She was quite surprised when Jarret, with infinite charm, asked the star-struck Rory, 'Would you mind if we did this alone? I would rather you and Walter saw them another time.' Then took the young man by the arm and ushered

169

him into the office, closing the door.

The Walter Cordigon Gallery was small, one large room, and way down on the list of galleries that Amy found interesting. Walter Cordigon was not an adventurous dealer, but he had been a dealer for many years and did on occasion hold a better than good group show. He knew how to get the paintings he wanted when he wanted them. Amy thought him a rather silly and pretentious man, kind but gossipy. She had always imagined he might have wanted to be a woman. More than once she had seen him flounce. But to his credit he did know good paintings and could be moved by great paintings that other art dealers had discovered and exhibited. She would not have chosen the Walter Cordigon Gallery for her lover, but knew that a show there could do him no harm and would give him the New York exposure he needed. She was therefore impatient and excited to see the work.

The paintings were good, very good. There was no question that there was a radical and sometimes inspired change in Jarret's work. It was thrilling to see an artist's canvases unfurled from the roll and suddenly become works of art. Amy experienced that same high she had had on first seeing Jarret's work at the *palazzo*. But good, even very good, is one thing. Showing the best of what you've got is another. The collection was uneven. Amy was relieved that Walter Cordigon and his assistant were not there. The problem was the canvases were good enough for a show, but not a show that the New York art world would talk about and the hot collectors buy from. Amy walked round them, studied them, thought about them.

'Well?' he asked her.

She remained silent, working out what was right and what was wrong with the collection.

'What do you think?'

Again she remained silent, this time composing in her mind what to say to Jarret.

'Will they get me a show with Walter?'

Amy turned to look at him. She walked to the chair that had been brought into the gallery for her and stood behind it, her hands clasping the back of it. Jarret went to her, sat sideways on the chair and looked up into her face. 'Come on, what do you think?'

Amy put her hand on his shoulder. He nervously shrugged it off. She stepped away from the chair and walked to one of the paintings then told him, 'This is a terrific painting worthy of any show anywhere. And so is this, and this one.' She pointed to a large, dark but vibrant

170

canvas, a painting full of energy, then walked to the far side of the room to indicate another. 'These are a thrilling breakthrough in your work. Jarret Sparrows that are new and inventive, inspired even, open and vulnerable. They've lost that tight, sometimes derivative thing that slips into your work. But the collection is uneven.'

She waited for him to say something. He seemed stunned with disappointment. But she could do nothing about that so she continued, 'My recommendation to you is that you stretch five of these paintings.'

At this point she walked over and selected the five and laid them on the floor in close proximity to one another, then moved the remaining paintings well away from them. Jarret never made a move to help her, merely sat there and watched and listened. When she had completed her work she stood back from the collection, arms folded across her bosom, and studied them.

Jarret rose from the chair and walked over to her and studied the collection. He remained silent, withdrawn. Amy told him, 'Now here we have the makings of a sensational show. Might I suggest to you, Jarret, that you have stretchers made for these and we roll up the remaining canvases and get them out of here before Walter returns? Bring them home. We can go over them then talk about them not just as paintings and your work but as an exhibition in New York at a very exciting time in the American art world. Whether you take up my suggestion or not, one thing is for sure: I would only show these paintings to Walter on stretchers, and better still framed, if that's possible.'

'Walter has been seeing my canvases unstretched and spread on the floor or draped over an already stretched canvas for years. He is a dealer after all.'

And has never given you a one-man show, was what Amy wanted to say, but that seemed mean and unnecessary. What she did say was, 'Yes, but he's never seen these paintings which are such a new departure from your other work, and he may not be expecting this change. Walter might find them thrilling but confusing because the majority of this collection is the work of yesterday. Well, I may not have said it very well but you know what I mean.'

'This is a nuisance.'

'Not if you want a show, it isn't.'

'You seem very sure about this.'

'It's only an opinion, Jarret. And a personal one at that. We're too intimate with one another for me to step into your life in my professional capacity, but I can't leave that behind when we're talking about your work.'

'And you think if he sees the new work stretched on frames and maybe one framed, he'll give me a show?'

'I'm only saying, I think you have a hundred per cent better chance.'

'But then I won't have enough work for a one-man exhibition.'

'We can talk about that later. But if you want to think about this or do as I suggest, one thing is for sure. We should roll these canvases up right now and get them out of here before Walter returns.'

'What can I say to him? He expects me to lunch with him and look at the work and talk about a show.'

'We go, we return, and you tell him the truth. You want him to see some of the paintings stretched. And then a little white lie. It was a matter of timing with the framer. You were sure he would not mind a day or two more. And then you take a gamble and say that if he does, you will go and get them from the framer's immediately. You won't have a problem, of that I'm certain.'

'Do you know someone who has stretchers or can immediately make them to the size I need, and do the stretching, and a proper job of it?'

'No. But I know a man who does and he owes me a favour. It's one phone call.'

'We might even get them for this afternoon?'

'We probably could but I would suggest you put Walter off for a couple of days. That would give you a chance to get into the galleries and see a great deal of new and exciting painting. The scene is rapidly changing here, Jarret. You've been away too long in Europe. Put *palazzos* and *things* and the high life aside and steep yourself in the New York art scene for a couple of days, then you'll know better what you're up against. And how to talk with Walter about the sort of show you can get together.'

'You really think it's so important?'

'This is a very exciting time to look at art in America. The dealers and museum people are all on edge. New painters are coming up fast, and the museums and dealers and collectors want to jump – but not over the edge. They're flailing about, worrying who to back, what to show. Do you think Walter is any different? They all want to discover the new winner. Your timing could be perfect but you have to steep yourself in the art world, and see what you think about what's happening in it. If for no other reason than to reassess where you're going with your own work.'

172

Jarret said no more. Swiftly he went round the room gathering his work together and piling the painted canvases carefully one on top of the other. Amy helped. She was feeling divided about what she had done. She had upset him, which was the last thing she'd wanted to do, but she loved him too much not to put him wise to the art scene that could further his career.

They made a hasty departure with the heavy roll of canvases, assuring Rory that they would be back at one o'clock. Amy made her phone call from a box in the street and came out all smiles and waving a piece of paper. She hailed a taxi. Jarret stopped her. 'I can't afford taxis, we'll go by bus.'

'Humping that load on your shoulder? No, I think not, and I'd be surprised if a bus driver let you on with that roll. I'll treat us to a taxi.'

At the framer's, excitement began to mount for both Jarret and Amy. The framer, who worked for Robert Motherwell and Hans Hoffman, Clifford Still and Jasper Johns, and was in the process of mounting a Jim Dine, was clearly more than interested in the first five canvases to come off Jarret's roll, the five that Amy and Jarret had agreed were the ones to be stretched. Amy stepped aside and watched Jarret charm the framer during the discussion of what he wanted done. They asked her opinion about a frame for one of them and excitement mounted as the framer's assistant arrived with stretchers and frame samples. Finally they chose simply carved and silver-leafed wooden picture frames for two of the paintings and merely to stretch the other three. They would be ready for five o'clock, delivered for half-past six to Amy's flat, the five pieces and the roll of canvases that remained.

Together Jarret and Amy walked arm in arm from the framer's back to the Cordigon Gallery. Briefly, they joined the surging crowds rushing up and down Fifth Avenue. There was a spring in their step, smiles on their faces. It had been so far a thrilling morning and Jarret was beginning to get the buzz of New York. The excitement of seeing the Motherwells and Jasper Johns in the framer's studio helped to make him understand what Amy was talking about.

It was less crowded on East Fifty-seventh Street. One thing about New Yorkers – busy as they are, they are lookers and can always find time for a glance at the beautiful people. To passersby that must have been how Amy and Jarret looked. A tall couple, handsome, well turned out, high on confidence and life, and obviously in love, they walked as if the world was their cupcake and they were eating every last morsel of it. They were somebodies, could even be celebrities, and deserved a second glance.

With a few minutes to spare before they were due back at the Walter Cordigon Gallery, they dashed into the Andre Emmerich Gallery for a quick viewing of the Sidney Nolan show. Impressive, bold, exciting, they had not enough time to do justice to it. On their way out they bumped into John Chandris, a curator from one of the city's most prestigious museums. He greeted Amy and seemed to be surprised to see her with Jarret.

'Amy, I had no idea you knew each other. Jarret, when did you arrive?'

'Only just.'

'Is Fee with you?'

'No, he's in Istanbul.'

'That marvellous *yalis* on the Bosphorus? What an amusing time we all had there! How is Savannah? Pity you two couldn't keep it together. Is she still in Paris?'

'London.'

'Where are you staying? With the Clarksons?'

'No, another friend.'

John immediately produced a pocket memo pad and pencil. 'Give me your number. You must come for dinner. I'll call you.' Amy felt as if she were invisible for all the attention he was paying her. A closet homosexual in love with her lover? Well, one could almost understand his rudeness.

John Chandris was flushed and nervously dancing from one foot to the other. He was so obviously smitten with Jarret, Amy found it embarrassing. Even more difficult was watching Jarret charm and flirt with the eminent curator. Amy, unable to bear it, looked away.

'I don't know the number, John. I have yours. I'll call you in the morning at the museum.'

Jarret did know the telephone number, she was the friend he was staying with, why couldn't he be straightforward and come out with it? She found that disconcerting.

'You won't forget?'

'Of course not, John.'

'How long are you here for, Jarret?'

Even Amy hadn't asked that question but now her ears pricked up. She too had been wondering how long he would be staying in New York. For a moment she allowed her fantasies to take hold and waited

174

for him to say, 'Indefinitely'. What he did say was, 'I only just arrived, John,' with a laugh, and gave John Chandris a flirtatious smile that made the man all but twitter.

The three said their farewells. Amy and Jarret were alone in the elevator. 'John knows the score. He just never gives up, the poor sod. After all these years and rejections, he's still as smitten as ever. It's actually rather sweet, don't you think?'

'No, I don't, *actually*,' she mimicked.

'You're jealous because I flirted with him,' he teased.

Amy gave him a harsh look. 'More amazed that you enjoyed it so much.'

He laughed even more, and placing an arm through hers said, 'Well, you needn't be jealous, it's you I'm sleeping with.' And whispered in her ear, 'And you I fuck.'

It was a silly incident and she would not allow it to spoil the great day they were having together. It was after all not her problem or Jarret's but John Chandris's.

The Cordigon Gallery was on the first floor of a large brownstone house on East Sixty-fifth Street between Park and Lexington Avenue. With Amy still on Jarret's arm, they climbed the flight of stairs from the pavement to the entrance of the building. Amy was astounded how happy they were. The world had never looked bigger or brighter. At last she had cracked it. So this was what life was all about, these special moments in time and space that could carry one through no matter what it delivered. Thinking how sad it would have been had she and Jarret not fallen in love, she felt the luckiest woman in the world.

They entered the gallery to find Walter placing a small red sold dot at the corner of a painting. 'What a break, he'll be in a very good mood,' whispered Amy.

Jarret smiled at her while removing his arm from hers. He took several strides forward, leaving Amy to walk into the gallery behind him. 'Walter!'

'Dear boy!'

Amy watched Walter Cordigon's face change on seeing Jarret. It was full of smiles and a sparkle came into his eye. She thought, Oh, no! He fancies my lover too. What am I up against here? Walter Cordigon walked forward and first shook hands then hugged Jarret. Only then did he see Amy.

'Do you know Amy Ross, Walter?'

'Yes, we've met. It's a long time since I've bumped into you, and a very long time since you've been in the gallery. How are you? Didn't know you were a friend of Jarret's. Known him long?'

She had seen him fishing for gossip before. With Walter Cordigon it was the major part of any conversation he had. Because he was basically such a pleasant and harmless person, people accepted it, treated it no differently than if he had a wart on the end of his nose, were merely careful not to make an issue of it.

Jarret was quick to interrupt. 'Not nearly as long as you have, nor as well.' That was followed by one of his handsome smiles.

Walter seemed to take that as a compliment. He became not exactly twittery but was clearly flattered. He all but threw back his shoulders and raised his chin just that little bit higher.

'Oh! Then you've not been to the *yalis*. I meant to ask you yesterday when we were catching up, how is the Countess Armida, Jarret? When I was in London I had lunch with Savannah and Billy Bolton . . . you'd better watch out there, Jarret, he's taken sides with Savannah, thinks you will lose in your fight to keep the Paris flat. Well, that's neither here nor there. As I was saying about the Countess Armida . . . somehow they got news that she was now bedridden, had gone into complete seclusion, given up seeing anyone but you and Fee?'

'Just gossip, Walter. She's very well. I think you offered lunch? I'm famished.'

'I've already sent Rory out for sandwiches and a bottle of wine, but I didn't expect another guest for lunch. Never mind, we can send him out for more. Have you met the Countess Armida Montevicini, Miss Ross? No, of course you haven't, she never leaves Istanbul and you haven't been to her wooden mansion on the Bosphorus. She must be getting on now – seventy-five, eighty. Whatever she claims she must be older, many years older. Women like the Countess Armida never tell their real age. I wish I had known her in her hey-day. She was one of the greatest beauties of her time. Her portraits and the photographs – no wonder men gave up their lives and their wallets for her, one even a kingdom! Oh, you must get to meet her. Even in old age she has charisma, a faded beauty that won't let go, and she can still seduce men less than half her age to her bed. Bed and sex . . . well, she was famous for that. They say that was how she enslaved the last ruler of the Ottoman Empire and she was a mere child then. She adores Jarret and Fee. And the people she knows who used to pay homage to her, well . . .'

Jarret looked neither disturbed nor discomforted by Walter's gossip, merely as if he had had enough of it when he interrupted the art dealer. 'About my paintings. Having looked at them, I decided I wanted five of them stretched. It was a matter of getting the framer on the job. I knew you would have no objections if we went through them together on Friday. We can still have preliminary talks about an exhibition today after lunch. You don't mind, do you?'

Of course Walter didn't, he was too carried away on the gossip he had just delivered and enchanted to see himself as part of Jarret's inner circle. The timing was perfect. Rory arrived with the sandwiches.

Chapter 12

The rare roast beef sandwiches on buttered rye had hardly been served nor the bottle of cheap red wine opened before Amy realised she did not belong at this lunch and the meeting that was to follow. But that alone was not what made her want to escape from Jarret and Walter Cordigon who was fussing unnecessarily.

'Amy, if you want me to, I'll send out for another roast beef on rye? But it'll be busy at the sandwich bar at this hour and we'll have to wait lunch, and Rory should be doing an errand for me. What do you suggest?'

Walter looked all dithery, and before she could answer him changed the subject, something he was known to do when he didn't want to hear something. Walter had a reputation for that but people forgave him for it.

'I remember Savannah used to love these little office lunches we three used to have here. They were her favourite, these roast beef sandwiches. She always said it was more fun than going out to one of those overcrowded chic restaurants. I do miss Savannah. Were you a friend of Savannah's too, Miss Ross? She and Jarret, the most beautiful and enchanting couple in the Paris art world! When in New York they were like visiting royalty. None of us believe you two won't get back together again,' he told Jarret, very nearly producing a tear in his eye for effect.

'It's not true about the sandwiches, Walter. Savannah loathed these dried-up excuses for lunch. She was always remarking how very mean you were, never taking us to a proper lunch.'

'She didn't?' Walter looked shattered by this news.

'She did. I think she might even have settled for a department store lunchroom for ladies, although she did always claim that one day she would get you to take her to The Russian Tea Room.'

'You're making this up, just teasing me?'

179

'Am I? You know better than that, and you know very well that you're mean, the meanest dealer in town, and take a perverse pride in being so. It's no secret, Walter, just one of the facts of life of the New York art world.'

Jarret went to Walter and placed an arm round his shoulder. He took one of Walter's hands in his: a large, plump and coarse hand with fingers like sausages, pink and soft, with well-manicured finger nails.

For a few seconds while Jarret patted it, Amy imagined Walter sitting in an elaborate Gothic oak chair, a white sheet wrapped round him like a Roman toga, pale pink flesh popping out: a naked arm here, a bare shoulder there. A beautiful catamite, a naked boy with blond curly hair, was sitting on his lap giving Walter a manicure. She had to hold back her laughter.

'I always think it's more intimate, these little business lunches in my office,' spluttered Walter to Jarret while staring admiringly into his eyes.

'And it is, Walter, it is. And I'm delighted to be here *à deux* with you.'

It was outrageous flirtation on Jarret's part. He was a tease, and Amy found something quite cruel and unsavoury about it. Charm was one thing, this was something else – and something she found unpalatable, not to mention that *à deux* excluded her.

'Don't bother about lunch for me, Mr Cordigon, I won't stay. Thank you just the same.' Amy buttoned her coat and took her handbag in a deliberately slow and easy manner, not wanting either man to see how offended she was, or how unwelcome she had been made to feel.

'I'll see you to the street,' offered Jarret.

'No. Please don't bother.'

'It's no bother at all, I insist.'

To protest any further would have been to make a scene. She managed a smile, said goodbye to Walter Cordigon, and walked with Jarret from the gallery to the hall and down the stairs to the street.

He stood with her there, buttoning his coat, turning up the collar. 'What's wrong?'

'Don't you think it's quite cruel to flirt with men who are clearly infatuated with you, lead them on?'

Jarret began to laugh. 'They love it, it gives them hope, although they know I only fuck women.'

180

'I don't see it as funny, Jarret.'

'Well, you should, especially since it's you I'm fucking and not them.'

'Oh, so that makes it all right?'

'Yes, I think it does.'

'They wouldn't.'

'But they don't know and aren't likely to.'

That quite stunned Amy. Though she had never thought of shouting to the world that she and Jarret were in love, she certainly had not expected their love for each other was going to be a deep dark secret. She was further taken aback when she saw a serious light come into his eyes.

She was about to walk away when he smiled at her and said, 'Please don't walk away from me like this. I'm sure that Walter is peeping out the window looking to see if we're having a lovers' tiff, and we wouldn't want that, would we? We'll talk about this at home this evening. Don't behave like a silly jealous woman – you have nothing to be jealous about. After yesterday and this morning, surely you must know that? You could have stayed for lunch, no one asked you to leave.'

'You must be joking! Walter did everything he could to discourage me from staying. As a matter of fact I didn't hear you make any protest about my leaving. What was that *à deux*, Jarret? In my book *à deux* still means two and implies intimacy.'

'Walter's gossiping was getting on your nerves. I was giving you an out in case you wanted one.'

'Well, you would be right there.'

The two of them began to laugh, as much at themselves as they were at Walter. 'I'll call you at home when I'm free from him and maybe we can do some more looking at art together.'

It was a long walk from the gallery to Amy's flat but the weather, though crisp and cold, was bracing. She somehow couldn't bear the idea of getting on a bus and never used the underground. The fact was she needed the air and a brisk walk to clear her mind. If anyone had told her that she would be happy to get away from Jarret, she would never have believed them. But she was.

He was such a different man in the way he related to other people from the one she knew in their intimate life. She saw clearly for the first time the two sides to Jarret's personality. Can one love a man and not like him? Now that was a question to ponder. By the time she arrived home she had already made up her mind that she would never

181

be upset by Jarret's behaviour again. Walk away but never close your eyes had to be the right solution.

On entering the flat she had to smile. He did have a way of making his presence felt. The room seemed no longer hers but theirs; evidence of him was everywhere and it warmed her heart. She missed him already. Her life seemed so such more full and rich, she was so much more alive, when he was with her. Just to watch him reading in the chair by the fire, to make him a cup of his favourite tea, to listen to him talk about his work, was already a part of her life. Would it happen that one day they would have to give each other up? She picked up his shirt and buried her face in it. Love for him overwhelmed her. She said aloud, 'Is it possible that to love a man as I love you, Jarret, is not prohibited, but to love you, Jarret Sparrow, for now and eternity, is forbidden?'

Amy curled up on the bed. She was suddenly exhausted, so very tired that she could not even manage to remove her coat. She fell asleep instantly, tears still wet on her cheeks.

It was the street door intercom buzzing madly that finally awakened her. The room was dark, she was disorientated upon awakening and felt as if her brain was scrambled. Then quite suddenly her mind cleared. It was Jarret at the door. She all but sprang from the bed, switching a light on as she rushed to the intercom.

'Jarret,' she called into it and buzzed him in.

Amy was surprised to hear a strange voice ask, 'Miss Amy Ross?'

'Yes.'

'Hampshire Holland, the framer's. What floor, ma'am?'

'Oh, of course, the first floor.'

Amy looked at her watch. Six thirty-five. They were on time but what had happened to Jarret? Had she slept through a phone call? The buzzing of the intercom earlier in the day? She opened the door to her flat for the delivery men and struggled out of her coat as she hurried to the telephone to call the Walter Cordigon Gallery. No answer.

She was in the bathroom combing her hair and fussing with her face when she heard the men enter the flat. First came Jarret's roll of paintings and then the five on stretchers, two of which were heavier for frames. They were wrapped in brown paper and tied with string and seemed to fill the room. On the one hand it was thrilling to have them there; on the other it was a disruption to her home, their love nest.

182

'Sign here, ma'am.'

Amy signed the delivery slip.

'Are you paying cash, or do we bill you, Miss Ross?'

That rather flummoxed Amy because she had no idea what arrangements Jarret had made with Hampshire Holland. It was a rush job and done as a favour to a friend of hers, and Hampshire Holland was such a nice man, one she would not like to take advantage of in any way. She started for her desk and her cheque book. 'I don't know what arrangements Mr Holland and Mr Sparrow made but I think I had better give you a cheque,' she told the delivery man.

'I think not! The invoice is to be sent to the Walter Cordigon Gallery. That's what Hampshire and I agreed upon,' said Jarret who had just entered the room.

Amy swung round to face him. How handsome and happy he looked, all charm with the two delivery men. One of them thumbed through the papers on his clipboard and said, 'Sorry 'bout that. Here it is, payment to be billed. Got my papers out of order.'

'No problem,' offered Jarret who ushered them from the flat.

On his return, he went directly to Amy and said, 'I don't want ever to take advantage of you, not for a penny. Anyone else in this world I don't give a toss about, only you. We're something special, private, personal, intimate, and I want to keep it that way. You do enough for me, loving me, giving me all of yourself, caring for me. You're in a secret part of my life. I want you for sex and love and nothing else. No matter how I behave with you, what you see and what you hear, as long as you know that we'll be all right.'

It was the speech every woman in love wants to hear but somehow not from the man who lights up her life and is wanted by her completely. The words were flattering and demeaning both at the same time. That was bad, but added insult to injury had to be the manner in which he delivered his little speech: matter-of-factly, without a semblance of emotion in it. It was as if he had come home to set love guidelines. Never step over the mark was not her idea of love, nor was a backstreet romance, and most especially not since they were both free and had no reason to slink around hiding anything.

'You don't look happy, Amy.'

'I'm confused.'

'Do you doubt that I love you?'

'No, but I would like to know why you're putting the brakes on. It's as if you don't want our love to get out of hand.'

He went to the fireplace and put a match to the well-laid fire which flared up at once. Then he turned to look at her. 'I suppose we have to have this conversation and now is as good a time as any. My love for you is already out of hand, stronger and more important to me than I ever wanted it to be. The kind of love I have for you is forbidden to me. I've made a pact with myself and Fee that a love that could take over my life is forbidden territory. If we keep it in bounds we'll be together forever, but it must not play havoc with my work, the plans and goals Fee and I as partners are working on. He has taken the same vow. And now so must you.'

'The only thing I *must* do in this life is die, Jarret.' Having said that Amy went to the drinks table and poured herself a whisky with a splash of water. She took a long draught of the drink and went to sit down on the sofa bed in the middle of the room.

Jarret suddenly went ashen. The firmness in her voice, her refusal to do as he asked, quite took him aback. He removed his coat, dropped it over a chair and went to Amy. Clearly her reaction was not what he had expected. He sat down next to her, removed the glass from her hand and placed it on a table in front of the *lit en bateau*. Then taking her hands in his, he held them and stroked them. 'Say you love me? I need you to love me. I'll give you everything I can of myself, we'll be happy together, you'll never know a better lover than I will be to you. Don't throw that away.'

Amy could find no words, emotions were running high for them both. They were involved in a deep and profound love that he didn't want and Amy knew he could not sustain.

They sat there holding hands, each of them silent, knowing that no matter what, they could not for the time being give up what they had together, each of them aware that they would do what they had to. Everything in Amy's life might have been entirely different if in those moments when each of them was making choices about how to handle their love for each other, Jarret had been able to take her in his arms, kiss her with the passion and love she knew he was capable of. But he didn't.

It was some time before he was composed enough to lower his head and kiss her hands, still held in his. Very nearly in a whisper he asked, 'Shall we look at my paintings?'

Amy wanted to reach out and stroke his cheek, push back the lock of hair that had fallen on his forehead. He looked so handsome and vulnerable, so in need of her love, just as he had claimed that he was.

It was then that she knew she would stay with him, love him, give herself to him utterly for as long as they were willing to add to each other's lives.

He would never marry her, they would never build a grand open life together that she would be proud to show to the world, nor would he be a father to her children, but just as he had told her, he would be the great love of her life.

Amy no longer had any need to tread carefully in her love for Jarret. She no longer had that fear that he would leave her if she put a step wrong; she knew for a fact now it was just a matter of time before he did. And so she did caress his cheek and did move the lock of hair from his forehead.

She answered him, 'Well, of course we must.'

'You won't leave me?' he asked rather pathetically.

'I think you know I won't.'

'I want to hear you say it.'

She began to laugh. 'Later, at the right moment. For now you'll have to be satisfied that I'm still here at all.'

With that she rose from the sofa and, removing her hands from his, walked away across the room to carry a painting back to him. On her return she sat down, placing the painting before them. Together they began to undo the string. Amy stopped him. 'Just one thing more, Jarret.'

'Yes.'

'We will never talk about or qualify our love for each other again. It's all been said, agreed?'

'Agreed,' he told her.

Amy suddenly felt as if an enormous burden had been lifted off her shoulders. She felt relief, a new freedom of the heart and soul. Now she could love Jarret any way she cared to, on her terms. He was a love story to which she knew the ending. It was like reading a romantic novel from back to front. The surprises, the excitement of lust and love, were still there to be looked forward to. Nothing else except the day when there wouldn't be any more. All she would have to do was cultivate the will that when that day came there would be no sad songs for her.

Ever since that first moment in Venice when Amy fell in love with Jarret there had been some inexplicable thing that troubled her about their togetherness. She kept fighting off something in her very soul that kept warning her that Jarret Sparrow was forbidden love. His passion in bed versus his cool indifference to her out of it; the distance and long periods of time apart versus the occasional letter of lust and love for her. The mixed signals. These were no longer a problem for her now.

She had been constantly trying to evaluate other people's hints, even warnings on both sides of the Atlantic about Fee and Jarret, her own concern about their lifestyle and how she could fit into it. And her obsessive love for Jarret, the power he held over her because of it. Now, thanks to this unexpected confrontation, the air was cleared, the sun had come out to kill the demons that were confusing her. The ghosts of other loves, Fee, Savannah, all those other people and places and things that haunted their affair no longer mattered to her. They were Jarret's problem not hers.

Strangely a feeling of happiness and freedom returned. She leaned over and kissed her lover. That kiss sealed their fate. It was no less filled with love nor passion; the moment her lips touched his she knew that she was no less in love with Jarret Sparrow, simply able to deal with the reality of loving him.

Once the brown paper had been removed from the painting they were balancing on the floor in front of them Amy and Jarret were once again swept into talking about his work. She had been right. The painting stretched and framed looked twice as powerful. Walter would be impressed. Within half an hour her room had been taken over completely by Jarret and his paintings. Once more she enjoyed his moving another part of himself into her life.

Only for a fleeting moment did she find it sad that she could not be a wife in every sense of the word to Jarret, support her husband, be the woman to nurture his talent, stand by his side and one day reap the rewards with him for a creative life and a body of work well worth giving a lifetime to. The potential for all that was right here in this room. And then that moment was gone. No sad songs for her.

It was nearly eight o'clock when Amy mentioned dinner. 'Oh, I forgot to tell you. I'm not in for dinner this evening. I'm invited out. I'll get back as early as I can,' Jarret told her.

Amy was neither surprised nor upset by the news. All in all it had been an emotionally exhausting day and the time and space alone would do her just fine. Living with Jarret, thinking about him all the time, sharing what was usually her solitary life with a man, did take some getting used to. She could do with a few hours to herself.

When Jarret returned from his dinner party it was well after midnight. The fire was blazing in the hearth and Amy was in bed reading. She had not touched a thing. His paintings were standing round the room, the unstretched canvases draped everywhere. Jarret dropped his coat on a chair and his jacket on another. He went directly to the fire and warmed his hands. 'You waited up, I was hoping you would. This room looks marvellous, a haven. Thank God for it and you.'

He went directly to Amy, tearing off his tie and his shirt and dropping them on the floor. He was naked and already rampant when he slipped under the covers next to her. There was something new and thrilling about his urgency to have sex with her. That night sex and lust took them over, both of them, and it was somehow different from ever before. They seemed more free, more ready to go that extra bit further into an erotic landscape they wanted to discover together. Their sexual life became even more vital, more full of adventure, and through it they sought those moments of sexual oblivion that could give them total oneness with each other and which they could achieve in no other way.

From that evening on for the next few weeks Amy had the best time any woman in love could possibly have. During the days they went their separate ways. Sometimes they met up to go to an exhibition, and sometimes gave up their evenings alone together for Amy to see her friends or Jarret to see his. Only occasionally did they socialise together. Within weeks they became one of the beautiful and intriguing couples on the art scene.

The gossip was out, not so much about Amy but Jarret, which made the lovers even more cautious and secretive about their love affair. Few people knew that they were living together, but most guessed that they were. Jarret claimed that he was living in the studio of the Greek artist Manatakis who was having a huge success in New York with kinetic art. He was currently living in Paris, which was were Jarret had first met him. Manatakis, like Jarret, found New York a hard place to live in, and so when the two met again at the party given at the Museum of Modern Art in honour of a Dada exhibition, several days after Jarret's arrival in New York, a glittering affair that brought everyone in the *Who's Who* of the art world out in force, they clung to each other as if shipwrecked. That proved to be a godsend because Manatakis offered Jarret space to work in while he was in the city. Jarret had not planned to work while in the States. Hustling and charming the art world, his

187

patrons, those socialites who bought his paintings, getting an exhibition with Walter, had been his objectives for coming here. But after a week the excitement generated by the new wave of young painters, the buzz and controversy they were creating, got to Jarret just as Amy had thought it would. She was somehow more thrilled than Jarret when he received the generous invitation and accepted it.

The Dada exhibition was by invitation only. Amy had one and so she and Jarret attended the affair together. That was where they bumped into Manatakis who was not at all fazed by his new fame. Amy was by no stretch of the imagination a celebrity such as he was in the art world. She was relatively unknown, a minor player in that world. She was astounded when Jarret appeared to be anything but a minor player, although the reality was he was an unknown artist still struggling to get a one-man show and find recognition. He seemed to know most every one of the wheelers and dealers, the heavy-duty collectors and millionaire patrons of the arts who kept the art circus going round and round. There was no question about it – Jarret was very well connected. She watched him work the guests with his charm, flirt outrageously, and saw him swept up into the social whirl. She still found that side of him unattractive, but somehow it didn't matter any more. The flaws in her lover were there for her to see as so many chinks in his armour, not hers.

Dadaism was a period of art that every painter and sculptor was fascinated by and so brought out the artists who could get an invitation and they brought those who couldn't. That made the show immensely exciting and fun. People were debating art and Dadaism in clusters throughout the exhibition rooms, critics and art historians having heated confrontations. And everyone was talking about where American Art was going to go now that Abstract Expressionism was seriously being challenged by the new young painters and their works.

When Jarret and Amy finally did leave the exhibition they went with Manatakis and a sculptress whose work he was raving about. From the museum they went to West Fourth Street and the basement studio where Manatakis was living and working. It was more like a mechanic's workshop than an artist's studio, a poor and wretched place that in daylight would need artificial lighting. It had a cot in one corner and a filthy loo in another behind a free-standing cupboard, the only piece of furniture in the room except for two cheap wooden chairs.

But none of that mattered once they saw the amazing sculptures that Manatakis created. There were small pieces and large pieces, and magnets in all shapes and sizes, bronzed and shining or in other metals polished to a patina of infinite beauty, assembled with other metals and wires. They were sculptures like all great modern sculptures where the empty spaces are a work of art in themselves. The spaces within Manatakis's sculptures were created with the help of the force magnets can create and the pieces of metal he could keep floating between them. They were magnificent works that stunned the imagination. Inspirational.

From there the four of them went to the sculptress's studio, a vast warehouse space she lived and worked in on the third-floor walk-up of an old unheated building. In the freezing cold they were given a viewing of one more exciting piece of sculpture after another: huge tablets of white plaster with hundreds of white plaster letters from the alphabet applied to them. There was about her work a certain magic combined with unsung genius. She was one of those artists awaiting her moment.

It was near midnight, and high as they were on art they were down to earth enough to know they were all starving. Amy invited them to go home with her where she had food and could cook a meal and their art whirl would not have to stop. They could see Jarret's work. It was dawn before the two artists left her flat and Jarret and Amy fell exhausted into bed. That evening the four of them became close friends.

The following day Jarret carried his paintings through the streets of New York to the Walter Cordigon Gallery. He stubbornly refused Amy's help and so had to make two journeys. Only on his return for the second batch of paintings did Amy realise that he no longer wanted her involved in his business. She made excuses for his suddenly cutting her out but for a few hours it hurt her more than it should have. He did promise to return and tell her what Walter thought about them, or at least call and tell her. He did neither.

It was two in the morning when Amy heard the key in the lock. She had not been sleeping, only lying in the dark coming to terms with the fact that Jarret was distancing himself from her. She switched on the lamp next to the bed.

'I'm dead. Can we talk about this in the morning?' he asked as he undressed. Amy drew the covers off her and he slid into bed next to

189

her, kissed her briefly on the cheek and turned on his side, instantly falling asleep.

As usual Amy was awake before him. When he did awaken he smiled at her. 'I know you watch over me while I sleep. Did I ever tell you how much I like that, your watching and waiting for me to come alive for you, for another day?'

He was naked and snuggled up next to her, removing her nightgown. Like a hungry child he fixed his lips upon her breast and sucked on the nipple. He bit into her flesh. They rolled round in the bed together, kissing and licking each other to a fever pitch until their urgency to be locked together in lust caused him to take her from behind, plunging deep inside as he bent her over the edge of the bed. There were the usual protestations of love and lust for her, some crude talk of things he wished he had the courage to do to her sexually. None of that was unusual; such talk did in fact excite them both. But for the first time he pulled on her hair between ravaging the back of her neck with kisses and told her, 'You have too much power over me. This fucking and lust is driving me wild, enslaving me to you.'

She had come several times and was only half in this world. The other half of her was lost in passion and sexual lust so that though she heard it she had not the clarity of mind to realise how dangerous talk like that was to their relationship. She would only remember those words when, much later over breakfast, there was something odd about the silence that was screaming between them.

She had handed two letters from Fee to him and he had sat reading them while she scrambled eggs. Now those pages lying on the table next to his plate seemed to reinforce the sense of danger Amy had briefly sensed when they had been in the throes of sex, and his words came back to mind. Waiting for him to speak was excruciatingly painful. She could bear it no longer.

'How is Fee?'

'Very well, he sends his love.'

'Does he?'

Amy knew the moment the words slipped from her mouth she should have kept quiet. They were provocative. She prayed that Jarret would let them pass.

He did. Went all silent again. Amy thought she could wait him out. That he would come out with the thing that was bothering him. He didn't. She finally asked, 'Aren't you going to tell me what happened at the gallery? What Walter had to say about the paintings, a show?'

190

'Oh, that.'

'Oh, that? Jarret, I waited all day and all night for a word about "Oh, that". "Oh, that" was the most important thing in your life a few days ago.'

The look that he was giving her was not one of anger for being put on the spot nor for her subtle chastisement of him for not calling. It was far worse – indifference. He seemed distracted, thinking of other things, other people. It was then that Amy realised that Jarret never said he was sorry. He apologised for nothing, took everything for granted.

He refilled his cup with hot black coffee and told her, 'He was thrilled with them, thought the new work impressive, but like all dealers at the moment he's nervous about the dramatic changes happening in the art world. He said yes, in principle he is interested in giving me a one-man show but he wanted to give me a final answer later in the day.'

'And?'

Amy's genuine enthusiasm seemed to perk him up and he continued with more vigour, 'And at five o'clock I returned to the gallery with Mamie Clarkson and Doug and Winnie Miliken, with whom I'd had lunch at the Knickerbocker Club. Walter almost fell over with excitement when I entered the gallery with them and because they came to see my new work. You know what a social climber he is. The Milikens bought your favourite of the five paintings and Mamie bought the one we named Green Gage. Walter asked if he could borrow them for my one-man show. Yes, was his answer. I did get a show out of him but I had to hedge my bets.'

'How thrilling! Wonderful, darling.' Amy leapt from her chair to go to Jarret and kiss him many times all over his face. He finally pulled her into his lap and they both laughed. Amy insisted on further details. He had pulled it off. It didn't matter how, it was done and now he had the break he had waited and worked so hard for. As they sat together, Jarret rocking her back and forth in his arms, both happy and at peace with each other and the world, Amy could not help but wonder why he had been so glum over breakfast. It could only be those letters from Fee.

Now that Jarret was off and talking he continued, 'The show is for the second week in January next year, and will run through to March the fifteenth. I want to paint an entirely new show. Walter will have the remainder of the rolled-up paintings stretched and keep them for back-up and subsequent sale. They will not go into the exhibition because we don't want the show to be a retrospective – unless of course he hates the new paintings, then we might slip one or two of the old ones in.'

'And you've already sold two? He must be thrilled.'

'Oh, he is. And so am I. The money has to go straight to Fee and into the house in Istanbul, and for supplies for the Cordigon show. And I have to return to Istanbul as soon as possible.'

'Is something wrong?'

Jarret's 'no' was much too sharp for Amy's liking. It was practically telling her to mind her own business.

'Then why must you go so soon?'

'I have a huge amount of work to get out in a very short time – eight or nine months. Which brings me to something else. I'm moving out, down to Manatakis's place for the remainder of my stay here, as soon as I can get a bed together. This place is too small for us both.'

Amy couldn't help herself, she was devastated. 'Not if you spend all day there and sleep here.'

'Don't make this difficult Amy. You know very well where I would rather be.'

'If that were true then you would be, wouldn't you?' she answered testily, and rose from his lap.

He held her tight by her wrist so she could not leave his side. 'I'll keep a key, I'll come home and fuck you as much as I can. I shouldn't have to tell you that. It's something you should know.'

'What's this all about? We're so happy together here in this hideaway.'

'That's part of the problem. Unless I move out it won't remain our little hideaway. Walter, the Milikens, Mamie . . . they all want to know where I'm staying, if it's with a lover. There are several grand houses where I'm welcome to stay, and I chose you. It wouldn't be good for it to be seen that I've fallen for you.'

'Why ever not?'

'Oh, please, Amy, don't be stupid.'

She wrenched her hand away and walked to the fireplace, sitting in the wing chair next to it. 'Don't insult me, Jarret.'

He went to her. 'If word of our affair leaks out and it's thought to be a fling, something on the rebound from Savannah, it will be considered forgivable. Anything more would be frowned upon. Savannah's mother arrives at Mamie Clarkson's the day after tomorrow. We're close –

she sided with me against Savannah. I'll be seeing her, have to have an address that I can give her. The starving artist sharing a studio with another artist. Better public relations, I think, than the address of the woman who has replaced her daughter.'

'You're not taking me into any of your life, are you, Jarret?'

'Only the most intimate part of my life, isn't that enough for you? All those wealthy socialites, movers and shakers of this city, every fag curator and dealer that I flirt with and party with . . . not one of them has what you have of me. The one thing they all want from me is what I give to you. Don't be stupid and bourgeois. Play the game, Amy, or we're dead.'

Tears were brimming in her eyes. There was a tremor in her voice when she asked, 'Is that an ultimatum?'

'No, just a fact of life.'

'Well, here's another fact of our life together for you, Jarret. For me, it's play the game as long as I can and *then* we're dead.' And all the while she heard herself saying those words Amy was aware that she was swimming with a shark, dancing with the devil.

She was astonished to see the colour drain from Jarret's face. In a matter of seconds he was white and looked as if he was about to faint. He had actually to cling to the fireplace for support. She rushed to help him. It took several seconds for him to recover himself.

'Are you all right?' she asked, the tears now streaming down her face.

He wiped them away with his hand and said, 'So be it.' But he never moved out.

A friend of Amy's lent them a folding army cot and bed linen which they moved to Manatakis's studio. Jarret did go to the studio every day for a few hours and it was there that he received his friends, and as many of the art world figures as he could get down there. It was that telephone number that he gave out and there where people called him. So he lived two lives: one with Amy and the other without her.

But in the remaining weeks that he was in New York, they were no less besotted with each other and Amy and he had the best of times in bed. They went to the Cedars bar with new artist friends, did the art world parties together, but behaved in public as discreetly as they could, outwardly no more than just good friends. They did not, however, fool as many people as they thought they had.

Their intimate life flourished. And slowly Amy came to terms with the fact that sex for Jarret was the motivating factor, not love.

Practically every day a letter came from Fee. Amy no longer asked what he had to say. She had only to look at Jarret's face upon receiving one to see that he was torn between two worlds, two lives, and greedy man that he was, thought he could have both.

Jarret had been in New York barely a week when letters from a woman started arriving from Istanbul: violet ink, feminine hand writing, fine stationery with a royal crest on it. He opened and read them impassively in front of Amy but never said a word about them. She made up her mind never to ask about the woman in Istanbul who wrote with violet ink. But something happened that made her change her mind.

Fee called. It seemed odd to speak to him from New York. He wanted to speak to Jarret who was not there. Fee was as always polite and charming, thanking Amy for taking such good care of Jarret who had it seemed been writing glowing letters about her and the New York art world every day. She thought it odd that she had never seen him put pen to paper.

'When is he coming home, Amy?'

'I don't know, Fee.'

'He's supposed to be here the day after tomorrow. Will you tell him he's expected?'

The news rendered her speechless. Jarret had said nothing about leaving so soon.

'Amy, tell him I can't be responsible for the consequences if he is not.' And Fee hung up.

When Jarret returned home, she gave him the message and Jarret made light of it. Two days later the telephone rang and when Amy heard a woman's voice she passed the telephone on to Jarret and took her hat and coat and left the flat. On her return the first thing she said to him was, 'Is that woman in love with you, Jarret?'

'That woman is seventy-five years old if she is a day,' was his answer.

'Jarret, I didn't ask her age. I want you to tell me if you're in love with someone else?'

'If I was, I would.'

They lived a blissfully happy existence, ignoring the daily letters and occasional phone call from Fee. And then one morning she awakened and for the first time since his arrival in New York, Jarret had awakened before her and was gone.

194

He called her from the airport. 'My plane leaves in twenty minutes. I didn't know how to tell you and I couldn't say goodbye. Thank you for everything. I love you just as much as I lust after you. Don't say anything, please. Write to me in Istanbul. God bless.'

Chapter 13

Extraordinary. There was actually no other word to describe how once Jarret had gone there was not the least sign in the flat that he had ever lived there with her. Her initial reaction was that a light in her life had been extinguished. She felt the world as huge, dark, a place of nothingness. She could not prevent uncontrollable floods of tears. Amy realised that she had sustained a serious shock, one she had mistakenly thought she had been prepared to handle. Struggling against falling into a lonely vacant place where she might vanish forever, she left her bed in search of something of his, any little thing to cling to that he might have left behind.

It was during those frantic and insane hours, searching wildly through the flat, that slowly her hysteria subsided. The hyperventilating eased, though it would take her several more hours before she could breathe normally with no relapses, and her body returned from its dehydrated state, having consumed gallons of water.

Only then could she crawl into bed and face the truth of it: her sexual life was over until her lover returned. That passionate love for him would have to be tamed, put on the back burner of her life, kept alive through distance and time as she had done the last time they had parted. The realist in Amy conquered the desperate romantic, and exhausted she fell into a deep and troubled sleep.

It was nightfall when she awoke, hurt, lonely for Jarret, but very much more in control of things. She switched on the lamps. The room was a wreck. She straightened up a few things, laid the fire and put a match to it. She made the bed and then went to the bathroom where she drew a bath, dropping almond and rose and gardenia oils into the water. She sat with hot scented bathwater up to her neck, sponging herself, thinking of him, the good and the bad Jarret Sparrow that she loved. His handsome face, as vivid as if he were there in front of her, was a fact of life for her and that was that.

Out of the bath, with a freshly made up face and dressed in her terrycloth robe, she continued to put her flat in order and marvelled that there was not a trace of him there. He had forgotten nothing, not a toothbrush or a sock. He had taken every brochure from every exhibition, every pencil, paint brush, every last one of the bits and pieces people had given him, the things he had bought. He had left her nothing.

'Every painting I paint is yours,' he liked to tell her. There was not a painting of his in her flat. Not a watercolour, a pastel or a pencil sketch. How clever he had been to have packed everything away without her realising it. Not to have dropped a hint by word or action that his departure was imminent. The sex the night before, his protestations of love, were no more and no less passionate, wildly adventurous and as thrilling as ever they had been.

No sad songs for Amy. No self-pity for the loss of the man she knew she could never really call her own. Only gratitude and joyfulness that she and Jarret had had the best time ever together. Three weeks of erotic madness and love that would bind them together forever was a better song to sing. She had lived with those lonely nights without sex before, she could live without them until his return. She had her own life and career to get on with just as he had his. So be it.

And so it was.

There were career and house moves and people to see and in time even men's invitations to accept and enjoy. There were marvellous letters from Jarret, the first few more erotic than he had ever written to her before. They were sexy and provocative and clearly written to remind her what she was missing and that what they had together could never be replaced with other partners. She believed him. There were other letters about his work and the people who passed through his life. It seemed that now at least he was sharing some of his life with her even though they were apart. There were postcards and the odd rare letter from Fee too.

My dearest Amy,
We talk about you all the time. Jarret is thrilled about the coming exhibition in New York. He has been working on getting that for years and deserves it. His new work is exciting, very well received by a Parisian dealer who was here last week – charming woman who's besotted with Jarret and his work. They spend a great deal of time together mapping out a campaign for exhibiting a show in Paris, and bringing round several men looking for things

198

*for the next Venice Biennale. What a coup if he gets in! She has
a house on a Greek island. We're going there to talk about
painting a mural for her. Hope you are well.*

    All love,
      Fee

Amy dearest,
*The unthinkable, my prayers have been answered! Savannah has
agreed to see Jarret. We are off to London. It would be so good
for his career if they were able to squelch these ugly rumours
that have been circulating since the break up. They have done no
good for either of our reputations.*

    Fee

    PS Jarret sends love.

What ugly rumours? Bad reputations? What were they keeping from
her? What was Fee hinting at?

    That letter upset Amy. She knew that Fee had sent it to do just that.
In letters from Jarret he told her how Fee adored her and how much he
looked forward to seeing her again but could not understand why Jarret
had not returned sooner to Istanbul. He blamed Amy. 'Be cautious in
what you write about us to Fee. I don't want him upset, or you for that
matter,' he had told her in one letter. In another his words had been:

> *Fee blames you for keeping me in New York longer than I should
> have stayed there, for my ignoring our friends. He can understand
> my weakness for you and is happy we have such an erotic love
> going for us, but thinks that will soon pass. He does not
> understand that how we feel about each other will not interfere
> with his and my plans or our lives. Have no fear, pay little
> attention to what he writes. You and I know it will not pass, that
> you love me, you're always going to love me.*

Who was telling the truth? Fee? Jarret? Was Savannah back in Jarret's
life? The very thought of it was frightening because without the truth
Amy didn't really know where she belonged. The Parisian art dealer?
Fee had implied an affair. Savannah? He was maintaining there was a
great love that had never died. Amy did not want to deal with loss and
jealousy. She called Jarret in Istanbul.

His voice. The very sound sent ripples of pleasure through her body.

'Oh, I'm so glad to hear your voice.'

'Amy?'

'Yes, of course it's Amy. How are you, darling?'

'How extravagant of you to call, but how good to hear your voice.'

'I miss you terribly.'

'I know what you miss.' There was a naughty lilt in his voice.

'This is not an erotic telephone call, Jarret.'

'Isn't it?'

'Well, it might be,' she admitted, and then couldn't help but laugh.

'Why are you laughing?' he asked, the amusement still in his voice.

'Because I find myself in a ludicrous situation. Me in New York, you in Istanbul, and with all that we should be talking about, it's sex through the trans-Atlantic telephone cables that says it all.'

'We're powerful stuff together in that department, you must agree?'

'Oh, I agree.'

'But?'

'But? But are we coming? Are we in the throes of great sex? Do you have me pinned beneath you while you take me leisurely with every deep thrust and mark me your own? It's too long since you filled me so completely and professed love for me. How crass to remind me how awesomely powerful the sex is between us. It sounds as if there is nothing else.'

'You see, this *is* an erotic conversation. A pretty good one! Your voice, your anger, and quite a sexy and vivid description of what we're like together. You've put me in a state. Would that you were here!'

'Would that I was.'

'What's wrong, Amy? You haven't replaced me? You're not thinking of leaving me?' The laughter was no longer in his voice. He had at last understood that something was wrong between them.

'I want you to tell me about you and Savannah.'

'Savannah has nothing to do with us.'

'I don't believe you. Fee implies that she is still the most important woman in your life.'

'You know differently.'

'Do I? She's always there, like the spectre at the feast.'

'Don't talk about her like that. And this is not a conversation to have on the telephone.'

'Then we'll have it when we're together. We'll talk her out of our lives once and for all. That is, if we still have a life together?'

'What's this all about? You *are* going to leave me. You can't! You love me too much and I want you to. Is there someone else?'

'No.'

'You swear that there isn't?'

'Can you swear that there is no one else in your life?'

'Yes. There is no woman in my life who means what you do to me, and you know that's true. I don't even know how you can question it. Those three weeks in New York, did they mean so little to you?'

'You know what they meant to me, Jarret.'

'I wish I was there with you right now. I would make love to you and tell you I miss you, even more than you miss me, and then I would show you in bed, take you to that magical place of erotic dreams and sexual oblivion. This separation is no easier for me than it is for you. A dozen times I wanted to hop on a plane and rush to New York to be with you.'

'Truly?'

'Yes, truly.'

'Is the Parisian art dealer you've been spending so much time with beautiful?'

'Yes, very.'

'I don't think I needed to hear that.'

'You did ask me.'

'Fee says she is besotted with you.'

'Yes, she is. She's beautiful and sexy and she's clever and she's business. I'm not in love with her. My heart and my passion lie in New York with you.'

'When next we're together, Jarret, there are many things I want to understand about the life you live. Do you promise me we'll have that talk?'

'My dearest heart, I have nothing to hide. Of course, when we next meet.'

As chance would have it six weeks after that telephone conversation they did meet but they did not play the truth game that Jarret had claimed they would. The time and the place were wrong. They had barely forty-eight hours together and the moment they clapped eyes upon one another the old magic was there, passion and love moved in and displaced all doubts.

It happened when quite suddenly Amy was called to Amsterdam to address the board of governors of the museum that was sponsoring the world tour she was organising. The meetings were scheduled for a

201

Thursday through to the following Wednesday which gave her a free forty-eight hours over the weekend. Amy tracked Jarret down. He and Fee were in Paris. They had two almost perfect days together there, marred only by Jarret's not extending her an invitation to stay with him in his flat. The excuse had been that Fee was there and it was too small for the three of them. Even though Fee had been charming and as amusing as ever she would have preferred not to have had to share her short time with Jarret, which she had been obliged to do. But the hours snatched in the day to rush back to her room in the hotel with Jarret for afternoon sex, and the nights, wildly erotic and full of passion, were newly fresh and vital. They were happier than they had ever been. Fee, once out of Amy's sight, was out of her mind.

The day she left to return to Amsterdam, Fee and Jarret left for Istanbul. Amy had hinted that she could manage several more days away from New York to be with Jarret, but no invitation for her to stay with him had been forthcoming.

He had actually said, 'Too bad my work schedule doesn't allow you to come and stay with us on the Bosphorus.'

Things were not going very well in Amsterdam and this was no time for Amy to get upset by Jarret and Fee's not very discreet hint that she was not welcome in their house in Turkey. So she let that pass, aware more than ever that there would come a day when she could no longer carry on her love affair with peace at any price as the linchpin holding her and Jarret together.

Amy returned to New York more calm and realistic about Jarret than she had been in several months. She loved him as much as ever but liked him less. Having seen him again with Fee on the scene, she came to understand, when she could distance herself from him, when he was physically out of sight and could not smile at her, caress her cheek, was not insinuating sexual passion and undying love for her, that there was something unacceptable about her lover.

Amy was settled into her new flat. It was five times the size of her bed sit, the rooms large and impressive. It was in an older Park Avenue building that she had only just been able to afford and that because it was rent-controlled and she sub-leased it from a friend who was moving to Rome. Her contract for the book and travelling exhibition had been signed months before and the news had been out in the art world for some time. It had brought, just as she'd thought it might, a great many new people into her life. Suddenly they were interested in her and her work. That hardly fazed Amy, who knew very well how fickle the art

202

world was. To be queen for a day in it held no interest for her. She had hired a part-time secretary and a part-time assistant and did what she was used to doing – staying as much in the background of things as possible, tending to the work in hand.

The only people who appeared to be really pleased for her if not impressed were Jarret and Fee. It was for the most part the other way round with everyone else. Fee had commented, 'If it happens it will be very good for your career. But will it happen?' It was then that she realised that he and Jarret saw her as insignificant in the art world, and certainly not someone who would further their careers.

So just how did they see her? Amy felt quite ill when the answer came to her. As no more than Fee had wanted her to be: a sexual diversion to answer Jarret's needs, a muse when he needed one, a woman when he wanted one, someone who would fall slavishly in love and would make no demands. A lady easily disposed of. Only one thing had gone wrong – something that Fee, playing pimp for Jarret that day he'd picked her up in Venice, had not counted on – Jarret was in love rather than infatuated, something Fee had never expected to have to deal with.

The months before Jarret's return were endlessly busy for Amy, and the art world was more frenetic than ever. Every gallery was now on the verge of taking new and exciting painters on board, but they were behaving as if they were playing Russian Roulette.

The New York dealers had a tight grip on the world art market, and in particular Modern American art. Millions upon millions of dollars were at stake and they had no intention of losing that or their clients by backing the wrong new -ism in art.

By the time Jarret arrived in New York for his one-man show the art scene was bursting with vitality, anxiety and power plays between dealers, artists, critics and museum curators, while the paying patrons were waiting and watching in the wings, fistfuls of dollars held tight.

But despite the precarious feeling of the time there was also a great deal of fun to be had. One could go to a party or two or three practically every night of the week: a gallery *vernissage*, the private view of an exhibition, to a showing in an artist's studio since he had no dealer. There was so much new and innovative that there were few dealing or collecting or writing or theorising in the art world who didn't go to every party they could, look at all that was on offer, for fear of missing out on the newest discovery. This was the beginning of the 1960s, a new decade where everything was in transition and had somewhere to go. It was a thrilling time, like jumping into the deep end, this breaking away from an era that had run its course.

Things were very different when Jarret arrived in New York this time. Amy was under enormous pressure. The backers of her world tour project were sceptical about the timing of the exhibition and were now talking of delaying it for another year, possibly two – an impossible situation for Amy who was walking a financial tight rope. She had budgeted for a two-year project. If they were to delay payments to her she would be in serious trouble, and what was worse so would others who were working on the project with her. She had obligations and Amy took her obligations seriously.

But she wanted nothing to cloud her time with Jarret and instinct told her to keep her problems to herself.

Amy saw the long, sleek, black limousine glide up to the entrance to her building. It was just before noon, the sun was bright but it was bitterly cold outside. People were rushing up and down the avenue muffled against the cold and the icy winds that blew off the rivers surrounding the island of Manhattan. It was a typical New York City winter scene: white smoke twirling up from every car's exhaust, steam rising from the mysterious caverns under the man hole covers. There had been a blizzard on New Year's Eve and snow was still piled high on the islands that ran down the centre of Park Avenue, hiding nearly half of the Christmas trees planted there that were still up and twinkling with coloured lights.

Amy had been looking out of the window for the past half hour waiting anxiously for her first sight of Jarret. Not having previously told her exactly when he was arriving, this time he had called from the airport to say he was on his way and had a ride into the city with a friend he had met on the plane.

She sensed the moment the Cadillac pulled up to the kerb that Jarret would step from it. The chauffeur opened the door for him. She saw the same black coat with its velvet collar, the same handsome face, big, broad-shouldered Jarret, wearing no hat, no scarf, no gloves, his longish hair whipped by the wind. The same devastatingly handsome smile. She watched as the chauffeur went to the boot of the car to get his things: the same small battered suitcase and a portfolio, black, worn and tied with string. A sable-clad arm and a black kidskin-gloved hand was held out from the darkness of the limousine. Jarret lowered his head and kissed the hand. The gentleman painter was back in town.

Amy actually laughed aloud. He waited for the car to pull away from the kerb and then looked up at the building. She didn't know why but she jumped away so he wouldn't see her. It seemed the right thing to do. Instinctively she felt he would never mention the woman in the sable coat who had given him a ride in from the airport.

There was something easier about this reunion than the last one in New York. She opened the door to the flat and he put down his small case and the portfolio, then picked her up in his arms and carried her into the drawing-room, kicking the door closed behind him.

It was marvellous, his being back in her life again, to have sex with someone she loved, reaching out together, always that little bit further into the erotic world they created for themselves where they could be totally free. With every sexual act Amy knew she was laying down her life for love with this man. She could deny him nothing of herself. The reward she reaped from such total submission was to retain Jarret's complete and utter passion for her. He thrived on her giving, but for a clever woman she was somehow unaware that although he professed everything he was belonged to her, every painting he painted was for her, the reality was that he gave nothing, shared nothing, voluntarily. Whatever love he did give her, whatever great sex they had together, it was in spite of himself, against his will. Cupid had played a trick on him, and he resented it.

It was after his *vernissage*, which was a great success though the exhibition itself was only moderately well received by the critics and sales were few, that Amy began to see signs of resentment that he was no longer bothering to keep hidden. They were small things, and at first difficult to understand.

Although he had always behaved impeccably with her, she began to feel that loving her was a strain on him. He was constantly bringing new people into their life to ease the powerful hold their togetherness had over him. She gave small intimate dinner parties with fascinating people from the art world; parties that were interesting and amusing, where great food was served. Jarret would insist on arriving with one of the guests and would leave with another, only to return to her in the early hours of the morning. Yet at other times at these parties, he would flirt outrageously with her and make it clear that they were very much together. He professed himself impressed by her artistic judgement and agreed to introduce her to people who might further her in her career, but did it in such a way as to make her feel he was trying to distance her, be less intimate with her.

205

There were also people and events in his life in New York that he refused to share with her. The beautiful French art dealer arrived from Paris to do the art scene and Jarret squired her round everywhere. Peggy arrived from Venice in time for his *vernissage*, and though he introduced Amy to her he saw to it that they never met again. When Peggy called the gallery for Jarret, he was found by Walter and would snap to attention. He charmed and danced round the art scene, showing up at every important exhibition with either Peggy or Amy, and that was indeed a dazzling year to view paintings. Jim Dine, Jasper Johns, Lichtenstein, Lindner, Arman, John Chamberlain and Claes Oldenberg were some of the artists shaking the New York art market by the tail.

The more Jarret became steeped in the New York art scene, the more restless he became, the more selfish and the more greedy. And something else had changed from the first time they had lived together – he was in closer contact with Fee. There were letters and phone calls from him three or four times a week. And the user of the violet-coloured ink? A letter at least twice a week, sent to the gallery but left on the chest of drawers in Amy's bedroom. None of this was ever discussed with her and Fee's postcards to her had stopped.

In many ways they were happier together. They laughed a great deal more and Jarret could still dazzle her with his charm. The sex was never better. People were affected by them. There was something outstandingly romantic about their love affair. It was, try as they might, impossible to hide. At this time a small scene took place in their lives that was to shake them both into a realisation of how deep their feelings for each other ran, in spite of the indications that their love was in trouble.

Amy had a friend, Andy Warhol, someone she advised on the purchase of paintings. He was the most singularly unattractive person she had ever met, and made even more so by the cheap, nasty white wigs he wore which always looked as if they needed a wash; a combing appeared to be impossible. He was a very talented artist who illustrated shoes in watercolour for a department store, and did twee little books for twee little shops like Serendipity where you could buy amusing tat – anything from a hat with an ostrich feather in it to a back scratcher studded with rhinestones – and where you could be served an extravagant ice cream concoction in an oversized champagne glass. He was a commercial artist and collector of art, artefacts and trash. He did so love trash! Andy was obsessed with the idea that Amy could tell him what to paint then he could be as famous a painter as any of

206

the artists whose work she was advising him to buy, rather than a public relations pet, hacking out what he did best, decorative illustrations.

Andy was always dazzled by other people's lives, other people's romances, and especially their sex lives. He particularly enjoyed hearing about celebrities or beautiful people, men and women alike.

The year before when Jarret had been in New York and he and Amy had been keeping themselves pretty much to themselves in her bed sit, they had one day bumped into Andy at an exhibition at the Betty Parsons Gallery. He was instantly dazzled by Jarret, and cruelly Jarret took advantage of that and turned on the charm. To watch them together was to view beauty seducing the beast. There was something pathetic about the contrast between the two men. Andy became obsessed by Amy and Jarret's love affair.

After Jarret had left New York, Andy would endlessly talk about her and Jarret and how romantic and beautiful they were together. He would beg to be told intimate details of their sex life which Amy would decline to discuss. The only thing that would stop him persecuting her was Amy's promise that on Jarret's return she would see to it that they met up with Andy for an ice cream at Serendipity. He held her to that promise.

Andy was working on a new book of drawings, *Famous Feet*, and wanted Jarret and Amy as models, assuring them they would be in good company as other famous people had agreed to sit for him. 'Feet, just feet,' he assured them. For all his vacuous personality Andy knew how to push. He never gave up. Jarret, much to Amy's surprise, agreed that they would sit for Andy.

The following Sunday morning he arrived at Amy's apartment with two friends, Ted and John. They were friends of Amy's too, and they and Andy often did the galleries with her on a Saturday. John was all apologies about crashing in on them, telling her that Andy was so nervous about being alone with them that he'd insisted that the two men be there. They had little choice in the matter and had thought they would get Andy there and then leave. Amy insisted they stay for the fun.

Coffee was made. They had brought warm fresh croissants. Jarret was amused and charmed by the flattery: the three of them had been to his show. Andy had ten thousand questions that he droned out in that thin voice of his, interrupting the conversation at the oddest moments with his inane queries.

Finally, shoes, socks and stockings dispensed with, Amy and Jarret sat for Andy. His foot, her foot. But Andy thought that not quite right: it had to be their feet together, her left, his right, entwined. And so Amy sat on Jarret's lap, their legs entwined, and Andy did his drawing during a quite mad and amusing conversation. Amy thought the whole morning quite bizarre. After they'd left Jarret said, 'There is something very surreal about that creature. And, you know, he really does believe that you can make him the most famous painter in the world. Will you?'

'Probably. If he doesn't stop pestering me,' she answered.

Chapter 14

That afternoon Jarret was very quiet and pensive. Every so often he would suddenly gaze at Amy and make the odd remark, such as, 'You are incredibly naive, I never realised that.'

'Oh, do you really think so?'

'You're very American. Basically bourgeois.'

'I don't consider myself bourgeois. I don't think I live a bourgeois life.'

'Most bourgeois don't! I think I might just prove you wrong. There's so much of real life that you're ignorant of, could never handle. You've never lost your innocence. It's part of your attraction. You should love me less.'

'Why? So I could give you a reason to abandon me?'

Amy had not the least idea where that came from. She said it instinctively, without thought, and was appalled by the look on his face. She had caught him out. That was exactly what he wished for, to be able to give her up. She felt so ill she had to leave the room. She walked past him and patted him on the shoulder. 'I'm going to take a nap,' she told him.

The signs were there; his love for her was on the wane, if not his lust. And without that love, as great as the sex was, their relationship was evolving into something less beautiful, more sad, that Amy tried to ignore. Several people warned her; friends not even of hers but his to whom she had now become close, a French girl who had confessed during a girls' lunch that she envied Amy because Jarret loved her, but: 'He will hurt you, the way he hurts everyone. He'll take everything from you and leave you empty and alone when he's had everything he can get out of you, and you won't even know how he did it. Please don't think I say this because I'm jealous of you. I am envious but not jealous because I know the pain you'll feel when your affair is over and would wish that on no one. He ruins women, and forever. You don't know him.'

209

'I think I do.'

'So did I. What do you know about him? You can't begin to fathom the selfishness of Jarret and Fee. The lengths to which they will go to get what they want out of art and life. They are without morals or heart. They do unimaginably evil things.'

'I can't believe that. Evil's a strong word.'

'Believe me, I know what I'm talking about. Evil is exactly the right word. Have you ever asked either of them for anything?'

Amy had to think. Amazingly she had not. She answered, 'It's not in my nature to ask for things.'

'I hope the day never comes when you have to! Those men are not givers, and in love as Jarret may be with you, he will refuse you in the nicest way.'

Amy was angry. This was not a conversation she wished to have, she wanted to cut it short. 'You're frightening me by describing a man I don't know. I know you mean well but can we change the subject?'

'All right. But ask him about the Contessa Armida Montevicini, his relationship with her and the *yalis*. I can't believe you know what Fee and he have done to her. Ask him how he managed to get all of his wife's fortune, to the extent of leaving her penniless and homeless when her money had bought three residences for them. He then ruined her reputation so as to deprive her of friends too. Ask him about how he used to make love to her mother, and still does. How he took Savannah in marriage but had a settlement and some bizarre agreement from Mama first. And he didn't do all this alone, Amy. Fee with his Byzantine mind masterminds their lifestyle together. Incredibly they get everything they want, leaving a trail of used-up and broken people in their wake. And still they manage to come out the good guys! They get away with their evil doings and are never caught out or taken to task. That should show you how professional at it they are. You were a mistake that never fitted into their scheme of things. They won't be forgiving about that. I won't go on. Just promise me you will confront him?'

'Have you seen this first hand, heard this from these women? Or from Fee or Jarret's mouth?'

'No, from reliable rumours that they are not even embarrassed about.'

'Rumours.' It was very nearly a shout. 'Do you actually think I could confront Jarret with a pack of rumours? He has given me no reason to question him about anything. He has always been honest about his feelings for me, to what extent they do and do not go. I should hope by now we have our love worked out.'

'Forgive me, Amy, but close your heart and open your eyes.'

When she arrived home she was still disturbed about what the French girl had had to say. She had previously heard mere hints and been given subtle warnings about her love affair with Jarret, mostly from men friends who warned her that on both sides of the Atlantic he had the reputation of being the most clever of gigolos, appearing a most vulnerable and charming man, dedicated to art and all things beautiful. And Fee? Was he brother, lover, mentor? No one really knew. But no one had ever come out calling either of them evil before.

Problems seemed to be piling up one after another for Amy. The date of the world tour of American art had been officially changed. That was a disaster. At five o'clock, after her lunch with Colette, there was a call from her landlord in Rome. The building had been sold and the flat with it.

They were old friends, and after he'd explained the situation at length to Amy she could see that he had little choice but to evict her. It was a dreadful situation for them both. In a matter of hours her world seemed to be collapsing around her.

Jarret came home at about seven o'clock. It didn't take him long to sense that something was wrong. 'You look upset.'

'I am. I've had a pig of a day.'

'What's happened?'

She tried to play down how disastrous her news was. 'The dates are changed for the tour and that means the book will be delayed for the same length of time.'

'Does that pose a real problem for you?'

'Yes, very real.'

'Well, you're a clever girl. You'll work it out.'

'Yes, I suppose I will. But almost worse, I'm going to have to move.'

'You have had a bad day! Let's light the fire and open a bottle of wine and I'll cheer you up by telling you about my day. I sold a painting.'

Amy was so glad for Jarret she forgot her own troubles. He took her by the hand and together they sat on the settee in front of the fire. She felt utterly exhausted and collapsed against him. He placed an arm round her and they drank their wine while he told her about the sale and of a new young painter he had met. Jarret was impressed by the young man and his work and asked if he could bring him round to meet Amy. It was all comfortable, cosy chit-chat, Jarret full of enthusiasm.

Only two things marred the evening for her. Just before they went to bed, he asked, 'Weren't you having lunch today with Colette?'

Here was her moment to say something about those rumours, to ask the questions that were troubling her. But she couldn't bear to give up the joy of being in his arms.

She answered, 'Yes, I wish you had been with us,' and quickly changed the subject.

The other thing to mar her bliss with Jarret happened in the early hours of the morning after a night sated with sex. In a half sleep he casually announced, 'I'm going to Palm Beach tomorrow. Four or five days, a week at the most. Ginger Woodruff has invited me, wants to introduce me to a gallery owner down there.'

In the morning she watched him pack his few belongings and worked hard trying to keep the panic out of her eyes and voice. For the first time since she'd known him she wanted to ask Jarret for something. Please give up Palm Beach, stay with me. But Colette's warning was too fresh in her mind and she could not bear the thought of what might happen when he refused. It would be her moment of truth, the time when she would have to give him up, and she knew that she couldn't.

Amy rationalised that it was a good thing that Jarret was away and she wasn't distracted by him. It would give her a chance to concentrate on her problems, make decisions as to how to cut back to the bone. Within days she knew what had to be done. The staff would immediately have to be made redundant. Her contract remained firm, as originally written, except for the change of date which meant she still had a plum of a job but a cash flow problem. The money would not even begin to roll in for at least two years. The advance she had had on it was already used up; further staggered payments which would have kept her going should have come in quarterly, with one due three weeks before. Now she was in debt, and in thirty days would be without a roof over her head or a current job.

How did all this happen to her? Where could she go? If only she had kept the Easthampton house, she could have worked from there. But Amy didn't believe in 'if onlys'. She would have to ask to be taken in for a while by a friend. Unless of course Jarret would ask her to go and live with him. To stay with a lover who had all those rooms in all those houses and a flat in Paris did seem the natural thing to happen. Or there was home to her family. Amy nearly laughed aloud. That was no longer an option.

She had invited her mother and father to the house warming party

212

she had given a few days after Jarret's arrival in the city. It had been a wonderful party with everyone having a good time. Everyone except her parents.

Amy could not fault Jarret who had made the most tremendous effort to charm Sylvia and Arthur Ross, both out of their depth at the party. Sylvia found a place for Arthur to sit and he never moved from the wing chair. She brought him wine and food, and when Amy wanted to take him round and introduce him to people, Sylvia would not allow it. She spoke to two or three people and after that stood alone, face dark and brooding. No drink, no food for her. Clearly she was not there for fun.

It was then that Jarret drew Amy away from a group of people she was talking to and told her, 'I think you have a serious problem about to break – your mother, she hates me! Best you try and smooth things over before she ruins the party with her scowls.'

Amy went to Sylvia immediately. 'Mother, no wine? Let me get you a glass,' she said, smiling.

'I don't want a drink.'

'Some food then?'

'I don't want any food. Is that man living here with you?'

'Jarret? He does have a name, Mother.'

'I don't like his name and I don't like him.'

'Well, that's too bad, dear, because I do, very much.'

'And I don't like this place and I don't like your hair, you should cut it.'

'Why are you so angry, Mother? I'm so happy. Can't you be happy for me?'

'You should be ashamed of yourself, loving a man like that and acting so proud about it. You look as if you're wearing your sex life on your sleeve, flaunting it like some badge of honour. The way you look at each other – it's all too disgusting. When it ends in tears, don't think you can come running home to me. You live with him, you forfeit your father and me and home. I don't know you like this! In love, big deal. He's not what I wanted for you.'

'He's my choice, Mother.'

'Then live with it. We're leaving.' And she walked away.

Now Amy had no family, no home to go back to. Jarret would be away five days. Amy worked very hard to get things on the move in such a way that when he returned the upheavals in her life would not be too evident. All she really wanted was for things in the flat to appear

213

as normal as possible so that she and Jarret could keep up life together without disruption until he left for Europe.

The first evening after his return Jarret was especially amorous and lustful. Their erotic night was filled with words of love and praise for what they shared together. It set just the right tone for troubled times ahead for her.

When she was with Jarret she knew she was not alone, she was sharing that most intimate part of herself and all her erotic fantasies with a man who loved and appreciated every nuance of lust he brought out in her. Work and troubles were only a part of her life; she also had love and lust from a man who adored her and whom she adored. There was someone there in her troubled life to fall back on.

Her love fed Jarret and his ego, her lust fired his libido, and he was able to say things to her from the heart, the soul, some inner self that he was helpless to hold back. He both loved and hated her for this because he had declared a long, long time ago that for him that kind of love was forbidden.

In the days that followed his return Jarret seemed unable to get enough of Amy. They were some of the best of the times they had ever had together. During those days and nights they saw a great deal of the young artist Jarret had befriended. It took hardly any time at all to see the young man, Philip, was dazzled by Amy and Jarret as a couple. He was of a younger generation and very outspoken, open as they had never been about all things, including sex. They talked about everything and how exciting a time it was they were living in, what it was like to be as sexually free as his generation. In the evenings they drank a great deal. Most times Philip was too drunk to leave and so slept over at Amy's flat.

The first morning he crawled into bed with them Amy was shocked to find another naked rampant man with his arms round her. Nothing happened that was untoward except that he kept telling Amy what a great body she had and that he wanted to make love to her. Another time he was more bold, told them he wanted to watch his two favourite people fucking, coming together. The easiest explanation for their having Philip around them so much of the time was that Jarret and Amy got used to him and nothing he said or wanted surprised them.

One night, weeks after he had become a part of their life, they all drank much too much. They were out of control. The three of them were lying on the floor in front of the fire. Jarret opened Amy's blouse and caressed her naked breasts, licking them and sucking her nipples.

214

Amy was in an alcoholic stupor. Everything was hazy, as if she were looking through a soft focus lens. It felt wonderful. Jarret looked sublimely happy and was so tender.

Only when she heard Philip's voice did she realise that he too was holding her in his arms, and he too was caressing her breasts.

'From the first time I saw you, I thought you were the sexiest woman I'd ever met. I wanted you. All I've dreamed about since I met you was fucking you. Oh, God, I want to be inside you. To feel the power and warmth, the softness of your most intimate self,' he told her in whispers filled with real passion.

Jarret was removing her blouse. 'Please, we want to fuck you, both of us, at the same time. Do it for us, for me, Amy, because you love me?'

It was extraordinarily erotic to have two men adoring you, desperate to make erotic love to you, want to take possession of you, ensure that you would reap the greatest sexual pleasure imaginable from their lust for you. What woman would not lose herself in lasciviousness, and acquiesce to her lover's pleadings?

Amy knew just as the men did that she could deny Jarret nothing. She kept telling herself she was a woman with a strong libido, and this was her sexual fantasy come true. Here indeed was a once-in-a-lifetime erotic adventure. Two sets of hands and lips, two mouths, two penises to enter her together, at the same time.

They were tender lovers, they were sweet, they were pure lust. Hours passed and they lost themselves in sex, but their passion was not only sexual. They recited exquisite love poems to her as they took her further and further down the road to oblivion, three people making love to each other. All was bliss until in the early hours after dawn the alcoholic haze began to wear off. It was during the time Amy was being riven by Philip from behind while Jarret took her from the front as she lay on her side. Jarret had of course been right when he told her she would never have experienced anything as sensational as having sex with two men to the same beat, of being the recipient of three people coming inside her together, or how raunchy it would be for her to flow with their many orgasms.

She was kissing Jarret. It was only Jarret that she wanted. For him only did she feel deep and abiding love. He was enough for her, had always been enough for her, and yet she was allowing another man to pleasure her. She had agreed to enter a world of depravity for Jarret, not because she wanted Philip or because she had any feelings for

215

him. She had merely used him as a stud to please her lover. Amy found that, not her going to bed with two men, deplorable. Fear, raging fear for how low she had sunk for the love of Jarret, now took possession of her. She tried to extricate herself from the situation as quickly and gracefully as was possible. The men thought she was exhausted, which she was. They never guessed that it was not tiredness but fear for what she had done that put a close to this night of depravity.

It was a Sunday morning. The three of them had breakfast together and miraculously there was no embarrassment. Not a word was spoken about the night before. The only thing Philip said as he was leaving the flat was, 'I drank too much, we all did, but I want you both to know it wasn't just sex. I was making love to you. I don't think I'll ever meet two lovers like you again. One always senses that about you two, but now I know it.' And then he was gone.

A few hours later three dozen white lilies arrived. No note, merely a white card that said, 'Thank you.'

As Amy was placing them in water, she turned to Jarret and told him, 'Don't ever ask me to do that again.'

There was a certain firmness in her voice, a look of determination in her eyes. He went to stand next to her and his only reply was, 'I thought you might say that.' Then he kissed her on the cheek and walked from the room. She was grateful he had not called her bourgeois.

A staff meeting had been called by Amy where she explained the situation and made her assistants redundant, giving them two months' pay each. Amy felt sad and depressed. She put on a brave face for Jarret, but her stress was visible. They didn't talk about it.

The eviction notice had been nailed to the door of the flat. It was Jarret who had torn it off and handed it to Amy one evening when they came in from a dinner party.

The bills were piling up on her desk and she was calling people, asking for longer to pay them. Her creditors were sympathetic and gave her time. She would sell everything she had except for her library and her clothes. That would get her out of debt but leave her penniless. The most dreadful thing was that, try as she might, she could not see this as a mere hiccup, and part of the reason for that was that her lifestyle would end and she would no longer be able to live with Jarret when he came to New York.

Jarret had done what he had always done when he was living with Amy: left his mark everywhere in the flat, making it his own. When he was there she thought of it as their flat, and he was comfortable to think of it that way too when it suited him.

It was about a week after their night with Philip. Amy was sitting by the fire going over the list of her belongings that would be going to auction, when Jarret sat on the arm of her chair.

'Amy, did you really mean it? That I can have that tea pot I like so much?'

'Yes, if you like,' she answered him, looking up from her list as she crossed the tea pot off it.

'I'd like it for one of the rooms in the *yalis*. I think I can fit it into my case.'

Amy's heart felt cold, her mouth dry. He was leaving. This time she could not afford the self-indulgence of ranting and raving in despair. 'When are you going?' she asked.

'In two days' time. I was going to stay longer, but frankly I can't stand being in the middle of your problems. There is nothing I can do for you anyway. You're a clever girl, you'll work it all out, and I'll come back when things are better for you.'

He rose from the arm of the chair and walked through the flat to their bedroom. After several minutes she followed him and sat on the end of the bed, watching him take his case from the wardrobe, open it, and place it on the floor.

'Why are you packing now?'

'Easy does it. I have so many things to try and fit into my case, I thought I would start now to see if there's room otherwise I might have to borrow an extra one from you.'

'I'll need all my cases for my move.'

'Do you know where you're going?'

'To whoever will take me until I get things sorted out and a job.' She waited for him to say he had a place for her. That was just what she needed, to have somewhere ready and waiting for her at a distance from the mess she was in here, and to be with him, have him take care of her for a while. To go with her lover – what could be more natural?

He wasn't even evasive but looked her straight in the eyes and suggested, 'To your parents?'

There was a slight smirk on his lips, a nasty sound in his voice. Many had been the time since he had met her parents that he had reminded her what a common, rude and abusive mother she had.

'No, I guess not,' he told her now.

'Any other suggestions?' she asked, not feeling at all inclined to let him get away so easily as the last time.

'No. None.' His voice was hard and firm.

Amy had expected he would not be forthcoming with an invitation, but to hear it so unequivocally from his lips was a shock. She simply did not believe that in the end he could do it, walk out on her when she was in need and with not even a roof over her head.

'I'm going for a walk,' she told him, and left the flat.

When she finally returned home, he was already in bed. She undressed in front of him as she always did then bathed and put on a fresh nightgown and got into bed with him. Neither of them spoke until he took her in his arms and then it was sex talk, love talk. Amy listened and thought: What a strange thing love is. She knew that Jarret was worthless, without heart, that he had no scruples. Yet she was suffering at the point of torture because he was betraying her. Had he been betraying her all along?

She found her answer. It was shortly after he stood in the doorway to her flat, ready to leave for the airport, having told her, 'Remember, let me have an address where you'll be staying, I'll be back when things are good for you again. Write. This isn't goodbye, you love me too much for that, and you know how I feel about you.'

Once the door closed behind him, Amy collapsed into a chair. She was emotionally drained. She had been determined not to break down in front of him, to deny him nothing, not in their sex life or the love she had for him. She had carried on hanging on to her love for Jarret as if nothing had happened. He had gone away thinking that she would recover and forgive.

How had he done it? He had ruined her. No, to be more accurate, he had allowed her to ruin herself for the love of him.

Amy had never felt so alone and adrift as she did now without him there, without loving him. She wanted to weep but no tears came. She went to the bedroom and began straightening the room. He had bought new shirts. The cardboard and clear plastic packaging was flowing out of the waste basket. She emptied the basket into a larger one from the bathroom then emptied that one into the waste chute in the kitchen and returned to the bedroom. Her eyes fell on a scrunched-up ball of paper that had been left behind. She picked it up and sat down at her dressing table. The ball still in her hand, she stared into the mirror. She hardly recognised herself. If only she could weep and wash away this stranger she saw reflected back at her. She sat there for some time, unable to move.

Finally she flexed her fingers, releasing them from the tight nervous fist she had made of them, and the ball of scrunched-up paper fell on the dressing table. She picked it up again and without thought began straightening out the sheets of paper, three pieces of fine stationery. She smoothed them out as best she could and recognised the violet-coloured ink. It was one of the letters she had always been so curious about but had never read.

Jarret, my darling, my life,

I do not know what I would do without your letters. Such declarations of love and passion would make any woman's heart spin. To hear such protestations during our hours lost in lust is to be alive, young again. Where are you now? There is no replacement for the warmth of your body next to mine, your lips upon my breasts, your kisses. Every day you are away from my bed it is as if death is knocking at my door.

I read your letters and re-read them every day. How glorious to know you miss making love to me, that you too can hardly bear these separations so necessary for your work. They have broken down my resolve not to assign any more of the yalis *to you and Fee. Since you have declared that we shall be together till death do us part, there is no point to my resolve. What is mine is yours, and what is yours is mine anyway.*

In celebration of your return, I will do what you have been asking for so long: I will make over the west wing of the yalis *to you and Fee, and move myself and my personal effects into the servants' wing. As you so rightly say, what does it matter who owns what when I have the run of my house anyway, and you both intend to keep me and care for me for always? You and I, of course, will keep the bedroom we share. My heart would die if I had to give that up. There! My gift to you for loving me, for coming home, for missing the erotic life we share and because you love me as no other. Save for a few small shabby rooms, your own* yalis *on the Bosphorus awaits your arrival.*

All my love, my life
Armida

And now they came, the floods of tears. Amy's heart was broken. She felt as if she were crying not only for herself but for the Contessa

Armida, for Savannah, and for every other woman who had loved a man beyond reason, for every woman alive who had ever been betrayed by her lover.

LONDON, SONNING,

VENICE, ISTANBUL

1994

Chapter 15

Amy slipped from the past into the present to the constant muffled drone of the 'plane's engine – the same sound that had sent her into a half-dream where she had revisited her past. It had all been buried so deep, and been forgotten so very long ago. Incredible that she should remember it so vividly now. It had run through her mind like an old black and white B movie: a melodrama. Had it all really happened like that? Had she really been so weak? Had Fee and Jarret been so very evil? Or had time and memory done their work, distorted events?

Jarret Sparrow had been the great love of Amy's life to date, neither time nor memory could change that. Now, on a flight from Geneva to London, her denial was over. She could accept that truth and need never run away from it again.

Reliving that was the catharsis that set Amy free to love again on a grand scale once more, if she so chose. Until now, her moment of truth, she had never really understood that she had been struck down by the cruel love affair from which she had never wholly recovered.

Suddenly Amy's inner perspective changed. She felt lighter in spirit, as if there was cause for celebration. Leaning across the empty seat next to her, she looked up the aisle. The air stewards were chatting together. She caught their attention and an attendant hurried forward to her.

'A bottle of Krug, please. A half bottle if you have one.'

'Only full bottles of Krug, Miss Ross.'

'That'll do.'

'You won't be able to drink it leisurely. We're due to land in less than thirty minutes.'

'We won't worry about that, let's just call it a self-indulgent celebration.'

One glass of champagne and Amy used the plane's telephone next to her seat. She slipped her credit card into the slot and punched in Charles's private number at Claridge's. His butler answered the telephone.

'Hello, Raskin, it's Miss Ross. Is Sir Charles at home?'

It seemed like an age before she heard Charles's voice. 'How would you like to take me to lunch?'

'I'd rather take you to bed.'

'That might be managed.'

'This *is* Amy?'

'Yes, of course it is.' She couldn't help but laugh.

'It's years since you've said that.'

'I said might, not yes. Let's just see how lunch goes. That is if you're free?'

'I'll make myself free. Where are you?'

'Sky high, so to speak.'

'What are you talking about, Amy?'

'I'm on a flight from Geneva, landing in about half an hour.'

'I'll send a car for you.'

'Great, then I can drink as much of this champagne as I like.'

'Champagne on a flight? You never drink on planes.'

'A special occasion.'

'The end of your desert of a sex life?'

Amy refused to answer, merely laughed and pushed the disconnect button.

The man sitting in the aisle seat across from her leaned over and said with a broad smile, 'I hope you don't mind my saying so but you've got a great laugh.'

Amy smiled at him. 'Do you think so? I would have said distinctive. People don't forget it.'

'I shan't. A great-looking lady with joy in her soul who can laugh as you do. I would imagine you to be a woman few men forget. I know I won't.'

'But you don't even know me.'

'That's not to say I wouldn't like to. That's what it's about. A man sees a woman – on a plane, a train, in the street. She has a certain beauty, a vibrancy that's appealing to him. For a fleeting moment she captures his total attention. He's not made a move, the moment passes, and she vanishes from his life, but remains lodged in his psyche, a fantasy of erotic bliss, possibly even the *grand amour*.'

'You're a romantic.'

224

'I confess that I am.'

'I like romantic men, but they must be honest, kind, and very sweet. Are you such a man?' she teased.

'To the letter,' was his answer. He followed it with a broad smile.

Amy liked his face. In his youth he must have been an outstandingly handsome man. In middle age he was a ruggedly good-looking one. A man who'd skied off piste all his life, who'd sailed against the winds, an adventurer who'd loved dangerously. He wore his age well, every line; the folds that appeared in his face when he smiled showed character, sensuality, and his eyes were intelligent, mischievous and very much alive. Happy eyes. They seemed to speak, to say what Amy was thinking: 'It's time to love again.'

'Then I invite you to join me in a glass of champagne.'

He was very tall with a slender but muscular body dressed very well in an Armani dark grey double-breasted suit and wearing the perfect navy blue silk tie with minute white dots woven in it. He sat down next to her after telling the steward to bring another glass.

'I saw you at the airport with the de Boulets.'

'You know them?'

'Very well. I have a house on the lake close to theirs.'

'Then you live in Geneva?'

'No, not exclusively.'

The steward, having brought a glass for the man, filled it and recharged Amy's. They drank the perfectly chilled wine, and then he said, 'I wanted to ask you to join me for a drink several times.'

'What stopped you?'

'You. You seemed to drift off into another place, another time. To have asked you then would have been an intrusion. The older I get, the less I can face rejection. That place where you were, was it a good place?'

'The best and worst time of my life. I was revisiting it.'

'So you could let it go or so you could hang on to it?'

Amy looked intently at this handsome stranger. She smiled and said, 'That's an interesting question, one I would not have expected from a man with so smooth a line as you cast to hook my attention. Does it work every time?'

'Pretty much every time.' He was clearly enjoying himself and took a long draught from his glass. 'Do you always answer a question with a question?'

Amy reached across him to take the bottle of Krug and top up their glasses. He removed the bottle from her hand and while he was pouring she answered him. 'I don't think that's a particular habit of mine. As it happens it was to let go, hence the bottle of Krug in celebration. But what is more interesting is that I had pulled out of the memory box something I thought had long ago been discarded, something I had no idea had been dominating a certain segment of my life.'

'Great love affairs can do that. They never quite go away unless you can stand back, step out of your skin and see yourself and the affair as an observer, not the observed.'

'Why do you assume that it was a *grand amour*? It could have been a business deal, the experience of seeing a great work of art?'

'Yes, it could have been.'

They remained silent for some minutes, drinking champagne. Then without thinking Amy told him, 'The last twenty years of my life have been the best years of my life. I've achieved everything I wanted in my career. I have had wonderful lovers, happy times, peace and contentment. Then a few weeks ago, I had a dream. I dreamt about an old lover. He returned to claim me after nearly thirty years. It was an unpleasant dream, disturbing. Several days later, quite by chance, I met the man I jilted for the man in my dream. I hardly recognised him, had never thought of him from the very last time I spoke to him decades ago. What a coincidence that they should both appear in one form or another within days.

'The first chance in weeks I had to relax and calm my mind, empty it of all thought, was when I unstrapped my seat belt and leaned back in this seat. I closed my eyes and thought maybe now is the time to review, to remember. I had no idea I was holding on to anything from all those years ago.'

'And now you feel wonderful?'

'I felt wonderful when I got on the plane in Geneva. Now I feel as if some invisible string that had been tethering me has broken and I can sail with the wind.' Amy gave a deep sigh then laughed.

'And the man you jilted?'

'He sends flowers.'

'The man in the dream?'

'I think he was always a dream, but I wasn't asleep.'

'I think you should have lunch with me.'

'Why?'

'Decades are a long time to wait between great love affairs.'

226

'How are you so sure that I have waited?'

'Lovers, affairs. A woman as attractive as you has had many, I'm certain. But the *grand amour* . . . you can't have had that because you never let go until now of the one that traumatised you.'

'I think you're too clever for me. I've known you for fifteen minutes and you know more about me than the men I have loved.'

'Too clever to have lunch with?'

'No, I think I could manage that, but I already have a luncheon date.'

She liked this man. Something was sparking between Amy and this stranger, something she had almost forgotten could happen between two people, that little something extra that is so rare and so inexplicable.

'I can't ask you to dinner,' he told her.

'But you would like to?'

'Very much.'

The steward arrived at that moment to collect the glasses and the champagne bottle and to tell them to fasten their seat belts and ready themselves for the landing.

They were the last two to leave the first-class section of the plane. He helped her on with her coat: brown cashmere with a huge lynx collar. 'You're nearly as tall as I am,' he remarked.

Amy turned to face him. 'You don't like tall women?'

'Wrong. I never fall in love with short tiny women.' He lifted some of her hair that had become caught under her collar. Their eyes met.

'Are you implying that I might qualify?'

'I'm not sure. I would have to know you longer than half an hour. If you could have made lunch I might have known by then.'

She laughed. 'You're a terrific flirt.'

'I am.'

'A smoothie.'

'I am.'

'A ladies' man.'

'I confess, I love ladies, and would like to love you.'

'You're very direct.'

'Not always. Only when there's no point in being otherwise.'

'We're strangers.'

'Most great love affairs begin with two strangers,' he told her.

'You seem very sure that we could be a great love affair.'

'Are you so sure we cannot be?' There was disbelief in his voice.

227

The steward approached them and asked if they would be kind enough to leave the plane. They walked through the terminal together. The silence between them was not awkward, more comfortable. At the baggage carousel she told him, 'I have no luggage.'

'Neither do I.'

They passed quickly through passport control and silently walked together through the busy terminal teeming with people. They were through the glass doors and out into the cold and crisp air. This was a busy hour at Heathrow airport: cars in a constant flow of coming and going, people rushing away to lives no longer suspended in mid-air, baggage being shifted and packed and unpacked into waiting taxis and cars. Amy and her stranger seemed the only two people oblivious to the goings-on and not in a rush to get away.

'See me again. Take a chance on me. I'll never hurt you. I think you might be someone I would like to spend the rest of my life making happy. I need time to find out.'

'I can't make lunch and you can't make dinner.'

At that moment Charles's Rolls-Royce drove up to the terminal building and directly to where Amy was standing. His chauffeur went round the car and, after tipping his hat to Amy, opened the rear door for her.

'This is madness. Wonderful romantic madness. I don't know if it's the memory of what it was like to be swept away by love, of being one and whole with another human being, of dwelling in erotic oblivion, or your seductive charm, but I thank you for making me see that I want such a love as I once had. Only this time not with a cad but with a good man who's not afraid to love me.'

'I can't leave this to bad timing, can you?' he asked her.

'There's tomorrow.'

'Not for us. I leave for South Africa tomorrow, almost at dawn. But there can be other tomorrows for us if we want them. We only have to want them enough.'

Amy saw a maroon Jaguar cheekily pull in between a taxi and Charles's Rolls. So did the stranger standing next to her proposing love on a grand scale. A toot of a horn, an arm through a window waving at him.

'You're being met too?'

'Yes. Look, we don't have much time, and time is what we need to have together. I'll reserve a room at the Connaught for tonight in your name. I don't even know that I'll be able to get away for a few hours to be with you but I'll try. If you're not there I'll understand, and if I don't make it – well, you'll know that I tried my damnedest.'

Together they saw the Jaguar's door open and a tall, long-legged beauty with long blonde hair unfold herself from the car. She could have been no more than twenty-two. Amy looked at her stranger and raised an eyebrow but said nothing, merely smiled at him and walked towards Charles's waiting car.

He walked with Amy for several paces before the girl rushed between them and threw her arms round his neck. From the comfort of the Rolls Amy watched them kissing. He placed an arm round the girl's waist. His smile for her was charming and sexy, the same smile he had given Amy, only now she recognised it for what it was. She liked it, wanted his smile to be for her again. For some weeks, ever since Peter came back into her life, ever since the Jarret dream, she had known that her years of celibacy were over. They were drifting away as naturally as she had drifted into them. She ordered the chauffeur to drive on.

Lunch with Charles was a joyous occasion. Amy was ebullient and Charles fell in love with her that little bit more. Over the smoked salmon mousse and triangles of buttered toast, he commented, 'I've never seen you as you are today. Something has happened to make you – well, I don't exactly know what. What's happened?'

How could she explain to him what had happened on the plane between a walk down a lane of memories that had set her emotionally free and meeting a stranger who in a few minutes was a more grand and exciting attraction than Charles had ever been? She answered, 'The Soutine? Maybe that's it.'

They ate wild roast duck and poached white peach, mangetouts, wild rice, and drank a red burgundy that dreams are made of. Charles watched Amy eating her food with appetite and pleasure, and remarked, 'No, it's not the Soutine, not the excitement of placing it with the right museum, nor the deal. I've seen you through dozens of exciting art projects, and this is different. It has nothing to do with your work and everything to do with you. It's a fundamental change in you.'

They were dining not in Claridge's dining-room but in front of the fire in Charles's suite. Amy tried to make light of his comment, and managed to change the subject; they talked about Geneva and her day there. Raskin, the butler, cleared the plates and produced the pudding:

caramelised orange set in its own gloriously delicious juices and encircled by a shallow ring of chocolate mousse.

Amy gazed across the table at Charles. When she had called him from the plane it had been instinctive: wanting to see him, wanting to have sex with him again after so many years. Accepting that Jarret had been the great love affair of her life that had cheated her from going for another, Amy now wanted Charles and she to have another, fairer chance at love. Charles deserved at least that after so many years of loving her, and so many years of her rejecting him. Though she no longer wanted to sell herself short in the love stakes, being with Charles now, and ready as she was to give love with him another chance, the magic quite simply was not there. Not even a hint of that inexplicable force that had bonded her and the man on the plane, a stranger, was happening here. Love, affection, an erotic urge to be with Charles, yes, all that was there, but Amy could not stretch that into the magic, the grand passion of a lifetime. And a taste of that once more . . . oh, to have that with a good man!

Lunch over, Raskin had cleared away the table and been given the afternoon off. Amy and Charles were taking their coffee, sitting together in front of the fire. They were quiet, content with the soft sound of a Mozart violin concerto, and clearly happy to be together. Amy was seeing Charles somewhat differently now, more as she had seen him when she had first met him and they had fallen in love. She thought of the many women he must have had in the eight years of her celibacy, how his having those women had never bothered her. Now she was thinking how lucky those women had been to have had such an accomplished lover. She marvelled that he had found no one to replace her. Amy told herself that had to count for something. Enough at least for them to try for another chance together.

She slipped the leather jacket off his shoulders, raised his cashmere jumper over his head and unbuckled his alligator belt as she kissed his nipples. She slipped her hand beneath his jeans. How warm was his flesh, how smooth and sexy his skin. He was trembling with excitement. Tenderly he eased her on to his lap and into his arms, then he rose with her from the settee and carried her to the bedroom.

Charles had a penchant for going down between a lady's legs. He was accomplished at oral sex on a woman, a cunt lover in every sense of the word, and Amy came quickly and often before he replaced his tongue with his penis. He was a man who fucked sometimes with a

230

grace and gentleness as delicate as a butterfly's; at other times he was near violent in his fucking, in his desire to hit the highs of sex.

For Amy, having sex again, it was as if she had never stopped. She was able to submit herself utterly to the erotic. Here was sex on the scale she had once known it with Jarret. To feel as she did now with Charles was to be born again, to be young again and in love. There was but one problem in this sublime erotic tryst: it was the stranger on the plane she really wanted; the stranger who thought he might like to spend the rest of his life making her happy to whom she was submitting. It was a surprise, a disappointment, to open her eyes and drift back from a state of sexual bliss to see Charles's face and not that of the stranger whose name she didn't even know.

It was nearly seven o'clock in the evening when Charles turned on the lights in the bedroom and, kissing Amy lightly on the lips, went to shower. He returned looking incredibly young – he was terribly young, Amy reminded herself – wrapped in his navy blue terrycloth robe. He slipped into bed next to her and placing an arm round her, said, 'Can we talk about this?'

There was a strange sadness in his voice that could not be missed. Amy had no need to ask about what, she instinctively knew. 'Would you mind if I bathed and dressed first?'

'No. I'll order a bottle of champagne. I'm famished again, and so must you be. What would you like with it?'

'Smoked salmon sandwiches?'

'Perfect.'

He drew the covers off Amy, smiling at her, caressed her breasts and kissed the nipples. Then he scooped her up in his arms and carried her to the marble bath already half full of steaming water. Gently he placed her in it and handed her a bottle of almond-scented bath flakes.

Charles had always liked to stay with her when she bathed. She missed him now, but could understand why he wasn't there. The water felt soothing and though she would have liked to linger in her bath, she didn't. In the dressing-room, she sat at the dressing table and very carefully made up her face. There was a bloom in it she had not seen in too many years. Amy was feeling young and full of adventure, just a little bit more in love with life. Could it be true, what she saw reflected in the mirror? The years rolled back to reveal a beautiful woman, ready and now able for love as she had not been most of her adult life.

She found Charles on the settee in front of the fire and sat down next to him. He handed her a glass of champagne and a bite-sized smoked salmon sandwich. She smiled at him before she popped it in her mouth and sipped her wine. Placing her glass on the table in front of them, she took his hand and kissed it.

It was a gracious smile that he gave her before he spoke. 'What happened to us back there was fantastic. You and I have always had great sex together, but this was something else, something different. We've never been anything remotely like that before. I sensed something changed about you today, the very minute I set eyes on you. It took the sex for me to figure out what it was. Amy, you were in bed with me but you were having sex with another man.'

Amy didn't know what to say. What was there to say? She said nothing.

He continued, 'It was the love, the adoration I sensed coming off you. It had never been there for me before. The giving up of yourself to sex, as if you were ready to expire in your lust for sublime bliss with your partner, gave you away. It told me you weren't with me but someone else.'

Amy took a long sip of champagne. 'I think I have drunk more of this in the last few hours than I have in years.'

'Isn't there anything you want to tell me?'

'That I love you, Charles. A phantom of a past love appeared like a genie from a bottle and set me free as you have never known me. It made me want to give us another chance to be the grand passion of our respective lives. Then fate delivered me a stranger whose name I don't even know.'

'Well, I guess that says it all.'

'Yes, I guess it does.'

'You do know that leaves us with little choice?'

'Loving and close friends, casual sex when we feel inspired towards that, nothing more? I would never want you to feel cheated by me.'

'I have two tickets for the ballet this evening, *The Sleeping Beauty*. If we hurry we can just make the curtain.'

'Yes, I would like that very much.'

He touched the rim of his glass to hers, and smiled. 'Would that I had been the prince to have placed that kiss upon your lips, my beautiful friend.'

How kind, how civilised. They smiled at each other with love and respect for themselves and their situation. *The Sleeping Beauty*. How perfect, how poignant, to end what could have been an awkward and even heartbreaking evening for them both with that particular ballet. How very apropos.

Charles asked Amy to stay the night but she declined, telling him she was anxious to get home. She had left her car in the hotel garage the morning she left for Geneva. It was brought round and Charles saw her into it and watched her tie her scarf round her hair. They kissed and she was gone. She saw him smiling in the rear view mirror. He always smiled when she drove away; somehow it amused him, Amy having that car and the way she drove it. It had become a part of her personality, one of the many things he loved about her.

Amy was on the other side of Hyde Park waiting for the traffic lights to change when she thought of her handsome stranger. She wondered where he and his lady had been that evening, where he now was. Surely not in a room at the Connaught booked under her name? He didn't know her name. They had been too lost in the growing attraction between them even to remember to exchange names. It made her laugh. It made her wonder.

And what if he had found a way to reserve a room for her without giving her name? Impossible. Not at the Connaught. She sped away from Mayfair to the next set of traffic lights just at the edge of the park. Exhibition Row was straight ahead. The lights changed and she raced a few hundred yards down the street. On impulse Amy flicked the direction signal and took a sharp left into Ennismore Gardens and pulled into the first vacant space she could find. The motor still running, she opened her briefcase and removed the mobile telephone. Directory Enquiries seemed to ring forever, then she asked for the telephone number of the Connaught in Carlos Place, Mayfair.

'Good evening, my name is Miss Amy Ross, I believe you are holding a room for me?'

'One moment, please.' But barely a moment passed before the smooth and welcoming voice said, 'Ah, yes, Miss Ross. We've been expecting you.'

Amy tried to dispel the surprise in her voice. 'Yes, well, it's quite late, I thought it best to make certain you were still holding the room, I'll be there in a very few minutes.'

She put her telephone away, knowing that she would sleep in the Connaught that night. She was not so much surprised that the stranger had done what he had said he would do as excited about an adventure that might or might not be unfolding. He did say he only *might* be able to get away to meet her there.

When Amy drew up to the entrance of the hotel the doorman rushed forward to greet her. Once she had handed her car over to his care and had been greeted by the night concierge and signed the register, Amy realised that she was at a distinct disadvantage. She could not possibly make any enquiries about the man who had made the reservation or whether he was there or not. She could say or do nothing that would cause any speculation about what she was doing here.

In this elegant and sedate hotel a few affluent, well-dressed people were around the hall and the sitting-room, the last diners drifting out from the famous dining room. In ordinary circumstances she might have been one of them. But these were extraordinary circumstances. She felt like a romantic but wondered if she should be feeling like an expensive tart.

The porter unlocked the door for her and switched on the lights. There were fresh flowers, white arum lilies, two dozen of them, looking spectacular in a vase set in the centre of a round table in front of the windows overlooking Carlos Place. She could hardly keep her eyes from the small white envelope lying on the black marble table top next to the vase. There was too a very decorative box of white chocolates, her favourite Belgian whites filled with fresh cream. She knew that because the silver-papered lid and gold bow had been opened and laid at an angle across the box. Several of the chocolates were missing. He had been there and was gone, and he had a sweet tooth. She knew at least that much about him.

The porter opened the door to the bedroom and switched on the lamps then returned to the sitting-room. Amy thanked him and handed him a five pound note. He was about to leave when there was a knock at the door. She hadn't realised how nervous she was until her heart gave a little skip and a beat. He was here.

But he wasn't. It was a waiter wheeling in a white damask-clad table with a bottle of champagne in a silver cooler, a single champagne flute, a pot of hot chocolate, a single cup and saucer, a plate piled high with small crustless sandwiches. A before-bedtime snack for one. For him or for her? When the waiter had left Amy rushed to the table and grabbed the white envelope, opened it and pulled the card from it.

234

Desire me, encounter us
in your secret night.
I kiss you.
  Brice

Chapter 16

Tillie Tyler heard the Lagonda's horn and looked up from the kitchen sink to see the car emerge from the dirt track through the trees. Wiping her hands on a tea towel, she opened the door and greeted Amy.

'Need any help unloading the car?'

'Just one trip between the two of us will do it.'

'I thought you were returning yesterday,' said Tillie as Amy handed her the two dozen long-stemmed lilies.

'I was, I did, but I stayed the night in London. It was all very unexpected.'

Now Tillie with the flowers and the large box of chocolates, Amy with her briefcase, walked together up the steps and into the house. 'What beautiful flowers and chocolates. Looks like someone's courting someone?'

'Could be, but at this stage of the game your guess is as good as mine. I got the flowers, the chocolates, but somewhere along the way I missed the man.' Amy could not help but laugh at the puzzled look on her housekeeper's face.

'I think I missed something.'

'So did I, Tillie, so did I,' said Amy, and laughed at herself again.

'Well, no matter, you look really happy.'

'You know, Tillie, I am.' They were in the hall when Amy added, 'God, I do like coming home.'

'Good trip?' asked the housekeeper.

'A great trip.'

The two women walked together into the kitchen. 'Coffee?' asked Tillie.

'Oh, yes, please.'

As Amy removed the paper from round the lilies she could not help but think about Brice, her stranger. He had never turned up at the hotel. He had never called. When she had awakened in the morning it seemed the strangest thing that he was not lying next to her in the bed. Unnatural.

He hadn't been there but she hadn't been disappointed because she knew that if he could have been, he would. They had missed each other. It was as simple and uncomplicated as that. But what a magnificent effort he had made for her, down to the last detail. When, after breakfast in her room, she called down to the desk to say that she would be checking out, within minutes the maid had arrived to wrap up the flowers and a white envelope had been handed to her, a paid receipt for her stay.

The aroma of freshly perked coffee drew Amy's thoughts away from her interlude with the stranger. With a knife she cut each stem on an angle before placing the blooms in water.

'Shall I put the chocolates in a dish?' asked Tillie.

'Put a few in that small Chinese one I like, the one with the pedestal, in my bedroom. And do have some for yourself. Anything happen while I was gone?'

'Mr Silberzog called twice, and said it was important you call him. Some things came in on the fax machine. The post is on your desk. Mr Whately came round looking for you – I gave him a cup of tea. That was yesterday afternoon. And a stranger, a man, looked very foreign, arrived in a London taxi. I knew you weren't expecting anyone so when I saw it coming down the track I went out to meet it. I know you don't like anyone coming to the door who's not invited.'

'When was this?'

'About two hours after you left for the airport to go to Switzerland.'

For a brief moment Amy had thought it might have been Brice, but she hadn't even met him at that time.

'How odd. Who was it? What did he want?'

'He was looking for you and said he was an old friend and wouldn't give his name because he wanted to surprise you.'

'What did he look like.'

'Very foreign.'

'Tillie, come on now. I need more to go on than that.'

'Sort of Chinese, I think, but not exactly. He had a lot of colour, like he sat in the sun a lot. Bald as a billiard ball. I didn't like his eyes, they were what I call sneaky eyes, and he was being too slimy nice to me. He asked if you lived here. I didn't say yes and I didn't say no.'

'What did you say?'

'I told him what I tell anyone who comes here who's not invited or

238

we don't know: "This is a private road and you're trespassing. As it happens I know Miss Ross, and the only way you're going to get to see her is to leave a message in the post office in the village, or if you want I can give her one when I next see her." '

'I wonder who it was?'

'An odd man. He smelled like a lady, of lavender. He wore a suit and all that plus a gardenia pinned to his lapel. Lots of gold jewellery round his neck and an embroidered shawl round his shoulders. I wouldn't have been surprised if he'd had a hand bag!'

Amy went quite pale, and had to sit down. It could have been anyone but she was certain it had been Fee. Ever since the dream, she had half expected one or both of them suddenly to appear.

'Are you all right? Did I do wrong? You look pale as a ghost.'

'Funny you should say ghost.' Amy recovered quite quickly from the initial shock.

'Should I get you a little brandy?'

'No. Coffee and chocolate will do me fine.'

Tillie poured the coffee and sat down opposite Amy, the silver-coloured chocolate box between them. 'By God, you didn't half give me a shock, Miss Ross.'

'I'm sorry, Tillie. You just took me by surprise with your description. I think I might just know that man from a very long time ago . . . You did very well to shoo him off this property. I have no particular desire to see him if he is indeed the man I think he might be, but if he does come back and I am here, I have nothing to fear from seeing him either. If it's convenient for me I will. He will give you the name Fee or Mr Yolu. There wasn't another man with him in the taxi?'

'No. He was alone.'

'If he returns, I doubt that he will return alone.'

'Is something wrong, Miss Ross?'

'Nothing. On the contrary, everything is terrific.'

In the days that followed Amy's return from Geneva she busied herself with the sale of the Soutine. Pierre de Boulet called to say that a courier would be arriving with the painting at her house in three days' time and that it was insured as she specified it should be. She waited for Pierre to say that he had given her name to a neighbour called Brice but he mentioned no such thing.

She rationed the chocolates out to herself one a day, wanting romance to linger that little bit longer. Once the chocolates had been consumed

239

and the flowers had wilted, the little bit she had of Brice would fade into memory, become a past experience, something delightful that had been. Strangely she felt no sadness about that. Quite the opposite, she felt alive, on top of the world, wanting only to be ready and willing and able to meet every day and what it might bring.

Anthony Kramer, Amy's long-time millionaire suitor, was a Sephardic Jew whose family originated in Turkey. They had even to the present day always been philanthropic to the country though they had been naturalised Americans for four generations.

Many years before, Anthony had told Amy that it was his intention to build a museum of modern art in Istanbul, a monument to his great-great-great-grandfather. He had been working on the gift with the Turkish government for years. He and Edward Silberzog had been dealing with the difficult preliminaries in Turkey. All was in place and now had come the time for Amy's input into the project. Hence the urgent calls from Edward, who had somehow forgotten to tell her that the project was on go and had been made official two months ago, the government now wanting to move ahead as fast as possible. Amy had years before been offered the position of curator. She'd rejected it but did agree to be one of the museum's chief advisors until it was opened to the public and the curator and board of directors took over. She, Edward and Anthony would each hold a seat on the board. It was a dream-come-true project for the three of them who had conceived of the idea on a cruise along the coast of Turkey when Amy had thought she might make a life with Anthony.

The most pressing things to be dealt with were the location and the building they might want to buy or construct to house the museum. A selection of photographs, floor plans and specifications of desirable properties, and maps of areas considered for the museum, had arrived for Amy to ponder. Edward and she had agreed that when each of them had evaluated what was on offer they would make a shortlist, then go on a reconnaissance trip to Istanbul with Anthony.

When the current *Art News* from New York arrived, Amy had something of a shock to see herself on the cover with a three-page article about the project inside. She called Anthony at once.

'I've just received the current *Art News*, Anthony.'

'I know that tone. You're angry?'

'What happened to anonymity, staying in the background of things?'

'You're *very* angry?'

'You've known about this for months and not said a word.'

'Because we knew you would be angry. Will you let me explain?'

'It had better be good.'

'They wanted to run the story and we had no idea that they were going to use you or any of us on the cover until it had already gone to press. I promise you, I tried to stop it.'

'Why me?'

'Because you're so accomplished and so fucking reclusive it gave the story more interest. Just what the caption says: "One of our more renowned art historians who prefers to remain in the background while acting in an advisory capacity to the Anthony Kramer Museum to be built in Istanbul." But don't despair, no address, no telephone numbers, not even a mention that you live in England, and not a word about your private life.'

'If there are any repercussions to this publicity I'm throwing them right back at you, Anthony, remember that.'

'I'll make this up to you.'

'That's not necessary, just keep me out of the press and let me do my work. I know you love riding the band wagon of the art world, and you know I don't. It has sent me away before, Anthony. It could easily send me away again.'

'I never have understood this obsession of yours with being a private person.'

'You don't have to understand it, dear Anthony, just respect it.'

'Am I forgiven for being a coward and not telling you about it, because honestly that's all I'm guilty of?'

There would be few people Amy knew who read *Art News* magazine who would call her about the cover or her role as advisor to the new museum; they knew her sentiments about being in the art world circus. But what about the people she didn't know who would be impressed by the story and try to involve themselves in the project by appealing to her? However, *Art News* and her concern about her subsequent notoriety vanished within the hour because the courier from Switzerland arrived with the Soutine. Once it was out of the crate and on to the large mahogany easel, the machinations of the art world became nothing at all to Amy. Only the fine work of art in front of her and her concern to place it with the right public institution, at the price she was asking, on behalf of the de Boulets.

It was here in the boat house that prospective buyers would come to view it. Two New York museums, the Chicago Art Institute, one Paris museum and one from Tokyo had already shown a keen interest, and that had been from mere telephone conversations and faxes. And Amy had given only the barest hint as to how important a work she was so very discreetly offering.

To sell it privately would have been no problem. The Whatelys saw it the second day it was on display in the boat house and wanted to buy it, offering a signed blank cheque. All Amy had to do was fill in the sum. But they had little hope that she would do that. They were very much aware of Amy's intention to sell to a museum where the painting would be permanently on display to the public. Dick could do little but play the waiting game and hope the museums, for whatever reason, would one by one vanish from the market place. Besotted by the two reclining nudes, every day he would boat over simply to sit and look at the painting.

A pattern emerged. Dick would arrive, would let himself in, and if Tillie was still there she would make him a pot of tea. Often he would bring cakes. If Amy wasn't busy in the library, she might join him; he did not however disturb her except to call out, 'I'm leaving, Amy, thanks.' Then he was gone as quietly as he had arrived. Those times that Tillie was not there he would let himself in quietly, take his place in front of the painting and light one of the large Havana cigars he was so fond of. It was only the aroma wafting through the boat house that signalled he was in the house.

Tillie had already gone home, Amy was on the telephone in the library, and Dick was contemplating the Soutine when he heard a car crunching the gravel as it drew up to the house. He called up to her, 'A car's arrived, Amy, shall I see to it?'

'Yes, please. I'll be there in a minute.'

It was a bright sunny day and the boat house was filled with shafts of light pouring through the windows, lovely angles of that special kind of sunlight that reflects off water. The beams of light criss-crossed dramatically through the ground-floor windows, from others puncturing the three-storey-high walls and those under the eaves at the roofline. Amy, finished with her conversation, could just about make out the sound of men's voices at the front door.

From the balustrade in the library high above the ground floor of the boat house and overlooking the main room and entrance hall, she saw Dick standing to one side of the front door talking to a man. With bright sunlight behind him, the man appeared only as a dark silhouette. He was a big man who seemed almost to fill the doorway. He looked a dramatic figure etched into the sunlight all round him. Even from

242

where she was, Amy sensed a powerful presence. Though she could not see his face, she knew that presence, just as on seeing it she knew the man's form.

She felt strangely calm for a woman whose heart was racing so fast. She was not surprised that he should be there. She had half expected him to appear. There had been enough signs that he might.

She called down from her vantage point, 'Dick, it's all right, let Mr Sparrow in.'

Amy watched him walk through her front door and into a shaft of sunlight. She had to close her eyes for a second and take a deep breath. Jarret Sparrow, after nearly thirty years, was as handsome and charismatic as he had always been. The hair glistened more silver than dark blond but it hadn't thinned with the years. The two men walked from the entrance hall into the vast drawing-room. He was wearing probably not the same but a similar black cashmere coat with a velvet collar. It was as if time had stood still. Well, for the moment anyway. She was gazing intently down at him, he in much the same manner up at her.

Neither spoke for several seconds, the atmosphere charged with something Dick had never sensed before in that house. He pulled his Zippo lighter from his pocket and held the flame to the end of his cigar as he rolled it slowly between his fingers. He had no idea what was going on but had no intention of leaving until he found out, as much for Amy's protection as the Soutine's.

She could not bring herself to speak. It was not distress, nor anxiety, she simply didn't know what to say to Jarret. 'Get out of my house.' 'What are you doing here?' 'How dare you invade my privacy?' They hardly seemed right since by saying any of those things she made his appearance in her life much more important than it was. Having invaded her dreams, having so recently caused her to review their affair, it no longer made any difference whether he was here or not. Indifference to Jarret at long last. How delicious! She walked from the library down the stairs.

It was impossible for him to lose sight of her in the open-plan house where nearly everything was visible. 'I'm sorry to take you by surprise, just appearing like this. I couldn't call, I had no telephone number.'

'You may be a surprise, Jarret, but not a shock. I half expected to see you. Is Fee not with you? It was he who found me for you yet again, wasn't it? My housekeeper tells me she sent away a bald-headed man several days ago, one who would not give his name. She thought he looked dangerous.'

243

Amy was standing directly in front of Jarret by the time she delivered those last words. She could not help but enjoy his discomfort. His precious Fee being called dangerous? He looked very displeased with that. Before he could say anything she continued, 'Dick, Jarret Sparrow is someone I knew a very long time ago – it seems like a lifetime ago. Someone else's lifetime. Jarret, meet my friend and neighbour, Dick Whately.'

The two men shook hands. Dick, who found the atmosphere strained and yet somehow electric with the meeting between Amy and Jarret Sparrow, was feeling not at all inclined to leave Amy with him unless she wanted to be. He offered, 'Shall I make us a cup of tea, Amy?'

'No, I don't think so, Dick, you make such a lousy cup of tea, but do pour yourself a drink.'

'Fee is in the car, and my son Tennant. Fee wants very much to see you, almost as much as I do, and Tennant has heard about you for years and longs to meet you.'

'It seems you brought all the family. Well, not quite. How is it you left your wife out of this uncalled-for reunion?'

'My wife and I are divorced.'

'And why am I honoured with this extraordinary visit? And more to the point, how did you find my address?'

'It wasn't easy. Bribery, sleuthing. Don't look for ulterior motives in my seeking you out, you'll find none. I'm just trying to find something I've missed and longed for for too many years.'

Dick was astounded at Jarret Sparrow's gall, the charm, the determination with which he delivered those words. He was already impressed by the handsome, charismatic presence of the man and understood that Jarret was there to seduce Amy back into his life in any way he could. He was blatant and Amy, though she looked calm, seemed to Dick to be undeniably on edge. Was that a glint of fright he saw in the back of her eyes? 'Amy, do you want me to leave or escort Jarret to his taxi?'

'No, don't leave, Dick, I will. I need to check the boat, make sure it's secured for the night. You keep Jarret company. I'll either return with his family or they'll all be leaving and we can see them to the gate.'

Jarret reached out and touched Amy's cheek.

She removed his hand. 'I won't be long,' she told him, and walked away before he could say another word. In the hall she slipped into a wool-lined denim jacket. The two men watched her and Dick noticed that she took a side door rather than the front entrance that would have brought her in direct contact with the taxi and its passengers.

'You had better give me your coat,' said Dick to Jarret.

He removed his coat and laid it over a chair. 'Look, I'm sorry about this intrusion but for a very long time I have been trying to find Amy. We were once very close friends.'

'You're Jarret Sparrow, the painter. I know your work, saw it years ago in Paris. Come on in, there's something here you'll appreciate – a great Soutine.'

Through the window Amy saw them walking towards the easel. She could not relate to Jarret through the past but only in the immediate present. She saw an attractive man to whom she was still sexually drawn. She knew who he was, what he was, what he was not. The bad, the good, the downright depravity of the man, but she was indifferent to all that. She had no need to deal with what he had been nor what they had been. She had known him as the great love of her life, but that was like some melodramatic novel that she had read somewhere and immersed herself in. She had finished it now. It was closed.

Amy checked the boat's lines, and then sat there for some time, but not thinking of the past. She was thinking about Jarret being in her house with Dick. Of meeting Fee again, of meeting Tennant, Jarret's son. She was thinking about herself. And of Jarret and her, how he would always be the great love of her life, past tense. What could they possibly be to each other now, if anything?

She walked from the boat round the boat house to the waiting taxi. The two men, Fee and Tennant, alighted from the taxi immediately.

'Oh, how wonderful to see you, Amy. You have hardly changed, you look marvellous.'

'Not changed in thirty years? You were always the consummate flatterer and liar, Fee. You look as dramatic and attractive as you always like to look, but by God, I see the years on you. And this is Tennant?'

'Hello.'

It was difficult for Amy to find words for the twenty-two-year-old. He was almost exactly like his father when Amy first met him, though Jarret had been older then. She was drawn to him at once, just as she had been to Jarret.

'Hello, Tennant.'

'Fee and Dad have told me all about you and your years in New York in the art world, and how exciting a life you and my dad led there. I wish I could have been a part of that scene.'

245

'Tennant is a painter. Better than Jarret, better than me,' said Fee.

'I wish you well, Tennant. Fee . . .' She held the taxi door open for him. 'Jarret is staying on for a bit. I'll drive him back to the city.'

For the first time in her life Amy saw Fee nonplussed. 'Might I just have a word with him?'

'No. And, Fee, if you ever want to return here, send a letter care of the post office asking if you might visit, but never trespass again. Don't be offended, that's what all my friends and acquaintances, and strangers especially, are asked to do.'

'Amy, I would like to see you again. We had great times together, a great deal of laughter, we were good friends. I would like that to happen for us again. When may I see you?'

'How strange that it should take you thirty years to remember we were friends, Fee. I had forgotten. Tennant, you and Fee go ahead. Maybe I will see you again when I return your father to London.'

Tennant took her hand in his and lowered his head and kissed it. The two men climbed into the taxi and Amy closed the door. Fee pulled down the window. 'He loves you, he has always loved you, like no other woman in his life.'

'Then he should have done something about it, shouldn't he, Fee?' Amy slapped the side of the taxi and the driver drove off.

Jarret filled her house with his presence. She listened and watched as he charmed Dick with that lethal combination of sensitivity, chic sophistication, good looks and deferential, almost vulnerable, lost boy manner. That sex appeal he always used on both men and women. How long had he been there? Half an hour? And already he had restored a dimension to her life that she had missed those thirty-odd years he had stayed away. Incredible, the chemistry between them was still there. She'd sensed it the moment she saw him enter her house.

He had won Dick over. She could see it in his face, in his manner towards Jarret. She could understand it. Jarret and Fee, like the devil himself, had many disguises that all worked. Had they ever come unstuck, been made to pay for the evil things they had done? They were such a clever partnership, Amy somehow doubted it.

'Your house is marvellous, Amy. And the Soutine's the best I've ever seen.'

'We've been talking art. Jarret was telling me about the *palazzo* he lives in in Venice, and his garden. You've been there, haven't you, Amy?'

'Oh, yes, I've been there.'

246

Something was happening between Amy and Jarret, that same old magic was at work. Dick couldn't help but see it and feel awkward, out of place. 'Jarret's friend and son, Amy?' he asked.

'I've sent them back to London. I'll drive Jarret in a little later.'

Dick needed no prompting from Amy, he could see that she had softened somewhat towards Jarret and was in total control of the situation. 'I'm going home. Nice to meet you, Jarret. If you're round for a while get Amy to bring you over to us, we're only on the other side of the river.'

Amy watched the two men shake hands and marvelled at how smooth an operator Jarret still was when she heard him say to Dick, 'Really nice to meet you and hear about your Bacons. Sounds to me you're that rare sort of collector who puts his heart into every painting he buys. I would really appreciate seeing them and your collection.' This to Dick who so rarely spoke about his collection to anyone, Dick who guarded every painting from outside visitors.

Amy walked with him to the door and stepped outside for a moment. 'Are you going to be OK with Jarret? I can stay but somehow thought you wanted to be alone with him. I am right, aren't I?'

'I'll be fine.'

'Amy, this guy . . . he's awfully smooth, a lady killer . . . but what the hell am I telling you that for? You're not blind.'

'Is he so obvious?'

'To a guy who was once a lot like him, yes. This guy is an interesting rogue. Just what women love.'

'Don't look so worried, Dick. I've been there, done that.'

'Ah, I see, a class reunion?'

'Something like that.' And they both smiled.

'Do I have to call before I come round tomorrow to visit my painted ladies?'

'No. I don't give up my life so easily any more when a man comes through the door.'

Dick laughed. 'Careful, Amy, all women *and* men do when the real thing walks in.' And he waved and ran across the lawn to his boat.

Amy closed the door behind her and entered the room. Jarret was putting logs on the fire. She couldn't help but think how presumptuous he was, how very quickly he was taking over her house, how sure he was of her. It was written plain for all to see: the look on his face, his movements.

'I'm going to make a cup of tea,' she told him.

He followed her into the kitchen. 'I wish you had asked Fee and Tennant in.'

Amy swung round, kettle in hand, and asked, 'Why, Jarret? I don't feel particularly well disposed to Fee, and I don't know your son.'

He removed the kettle from her hand and placed it on the table. Somewhat roughly he pulled her into his arms. She could feel the emotion emanating from him. He pressed a kiss upon her lips. His were trembling. To be held in his arms, feel his need for her, his lust for her, was thrilling. With Jarret sex was something much more than with any other man she had known. Against her will, she felt her body giving in to him.

He slipped his hands under her jumper and found her breasts. Caressing hands, Jarret's hands, hands that she'd never dreamed would touch her again. It had always been as if she had found the other half of herself when she was in his embrace. How could that still be? It was a mystery to her that love should be gone and she still feel so strongly sexual with him. She could understand the many sex-without-love experiences she had had with other men, but for it to be so with Jarret seemed somehow immoral.

She tried to remove his hands but he was too quick for her. He had her jumper off and his mouth was sucking at the nipple of the breast that overflowed his cupped hands. She could feel the hardness of his erect penis pressed against her through his trousers. She came, an unwanted orgasm, light, almost imperceptible. He picked her up in his arms and carried her from the kitchen to a chair in front of the fire, all the while reaching underneath her skirts and beneath her silk panties.

'Jarret, there is no point to this.'

'Love, lust, those same things we've always had for each other, that's the point. And don't tell me you've forgotten.'

'Not forgotten, but I don't live in the past, Jarret.'

He had her panties off and felt the moisture on her inner cunt lips. 'I have my proof,' he told her.

He draped her legs over the arms of the chair. She leaned against the pillows on the chair, exposed and raunchy, and enjoyed the lust she was exhibiting to Jarret. Amy enjoyed her sexuality. Men who fed her libido with their lust reaped their just rewards from her. She watched Jarret as he unzipped his trousers and dropped them. He went down on his knees and roughly pulled her by the legs tight up against him, half lifting her bottom off the chair. He thrust into her. The force of his entry took her breath away. She called out, a near scream to God to

248

save her, and came in a copious orgasm. Jarret pulled her tight into his arms. His kisses were wild, full of passion. They were interspersed with protestations of love while he fucked her in long, deep thrusts that caused her to come again and again as she wrapped her legs tight round him.

They were both out of control, voracious for all things sexual. This was a more sexually violent, a more sexually desperate Jarret than Amy had ever known before. She herself felt a kind of anger at their erotic games. They were two strangers caught in the lust trap and nothing either of them could say or do could free them. Amy and Jarret would fuck until the energy ran out or death came. And it seemed to Amy that it made no difference to them which came first.

Chapter 17

Amy awakened still in Jarret's arms. They were lying on the floor in front of the hearth, the fire now nothing but cold white ash. Jarret had covered them with a blanket of Norwegian wolf skins that usually lay on the end of one of the pair of Georgian settees in the room.

'I remember you used to be the one who always awoke first, ready and waiting for me. I love you, Amy.'

'You used only to be able to tell me you loved me when you were fucking me.'

She rose from the floor, wrapping her nakedness in the blanket, and walked round the room picking up her clothes. She went through to the kitchen where she filled the kettle and put it on the Aga. When she returned fully dressed to the drawing-room Jarret too was dressed and laying a fire in the fireplace.

'I did mean to be more subtle about wanting to fuck you. I had planned at least to seduce you with some finesse.'

'Finesse? Tennant and Fee as back-up, you call that finesse?'

'This wouldn't have happened had you not sent them away. I hadn't planned it. We just happened as we always just happened.'

'Yes, I guess that just about sums us up. A love never planned, something that just happened.'

Jarret went to Amy and placed an arm round her. 'You've always been the sexiest woman I've ever wanted and had. You still are. You loved it so much, you loved me so much, and you still do. I once told you there would never be a man to replace me, and there hasn't been.'

'That's true,' Amy told him as she extricated herself from his arms and left the room to make the tea.

Jarret followed her into the kitchen and sat down at the table.

'We'll have this, and then I'll drive you to the nearest railway station.'

Amy poured the tea and placed a plate of ginger biscuits on the

251

table. She took a chair opposite him. Jarret was looking round the room. It charmed him. A real country kitchen of period wooden tables and handsome chairs of which no two matched, a ten-foot-long butcher's block, worn into waves of polished yew, that was used as a working surface. Marble surfaces surrounded the old-fashioned butler's sinks. Glass storage jars of all shapes and sizes were filled with preserves and pasta, nuts and honey, rice and sugar. Extra virgin olive oils and a variety of vinegars vied with handsome pottery pieces, marble and copper bowls, for room on the open shelves that circled the walls. Pots and pans gleamed on a rack above the Aga. And from other hooks suspended on chains from the ceiling hung bunches of drying herbs: rosemary and thyme, bay leaves and lavender, tarragon, dried marigolds, garlands of garlic and onion.

'This room is great. Your whole house is great. I want to see it all. Very impressive. I never pictured you in a place such as this. It's stunning, full of grace and peace and quiet. It has something special, uplifting about it. It's a home put together by someone who cherishes all things beautiful. I never realised a home was so important to you.'

Amy was taken aback, not only by what he was saying but his tone of disbelief that she should want and have a home, live as she did. The only thing she could think to say was, 'Why not, Jarret?'

'You gave up that first little flat we lived in together so easily to me. And, well, the second place . . . that hardly counted, did it, though you did move there for me, so we could have a larger living space. I always knew that. But this! A wonderful place to live and work in, and so close to London.'

'I had never thought of it before, Jarret, but until I met you I always lived in beautiful houses. Possibly not as large and grand as a *palazzo* or a *yalis*, more the size of your Paris flat. Do you still think all the houses, like all the flowers in the world, are for you and you alone?' She was being facetious but he didn't realise that.

He laughed. 'May I have a biscuit?' Amy offered him the plate. She watched him eat his biscuit and take a second, and a third, then drink from his cup. He gazed at her across the table and she recognised that meanness that could come into his eyes, that hardness that once had frightened her. It did no such thing now. She left the table and returned with a biscuit tin, opened it and sat down again.

'You remember that?'

'I'm not likely to forget it, Jarret.'

252

'Nothing has changed,' he told her, reaching for another biscuit and refilling his tea cup.

'How greedy you are!'

'Yes, that's true, but you've always known that. I have never pretended to be other than I am.'

'I may have known it but I never understood to what lengths your greed could extend itself.'

'Amy, I loved you as I have loved no other woman, and you know that is true.'

'Yes, I believe you did, in spite of yourself. But the kind of love we had for each other was forbidden, not in your plans.'

'Not did, do. I still love you.'

'I don't think we should be having a discussion about love, Jarret.'

'Why not?'

'Because I know only too well what your particular kind of love is. You loved me so well, Jarret, that when problems swamped me you packed your bags and left, telling me, "I'll be back when things are better for you again." Ah, to be loved by you was really something, Jarret! A flat in Paris, an enormous *palazzo* in Venice, another mansion on the waters of the Bosphorus – and when I was in debt and had nowhere to live, you couldn't offer me so much as a box room in any of your residences. I never heard: "Share my bed with me, dear Amy, until you can make things better." All I heard was, "Send word when you have an address."

'You have no idea what it was like for me to survive in New York City alone and adrift, without money nor a roof over my head, without love; no friends forthcoming to take me in and with a lover who cared so little he vanished without a thought. A stranger, a casual acquaintance, heard of my plight and told someone just in passing, as no more than a bit of gossip about an art name who lost all because of bad timing and love for the wrong man. That stranger lent me his flat while he was in Europe. The pity of a stranger saved my life. I hid from the art world trying to survive any way I could until I could get myself on my feet again. I will say one thing about New York, it's a very easy place to disappear in. And there's always a way to make money if you cast your sights low enough.'

'You managed very well, though, didn't you? Eighteen months later I was knocking at the door of your new flat in New York. This isn't the first time I've turned up on your doorstep to remind you that I love you and want to be with you. You turned me away for some second-

253

rate lover you could never love as you loved me.'

'Is it second-rate love you would like to talk about? All right, let's talk about that. No, better still, let's talk about despicable love, the sort of love that does as you did to me when I turned up in Venice three months after you left me alone to cope with my problems. The one bright note in my life, something wonderful from a grand romantic love: a child. Nothing else but that news would have made me swallow my pride and go to you. Like two long-lost souls we fell into each other's arms. A million ways of how to tell you kept turning over in my mind. I intended to go there and break the wonderful news because, as the father of my child, I felt you had the right to be part of that miracle. And when I saw you I felt as I always did when we were together, whole, as if I had come home. Only to hear, "Where are you staying? How long will you be here?" Those were your first words to me. Then, "What are you doing here?" '

Jarret said nothing. Amy gave him credit for that at least. Finally when he did speak it was to ask if she might add some hot water to the tea pot. There was no remorse in his voice. She rose from her chair, poured more fresh water into the kettle and removed the tea pot from the table. A fresh pot seemed in order. He walked up behind her and placed his arms round her, holding her close to him as she was rinsing the china pot clean.

'I didn't want a baby. You knew that was not in the scheme of things for us. You shouldn't have been surprised when I told you your having one was not my problem.'

'Well, as it turned out, it wasn't mine either.'

'I never did ask you what happened?'

'Do us both a favour and don't ask now. What are you doing here, Jarret? What do you want?' She slipped out of his grasp and made the tea, then sat down and waited for it to steep.

'I want you to love me again. We were once so good together. The best.'

'I don't live in the past, Jarret. If I did, I wouldn't have let you through my front door.'

'What just happened between us, that wasn't the past. It was wonderful, thrilling sex.'

'So what?'

The moment Amy said those words, she broke into raucous laughter. A smile crossed Jarret's face, and he too had to laugh. When he finished he told her, 'You've become a hard woman.'

'Well, let's just say age and experience have taken their toll on my innocence, and leave it at that.'

'Amy, my love for you will not die. I have taken wrong paths away from you, I've been foolish and vain, have flirted and charmed, seduced any number of women and men for the sake of ambition and dreams. For all the years we've been estranged, I've been in search of a love to replace yours, the great love of my life that I used and abused and threw away. Yet for me, you've never been replaced. I want us to make up for the years that we've been apart. We've all had our successes. You're a woman of substance in the art world, one with more power than I ever dreamed you would have. Fee is painting successfully and has become moderately well known. I have my work and now Tennant has come into his own as a painter. I want us to be a great art family. You're the woman of my life. I know that now, granted almost too late, and I want to prove it to you.'

Amy felt a sincerity emanating from Jarret that was difficult to ignore. She had never dreamed that he might feel remorse for the way he had treated her. But once more that strange sensation of knowing the man down to the marrow of his bones interposed a warning. Was Jarret Sparrow, in the final analysis, the man she would choose to end her life with?

Amy did not take him to the railway station. Instead she drove him into London and to a house in Belgravia where he, Fee, and Tennant were staying. Jarret insisted that she see Fee and Tennant again. Amy felt herself slipping under the Sparrow spell, and acquiesced.

The house was beautifully appointed, grand even. Fee seemed very much at home there. Their hostess was at the opera and had taken Tennant with her. Amy greeted Fee, and the moment she did felt something was wrong. She really didn't want to greet Fee or even see him again. She asked herself what she was doing there. Felt quite embarrassed about being in the house there with them and made a decision to be courteous but to leave as soon as possible without making a scene.

She felt quite sick when she heard him say, 'And now the tables are turned and it's Jarret who has brought you home to me.'

'No, Fee, I've brought Jarret back to you,' she quipped.

'What does it matter as long as we're all together again and have made things up? Though I do confess I don't know what has happened that we haven't seen each other before this. There's so much to catch up on. So many good times we shall all have together once things are sorted out.'

A look more like daggers than a mere glance passed from Jarret to Fee. He fidgeted. He had obviously given away more than he should have. Devious as ever! Amy could hardly believe it. She had been taken in once more by Jarret and his protestations of undying love for her. For a brief moment during sex with him she had thought that maybe destiny had looked favourably on them and their love was no longer forbidden.

A brief delusion of love and then there it was right in front of her: Jarret and Fee's greed, their self-serving manner. She was no longer blind, saw those things in them so clearly. Amy was genuinely shocked that Jarret should return to her after half a lifetime only to use rather than to love her. At least the last time round he had loved her as well. She could have run out of the house but that seemed too dramatic. She was more curious than upset. Amy credited that to her own indifference, her no longer loving Jarret.

She held on tight to her emotions and coolly asked, 'Do you think I might have a drink?'

While she sipped it, Fee jabbered on continuously. Amusing banter – that was as much his profession as painting was. But Amy hardly grasped what he was saying. She was preoccupied with her own feelings. For the first time she was experiencing the dark side of Jarret and Fee's nature as she had never known it before. She realised that in the past she had had nothing to offer them except a pure and innocent love and sexual passion for Jarret. For them she had been only a harmless plaything, while Jarret had been her life. How very changed things were now!

She listened, she even laughed, and found herself contributing to this unsavoury reunion. Amy felt herself drawn into it while at the very same time seeing clearly that Jarret had destroyed something in her that had never allowed her to love a man again as she had loved him. Seeing Jarret again, and Fee, who had always played his part in their love affair, laying the great seduction scene upon her for some yet unrevealed reason, Amy waited cynically for them to play their hand. They had known what they had done to her, and were prepared to rekindle her love for Jarret and to use it. A serious mistake.

The small revenge she had taken upon Jarret all those years ago had never really fazed him and had given her no real satisfaction. Now she understood why. When she wrought that pathetic bit of revenge she'd still believed that he had loved her, that she had been his only great love.

256

It had happened some months after he had tried for a reconciliation with her in New York and she had thrown him out. Fee was away on a trip to Nepal, had sent a postcard to say so. For some years after Jarret and Amy's break-up Fee continued to send her postcards. Amy made arrangements to meet Jarret in the *palazzo* in Venice. He assumed that she much regretted not taking him back and was sorry, all was forgiven and she was as much in love with him as ever. She stayed with him for several hours of sex. And then, when she knew he was once again erotically besotted with her, over the edge sexually, replete, and relieved he had her back in his life again, she rose from the bed and dressed. She had listened to him making plans to stay with her when next he came to New York. He began to sense something was very wrong. Amy said not another word to him from the time she rose from his bed. Soon she was walking away from him, he following behind her, through the many rooms of the *palazzo*. Catching up with her, he had spun her round and asked her what was going on.

Here, in a drawing-room in Belgravia, nearly thirty years later, she remembered her very words: 'I only came to use you for a great fuck, Jarret. Now I'm going home. How do *you* like being used?' He had slapped her face so hard she had fallen to her knees. But she had gathered herself up and walked away. That was the last time they had ever seen or spoken to each other.

Amy was not proud of that pathetic revenge. It had, she remembered, been sweet for a very few hours, but nothing more than that. And here Jarret was again, and Fee, trying to take advantage of her, she was certain of that, though she had yet to find out how. She knew that she could never allow that to happen. How very cruel and evil these men were, how clever and devious. The realisation dredged up a strange cunning and desire for greater revenge in Amy than she had ever known before. She could hardly equate these feelings with herself. At a certain moment Amy knew that this time round she would not walk away in a false glory of pathetic revenge, but would stay the course and fight Jarret and Fee. It was to be fire meet fire this time.

Almost without thought she found herself playing along with Jarret and Fee, allowing them to believe that Jarret's advances had worked; that Fee's eccentric charm, his desire to make her one of the family – how she detested the way in which he referred to Jarret and Tennant and himself as 'our little family' – was winning her over.

Amy thought of those other women who had been part of that inner circle they squirmed in. It nearly prompted her to ask Fee what had

257

happened to Savannah and the Contessa. Those two and how many more had once haunted her life with Jarret. But she saw no point. They would have been destroyed in one way or another, as Jarret had destroyed her by his so-called love. She could not help but wonder at how foolish she had been, and those other women, to have believed that he had loved them. Must a woman always delude herself that the man she loves loves her in the same way, with the same intensity, no matter that his actions decree differently?

Once she had thought of those women as the ghosts of past loves who haunted her life, and had hated them for that. Not now. Now she saw Savannah and the Contessa, and so many other women Fee and Jarret must have exploited, as sisters under the skin. She was about to go into battle against Jarret and Fee not only for herself but for them as well.

Fire with fire. Slowly, methodically, with incredible deviousness, she would strip them of all they possessed, destroy them publicly, and then she would walk out on them. She had hardly even to think about it, the plan seemed to formulate itself.

Very sweetly she told them, 'I can't believe this is happening to us after all these years. I think it's going to take me some time to get used to the idea that dreams do come true. I have a great deal to think about, I must go.'

Amy went to Jarret and placed her arms round his neck. She whispered something explicitly erotic in his ear and then kissed him on the cheek. When she released him she just caught the glance that passed between him and Fee and knew that she was not over-reacting to their reappearance in her life.

'I wish I could come home with you but I can't, my hostess would consider that very rude. She's been wonderful to us, having us all here for so long.'

'Still the great flirt, my dear Jarret.'

'It means nothing and will mean even less now that I've found you again.'

'Let's spend the day together tomorrow, the three of us?' suggested Fee.

'And what about your hostess?'

'I'll work it out,' said Jarret.

'What time should we come to you?' asked Fee.

'Don't, I'll come to you.'

'I would love Fee and Tennant to see your house.'

258

'Not tomorrow.'

'But here is impossible. We shan't be able to talk or make plans,' he said.

'Oh, we're going to make plans?'

Now Fee took over. 'Jarret loves you so much that he forgets all the important things in his life – our lives. He's always been that way when he's with you.'

'And that has always caused you a problem, hasn't it, Fee?'

'Frankly, yes.'

'Oh, yes, let's do be frank, Fee.'

'Fee! Not now.'

Here it comes, thought Amy. She looked at Jarret. He was his usual calm, self-assured self, with that touch of incredible arrogance.

'What's wrong, Jarret?'

'I don't want him to impose our problems on you.'

'What problems?'

'Very serious problems that have to be solved because if they are we can all have the most wonderful, happiest years of our lives together. And if they are not . . . well, best not to think about that,' said Fee.

'I'm not very good about solving other people's problems. I'll come back when you've worked them out. Does that sound familiar, Jarret? Now I really must go.'

He went to Amy and grabbed her by the arm. 'I thought we'd left the past behind us, forgotten?'

Amy removed his hand from her arm and caressed his cheek with her hand, leaned forward and kissed him lightly on the lips. 'Forgotten but not forgiven.'

She was walking from the room. Once more Jarret stopped her by taking her arm. They gazed into each other's eyes. 'Please, I want us to begin again. I'll prove to you that I love you – I began and you responded. You knew that it was right for us to be together. We need to begin anew, start a fresh life. In time you'll forgive me because I'll leave you with no other choice. There is no other man who can love you as I will, and we know you will never love another man as you loved me . . . as you will love me again. I'll make you happier than you've ever been. I need you, Amy. I've always needed you in my life.'

'Let me think about us tonight.'

'It isn't just us, it's my life, my son, the son you and I never had. I want to share him with you, make him too a part of your life. He's the most important part of mine.'

For Amy that was the lowest, the cheapest shot he could have delivered. Unforgivable! She had been all alone when she carried their son, alone when she had buried her beautiful six-week-old child, alone when she mourned him, alone every day of her life when she remembered him.

'Once you told me all the paintings you ever painted were mine, yet you never gave me one. Now you tell me you want to share your most precious possession: a son. Don't ever again promise me things you have no intention of delivering! Next you'll be promising me a *palazzo*, or maybe a *yalis*. And when I arrive with my luggage? A closed door. My dear, handsome, charming Jarret, I've been there, done that. You'll have to do better than tempt me with poetic promises this time round.'

'Then there is another time round for us?'

The look of relief on his face was a sight for Amy to behold, but the look on Fee's was astounding. Amy was more curious than ever to know what they wanted from her.

'Let's talk about things tomorrow.'

'And make love tonight. Take me home with you.'

'You've forgotten the Belgravia lady.'

'Tomorrow, then.'

'Yes, tomorrow. I'll come early and we'll do some of the London galleries and lunch with a friend of mine, and by then I expect you to tell me why, aside from your grand passion for me, you have sought me out and are promising me undying love until death do us part.'

'You don't believe how important you are to me?'

'Oh, but I do. Two taxis to seek me out? That's more money than you've spent on me since the first day I met you.'

Fee began to say something and Amy swung round to face him. 'Not a word. I would tread very carefully if I were you.' And she left the room.

Jarret walked her to the car. 'You mustn't be too harsh with Fee. He has always praised you, wants to be your friend.'

'Jarret, Fee needs me just as once before he needed me. At that time he found me and brought me to you to help you over a depressing time in your life. I lost my illusions a very long time ago. It would be no bad thing for you to remember that this time round and inform Fee of the fact. See you in the morning.'

All the way home from London there was not one moment given over to thoughts of Jarret and Fee. They were out of Amy's mind immediately she drove away from the Belgravia house. Her mind was instead focused first on the traffic leaving London and then on her work in progress. Lastly, as she drove down the track through the trees to her house, now brightly lit, about the sex she'd had with Jarret and the thrill of intense sexual attraction.

She entered the house and called out, 'Dave.'

'I'm in the kitchen, Miss Ross,' answered the off-duty policeman who acted as a guard over Amy's house when she had something as valuable on the premises as the Soutine. It was an extra precaution against theft. The house would remain inhabited by someone at all times while the Soutine was there.

The two had a cup of coffee together and then Dave went off duty. Amy made herself an omelette and called Charles.

'Hi, it's me. I'm not disturbing you, am I?'

'I have people here for dinner, but if it's brief, what can I do for you?'

'You could lunch me tomorrow and three others who might amuse you.'

'Sure, do you want to explain further?'

'No, I want an objective opinion. All you have to remember is, it's past tense. People who popped up from nowhere.'

'Say no more. One o'clock in the dining-room.'

Amy turned lights off and made certain the security alarms were on, then went up to the library. She should have felt tired, but she didn't. She felt restless, somehow unable to get the sex she had had with Jarret out of her mind. He was right about one thing: the chemistry between them was still there, but how strange that it meant absolutely nothing to her. She didn't even feel sad about that.

A fax came through with a list of dates suggested by the curator of one of the New York museums for a viewing of the Soutine. They wanted assurances of a first refusal. She faxed back the date that suited her best. Exhilarated that they were off the ground with the Soutine, Amy decided to take the Kramer Gallery file up to bed with her and make a stab at looking through it. She was halfway up the next flight of stairs to her bedroom when several photographs in the folder slipped out and fell on the stairs. She gathered them up and tossed them and the folder on to her bed before going to the dressing-room where she drew herself a bath.

Half an hour later, smelling of almonds, her skin glistening smooth, and wrapped in a celadon-green terrycloth bathrobe trimmed with robin's-egg-blue bands of satin, she approached the bed. Amy's

261

intention was to scoop up the file and photographs that she had tossed there so she might remove the eighteenth-century Persian embroidered coverlet. But she never touched it. Her attention was drawn to a large glossy black and white photograph of a magnificent eighteenth-century wooden mansion, a *yalis*, garden and hills rising behind and above it. The photograph had been taken from the water, the Bosphorus. Amy's blood ran cold. She stood next to her bed, looking down at the photograph, frozen to the spot. She knew without reading the documentation that went with that photograph that it was Jarret and Fee's house.

An image of that heartbreaking letter in violet-coloured ink from the Contessa Armida Montevicini flashed before Amy's eyes. That letter that had revealed to her what a grand passion can do to a once proud woman of character and substance. The romantic, elegant scrawl in violet ink had been for Amy the final humiliation of loving a bounder who could so cruelly strip a once remarkable lady of all dignity by making her beg for his favours in bed. The elegance, the splendour of that house, it was all there in that photograph. It could have been no one else's *yalis*.

Instinctively she knew the house was why Fee had arrived at her door when she was on her way to Switzerland. He and Jarret somehow knew that she was going to have something to do with the *yalis,* or could have, or might. But how had they known when she had no idea herself until the very minute she saw the photograph?

When Amy did finally reach out and take the photograph in her hands, she sat down on the bed close to the lamp and studied it in a better light. This house that had caused her so much anguish was an amazingly romantic place. One had only to look at it to imagine the gaiety, intrigue and assignations that once had taken place there. It seemed to have a life of its own. It seemed all wrong that it should have fallen into the hands of Jarret and Fee. Amy opened the folder on the bed and sought information on the house, but before she found it she discovered several other views of the *yalis*. Two photographs were quite old and in one she thought she saw the shadow of a woman standing in an upstairs window.

Photograph in hand, Amy ran downstairs to the library and her desk. There she switched on the desk light and took her magnifying glass and saw for the first time the Contessa Armida Montevicini. Her image was grainy, but made an impression not easily forgotten. She was old, her hair white, and dressed elaborately. Her face was impressive, more like a queen's than a countess's. Amy sensed that she must have been magnificent once.

She put the photograph down on the desk. To think that once she had dreamed she would live with Jarret in that house: the house he'd coveted so much, that he had never invited her to visit, that she had never seen until now. What was it in Fee and Jarret that made them ruin women for houses, give up love for their passion to possess? If Amy had not understood it thirty years ago, she understood it even less now.

Taking the photograph to return it to its folder, she was about to switch off the desk lamp but hesitated. Light was falling on her picture on the cover of *Art News* magazine. The Terry O'Neil photograph did her more than justice – that was something else she would take Anthony to task for; he had given it to the magazine, no one else could have. It was a portrait he had had the photographer take of Amy and the one he kept on his desk. She picked up the magazine and read the date. It had been three weeks getting to her, the magazine was nearly a month out to subscribers.

Then it clicked into place. Jarret and Fee had read the magazine. She had become over a period of decades a woman of position and power according to the art press. In the eyes of her former lover and his Byzantine friend, she had graduated from B list to A, a woman now worthy of being pandered to by Jarret and Fee as they had done all women who could enrich their lives. Desperation not love had made them seek her out.

Amy switched off the light and returned to her bedroom. Propped up against the bed pillows she put the Kramer file in order and then began to read. Two hours later she knew a great deal more about the houses available for the Anthony Kramer Museum in Istanbul. Only one was a *yalis*. It was called the Yalis Contessa Armida, and there was no mention of Jarret or Fee as being connected with the property. An excellent floor plan and several renderings of the interior gave Amy a clear and concise picture of the place.

There were other more impressive buildings but Amy was too distracted by the *yalis* and the mystery surrounding it to pay much attention to them. A mystery not only because of the reappearance of Jarret and Fee so suddenly in her life, but for the *yalis* being made available for the museum by the Turkish authorities. It was the odd building out compared to the others. Before Amy went to sleep she knew every nook and cranny of it. That the *yalis* had come to her attention was something she would never let on to Jarret and Fee.

'For old love's sake', that was the game they were playing with her. She too could play that game, if for no other reason than to see how far they would go to get whatever it was they wanted from her.

Amy reached out to the small pedestal dish on the table by her bed and plucked the last white chocolate from it. She looked at the delectable confection before biting into it and said aloud, 'And you? Where are you, Brice, whoever you are?'

Chapter 18

Amy had never realised she could be so very wicked. All morning as the three men, Tennant, Fee and Jarret, accompanied her round the London art galleries, they made repeated attempts to engage her in more personal talk. Each of them tried in vain and as the morning stretched out to lunchtime, they became less subtle about it. Amy saw it all and deliberately ignored it. She had no intention of making it easy for them. In fact, she rather enjoyed torturing them.

She was amused at the manner in which each of them, in their own way, was laying the seductive charm on her. Jarret's constant erotic insinuations; Fee's reminder of Jarret and Amy's love for each other; and Tennant reiterating how beautiful and vital she was, and how right his father had been to have loved her so long and so well. Jarret and Fee were as good at it as ever. And the young Tennant? They had taught him well. He was as irresistible as his father had been, a flirt who knew when to sparkle, how to kiss a lady's hand, how to turn on the soulful gaze. He would love women just as his father had, would be as self-serving and conniving as Fee had ever been. How many women would he ruin? He had been taught by masters.

She saw it in Tennant's eyes just as she had seen it in his father's when she had first met him. Erotic desire, passion to be used as directed by ambition, a quiet arrogance and a toughness hidden behind a guise of being the most sensitive and talented of people. The amoral son of an amoral man, born and brought up in an amoral lifestyle. What chance did he have of being anything other than the way he was? Amy had no doubt that women would fall madly, passionately, in love with him. Obsessively so even. They would accept him for what he was, flaws and all, and pay the price for their great romantic idyll. Hadn't she, after all, done so herself?

Still, all in all Amy was having a great time, swanning round with her three escorts. They were an impressive and interesting-looking entourage. She had dressed for the occasion, looking more glamorous than most art dealers had ever seen her. They rushed forward when the party appeared at a gallery; after all, they rarely had a chance to see Amy Ross doing the galleries with friends. Speculation was rife when she introduced the three artists to the various gallery owners. Did she know something they didn't about these men? Was there a talent here they had missed? Amy Ross was known not to waste her time.

Leaving the Marlborough Gallery, the last they would do before lunch, and walking up King Street, Amy between Jarret and Fee, Tennant just in front of them, she was reminded of those marvellous days in the early sixties when she and Jarret used to do the New York galleries. She was surprised when he picked up on her thoughts.

'This is great but I miss that frenetic buzz of the New York art world when you and I were there, Amy.'

'That was when you had that big breakthrough in your work, wasn't it, Pa?'

Fee looked pinched. Amy had her arm through his and actually felt him tense up, though he continued to keep pace with her and Jarret. 'That happened in Venice. And Jarret has had many breakthroughs, we all do. That's called progress in one's work.'

Amy tried not to gloat. She had always known that Fee could never accept her as Jarret's muse during the time they had been together. That had not been the role Fee cast her in. She could almost feel sorry for him. But almost was not enough. She was having too good a time enjoying his discomfort.

They crossed Piccadilly and were walking down Bond Street towards Claridge's. Amy directed a casual glance at Jarret. He was still one of the most attractive men around. She could understand why she had fallen in love with him, how she might do it all over again, except that she knew the dark side of his nature, that his self-absorption killed any love he might have for her or anyone else.

They were meeting Charles in his rooms for drinks before going down to the dining-room. Fee primped in the lift. Someone new to meet and conquer. Jarret put on his aloof manner. It never failed to draw attention to him. Tennant was just young and impressed with his morning and now Claridge's.

They were early and Charles was late and that gave Fee the opening Amy had been depriving him of all morning. Raskin offered drinks but no one accepted. The men were dazzled by Charles's drawing-room, especially the paintings. They walked round looking at them and Amy sat quietly and watched them. Fee went to sit next to her. He was about to say something, but she stopped him with a question.

'What are you doing in London, Fee?'

Both Jarret and Tennant turned round. She hadn't meant the question to sound so aggressive, but it was and clearly put them on the spot.

'Looking for you,' Jarret answered very matter-of-factly, and went to sit on the settee next to her. Tennant took a chair close by.

'I know you're here on a lost love mission, Jarret. You and your family have told me that enough times. But I still don't know what Fee is doing here, why he came to my house without you to seek me out. To plead your case and make sure I would see you? I think not. And Tennant? Tennant, while it's really nice to meet my one-time lover's son, and I find you an interesting and very handsome young man, I find it all a bit strange that you three should appear at my door at this particular time in my life when I was left behind so many years ago.'

'Are you angry with us?' asked Tennant.

'Oh, dear! Do I sound angry? I'm not. Tennant, your father and Fee and I, once, long before you were born, were rather more than friends. And then, hey presto, they vanished from my life. I think my anger, if indeed that was what I felt, has had enough time to peter out. Maybe I just need to know what this is all about?'

At this point she picked up Jarret's hand and raised it to her lips. Kissing it, she added, 'I mean, aside from love and passion the second time around.'

Clearly here was an Amy Ross that Jarret and Fee had never seen before. Jarret considered her: this woman so assured and in control of her life, so content with herself and her world, her sexuality. This woman whom they had never believed could make anywhere near the mark she had done as an art historian. It was true they had had something between them once that he had not forgotten. He felt almost sad that now thirty years later she had all the things to add to his life, and Tennant's and Fee's, that she had not had then.

Amy had toughened over the years. Her naivety was gone, although that innocence and unworldliness had been what set her aside from the other women he had had sexual affairs with. It had been such a burden for him, and for Fee as well.

He knew her far better than she thought he did. She loved him still. A love where you would happily give your life for your partner? That sort of love never wholly dies, it merely gets put aside when life

267

intervenes. He had no doubts that Amy still felt deeply for him. He was giving her another chance to love him. When she knew the facts, and what she must do if there was to be a chance for them to be as happy in love as they had once been, she would play.

'We need your help, Amy. You're in a position to help us. Possibly the only person who is. If you don't we'll have lost everything, be on the streets in our old age.'

'I somehow don't believe that, Fee.'

'It's true, Amy,' said a concerned-sounding Tennant.

'Maybe you had better explain?'

Jarret began to speak but she interrupted him. 'No, not you. I want to hear it from Fee. And Fee, don't dress up the truth in the colours that suit you. Do that and I'll walk out of here right now.'

Amy could see the look of surprise in the men's faces. She realised that that was just what they had planned to do and she had caught them out. Looks of desperation replaced their surprise, giving Amy no satisfaction.

'I don't know where to begin.'

'The beginning, Fee, and tell it straight. There's too much at stake for you to manipulate and play games with me this time around.'

Amy was astonished that not one of them looked embarrassed at her directness. Hardened criminals, she thought. But at the time had no idea how right she was.

'The first ten years after we met you were wonderful years for Jarret and me. There's no need to go into detail – you know what our life was like. Jarret's work, his successes, and I too began to paint again. Money was never in abundance but we lived well, travelled, saw amazing things – in some cases very spiritual. Tibet, India, China. We did incredibly interesting things, and there were always patrons to ease our way. We lived a social life when we wanted it and a reclusive one when we were working. The *palazzo* in Venice, the *yalis* in Istanbul, the flat in Paris.'

'Savannah?'

'Maybe you should ask Jarret about Savannah.'

'I'm asking you, Fee.'

'It doesn't really matter, Fee. There are no secrets from Amy any more.'

'The relationship between Savannah and Jarret always remained a tortured one. She fought him through the courts to get the Paris flat back, but we won. She fought for financial compensation, claiming

268

that we had robbed her of her wealth, which simply isn't true. There had been a pre-nuptial agreement. After years of litigation she lost that too. Still she haunted our lives, insisting on living in near penury and embarrassing us at every turn. There were any number of men who wanted to marry her but she refused. It got much worse when Jarret married Tennant's mother. Savannah called herself Mrs Jarret Sparrow till the day she committed suicide.'

Amy felt sick with despair for Savannah whom she had never met. As if someone had winded her with a punch deep into her belly. She saw not an iota of sympathy for the dead woman in the men's eyes, and Fee had spoken of Savannah's suicide with no emotion or regret for the poor, unfortunate woman. The very one whom he had once professed to love and care for and whom he'd dreamed would one day get back together with Jarret. There by the grace of God go I, thought Amy, and managed to hide from the men how deeply disturbed she was by their news.

Fee, hardly catching his breath, continued, 'It was Tennant's mother's money that for years helped us to fight off Savannah. There was all sorts of treachery. Savannah's mother agreed to pick up the legal fees for her though they remained estranged from the time Savannah and Jarret divorced.'

'Why was that, Jarret?'

'Because they were both in love with me.'

Amy had insisted on honesty and now she was getting it. Would that Jarret had been this honest with her when she was obsessively in love with him all those years ago. Lie upon lie, evasion upon evasion, had been the foundation of their love affair then. It was with such a degree of indifference that he delivered the information that Amy felt spurred on to ask anything she chose. It was like laying the ghosts that had haunted her love affair with Jarret.

'What happened to your mother, Tennant?'

'She and Pa decided they wanted to lead separate lives.'

'An amicable divorce,' interceded Fee.

'And you chose to live with your father, Tennant?'

'Yes. I have more in common with my father and Fee than I do with my mother.'

'You love your father and Fee and their lifestyle and their work?'

'I sure do. We're a team.'

Amy was horrified. These two men who adored Tennant were creating him in their own image. Would another generation of women

269

be taken in by him, used and abused? Where would it all end? What had happened to love?

Amy thought that it was about time she got round to the Contessa Armida and her *yalis*. The photographs of the house and the woman she had seen the night before were still fresh in her mind. She realised that she had been putting it off by asking questions she really wasn't interested in, not only to frustrate Fee but because the memory of the Contessa's love letter to Jarret still haunted her. A letter written by a woman very old in years yet young in heart, and in love with a man who, if rumour was to be believed, was taking over her mansion on the Bosphorus, room by room, reducing her circumstances while his own flourished.

Amy had always felt that that letter was one she could have written herself if the Contessa hadn't done it for her. She had always felt that she owed this woman, whom she had never met and would now never meet, a debt of gratitude for saving her from such an indignity.

'The Contessa Armida Montevicini – I'm sure she's long since dead?'

Amy had seen Jarret and Fee turn cold on someone before. It had always been in their eyes, that coldness and anger. In their deportment they never showed emotion, but remained charming, Jarret a little aloof, Fee eccentric. Wonderful cover-ups for the real Fee and Jarret they never showed the world. Now it was there in their eyes, that coldness – and something else. Hatred. Was it for her or the Contessa? Amy was astonished to see how she had ruffled them.

'Why do you mention her death?' asked Jarret, his manner cool and very icily under control.

'I was not *mentioning* her death, merely stating that she must be long since dead. Unless she's lived to be over a hundred years old?'

The look that passed between Fee and Jarret was one Amy hoped never to see again. It came from some dark recess of their souls. She knew these men well. At least she'd thought she did until she saw that look pass between them. It actually sent a shiver down her spine.

Fee, having recovered himself somewhat, said, 'How strange that you should remember the Contessa Armida.'

'I don't exactly remember her, more the violet ink she used to write her letters, and a charming, seductive voice which I heard when she called my flat, trying to talk to Jarret. Surely she's not still alive and living with you in the *yalis* in Istanbul?'

'Amy, I don't know what you've heard but . . .'

'I've heard a lot of things over the years, Jarret, but you would do better to ask me what I listened to.'

It was at that point that Charles arrived. Everyone stood up and Amy walked forward to meet him. Looking over her shoulder, she said, 'Rest easy, Jarret, I've not heard her name mentioned since you last lived with me in New York.'

She kissed Charles affectionately, then slipping her arm through his, made the introductions.

Charles's entrance into the room immediately instigated a change of atmosphere. The men took to him. He was young and handsome and an aristocrat. He had flawless taste and obviously a great deal of money, but he had something else too: the ability to enjoy any situation at any given time. The intrigue and angst that had permeated Amy's conversation with Jarret and Fee vanished as if they had never been.

Amy tried to remain detached as she watched the four men, always keeping in mind that dark side that the visitors hid so well. Yet by the time they had all gone down in the lift to the dining-room she had been swept into their orbit and was enjoying them as she had once done in those very first days over thirty years before. In many ways the years vanished as if they had never existed. She felt young, and full of life and energy and love.

There was no question that Jarret and Fee knew how to stroke people, make themselves lovable. They were the best strokers in the business. They had the ability almost instantly to inspire some sort of devotion from everyone they met. Amy had seen captains and commanders of industry and the art world who were only too willing to cosset and coddle these toy boys. Hadn't she done it herself, and without realising it? How many husbands had fallen in love with Jarret while their wives played a mothering role to him, with the promise of a secret sexual liaison always hovering in the back of their minds. Minor royals, aristocrats, millionairesses and women of consequence, all had been there for him.

Jarret, Fee and Tennant stroked Charles and he loved them. They stroked Amy and she forgot that they were three of nature's tarts. Professional party-goers working the table and Claridge's dining-room, ruthlessly exploiting their charm to promote themselves and their careers.

Over a long and extraordinarily amusing lunch that had many of the diners looking away from their own meals and wishing they were a guest at that table, part of that scene, Amy succumbed. She fell for Jarret all over again. Only this time she was aware of who she was falling for.

At four o'clock they were the last people in the dining-room except for those few waiters who were hovering round their table in the hope that Charles would call a halt to the extravagant lunch he had provided so they might go home. But it was Tennant who came to their rescue. He looked at his watch and all but jumped out of his chair.

'The time has just flown, Charles, I must go. I'm supposed to be leaving right this minute for the country with our hostess.'

Charles rose from his chair, as did Fee and Jarret. 'I am off to the South of France this afternoon and so I too must leave. But it's been great fun, and many thanks for joining me for lunch. I hope to see you all again. Amy will arrange it.'

The party left the restaurant and Charles walked with them to the lobby, offering his car to take Tennant to his destination and tea to Fee, Jarret and Amy in the lounge where a string ensemble would soon be playing. A shaking of hands and many flattering words and thanks and Charles left them there to get on with his preparations for leaving London.

Replete with too much food and wine, Jarret, Fee and Amy waited for their tea to arrive. 'He's wonderful. It was really nice of him to take us all on at such short notice. A lover?' asked Jarret.

'Yes.'

'I think I could be jealous.' And he took Amy's hand in his and lowered his head to kiss it.

'Then why aren't you?'

'Because you love me more than you ever have Charles.'

'You're always so sure of yourself, Jarret.'

'Amy, you must keep Charles as a friend, he's charming. Bring him to Venice,' said Fee.

'Oh. Am I coming to Venice, Fee?'

'For my part, you're welcome to come.'

'More to the point, where shall we go now?'

'To your house, Amy.'

'I think not, Fee.'

'I somehow thought you might say that, so I have arranged that we might be alone in the Belgravia house. We've sent Tennant off to the country with our hostess and have promised to follow later this evening. This has been charming but we *must* talk.'

'With you guys it's always pay the piper, isn't it? Well, let's go then.'

As the doorman opened the door of Amy's car for her, she thought she had never seen such a look of envy, surprise, complete disbelief on anyone's face as she saw on Fee's at that moment. 'Once you thought me not stylish enough to share your lives. Not now by the look on your face, Fee?'

'Too stylish. I think I'll walk and meet you at the house.' The three of them had the good grace to laugh at themselves.

As Amy circled Belgrave Square they saw Jarret's hostess and Tennant sneak a kiss in the back seat of her black Bentley on the other side of the square, just pulling away from the house. Amy somehow found it too embarrassing to comment on. She parked her car and together she and Jarret put the top up and locked it into place. Jarret used his key at the front door.

'All the servants have gone to the country. We have the house to ourselves. Come to bed. I've been wanting you all afternoon.'

'Fee will be here soon.'

'No, he won't. Two hours at least.'

'To walk from Mayfair?'

'You forget the window shopping. A stop to rest his feet and play the charming foreigner in some little shop, looking at something that takes his fancy and which is the last thing we need. No, two hours at the very least.'

Jarret had Fee down pat. It made Amy laugh. While he had her at her ease Jarret wrapped his arms round her and drew her to him. 'You've been wonderful, a star all day. But then, you always were a star for me. Always sparkled and brought me luck, made me the happiest of men.'

His kiss was full of love and passion and Amy felt herself slip under its spell. How she had once burned for those kisses! Now they were like an old friend that had returned to nourish her. Together they walked up the stairs to the bedroom floor. Jarret double locked the door. Who was this man who kissed her like her lover of long ago? Amy forgot to be confused about that. They slipped beneath the silken sheets and their erotic life took them over.

It was dark when they dressed and walked down the stairs to the small sitting-room where Fee was waiting for them. It was the dark that comes with late autumn when the time of day doesn't seem quite to fit the degree of light. It was only half-past six.

'The last train we can make to get to the country tonight is ten-thirty, Jarret.'

'Then let's get on with it, shall we, Fee?' said Amy.

273

'Well, that's what I've been trying to do. This isn't easy for us, to come begging a favour from someone we've been out of touch with for thirty years.'

'I can appreciate that, Fee. Well, cards on the table then.'

'That day I came looking for you at your house, it was to ask you to help me . . . well, us. Jarret didn't want to be the first to approach you. You had rebuffed him before, he expected it again. It was I who insisted. The idea came to us when we saw your face on the cover of *Art News* and read the back-up story.'

Amy very nearly stamped her foot in rage, not against Fee but Anthony Kramer. Here was a perfect example of why she preferred to stay in the background of things. 'Go on, Fee.'

'I know my countrymen very well. This position you hold with the Kramer Foundation, you do know that makes you a serious power broker in Turkey? You can ask any favour and it will most assuredly be granted. You can make any demand. The powers that be will do anything to keep you sweet. That will be the prime directive of any number of departments in the government, and will go right to the top. The last thing the government wants is to lose that museum, or the money for the foundation to keep it going. Turkey's a poor country with only an ancient culture to fall back on. The new museum will change all that.

'We're in serious trouble in Turkey, and you, Amy, are the answer to all our problems. If you are willing to help us.'

'And why would I do that, Fee?'

'Because for you love is everything,' he answered.

Jarret, who was sitting next to Amy, took her hand in his and squeezed it. Confirmation from him that he too knew that and appreciated the fact?

Amy managed to keep the emotion from her voice when she said, 'What's the problem, Fee?'

'The *yalis* and all our possessions and paintings, the bulk of a lifetime's work for both of us, have been impounded by the high court in Istanbul for nearly ten years now. Jarret and I are unable to return to Turkey. If we do we'll be arrested and tried for fraud, and must answer to charges of the attempted murder or murder of the Contessa Armida Montevicini.'

Amy gasped. She placed her hands over her face and lowered her head. Tears welled into her eyes and a near scream of 'No!' escaped from the depths of her soul. Jarret rose from the settee and walked to

274

the fireplace and stood there. Fee went to the drinks table and poured her a glass of sherry.

'Drink this. It might help.'

Amy was trembling so badly she had to take the glass with two hands. She drank it down in one swallow. It did help. She had gone cold and the sherry brought some warmth back to her body. Ever since that horrible morning thirty years ago when she had read that crumpled letter written in violet ink, she had feared for the Contessa Armida. But sinister death at the hands of Jarret and Fee? Not in her wildest dreams could she have imagined that.

'I know it's shocking to think of us having been put in this awkward position, to have such allegations made against us. Are you all right? Shall I go on?'

Of course that would be what they thought had shocked her. They did not know after all that Amy had read the letter from the Contessa, crumpled up and thrown away in a wastebasket. They had no way of knowing her anguish was not for them but for the last years of the foolish, love-besotted countess.

'Yes.'

'I think you know that we bought the *yalis* and all its contents from the Contessa over a period of many years. When we first met her, she was still beautiful and vivacious and had her house open to a côterie of friends from all walks of life. She ran a salon that was internationally known and famed for its wit and intelligent conversation. She had always been a well-loved and respected character in Istanbul and I had grown up with her name as part of the aristocratic legend of my city. We were introduced to her the first few days after I brought Jarret home to Istanbul. She swept him off his feet. Even in old age she was a woman of infinite female charm and sexuality. The Contessa fell in love. She offered us rooms to live in in her *yalis* – there are, after all, forty-odd rooms in it – and we moved in. It was rent free and a wonderful place to live and work in, and she cared for us and kept us in a style that was grand and amusing. We were all very happy. She was above all a realist and when we would go off to travel or to live for a few months in Venice, she remained in the *yalis* talking care of our things and affairs.'

Jarret picked up the story from there. 'She was outliving her money, so she cut down on her hospitality and made economies, and then finally, as she grew older, became quiet and reclusive. She had wonderful treasures that she kept selling off to keep herself. We and her precious *yalis* were her whole world. Eventually we started to buy the *yalis*, room by room, by taking on the upkeep and the taxes. We needed larger premises to exhibit our work to the dealers who by now were coming to visit us. She'd lost interest in the running of the house so we took over. She had a very happy life with us except for the few years when I was married to Savannah. We brought Savannah to Istanbul, but that didn't work out. Too bad. They could have been very good company for one another. Then Armida was very unhappy when I met you.'

After a few moments of silence Fee continued, 'There were ancient servants who had been with her in their youth and they and some of her friends resented the relationship we had with Armida and the fact that she was passing the house on to us room by room. Every time we took over a room we had a paper drawn up and we three signed it and had it notarised. As she became old and frail she needed less of the rooms to wander in and so we redid the servants' quarters and made her very comfortable there. When the last of her servants died, and because we were away so much of the time, we decided she would be happier in a small farm cottage she owned on a pretty estate on one of the Princess Islands. So we fixed that up and moved all the things she loved into it. There was a woman in the village who was paid to do her meals and to see that she had everything she wanted. It was there that she died in an unusually cold winter. We were in Tibet at the time, so you see we had absolutely nothing to do with her death.

'At the time, though we mourned her, we thought her death was a godsend. She had no quality of life left, and in her dotage she had turned against Jarret and me, the only two people who stuck by her to the end.'

Jarret walked back from the fireplace to sit next to Amy again. He told her, 'There was no inquest. She was buried on the estate where she died by the woman who took care of her. We, of course, immediately on our return from Tibet, went to pay our respects at her graveside. Then we had everything moved from the cottage back to Istanbul and got on with our lives.'

'You had already married your new wife then?'

'Yes, years before, and Tennant was a young boy.'

'You don't know my country, Amy, they can make a mystery, a Byzantine intrigue, out of anything, even death from natural causes,' said Fee.

'And that's what they did?'

276

'I'll say! Because Armida died on a remote estate on an island that has little contact with the mainland, never mind Istanbul, news of her death was not revealed until months after it happened, and then only as rumour until we returned to verify that it had taken place. Even then the news travelled slowly. This is the East after all.

'People began to talk, and jealousy began eating away at old friends of Armida's because now we owned and controlled one of the finest properties in Istanbul. But no one did anything about it. We never realised that for years she had been writing to friends telling them of her poverty and how she was living in penury, that she wanted to return to her house on the Bosphorus and soon we would be coming for her and taking her home. An old woman's delusions, of course.

'The most despicable rumours were circulating about the conditions she was forced to live in by us, and how she met her death. They increased because we refused to have her body exhumed and brought back to Istanbul for burial in the garden of the *yalis*, which it seems she had told everyone she had ever known, except Jarret and myself, was what she wanted done with her remains. We ignored all the rumours and some threats from several of her friends that they would not rest until she came home to her *yalis*. And, of course, nothing happened.

'For ten years we got on with our lives, moving between Paris, Venice and Istanbul. That's as long as it took them to cook up a case of fraud and attempted murder against us. I was tipped off by a young friend of mine in the police that papers containing serious allegations were about to be served on us within the hour, that Jarret and I should flee from the *yalis* and get out of Turkey by five that afternoon because the police were planning a raid and intended to impound the house and contents and take us into custody for questioning on the death of the Contessa.'

'This is a horror story. What did you do?' asked Amy, who was by this time a bag of nerves, finding the whole thing unsavoury beyond words.

'I called a lawyer friend and told him what I had just heard, and he said to leave the house at once, to waste no time in long discussions on the telephone, not to bother to pack, but to grab our passports and run, just get out of the country as fast as possible and call him from abroad. We could see the process server walking through the garden as our motor-taxi pulled away from the *yalis*. Genevieve, Jarret's wife, Tennant, Jarret and I fled the country, took the first flight available. We had a late lunch in Damascus.'

'And you've never been back?'

'No, never.'

'Then you were never served the papers?'

'Yes, *in absentia*, and have been made *persona non grata* in Turkey. The position as it stands now, and has done for ten years, is that if we set foot on Turkish soil we will be arrested and made to answer the fraud and other charges laid against us. I daren't even enter a Turkish embassy anywhere in the world for fear they might kidnap me and send me back.'

'And have you tried to fight this from abroad?'

'Right from day one,' answered Jarret.

'We have an excellent lawyer in Turkey who represents us. He's investigated every aspect of the allegations placed against us, and I won't lie to you – although he's made progress on some fronts, he's not done well enough without a real power broker who can twist people's arms and get the case thrown out of the courts. Time is now on our side rather than theirs because they haven't been able to prosecute so far.'

Jarret told Amy, 'You can well imagine we have had some seriously influential people from France, Italy and the States, even Turkey, who have come forward with statements and character references supporting us, but so far nothing has worked. Now we think we have something that might.'

'What's that?'

'You,' said Fee.

'How?'

The two men looked at one another. It was a gaze of relief. *Amy Ross was going to play. Love had won out.* She could almost hear what she saw pass between them in that gaze.

'We were advised by a Turkish judge friend of ours a few years ago that the only thing that would make the charges go away was if it was proven that we had sold our interest to someone of influence, preferably an American who was going to do something for the country. A request from that American could then be made that the courts drop the case since Jarret and I were no longer owners of the *yalis* and the new owner wanted no litigation attached to their property.

'The Byzantine mind is not stupid. The Turks would not offend a generous patron of their country. The fraud charges would be dropped as well as the absurd accusation of attempted murder, so as not to create a scandal that would offend the new money moving into Istanbul.

'The decree of *persona non grata* against Jarret and me would fade away to save embarrassment. In six months we could be back in the *yalis*, and if we kept a low profile for a year it would be as if it never happened at all. That's the way of the East. It's such a simple solution. Everyone saves face and no one holds any grudges. Very oriental. A brilliant plan but not easy to achieve. Who to find? Who to trust? We had no idea until we saw the cover of *Art News*.'

'Fee, this is a great deal to take in. Jarret, what do you want me to do?'

'Forgive me the past, help us, and believe that whether you do or you don't, I want you in my life again.'

What sweet and winning words from any lover! 'When are you leaving London?' asked Amy.

'We're supposed to go straight from the country to the airport on Monday morning. But we can change our plans, come and stay with you and work it all out,' replied Jarret.

'No, I don't want you to do that. You return to Venice. I'm going to go home now and I would like to take any documents that are relevant to your problem back with me to my place. I want to read them and have my lawyer look at them.'

'Is that necessary?' asked Fee.

'It is to me, if I'm going to help you.'

'I thought you might like to see some paperwork,' Jarret interrupted. 'Fee, go get the files.'

'Are they the originals?' asked Amy.

'Yes.'

'You have copies in Venice?'

'Yes.'

'Don't look so worried, Jarret, I won't lose them.'

Fee returned with the files and presented them to Amy. 'You will help us?' he asked, seemingly still reluctant about giving the documents to her.

'I don't know is the only answer I can give for now. I need some time to think about all this. Give me two weeks to consider things: you and Jarret coming back into my life, your problems, our futures.'

Chapter 19

On returning home, and after sending Dave off, Amy placed the files on a table in the library and went directly to her room where she bathed and slipped between the sheets, falling almost immediately into a deep and dreamless sleep.

In the morning she rose from her bed feeling extremely unnerved, sick even. She made herself tea but soon brought that up. She needed no doctor to tell her that she was not ill. Amy knew she was distressed by the reappearance of Jarret and Fee, the memory of love, the sad death of the Contessa, most particularly the injustice of all she had seen and heard. It seemed always to come down to the same old question for Amy. How to measure love.

She fed the ducks and dressed and went for a walk along the river, feeling the better for it. On her return she walked past the library table with the files on it and straight to her desk to call the florist.

Flowers for the house: dozens of huge white stargazer lilies and branches of shiny dark camellia leaves. The house must look its best for the curator arriving to view the Soutine.

Then a lunch menu to be planned. Keep it simple: cups of hot vichyssoise, thick with cream and sprinkled with freshly snipped chives, followed by thin slices of smoked salmon stuffed with light and fluffy eggs scrambled with paper-thin slivers of white truffle. Hot buttered slabs of toasted brioche. A bottle of Chablis Grand Cru, and demi-tasse cups of espresso with a twist of lemon. For pudding pears poached in red wine, sugar, cinnamon and cloves, lemon and orange zest, the wine reduced to a thick syrup, a shallow pool for the pear to stand in. These would be served with rivulets of thick white cream running over the voluptuous fruit. All simple to make and no problem if her visitor didn't want lunch.

After the call to the florist Amy rang through to several shops for provisions. She was still on the telephone when a fax started coming through from Japan. She tore it from the machine and read it while talking to the fishmonger in Scotland about posting the salmon: Please would she advise the first possible time the Soutine might be available to be viewed?

Unable to contain her excitement Amy shouted, 'Yes, yes, yes!' into the telephone, and then her arms shot up and with tight fists she punched the air. The telephone fell on the desk.

She collapsed back against the tapestry wing chair she was sitting in and a broad smile spread across her face. Now the game of selling the Soutine had two serious contenders. Here was where the fun and the real money would begin. She heard the sound of a Scots accent somewhere in the distance. It took her several seconds to realise it was Mr Burns from Aberdeen still talking about smoked salmon. She grabbed the telephone and was hard pressed to hold back her laughter.

The curator from New York came. Amy lunched him, as she had planned to, in front of the fire, the Soutine lit magnificently on an easel before them, several handsome Etruscan vases proffering white lilies dramatically displayed at the base of the easel. They ate off their laps, draped with huge white damask napkins trimmed in ecru lace. The curator was besotted with the Soutine, comfortable with Amy whom he'd known only slightly before his arrival at her house. He only left at dark and then reluctantly. Amy was certain that had he had it in his power he would have paid her the asking price then and there and walked off with the Soutine. Instead he asked her to hold it exclusively for him for one week so he might meet with the board at his museum. She would have her answer before the week was up as to whether they would or would not purchase. Then he was gone.

Several days after the visit from the curator, Charles called. He was back from the South of France and with a dozen questions about Jarret and his entourage. They laughed all over again at some of the most amusing things that had been said at lunch. Amy was not surprised by Charles's comment: 'I can understand very well how you could have been in love with Jarret, Amy, but what surprises me is that you were prepared to live so dangerously for love. That's a side of you I've never seen before.'

It was that conversation and having a little space in her own negotiations that prompted Amy to sit down at the library table and consider the documents she had been given. Several hours later she arranged the papers neatly in their file then went to sleep.

The following morning her first call was to her solicitor for an appointment. Her second call, made much later in the day, was to Edward in New York. There was the usual chit-chat and gossip and then she told him, 'Well, you'll be pleased. I've come up with my shortlist for a building for the museum. What's yours?'

Amy gave a sigh of relief to hear Edward had not put the *yalis* on his list. Neither had she. She was over the first hurdle.

When she called Anthony he was unavailable but did return her call several hours later. He had his shortlist, and that did not have the *yalis* on it either. She was over the second hurdle.

'I'm still angry with you about that *Art News* cover, Anthony.'

'Oh, do drop it, darling. I told you, I'll make it up to you.'

'Oh good, then you can do me a favour.'

He sounded relieved when he told her, 'Anything.'

'Your Mr Fixit man in Istanbul. Do you think I could ask a favour of him?'

'Is that all? Yes, anything. I'll call him and tell him to make himself available to you and have him call you. You mean that'll do it? I'm off the hook, forgiven, and you'll never mention that bloody story again?'

'Never.'

'Thank God for that!'

'Now. Could you call him now?'

'This very minute?'

'Yes.'

'Do I want to know what this is about?'

'No. It wouldn't interest you.'

Not twenty minutes later the phone began to ring and ring and ring. Amy was sitting next to it but made no attempt to pick up the receiver. She kept staring into the black instrument. Instinctively she knew that this call would set off a chain of events that she might one day regret. To answer that telephone would be to send herself down a path from which there was no return. By now the incessant ringing was splitting her ear drums. She picked up the receiver.

'Hello.'

'Hello, I believe you would like me to assist you in something? My name is Suleyman Gazi.'

'Yes, I think that's exactly what I want.'

'I am at your service.'

'Mr Gazi, I need some information. Two men of my acquaintance

283

are not in very good standing with the Turkish authorities. I would very much like to know as much as you can find out from the prosecution about the case, and just what exactly these men are accused of. What evidence the prosecutor's office has interests me greatly as well.'

'The men's names?'

'They are Jarret Sparrow, an American, and Firuz Yolu, sometimes called Fee, a Turk. The case involves the death of a woman, the Contessa Armida Montevicini, and possession of her *yalis* on the Bosphorus. Is that enough for you to go on?'

'Yes, quite enough. I will call you in a few days.'

'That would be just fine.'

After Amy put down the telephone she locked the file in the wall safe and put the whole business out of her mind. She called Amanda Whately and asked if she and Dick wanted to take a ride upriver for lunch. They did, so Amy dressed for the river and went down to make *Arcadia* ready. A day on the Thames and a luscious three-star lunch . . . just what was needed. The treat of slowly cruising by some of the most beautiful English riverside property was always a joy. The peace and quiet of country manicured through the ages into something rare and unique, England at its very best, its most privileged. Amy appreciated every nuance of that.

It took four days for Mr Gazi to call back and that was a good thing because it gave Amy time to consider what she was doing and steel herself in order to carry things through.

After the usual civilities Mr Gazi said, 'I have that information you are interested in.'

'All of it?'

'Yes.'

'Reliable? It must be reliable.'

'I can assure you, it is. I've spoken to all the right people, most discreetly, and even have copies of what's on record. You may be surprised by what you read.'

'Mr Gazi, I may be unhappy but I won't be surprised.'

'Oh, I see.'

'How shall we do this? Can you put me in the picture now then post the written information?'

'Not a good idea. Most of it is written in Turkish and I would rather not speak about any of this except face to face. Shall you come here, or shall I come to you?'

284

'What do you think best?' asked Amy.

'The latter.'

'Then how soon can you come?'

'Day after tomorrow. When I come to England I always stay at the Savoy. Shall we say eleven a.m.?'

'I'm very grateful to you for your help, Mr Gazi. Until the day after tomorrow then.'

Several hours after that another call came through from New York: the curator with an offer on the Soutine. Amy rejected it outright. The following morning he was on the telephone again with a better offer but Amy rejected that as well.

'You have someone else interested?'

'Yes.'

'I thought you gave us first refusal?'

'I did. And you are the only person who has seen it, and as I promised no one else will view it until your week is up, in two days' time.'

'What's the best you'll do for us on price?'

'You already have it. And I'm sure you would not like to have to pay more – which you will have to if it's to become a two-horse race.'

'I'll have to get back to you.'

'Fine.'

He did get back to her in the late afternoon that day. They made a provisional deal. The museum would buy the Soutine at the asking price, but there was still the matter of where they would obtain the funds to pay for it. He needed thirty days to work that out, and if he couldn't he would then give up his exclusive rights to purchase the painting and she could sell it on the open market. Amy refused this suggestion. He called her uncompromising then said he would get back to her.

Time seemed to fly by for Amy and before she even realised it it was time to meet Mr Gazi. She called from a house phone in the lobby. He told her he thought they needed privacy. They could talk in the sitting-room of his suite if that was all right with her.

He answered the door and until that moment Amy had not even thought about Mr Gazi or what he might look like, though had she he would not have been a tall, slender man of considerable years, with a head of white hair, elegant rather than handsome, and dressed by a

Savile Row tailor. Leave it to Anthony, she thought. It was rarely that he got things wrong.

Amy and Mr Gazi shook hands and immediately each knew that they liked each other. He ushered her into the elegant but somehow very English sitting-room overlooking the river. A table draped in white damask and with a bowl of white and cream-coloured roses on it was standing in the window, set for two. A waiter stood at attention. Mr Gazi helped Amy off with her coat and she was amused to see him stroke the lynx collar as he handed it to a man who was standing by to take it.

'I thought mid-morning coffee would be acceptable.'

'How kind. Perfect, actually, I've just driven in from the country. But this looks like more than mid-morning coffee.'

He smiled. It did indeed. There was a pedestal dish of luscious-looking Danish pastries, a silver basket of small brioches, another of croissants. A silver coffee service. They sat down and the waiter poured coffee and whisked a silver-domed cover off a platter of warm coronets of puff pastry oozing melted Gruyère cheese. Once they were served Mr Gazi dismissed the waiter and the maid and he and Amy were left alone.

'There's a great deal to tell you. Do you mind if we talk while we take coffee?' he very politely asked.

'That's fine.'

'I don't really know where to begin. Where would you like me to?'

'Have you read the material?'

'Yes, everything, otherwise how could I inform you of the contents?'

'How stupid of me, of course. Then you are familiar with every aspect of the case for the prosecution?'

'I would say so. I have also obtained from the men leading the case their opinions and how they plan to proceed or not proceed as the case may be.'

'I think you should be aware that all I know is what the men themselves have told me. I have brought their statements of how they intend to defend themselves and documents on any action so far taken against them. So, in fact, you've got one side of the story and I have the other. What I want is for you and I, Mr Gazi, to put these two sides together and see what we consider to be the real truth – or as close to it as we can come. Now shall we begin by my telling you what I know, and then we can match it up with what you know?'

'I think that might be a good beginning.'

Amy explained who and what she was and her connection to Anthony and the new museum they were building in Turkey. Then she began telling Mr Gazi what she knew of Fee and Jarret and what she had read. When she was finished he suggested they move to a pair of chairs set opposite each other in front of the open fire, a round table between them and on it papers neatly stacked. He rang for the waiter to take away the table in the window.

Mr Gazi began, 'What I am about to tell you is free from personal comment. We will deal here only in facts. Any opinions I have to offer, if you wish to hear them, I will make later. This way we can be completely objective.

'Let us begin with the *yalis*. There is no proof that will stand up in the courts that Mr Jarret Sparrow or Mr Firuz Yolu either together or separately own the property in question. The registered deeds of ownership have never been changed. They are still in the name of the Contessa Armida Montevicini. The receipts that the men have are virtually useless in this fight and made so by their own greed. The notarised papers they have merely state that in exchange for the care and maintenance of the property to the standard to which the Contessa had always maintained it, and for their taking over the costs of the lifestyle to which she was always accustomed and wished to continue to live in, she has given them the drawing-room or the dining-room, etc., etc. They used that ploy until they had every room in the house made over to them. She allowed them to believe they owned the rooms and later it was they who made her believe they did. In fact, this was never the case. The notarised papers mean nothing because no sums of money were mentioned, and they are null and void because the men did not live up to their promises. They never maintained the house nor kept the Contessa in the manner in which she had lived all her life – until she met those men.

'That brings me to the last years of the Contessa's life. There is overwhelming evidence to prove that at the time she met these men she had sufficient money to maintain her grand lifestyle if she lived to be one hundred years old. When the authorities raided the house and confiscated its contents those villains had not had a chance to dispose of the Contessa's private papers before they fled the country. She kept ledgers, diaries, every receipt for the money she gave them, and all were marked loans. They also found letters, many from the two men. Very damaging against them. She was a woman obsessed with love for Mr Sparrow, but in reading his letters to her one would have

287

thought, as she must have, that he was equally as obsessed with love for her.

'An old woman foolishly in love with a younger man she may have been, but a fool she was not. She never signed a thing over to them legally. What it comes down to is that so long as she was alive and with them, they had everything.

'Which brings me to their ugly, unpleasant, despicable behaviour. I have evidence here that Mr Sparrow and Mr Yolu condemned the Contessa to a slow and painful, not to mention humiliating, death from lack of love and neglect to satisfy their own greed. And whereas they might have been clever enough to take over her home and her life, they were not so adroit once they finally had complete control over the Contessa. They kept her in pathetic circumstances for years, and they flaunted their unkindness. They were disrespectful towards her and enjoyed humiliating her in public. Befuddled but still in love with Mr Sparrow, unable to believe that he wanted anything but the best for her, she trusted him and Mr Yolu to her death.

'I think you mentioned a cottage they fixed up for her? It was no more than a shack.'

Here Mr Gazi opened a large white envelope and produced a black and white photograph. 'This is the so-called cottage where she died.'

Amy took the photograph in her hands. Mr Gazi was right, it was no more than a wooden shack. She said nothing and placed the photograph on the table in front of her.

'I have others here of the interior of the shack. I don't think you want to see them. But I would like you to see these. The Contessa when she met them, in the early 1950s. And as you can see in this photograph, even in old age she was still a beautiful and vivacious woman. And this is how she looked ten years later. The photograph was taken by a villager who went to the authorities for help in saving her.'

The tears were brimming in Amy's eyes when she asked, 'And the authorities could do nothing?'

'They sent for Mr Yolu and told him to take better care of his responsibilities. He was irate and returned with a letter from the Contessa saying that Mr Yolu and Mr Sparrow had assured her that as soon as the *yalis* was fit to receive her she would be returning to live there. I need not tell you she never left that shack. She believed every last one of their promises, every story they told her about how difficult their lives were and how they struggled. It was just a matter of time

288

before they had their successes and then they would all be living together in the *yalis* . . . on and on they lied to her. For the first few months that she lived there, even the woman who brought her food believed it. But when their visits stopped, and the money for food and tending the lady didn't come, sometimes for months at a time, she stopped believing it.

'The Contessa died of hypothermia and starvation. In the end she was lucid and understood what they had done. A note in violet ink on her crested paper is proof of that. Everything I've told you can be substantiated by documentation and by the testimony of the detective in charge.

'The authorities would like to see this case resolved. The *yalis* is the finest in Istanbul and will crumble away because no one can do anything about it with a legal mess like this hanging over it. But they insist upon justice for the Contessa. She deserves it. I don't know if you ever met her? I did, and dined in her company many times. She was far from the frivolous fool she may have come to sound like in this story. She was one of the most intelligent and interesting women, a patron of the arts her entire life. She was generous and kind. She was not the famed mistress of some of the most eminent men of her time for nothing. When she was alive and well she made life sweet for everyone with her wit and her charm.'

Amy rose from the chair, the tears trickling down her cheeks. She walked to the window and stared down at the fast-flowing Thames. After several minutes, Mr Gazi went to her and handed her a clean white handkerchief.

She turned to face him and said, 'I once loved a man as much as the Contessa Armida Montevicini loved Jarret Sparrow. When you can love like that it's unthinkable that he should be the wrong man. She didn't believe it, I didn't. I could so easily have gone the same way as the Contessa did but I found a letter written in violet ink and it saved my life. The Contessa had written it to *my* lover, Jarret Sparrow. That was over thirty years ago. Mr Gazi, I want that *yalis*, for me and for the Contessa Armida, and I intend to have it. Now, will you think about that while I go powder my nose and put on my imaginary armour? I'm going into battle!'

When Amy returned to the sitting-room Mr Gazi was sitting back at the table in front of the fire, leafing through some papers. He stood up while she took her chair. Amy then spent the next half hour telling him about the reappearance of Jarret and Fee and what they wanted from her. Their scheme as to how she could get the *yalis* back for them.

Having told him everything, she added, 'I know myself very well, Mr Gazi. Destroying another human being as I intend to destroy Jarret Sparrow and Fee will not come easy to me. I will become fire to fight fire, but in the end I could very well be burned out. I need a Byzantine mind to help me in this. Will you work with me until the *yalis* is mine?'

'I need some time to think about that. But for the moment, why don't I work with you on formulating a plan?'

Smiles crept across their faces. 'You have a lovely smile, Miss Ross, I think we must work on seeing more of that and fewer tears.'

'And you, Mr Gazi, have a very handsome smile.'

'I've made a reservation for lunch at Wilton's. I never come to England without visiting it. I had my first lunch there with my father when I was seven years old. And it's a perfect day for oysters, don't you think?'

'Every day is a perfect day for oysters, Mr Gazi.'

They dined well at Wilton's but wasted no time in idle chatter. Mr Gazi was convinced that the first thing that he and Amy had to work out was a method by which she could gain title from Jarret and Fee to the property, the *yalis* and all its contents. Mr Gazi was not convinced that they would give that to her in a manner that they could not contest later on if Amy was successful with the next plan – getting the case against them thrown out of court because she was now the owner of the property. The more they talked, the more complicated it became. But by the time they had finished their bread and butter pudding, they thought they had a plan that would hold up. The next stop was to visit Amy's solicitor the following morning.

It took four days before the final transfer papers for the property and its contents were drawn up and ready for signature by Fee, Jarret and Amy, and by that time the museum in New York had committed itself to purchasing the Soutine. They paid the asking price and agreed to keep the original owner's name a secret. The de Boulets were thrilled. They could go forward with their private museum. They were besides extremely impressed and grateful for the swiftness and discretion with which Amy had acted. For the de Boulets discretion was everything. It therefore took Amy by surprise when Pierre de Boulet said that his wife Annette had something personal she wanted to discuss with Amy.

290

Once on the line she hemmed and hawed and simply couldn't get out what she wanted to say. Amy finally stepped in. 'Annette, is there something you want to tell me?'

'Ask you, Amy.'

'Well do, then. If I can be of any help . . .'

'Oh, no, I don't want anything. Pierre and I have talked this over for days and he thinks I should ask you before I do it . . .'

'Do what, Annette?'

'Give your address and telephone number to a friend of ours who is making enquiries.'

Amy felt a surge of delight. She knew of course who it had to be. 'If he is a friend of yours, then I don't mind, Annette.'

'Oh, good, he is such a fascinating man. His name is Brice Chatto. He's a neighbour of ours on the lake. I'll tell him the next time he calls.'

'Do you know why he wants it, Annette?'

'I don't think it has anything to do with buying a painting, Amy!'

She immediately went down to the kitchen and told Tillie, 'If any calls come from a Mr Brice Chatto, or flowers, or anything, he's on our very important, we want you list. We do not want this man to slip away! Got it, Tillie?'

'I'd better! My God, I haven't seen you sparkle like this in ever such a long time, not since you came home with those flowers and chocolates,' said Tillie, a teasing note in her voice.

'Don't get carried away. I just don't want to miss my chance this time.'

'It's been all go round here and you've been working too hard. I was beginning to worry because you've been busy but sort of depressed at the same time. I like you better this way. It was that oriental, wasn't it? I thought he was terrible.'

'Well, you have my permission to call the police if ever he shows up round here again.'

Amy walked away from the kitchen to light the fire in the drawing-room. She was bathed and dressed and ready for Mr Gazi's arrival. This was his first visit to her house. They were going to go once more over the papers that she would present to Fee and Jarret, and Mr Gazi was to brief her on every possible change they might ask for.

The faint scent of steak and kidney pudding came from the kitchen. That was Mr Gazi's request when Amy asked him for lunch. He wanted spotted dick for pudding. His comment was: 'Once an English public school boy, always an English public school boy.' But had then admitted that he only allowed himself the luxury of acting like one about once every four years. For all his kindness to her, Amy was serving oysters for their first course.

He arrived, was charmed by the house but fell in love with the Soutine which was still on display in Amy's drawing-room. He was also enchanted by *Arcadia* when they walked down through the garden to the river to have a look at her.

It was while they were standing there that he asked Amy, 'Miss Ross, are you sure you want to go through with this? You know you can walk away from it and those men, and that will be the end of it?'

She remained silent for several seconds and then slipped her arm through his. While they were walking back to the house for lunch, she told him, 'I want to walk away, but I can't. They came back into my life to exploit me, and I simply cannot allow that, any more than I could allow them to do to me what they did to the Contessa. And there would always be that possibility: that they would try to, no matter how much love for me Jarret professes. If you were to ask me why I am doing this, I would have to answer because I simply do not want them to have the Contessa's *yalis*. I want them to know that it is restored and flourishing and full of life and joy, and that they will never see it or the gardens again. I want all trace of them wiped from that woman's past. I owe her that.'

'And if you can't do it?'

'I will have had a damn good try.'

'I don't think you can carry this off alone, even with my help. We need more sympathisers with the same goal.'

Amy stopped walking and looked at Mr Gazi. 'Did I hear you say *we*?'

'Yes, I believe you did. Mr Kramer said, "Give her whatever she wants, I'll back her." So we have him as a solid ally as well.'

'Mr Gazi, I'm very grateful to you.'

'First things first. We go to Venice to present our plan to Mr Sparrow and Mr Yolu. You will have to make them believe you're doing this for love, Miss Ross, your love for Jarret Sparrow. They must not get the least inkling of what you really have in mind.'

'Well then, I think I had better go into the house now and call Jarret. I'll tell him how much I love him and how I have decided to help them. We'll make a rendezvous to discuss our plan of action.'

292

'Now you're very sure about this, Miss Ross?'

'Please don't ask me that again, Mr Gazi. I'm not sure about any of this. It's more like taking on a job and getting it done.'

Mr Gazi, Amy, and her lawyer James Hardcastle arrived in Venice one week later and checked into the Gritti Palace Hotel. James Hardcastle was not wholly aware of Amy's intentions. Mr Gazi thought they should remain a secret between Amy and himself for the time being.

Amy and her men went to the *palazzo* very soon after their arrival in Venice. Jarret impressed and charmed the visitors with his handsome good looks and that injured, somewhat aloof manner which won over most people. Fee seemed more eccentric and nervous than Amy could ever remember seeing him. She put that down to the presence of Mr Gazi, who was a grand Turkish gentleman whom Fee must know was a key factor in their plan for returning to Turkey.

Immediately after the introductions Jarret asked to see Amy alone for a few moments. He took her into the hall. 'Amy, I will love you as no man has ever loved a woman, as you have always wanted me to love you, for the rest of my life for what you're doing for us! I mean you and I, not just Tennant and Fee and me.'

He placed his arms round her and kissed her lovingly. Stroked her hair and kissed her eyes, raised her hands and lowered his head to kiss them, first one, then the other. He caressed her breasts.

They kissed again and she gave in to his kisses and licked his lips, and told him, 'New beginnings, Jarret. I'm doing this for us, for new beginnings.' And this time it was Amy who took over the kissing and sucked his tongue into her mouth. Their hearts raced and it was Jarret who had to pull away, obviously aroused.

'This will have to wait, Amy. We have the rest of our life to make love in. Let's just get out of this mess. And, remember, time is of the essence.'

Together they walked back into the drawing-room and Amy very casually asked in a low voice, 'Why of the essence, Jarret?'

In an equally low voice he told her, 'Because unless we show our bank that the Turkish property is ours, that it's an asset and can be used as collateral, it will foreclose and we might lose the *palazzo*. Once you've won the case against us and the *yalis* is legally yours, then you sign the house back over and we can go to the bank.'

A voice kept screaming in Amy's head: 'We've got you, we've got you! Now I know you'll have to sign it over to me on my conditions.'

293

They all sat round a table, each of the men with a pile of papers in front of him. But it was Amy who opened the meeting. 'I have explained the plan you and Fee worked out to Mr Gazi. He agrees with you that it is your best and probably only chance of settling this affair and getting everything you want.'

She stopped at this point and gave Jarret a warm and loving smile. Fee, sitting to one side of her, received a pat on the hand. He grabbed hers and kissed it. A look of joy, relief and greed came flooding over his face. With an arrogant twitch of the head, he told her, 'Amy, you will never regret this.'

'I'm banking on that, Fee.'

Jarret, who was sitting on the other side of her, leaned forward and kissed her on the cheek. 'Excuse me, gentlemen, but a kiss for a generous angel does not seem out of order.'

'Mr Gazi has agreed to act for me once I have the property legally passed from your hands into mine. It will take some time but he agrees with you, Fee. If those in charge can save face and they get the museum, they will grant me everything they possibly can.'

None of Amy's team missed the look of relief that passed between Jarret and Fee. She continued, 'Now, having found your plan feasible, Fee, I then went to my solicitor here, Mr Hardcastle, to draw up documents that would make the transfer legal and binding in international law so that it would protect us all and be credible to the Turkish authorities. Now I'll pass you over to Mr Hardcastle who will explain it all to you as he has explained it to me.'

For the next hour and a half James Hardcastle went over every detail of the contract he had drawn up for Amy. Fee and Jarret questioned everything they possibly could. They suggested loopholes, wanted escape clauses, anything to be certain they could grab the property back from her any time they wanted to. James Hardcastle rejected every suggestion. The contract was iron clad in Amy's favour or he would advise his client to walk away. Mr Gazi and Hardcastle explained endlessly that if even a hint of such a thing was in the contract, there was no point in doing the deal at all. For if it was there for anyone to see, the Turkish government would see it and scream fraud.

It surprised Amy when it was Jarret and not Fee who said, 'What recourse do we have if Miss Ross should not wish one day to return the property to us?'

Amy jumped out of her chair, her face full of hurt and anger. 'None! Unless my love and devotion and my word mean something to you, and obviously they don't. What am I doing here if not for those things? I'm leaving.'

It was Mr Gazi who spoke now, in Turkish to Fee. Amy merely stood there, Jarret trying to calm her with words of gratitude and love. Finally the two men stopped talking and Fee spoke. 'Jarret, Mr Gazi suggests that we remain as we are and do nothing or else make the property over to Amy and hope for the best deal she can achieve for us. Now we have nothing. With her, maybe we'll get something.'

'In other words, sign is the only game in town?' said a very unhappy Jarret.

'That's about it, Mr Sparrow,' said Mr Gazi.

'I don't want you to sign, Jarret. Love is obviously not enough of a guarantee for you.'

They were gazing deep into each other's eyes. Amy read in his anger, hatred, love, desperation. He saw in hers what he thought was a woman in love, a giver unto death. He put a finger under her chin and tilted it up to place a kiss upon her lips. Then he turned to Mr Hardcastle and asked, 'Where do I sign?'

Chapter 20

It was the second week in December. The Soutine was on display in New York, and all the art world was talking about it as being the finest of the artist's work. Mr Gazi was in Istanbul, fighting the good fight for Amy with some success. They were negotiating terms. Edward, Anthony and Amy were making ready to visit the sites on their museum shortlist. They would be in Istanbul the following day. Jarret and Fee were in India, guests of a minor Danish Royal. Peter Smith was disappointed by Amy's refusal of his invitation to Christmas in Easthampton and philosophical when she told him she could not see herself visiting him in the near future but that he and his delightful family were welcome to visit her when they were next in England. Brice Chatto was walking through Heathrow airport, trying to get through to Amy on his mobile telephone. Busy, busy, busy.

Amy was feeling just a little sorry about Peter Smith. Weeks before, on that morning his flowers had arrived, she'd had high hopes that it might go right for them. Now she knew she was still looking for the magic that can accompany love and that it simply wasn't there for Peter Smith and Amy Ross. She put the receiver down and hoped she hadn't sounded cold and cruel. No sooner had she done that than the telephone was ringing again. She picked it up.

'I'm feeling deprived.'

Amy recognised the voice at once. It sent a shiver of pleasure through her. 'Of what?'

'Of laughter with sunshine in it, the sound of joy, and a touch of wickedness.'

'I don't think I could ever deprive you of anything,' she told him, and then laughed – not for him or to impress but because she felt genuinely gleeful that he still wanted her.

'May I come and see you?'

'As quickly as you can.'

'Directions?'

She gave them and then he said, 'I'm leaving Heathrow *now*.'

Amy went into high speed, rushing round the house, wanting it to look its best. Tillie was informed of a visitor, *the* visitor, and got herself into a state because there wasn't much food in the house and the tumble dryer was going. Amy hated the sound of machines at the best of times, *never* allowed them when there were visitors. It was too late to do anything about flowers. Everything settled down when Tillie suggested, 'He's not coming to see the house, why don't you do something with yourself?'

Tillie was quite right. Amy took one last look at her house. It looked perfectly enchanting, just as it always did. She went upstairs to her bedroom and bathed and changed into a full-length paper-thin suede skirt the colour of grey pearls, slipped into a cream crêpe-de-chine long-sleeved blouse, and clasped round her waist a plum-coloured soft leather belt, the buckle of which was a huge elliptical black opal set in a slim pink-gold frame.

When Amy looked in the mirror at herself she could not remember the last time she'd looked so happy, so young and full of hope, so filled with excitement for a man. She ran her fingers through her luscious dark silky hair. She was at her best and waiting for the best, of that she was certain.

When Amy walked down the stairs Tillie had just put a taper to a newly laid fire. She watched Amy and had to take a seat. Never taking her eyes off her employer, she watched her cross the drawing-room. 'I don't know when I've ever seen you look so happy, Miss Ross, and so really beautiful. I almost don't know what to say.'

Amy laughed and told her faithful housekeeper, 'If I know you, you'll find something.'

'I hope he brings some more of those chocolates!'

Then they both laughed and Tillie rose from the settee and went to the kitchen. She could at least manage scones for tea.

Two hours had passed since his call and still there was no sign of Brice Chatto. Amy wasn't at all anxious about his not coming or getting lost, she somehow knew he was a man who never got lost or broke his word. Hadn't he already proved that to her when they had missed each other at the Connaught? No, she was more curious as to what was delaying him than anything. It was nearly four o'clock when a chauffeur-driven Rolls-Royce pulled up to the boat house.

It was dusk and mist was rising on the river and drifting across the garden. It was frosty and damp and cold, yet a romantic way for Brice to see the boat house for the first time; better even than if he had arrived in sunshine.

Tillie and Amy arrived in the hall at the same time to answer the door. 'Not this time, Tillie. This one is all mine.'

Tillie gave a broad smile and suppressed giggles, vanishing back into the kitchen, and Amy opened the door.

Brice was wearing a rust-coloured Harris tweed coat, its collar turned up. He looked at her, really looked at her, from the tip of her head down to her toes, and only then did he say, 'Hello.'

'Hello.'

He ran the fingers of his right hand through his hair, and then said, 'I remember you as less stunningly beautiful.'

'That's because you remember the sound of my laughter more.'

'Do you think I can come in?' he asked with a smile that crept into her heart.

'Please.'

He turned to the chauffeur and asked him to bring in the parcels. 'Hence the delay.'

'You didn't have to, Brice.'

'It's not a matter of have to. More that I heard a lady laugh and it touched my soul. Then when we met something in my heart went click. I would like to spend the rest of my life laying the world at your feet. I hope you'll not deprive me of that? Bond Street would be the less prosperous for it if you did.'

They entered the hall and the chauffeur followed, loaded down with an array of beautifully wrapped parcels.

'I feel like it's Christmas,' said Amy.

'I intend to make every day of your life Christmas. By the way, how would you like to spend it with me?'

'Very much.'

Brice didn't have to say a word. The moment he was in the hall there was a hint of a smile on his face. He got the very specialness of Amy's house, understood it, and was uplifted by it. They seemed to forget the chauffeur standing with the parcels. Brice unbuttoned his coat and said, 'I want a tour, I want to see it all.'

His eyes missed none of the beautiful things in the hall. Together they walked through it into the drawing-room. Brice looked over his shoulder and said to the chauffeur, 'Don't forget the flowers in the back of the car.'

'And flowers?'

'For you, always flowers.'

'There's not one in the house because I'm away tomorrow. I wish there had been, and glorious food and wine to welcome you home.'

Amy had meant to say 'to my home'. She could only put it down to a Freudian slip. He didn't miss it either, the look in his eyes told her that. He dropped his coat over a chair and wandered round the room. Amy stood by the fireplace watching him. Stopping at the Bechstein concert grand he sat down and briefly played something to check the tone, then stood up and shook his head in approval. 'Perfect.'

He went to Amy and took her hand in his. They stood for some time just looking at each other. Finally she broke the spell. 'There's the kitchen yet to see on this floor.'

'Are you a great cook?'

'No, just good.'

He made no comment and they went to the kitchen. On the table lay masses of large-headed white lilies on long stems, dozens of them, together with white lilac. Tillie was already filling the white marble vase. 'They're lovely, Brice! Now you will see the house as I would have liked you to. And this is Tillie, my housekeeper.'

'Hello, Tillie.'

'I made scones for tea,' she told him, and Amy couldn't understand why since Tillie was never familiar with her guests.

'And I've brought chocolates.'

'The best Belgians with cream centres?'

He laughed and said, 'Yes, how did you know?'

'You look that kind of man.'

Amy rushed Brice from the kitchen. Tillie was already acting out of character and Amy thought she might say too much. 'Tea in front of the fire, Tillie.'

There was that something special between them that can happen only when a person meets the other they have searched for all their life. They both knew it, and it was so very strong and right that neither of them felt the need to talk about it. It was all so easy and right between them. Amy had the strange sensation of having loved him all her life, of having known him forever, and yet there was that thrilling time between a man and a woman of discovering each other. A sexual attraction that kept her slightly on edge and full of anticipation.

Together they watched Tillie walking across the drawing-room with the silver tray laden with tea. Brice whispered, 'Can she be bribed to take the rest of the afternoon off *immediately*?'

'I would think it would take no more than the offer of a chocolate.'

'Ah.'

He rose from his chair and went to the stack of parcels. He removed two boxes, and the lid from one. The chocolates. Once tea had been set on a table in front of the settee, Brice spoke. 'Tillie, these are the Belgian chocolates you seem to like. Because I have a sweet tooth I always buy two boxes. Why don't you take the afternoon off right this minutes and go home and enjoy this one?' And he handed her the other box.

Once Tillie left the drawing-room Brice put the lid on the box of chocolates and whispered sexily, 'I never take tea, and find scones like dust in my mouth. I would prefer taking the chocolates to bed with us and discovering each other there. Is that a good idea or a bad one? *And* you can show me the rest of your house on the way.'

'Will you always be able to anticipate my heart's desire?'

'You know I will,' he told her.

Together, arm in arm, they walked up the first flight of stairs to the library. Amy watched him as he briefly scanned the bookshelves. He leaned over the balcony and gazed through the boat house and down to the drawing-room. Brice seemed to her to be very much at home here. Amy actually found it difficult to believe this was his first visit. He put his arm round her shoulders and together they walked up the next flight to her bedroom. He put the box of chocolates on the table next to the bed and they sat down side by side, then turned to face each other and gazed into each other's eyes.

Brice was wearing the same Armani suit he had worn on the plane the first time she had met him. Now he unbuttoned the jacket and leaned against some of the many period embroidered Persian cushions scattered against the headboard of the narwal ivory four-poster bed. He took her with him, lying on her side, and told her as he was undoing the button on the cuff of her blouse, 'There is more here than meets the eye or has to do with carnal desire – although there were those things immediately we met on the plane. I think you would agree with that?'

'Yes.'

She watched him as he unbuttoned the other cuff of her blouse and rolled the sleeve back, kissing her wrist and licking it briefly with the point of his tongue. She actually trembled with the intensity of her desire. Brice sensed it and kissed her lightly on the lips – a kiss that was still extraordinarily sensuous. Amy slipped her hands under his jacket and eased it off his shoulders.

She unbuckled the opal clasp of her belt which fell from her waist. Brice began to ease her silk blouse from under her skirt. 'Such a simple thing, removing a lady's blouse and yet I sense this is one of the most important moments of my life,' he told her, his gaze still locked with hers.

'And mine,' she told him.

They disrobed slowly and lingered over each other's body with eyes and hands and mouths. They delighted each other with caresses that excited the flesh and the mind and the heart. They rolled each other over on the bed and discovered every curve, every crevice. They romanced their bodies in a courtship the likes of which neither of them had ever experienced before. They knew intimately every inch of each other's skin, their body scent, the texture of their hearts and souls, before Brice licked the warm, silky-smooth come of Amy's many small orgasms from his lips and told her yet again how much he loved her. He placed many cushions under her bottom, making her ready to receive him, so that he might bring them both to greater pleasure yet by their first sexual experience.

He was extremely well endowed: a long, thick and handsome phallus, strong and throbbing with lust. Amy's silky moist come, blanketing her, would ease the way for his sex she was so hungry to have within her. She could think of nothing else but to have it fill her so completely that she might feel every nuance of sex as Brice made lustful sexual love to her. All that was what she wanted, and to give him every sexual delight, every pleasure that she possibly could.

It was almost as if he were reading her mind when he said, 'I tell you again, I love you, I will love you for always. There is a time for romance and courtship and I will always find time for those things with you, but there is too a time to exchange them for sex, pure lust, erotic abandonment. Like now.'

And having said those words, on his knees, he went between her legs now spread wide apart to accommodate him. He separated her soft sexual lips with his fingers and inserted his handsome knob in place. Then he leaned forward and put his arms under Amy's and

302

his hands over her shoulders. With his lips now trembling with emotion, he placed them upon hers in a kiss so passionate she opened her mouth to meet it. It was then, in that kiss, that he thrust as hard as he could and at the same time pulled her down by the shoulders on to him so they might take each other together with his amorous member. And then began the most exquisite, loving sex of Amy Ross's life.

Rather than being exhausted from the hours of sex they had experienced, they were exhilarated to discover they were so erotically in tune with each other. They lay in each other's arms, eating white chocolates filled with fresh cream and discovering who and what they were.

Both were surprised that neither of them had ever married. They had no children. Everything they learned about each other was unexpected because neither of them had laid any expectations on the other, not even in imagination. Brice told Amy, 'I'm a doctor, a plastic surgeon. Sometimes it's fancy noses and playing God to ageing ladies in a clinic just outside Geneva, but most of the time it's serious reconstructive surgery that saves people from having to live miserable lives. I spend six months of the year as a volunteer doctor with a team of five others in the third world. I'm a keen sportsman: skiing, tobogganing, sailing, hunting. I can afford to run my life any way it pleases me – inherited wealth, an obscene amount of it, and one brother, unmarried. I want you to know what you've got here.'

Amy said nothing.

'No comment?' he asked.

'What's to comment? That's you, and I want whatever you are.'

He kissed her and smiled and fed her a chocolate. 'If you want to we could spend the rest of our lives discovering each other, but before you answer that I think I should tell you the worst thing about me.'

'Must you?'

'Yes, this is not a fantasy love where everything is perfect. Just almost perfect.'

'Are you trying to put me off you?'

He laughed. 'We both know it's too late for that. Real love has struck and thankfully we're stuck with it. So for what it's worth, I am as you see me, always. What you see is what you get, *but* when I have to be I can be as hard and ruthless, as devious, as you can possibly imagine. It's never personal, always to do with my work and for the welfare of my patients. I can manipulate heads of states, influence kings and politicians to get what I want, and I do. I have no qualms about wielding what power I have.'

Amy released herself from Brice's arms. She pulled the bed cover off them and, sitting up, leaned over and kissed his eyes and his lips, the side of his face. She slipped on top of him, straddling him she sat down in his lap. He stroked her hair and caressed her breasts. He felt the weight of them in the palms of his hands and lowered his lips to them and kissed first one and then the other, sucking on her nipples. Amy stopped him by taking his hands in hers and kissing them. She pulled the bed cover up over her shoulders and sat there gazing at Brice.

'I used to think that I was a very nice person, a good person. I'm a woman who prefers love and laughter, all things beautiful. Hatred, revenge, bitterness, people exploiting people . . . I never closed my eyes to the fact that that too is a part of real life but I never dreamed that I could be involved with such things. And then, shortly after we met, all those things rolled into one landed on my doorstep. Literally. Here, in this wonderful place.'

Brice pulled the cover tighter round her so that it brought them closer together and then he kissed her on the lips, the side of her face, stroked her hair. She removed his hand, kissed it, then continued, 'I didn't want those things to touch me in any way, to chase me away from my life. I saw what was happening and then, without thought or intention, knew that this time round I was going to become fire to fight fire. I have become as dark and evil, devious and manipulative, as those people I am no longer running away from. Until the telephone rang and I heard your voice I was experiencing an unloving existence, one where I had become devoid of compassion. Being fire was burning my heart out, wreaking a terrible price on me. It was on the verge of causing permanent damage to the real Amy and who and what I am. I have no regret for what I was doing nor the fact that I must finish doing it, but I can see that it's making me no better than the men I am dealing with and I cannot bear that for much longer. I'm doing so only to destroy them and win through.

'You here loving me, your generosity of heart, your passion for us . . . it's like coming out of the dark and into bright sunshine to be part of that. I adore you, love you. I knew it before your call came, I knew it when I went to the Connaught that night. We missed each other then but we've never been apart, not for a minute.'

Amy clasped her arms round Brice and slid down his body to cover it with her own. They held each other for several minutes then he asked her, 'Marry me for Christmas, love me for always, Amy Ross.'

Epilogue

Brice and Mr Gazi were with Amy when she saw the Contessa Armida Montevicini's *yalis* for the first time. It was late April and Mr Gazi had arranged for them to approach the wooden mansion from a motor launch so she might view it from a distance as they travelled up the Bosphorus. He wanted her to see her prize in all its glory.

It was late afternoon and the sun was casting a coral light over the faded russet colour of the large and sprawling, dramatically romantic building. Amy had thought she knew what to expect after the many pictures she had studied and the long, arduous wrangling with the authorities over the *yalis*, but it was more, much more.

The gardens on either side of the house and rising up the hills behind it were overgrown, gone quite mad, but were a blaze of flowering shrubs: purple and magenta, bright yellow, white and cream, red and coral and rose pushing their way through the green leaves. For all its wildness the garden was still impressive, particularly its trees. Cypresses like aged sentinels rose high and handsome among them. As they stepped from the boat on to the marble stairs rising from the water, Amy could see blankets of tulips and hyacinths, and masses of wild flowers.

The men who had fought so well to give Amy everything she wanted, and to save face for themselves, and to see justice done as best they thought they could get it, were there to welcome her and officially to break the seals that had closed the house for so many years.

They walked together and cleared a path as they went, finally reaching the main entrance to the house. The seals were broken and three padlocks rusted solid were spliced by a giant cutter. It took two men to fold the wooden shutters back on their rusted hinges and to reveal a pair of ten-foot-high glass and wood doors.

'The key to your house, Madam Chatto.' The man handed her the original giant-sized iron key to the *yalis*. The look of admiration on his face and on every other man's there for Amy was what stilled the emotion that might have brought her to tears. Instead she gave an enormous deep sigh and a smile crossed her face. She tilted back her head and laughed, throwing her arms round her husband's neck. Brice swung her round and round in a circle, laughing with her. Their laughter was infectious and once he put Amy back down on her feet everyone began shaking hands. Things only calmed down when Amy inserted the key in the lock and entered the house.

It was dark and gloomy until they opened the wooden shutters and let the light pour in. The rooms seemed to spring to life. Until Amy had walked through these rooms she had not made up her mind what to do about Jarret and Fee, if anything. Now it was all hers. The *yalis* and its contents, which included the bulk of both Jarret's and Fee's work, and their private collection of other artists' work, which was extensive.

In return for getting everything she wanted from the authorities, including a document for Jarret and Fee which stated that any and all legal actions and sanctions against them had been dropped, Amy was obliged to restore the property and open it to the public four days of the year as a private residence and museum in memory of the Contessa Armida Montevicini. She had that document now, signed and sealed, in her handbag. Jarret and Fee were free to enter and travel anywhere in Turkey except within a quarter of a square mile of the Contessa Armida Montevicini's *yalis*. If they were to break that restraining order, they would be arrested and placed in prison forthwith.

Now, walking with Brice through the rooms, Amy was astounded. Fee and Jarret had told her the Contessa had had to sell off most of her treasures to survive. But the house was filled with them, and not the broken trash Jarret and Fee had lived with in Venice. They had lived in the lap of luxury and beauty while the Contessa had suffered in filth and poverty. For years after her death, till the very moment they were made to run away, they'd lived in splendour. Even the magnificent period draperies were still hanging at the windows. Fee and Jarret's work was exhibited everywhere and there were rooms stacked with their paintings.

'I will wipe those men clean from this house. Leave not a trace of them or their things in it,' she told Brice.

'And restore it?'

'Yes.'

'And then what?'

'I don't want to live here. Do you, Brice?'

'No.'

'Good. Then I'll lease it out to the Anthony Kramer Museum, as an annexe for museum functions, a residence for VIPs when they're visiting. We'll make it a cultural centre for the Turkish people and tourists – and all in the name of Contessa Armida Montevicini. I will also offer Mr Gazi the directorship of the *yalis* trust I will form, and a lifetime's residence here in the *yalis* if he would like to have it. A just but small reward for all he's done for me and the Contessa.'

That night, while sitting in bed next to Brice at the Pera Palace Hotel in Istanbul, Amy signed the letter she had just finished writing and which Mr Gazi had agreed to deliver to Jarret and Fee in Venice. Brice put his arm round her shoulders and she leaned against his chest and read it to him.

Pera Palace Hotel

Dear Jarret and Fee,
Enclosed you will find a most precious document which I have managed to secure for you. You are free now and forever from the charges that were laid against you. But at a price. You lose everything, and the right ever to go near the yalis *again. A few things I think you should know: they never could have made a successful case against you for the death of the Contessa. Other charges possibly. It was her love for you, Jarret, that killed her. Your cruelty and greed that has cost you everything.*
Amy

The letter was written in the violet-coloured ink that she had found in the *yalis* on the Bosphorus.

309